FIRE
AND
VENGEANCE

FIRE AND VENGEANCE

A KOA KĀNE HAWAIIAN MYSTERY

ROBERT McCAW

OCEANVIEW PUBLISHING
SARASOTA, FLORIDA

ISBN 978-1-60809-441-7

Published in the United States of America by Oceanview Publishing

Sarasota, Florida

www.oceanviewpub.com

10 9 8 7 6 5 4 3 2

PRINTED IN THE UNITED STATES OF AMERICA

To my wife Calli and my daughter Anne
who have been wonderfully supportive throughout
the lengthy process of bringing this book to life

ACKNOWLEDGEMENTS

Among the many people who helped make this book possible are my dear friends in Hawai'i who generously shared their knowledge of the culture, history, and language of the Hawaiian people. To them I owe an enormous debt of gratitude.

Special thanks must also go to Makela Bruno-Kidani, who has tirelessly reviewed my use of the Hawaiian language, correcting my many mistakes. Where the Hawaiian words and phrases are correct, she deserves the credit. Any errors are entirely of my doing.

Lastly, this book would not have been launched without the amazing support of my agent, Mel Parker of Mel Parker Books, LLC. His faith in my work and his tireless efforts made the publication of this story possible. I would also be remiss if I failed to acknowledge the support of Pat and Bob Gussin, owners of Oceanview Publishing, who have devoted their phenomenal energies to supporting and publishing my work and that of many other aspiring mystery and thriller writers.

FIRE

AND

VENGEANCE

CHAPTER ONE

DISASTER RODE THE gale-force winds of Hurricane Ida across the Big Island of Hawai'i from the southwest. Ferocious gusts felled century-old trees. Sonic booms of thunder chased lightning bolts sparking through ominous black clouds. Torrential rains pounded the mountains, filling gulches and gathering into flash floods. On Hualālai Mountain, one of the five volcanoes that make up Hawai'i Island, ten inches of rain fell in a single hour. Water cascaded into cracks and caverns, pouring deep into the earth. The pressure of the floodwaters opened long-sealed fissures in the faults on the west side of Hualālai. Water entered the volcano's magma reservoir and flashed into steam. Steam under astronomical pressure.

Catastrophe struck. Devastating news flashed through the Hilo police headquarters. Disaster at KonaWili School on Hualālai Mountain. Dead kids. Injured children. Stricken teachers. Panicky reports of a mass shooter, a terrorist bomb, a deadly poison gas attack, or something even more sinister. Confusion swirled like the storm still raging.

Conflicting disaster scenarios swarmed the airwaves as Chief Detective Koa Kāne, Sergeant Basa, and four patrolmen dashed through the downpour to a police helicopter. *Why does shit always happen when the chief's off-island?* Normally, Hawai'i Police Chief

S. H. Lannua, took the lead in disasters, but *ʻaʻole i kēia lā*, not today. With the chief preparing for surgery in California, Koa would be the senior police officer at the scene. At least he had Sergeant Basa, whose piercing dark eyes missed nothing. The thirty-five-year-old, bear-like police sergeant was one of ten brothers, all immensely proud of their Portuguese heritage. No one in the police department topped Basa for reliability under pressure. In a crisis, he stood like lava against every tsunami.

What the hell happened inside the school? Koa asked himself as the chopper rocked and bounced through the vicious wind and pelting rain. When the helo rounded Hualālai Mountain, an eight-thousand-foot volcano towering over Kona on the west side of the island, Koa glimpsed the elementary school through the driving rain.

Emergency lights flashed from fire trucks, rescue vehicles, and ambulances. Dirty yellow smoke obscured the south end of the year-old elementary school. More emergency vehicles, lights blazing on and off, converged on the scene from nearby Kona. The chopper's radio squawked horrific news—more than fifty children and teachers dead or injured. The mayor had activated the disaster management plan for the western side of the island. Nine-one-one operators were alerting all medical personnel to report to their emergency stations.

Wind slammed the police helicopter while it circled the school grounds waiting for a fire department medevac chopper to lift off and another to land on the flooded athletic field. Koa saw dozens of kids on the soaked ground in front of the school, some on stretchers and others lying helpless where they'd been dragged. He'd seen children bloodied during his Special Forces days in Afghanistan. Children caught in the crossfire. Youngsters killed by misplaced bombs. The sight sickened him then, but not like this. This was America. Kids should be safe in school. Instead, they were dead and dying.

When the police chopper settled onto the soggy softball diamond and Koa slid the door open, an overpowering smell of noxious gases washed over him, burning his nostrils and making his eyes water. He knew the awful smell—nearly everyone on the Big Island knew the odor of volcanic gases—but the stench was strangely out of place. Koa glanced up toward the top of Hualālai. The volcano hadn't erupted in over two hundred years, but it wasn't extinct. Had *Pele*, the Hawaiian goddess of volcanic fury, erupted *under* the KonaWili elementary school? If Hualālai went up, lava could rush down its steep slopes, cutting highways, disrupting electrical power, destroying Keāhole airport, and propelling death through the streets of Kona. The thought made him shudder.

Despite the torrential rain, thundering like a waterfall, firemen with two-and-a-half-inch hoses shot canons of water onto the south end of the school building. In defiance, the water vaporized before it touched the building, creating superheated steam clouds whipped in all directions by the wicked *makani*, the wicked winds. Try as they might, firefighters couldn't get close to the south end of the building. No amount of water dented the inferno.

Koa ordered the police helicopter back to Hilo for reinforcements before fastening his poncho and dashing into the foul weather. Chaos reigned around him. People ran everywhere. Kids and teachers screamed. Since he didn't yet know what had happened, Koa designated the whole area a potential crime scene, and assigned Basa and his patrolmen along with other cops from Kona to set up a cordon around the school. The five-foot-eight, barrel-chested police sergeant swung into action. Koa ran toward the building.

Firefighters in protective gear with breathing tanks, along with EMTs and policemen with bandanas over their faces, dashed into the north end of the building—the end away from the inferno. Others carried children from the building to a pair of raingear-clad triage nurses who categorized the injured. Green tags for the walking wounded, yellow tags for the injured not in immediate danger, red tags for the critical, and black tags for the dead. Way too many red and black tags.

Black-tagged kids lay in a row on the wet grass. Unconscious, but still breathing, children occupied stretchers, covered with makeshift ponchos waiting for ambulances or medevac helicopters. Youngsters suffering only mild signs of distress straggled toward buses four blocks from the building, guided by a phalanx of teachers. Anything to get the kids away from the crippled school and out of the driving rain. Teachers, some with rain protection, but many soaked to the skin, moved from one group to another trying to account for all the students. Even as Koa watched, more doctors, EMS, and nursing personnel poured in to help stabilize the situation.

Koa called Hawai'i Mayor George Tanaka, stunning him with the gruesome scope of the disaster. The mayor, saying, "This is the damned Education Department; that makes it Māhoe's problem," hooked Governor Bobbie Māhoe into the call. Koa focused on the most urgent problem: "We need state-wide disaster help." A rumble of tearing metal distracted Koa as a portion of the school roof ripped away. "There aren't enough doctors or medical facilities on the Big Island to treat the injured." He heard the governor instruct his staff to alert Maui Memorial Hospital and the Queen's Medical Center in Honolulu to prepare to receive patients. Koa then requested additional medevac helicopters to airlift wounded children.

"What the hell happened?" the governor demanded.

"No one knows, Governor, but it smells volcanic. The heat is horrendous. If Hualālai erupts, thousands of people in and around Kona are in harm's way. You should put the national guard on alert."

"Jesus," the governor responded. Both he and the mayor fired more questions, but Koa had no answers. The politicians demanded hourly updates, and the call ended.

Harry 'Ōhai, the short, squat, titanium-tough Kona area deputy fire chief, trotted by, heading into the damaged building as fast as his bulky gear allowed. "C'mon," he yelled over his shoulder, "still got *keiki* inside," using the Hawaiian word for children. Koa covered his face with a handkerchief, like other police officers trying to rescue children, and sprinted after 'Ōhai. "We've cleared the north end, but not the south classrooms," 'Ōhai shouted. Inside, they turned down the south hall. Thick yellow smoke billowed at them. Heat blasted Koa's face. 'Ōhai turned into the first classroom.

Koa ran straight into the thick yellow smoke. The rotten egg stench overpowered all other smells. He began to choke and dropped to the floor as though back on the battlefield, crawling under the worst of the fumes. The building rumbled and the floor vibrated. Turning into a classroom marked First Grade, he saw a child lying on the floor ahead of him. He scrambled forward, grabbed hold of the child, a little girl, and pulled her toward the door. At the doorway, he scooped her up in his arms. Holding her tight to his chest, he felt her shallow breathing. Still alive. Crouching low, he dashed down the hallway. Coughing from the acidic smoke, he carried the first-grader to safety.

Handing the child over to a teacher, he raced back into the building. The smoke had grown thicker, and he again crawled down the hallway. The floor grew hot. His eyes burned. He scrambled past the first two classrooms before turning into another. The building shook. A deep growling sound reverberated. He couldn't see. He banged into a desk, and then something soft. Another *keiki*. Choking uncontrollably, he became disoriented. Which way to the door? Clenching his teeth, he told himself not to panic. That instinct to remain in control had saved him many times.

Clutching the limp child, he inched forward. When he hit a wall, he followed it until he reached the door. A hacking cough racked his chest. He made it into the hall. Barely able to stand, he hauled the child into his arms and stumbled forward. His eyes, the inside of his nostrils, and his throat burned like acid. The hallway seemed to go on forever; he wasn't sure he'd make it out. Finally, he reached the entrance and stumbled outside. His lungs were on fire. A teacher rushed forward to take the child from his arms. Koa gasped for air. He couldn't breathe. He felt his legs go weak. The world turned gray, and he collapsed.

CHAPTER TWO

TEN MINUTES LATER, Koa awoke with an oxygen mask over his face. In another minute, he was sitting up and then standing. He'd have a sore throat and hacking cough, but that didn't prevent him from getting back in the action.

By late afternoon, emergency personnel had achieved some measure of control. Police had cordoned off and evacuated a mile-wide circle around the crippled school. Braving the unrelenting noxious air inside the building, professional firefighters with protective gear had retrieved all of the children and bodies they could find. Hostile temperatures in the south end of the school blocked rescue personnel from checking the last few classrooms. The most severely injured, all of them children, had been evacuated to hospitals.

Big Island Mayor George Tanaka arrived on the scene with his aides—Ben Inaba and Tomi Watanabe. The mayor never went anywhere without his political operatives. They made an odd pair. Watanabe, the mayor's press agent, stood no more than five-feet-two, wore ill-fitting clothes, sported an ugly black mole on his right cheek, and had an attitude to match. Inaba, eight inches taller, and smooth as polished obsidian, might have stepped out of a Tommy Bahama's catalog.

Tanaka's grim expression grew darker when Governor Bobbie Māhoe appeared with Francine Na'auao, his Department of Education chief. Both mayor and governor had reason to look distressed, but KonaWili wasn't the sole cause of their sullen faces. They were political enemies with wildly different agendas and personally disliked each other. That Tanaka made no bones about angling for the governor's job didn't help. Given the animosity between the two men, Koa could be forgiven for feeling like he was walking on fresh lava.

Māhoe, unlike Tanaka, the short, heavyset Hawai'i County mayor, looked movie-star handsome, resembling a somewhat younger and taller George Clooney with jet black hair. A Republican in a heavily Democratic state, he'd taken the governor's office by storm with a whopping 60 percent of the vote. Pundits attributed his victory to his good looks and friendly manner rather than his pro-development policies. His reputation as a charming ladies' man hadn't hurt. Now in the face of the KonaWili disaster, he wore a bleak expression and looked older than his sixty-three years.

Gearing up for a press conference, the politicians gathered in a police command vehicle. They wanted answers. Koa and 'Ōhai did their best to lay out the sketchy facts. 'Ōhai, still wearing firefighter's boots and insulated pants, reported thirteen known fatalities, three teachers and ten children. One teacher and four children remained missing. Ambulances and helicopters had transported forty-five children to medical facilities—fifteen to Hilo Memorial and ten each to Queen's Medical on O'ahu, Maui Memorial in Kahului, and Kona Community Hospital.

When 'Ōhai completed his accounting, Koa took over. "We've sealed off the site. It's still early, but we've found no evidence of a terrorist attack. No one shot. No bombs. The medics report injuries consistent with extreme heat and volcanic fumes like we'd normally see in Hawai'i Volcanoes National Park. All signs point to some kind of volcanic venting from Hualālai Mountain."

Koa paused to scan the ashen faces of the state's political leaders. "When I smelled sulfur gases, I called in Richard Tatum, a volcanologist from the USGS at Kīlauea. He's here with us now." Koa turned to the government geologist. "Richard, tell 'em what you've already shared with me."

Tatum, a tall skinny man with wispy arms, a pinched face, and a high-pitched voice, began, "Hualālai is an active volcano. It last erupted in 1801, sending streams of lava through Kona into the sea. Keāhole airport, just down there—" he pointed downhill toward the commercial airport at the edge of the ocean—"is built atop one 1801 flow."

"But that's over two hundred years ago," Na'auao, the DOE chief, objected. In her sixties with thinning gray hair and dressed in an expensive, but conservatively tailored, charcoal dress, she carried herself with a presence that warned against challenge. Her patrician face, once attractive, had hardened into a statue-like caricature of itself, and her arrogance confirmed what little Koa knew from press reports.

"True," Tatum acknowledged, "but Hualālai hasn't been quiet. Pu'u Wa'awa'a, the many-furrowed hill that looks like a Jell-O mold on Hualālai's northern flank, erupted in 1859, and lava vented under the ocean south of Kona in 1877. More recently, in 1929, a month-long swarm of 6,200 earthquakes, including a couple of big ones, shook the mountain. Probably a failed eruption. Hualālai's not extinct, and she's gonna erupt again. It's just a matter of time."

The politicians reacted with dour faces and deep frowns. "Get to the point, man," the governor insisted.

"Hualālai," Tatum continued, "has three rift zones—fault lines where volcanic activity is most likely to occur. One of those faults runs directly under the KonaWili school building. Looks like the volcano vented along that fault under the school."

"Holy shit," the governor swore uncharacteristically. "Do we need to evacuate the area between here and the coast?"

"Not right away," Tatum responded. "Our monitors haven't detected the kind of earthquakes or ground swelling signaling a major eruption. You'll have some warning—at least a few hours—before a full-scale eruption. It would be prudent, however, to begin planning for an evacuation."

"Shit is right," Mayor Tanaka interjected. "We'll have mass panic on our hands if we're not careful."

"You can't hide the problem, Mayor," Tatum warned, his voice rising to an even higher pitch. "Hualālai presents one of the most severe volcanic risks in the United States. We've been warning about the threat of runaway development along this coast for years."

"I recommend," Koa said, once again taking the lead, "we state the facts in a calm, straightforward manner, emphasizing we're at the early stages of this crisis, and there's no cause for panic."

Heads nodded in agreement. They decided the governor and the mayor would speak first, expressing condolences and emphasizing the extraordinary emergency resources made available by the state and county. Koa and ʻŌhai would then lay out the facts and answer questions.

When their meeting broke up and the group headed out into the storm to brief the press under a makeshift tent, Koa's cell phone rang. He looked at the screen and recognized the number. He answered the call he'd been expecting from Deputy Sheriff Mary Perko. "Your brother's here in the lockup," she reported.

"*Mahalo*," he responded. Ikaika, Koa's youngest brother, serving a minimum four-year sentence for burglary, had been subpoenaed to testify against another felon. Mary Perko had retrieved Ikaika from a contract prison in Arizona where the state of Hawai'i had sent him after revoking his parole. Ikaika, the black sheep of Koa's family, stuck like a thorn in Koa's side, causing conflicts for him as a police officer and embarrassing him at every turn. The chief blamed Koa every time his brother got in trouble, and, in his early days as a detective, Koa had feared that Ikaika would get him fired. Still, now that Ikaika had been hauled back to the Big Island, Koa would have to make time to see his brother. It would be a difficult reunion.

* * *

The press conference quickly became a zoo. Thick sulfur fumes hanging over the school forced authorities to hold the press conference in a makeshift tent half a mile away. Over a hundred media and print reporters, many from the neighboring islands, gathered in an unruly semicircle around an improvised public-address system. Governor Māhoe expressed condolences for lost loved ones and offered prayers for the injured children. Mayor Tanaka repeated much the same themes.

'Ōhai briefed the press on the fatalities, promising to release the names of the dead after completing family notifications. He identified the hospitals treating the injured kids and confirmed four missing children and one missing teacher. Finally, he recounted various acts of heroism by teachers and first responders who'd raced into the building to save youngsters.

When Koa stepped to the microphone, he told the press about the likely volcanic nature of the episode, repeatedly emphasizing the lack of evidence of terrorism and dismissing any immediate need for evacuation beyond the area already cleared by the police. He declined requests for pictures from inside the school building, citing safety concerns. The police, he disclosed, had ordered a robotic vehicle to search those parts of the school building first responders had yet to reach.

Concluding his remarks, he took questions, which came flying from every direction. He answered those where he had solid information and deflected the others until the authorities had more information. When the press conference wrapped up, he breathed a sigh of relief but realized his ordeal with reporters had only just begun. The KonaWili school disaster would be front-page news around the world, and this first press conference offered just the barest glimpse of what was to come.

Not long after the press conference ended, reporter Walker McKenzie—widely known as CNN's "Mister Disaster"—arrived with a camera crew in tow and a bevy of assistants to prepare a KonaWili segment for the next day's *From All Angles* news show. Koa recognized the handsome, urbane reporter, dressed in his trademark white dress shirt with rolled-up sleeves, and knew he was about to enter a maelstrom of international publicity. He filled the celebrity journalist in on the information already made public. McKenzie, unlike local reporters, raised the question nagging Koa: "Why had the department of education built an elementary school atop a volcanic fault along the slope of an active volcano?" Koa wanted to refer the question to the DOE chief but instead told McKenzie the location of the school would be addressed as part of a comprehensive investigation of the disaster already underway. Still, Koa knew the reporter had opened a Pandora's box as deep and dangerous as Hualālai's volcanic cone.

CHAPTER THREE

FIRST RESPONDERS WORKED through the stormy night. By six o'clock, technicians in Honolulu had loaded a bomb squad truck aboard a Coast Guard C-130H cargo plane. The turboprop carried the vehicle to Kona's Keāhole airport, and by nine, it arrived outside the school. Koa watched technicians steer an Andros F6B robotic vehicle down a ramp and prepare it to reconnoiter the school.

Four and a half feet long, the contraption featured eight wheels and a cart-like body with a complex manipulator arm extending out over four feet. It could go where no *kanaka*, no human—even in the best protective gear—could survive. Techs attached two cameras to its arm—a fire-resistant video camera and a thermal imager. The robot's two powerful halogen lights allowed it to capture video in the otherwise pitch-black interior of the school building, while its thermal imager needed no light to detect heat sources, even those obscured by heavy smoke. They activated and tested the robot's microphones.

The bomb squad truck featured a filtered ventilation system, so they positioned the vehicle close to the school despite the gases continuing to pour from the wrecked building. 'Ōhai obtained architectural drawings and construction plans for the KonaWili school, which he taped on the wall of the truck to guide the search.

Koa and ʻŌhai watched a technician use video-game-like controllers to direct the robot into the school. Monitors showed readouts and pictures from the robot's video camera and thermal imager. Bright red numbers flashed the temperature—120 degrees, twice as high as the rainy night air outside. The tech swiveled the robot's camera for an overall view of the situation. All of the heat and gases appeared to come from the south end, leaving only haze in the northern end. First responders had already cleared the north area.

The robot headed south, checking the main office and classrooms until it reached the last third of the southernmost wing. Here the Andros F6B reported temperatures above 280 degrees. An impenetrable yellow sulfurous haze reduced visibility to near zero. An ominous rumbling sound filled the air and echoed off the walls. Blistered paint turned cinderblock walls black. Fire-resistant ceiling tiles lay crumbled on the floor. The wooden classroom doors had disintegrated into charred heaps. Remnants of twisted metal, seared clean of wooden parts, stood as grim reminders of children's desks.

The robot painstakingly circled the room, lowering its mechanical arm close to the floor to see as much as possible under the layers of yellow smoke, until the video camera stopped on an elongated patch barely visible against its surroundings. The robot crawled forward until the video revealed the image of a small child, its clothes burned away, its body charred.

"God, that's one of the missing *keiki*," ʻŌhai said, choking on the words.

Koa was no stranger to death. As a child, he'd discovered a childhood friend hanged. As a teenager, he'd killed a man. His closest Special Forces buddy had died in his arms. He'd seen dead children in Afghanistan and killed his share of fanatics in Somalia. As a cop, he'd investigated gruesome murders and lost witnesses he should have protected. Death and guilt were irrevocably intertwined in his psyche. Still, the sight of the tiny charred body hit him like a fist to the gut.

The robot found the bodies of two more children and the missing teacher before approaching the door to the last classroom—the one on the southeast corner of the school. The robot's thermal camera registered white-hot temperatures over six hundred degrees. Yet, the door to this last classroom, although ravaged charcoal black by fire and bent out of shape, remained intact.

"What the hell?" 'Ōhai said. "That's a fire door—a steel fire door. We don't put fire doors on classrooms. And it looks like that sucker suffered bomb damage."

The tech moved the robot's claw to the handle, but the door wouldn't budge. The robot tried again to no avail, and the tech turned to 'Ōhai. "What do you want me to do?"

"Can we send it downstairs into the mechanical spaces?"

"There's a basement?" Koa asked. The island's rocky volcanic soil made basements expensive and rare.

"That's what the blueprints show," 'Ōhai responded.

"Got to be the only *kula*, school, on the island with a basement," Koa mused.

"Tell me where to go," the tech requested.

'Ōhai turned to the floor plans spread on the wall. "The stairs are back down the hallway, just south of the main office."

The Ardros F6B retreated back toward the main office and found the stairs. Koa watched the monitors as the odd-looking machine extended and lowered its front wheels, descending step by step down the stairs with remarkable agility. At the bottom, the robot turned to reveal a smoke-filled corridor with a concrete floor, walls, and ceiling. The thermal imager showed the walls to be a relatively cool one hundred degrees, but when the robot faced the south end of the hallway, its thermal imager registered solid white reflecting temperatures above 600 degrees. Reading from the plans, 'Ōhai announced, "It should be 300 feet to that end wall."

A rumbling sound reverberated through the speakers. The concrete tunnel shook, sending particles of cement into the air already laden with sulfur gases. The robot crept slowly down the hallway. Even with its powerful halogen lights, they could see less than a yard. The tech repeatedly stopped and turned the robot to avoid broken pipes and other obstructions. The sound grew deafening and the tech turned the volume down. Vibrations shook the images. The robot did not, however, transverse 300 feet.

After 240 feet, it encountered a concrete wall—or rather the remnants of one. The whole middle section had collapsed, leaving a gaping hole. The remains of the barrier stood no more than three feet high at its midpoint with crumbling concrete and twisted reinforcing rods protruding all around. Broken electrical cables hung like spaghetti and a ruptured pipe gushed water that flashed instantly into steam.

"I don't understand," 'Ōhai said. "There's not supposed to be a wall for another sixty feet."

"I thought it was impossible to burn concrete?" Koa said, adding a question mark.

"*'Ae*," 'Ōhai agreed, "but at temperatures above a few hundred degrees, concrete loses its strength. The cement and the reinforcing steel inside expand at different rates and the stuff rips itself apart."

"*Auē*, my God," Koa exclaimed, pointing to the monitor. "*Look!* Look at the edge of the hole. That's no ordinary wall." Smoke poured through the opening, but gaps in the opaque cloud revealed the remnants of a slab of concrete at least six feet thick.

"Christ," 'Ōhai exclaimed, "it looks like a bank vault."

"Why would anyone put a six-foot-thick wall in an elementary school?" Koa asked.

"It's like the contractor tried to seal off the end of the building," 'Ōhai responded.

The fire door on the classroom and this ruined basement barrier made sense only if they were intended to isolate the south end of the building. "Exactly!" Koa exclaimed. "The damn contractor must have *known* about the volcanic risk and tried to seal it off."

The two men stared at each other in disbelief. "Hard to believe anyone would do somethin' so stupid," 'Ōhai said.

"And criminal. The builders deliberately put those kids at risk. That's murder by reckless endangerment." Koa's voice rang with barely contained anger. "Somebody's going to pay for this. And pay big-time."

"Wonder where all that concrete came from," 'Ōhai mused. "With six-foot walls, they must have poured over a thousand cubic yards of concrete just in this one corner of the building."

"Had to be West Hawai'i Concrete," Koa responded. "One of Sergeant Basa's brothers is a manager up there. It's the only place on this side of the island big enough to handle the volume."

At that moment, an explosion rocked the truck. Rocks and other debris battered the side of the vehicle. The screens and readout from the robot went black. "Jesus," the tech said. "We lost the robot."

What had begun as one of the worst civil catastrophes in Hawaiian history had suddenly become one of its most horrific crimes. The deliberate concealment of a deadly flaw inside an elementary school had killed *keiki* and their *kumu*, children and their teachers. Murder . . . reckless endangerment murder.

CHAPTER FOUR

KOA NEVER MADE it to bed. Bleary-eyed, he found his way back to the police headquarters in Hilo. He stopped in the command center for a large Styrofoam cup of strong coffee. No cream, no sugar. Black and bitter. He'd always liked it black, and the Army taught him to like it bitter. The Army had taught him a lot of things and was the reason he'd become a cop.

Jerry, his closest Army buddy, had planned to leave the service, return to his hometown of Seattle, and, like his father, join the police. Only Jerry had died in Somalia, killed by a bullet meant for Koa. That moment when Jerry had died in his arms set the pointer for Koa's life. He returned to Hawai'i, joined the police, and channeled his guilt into fighting for justice.

His coffee had the acrid taste of sulfur dioxide, and he realized the chemical smell permeated his hair and clothes. Jolted by the caffeine, he made his way toward the jail. Waiting for one of the wardens to bring his brother to an interrogation room, he wondered which Ikaika would show up—the troubled boy he'd known as a child or the foulmouthed con he'd become.

It bothered Koa that he couldn't connect with his brother. In reality, they both had a criminal past. After Koa's father had been killed in a supposed sugar mill "accident," Koa, then eighteen, had talked to his father's mill coworkers. They shared their suspicions that Anthony Hazzard, the mill manager, had arranged the fatal accident because of Koa's father's union activities. Blaming Hazzard for his father's death, Koa had tracked the man to his remote mountain cabin.

He'd watched Hazzard, biding his time. By late in the evening, after Hazzard had downed nearly half a bottle of bourbon, Koa had jumped the heavyset mill manager in a chokehold. Wanting to punish, but not kill the man, Koa had released his death grip. Hazzard had rebounded and they'd fought. Sensing he was outmatched by the older, stronger man, Koa had grabbed an iron fire poker to defend himself. Hazzard had charged, his huge fists swinging. Koa struck and Hazzard had gone down.

Koa would never forget the waves of fear and self-revulsion that consumed him when he'd realized he'd killed Hazzard. He sat for hours blaming himself for his recklessness and stupidity. The sugar barons who still controlled the police and the courts would have him locked up for life. He considered fleeing to a foreign country or even ending his life. After hours of agony that seemed like days, he decided to hide the killing. He considered, but rejected, burning the cabin with Hazzard in it, and instead, disguised Hazzard's death as a hanging suicide in which the rope broke, allowing Hazzard's body to topple onto the iron fire tools, explaining Hazzard's head injury. Koa then left the cabin door open, hoping that *pua'a*, wild pigs, roaming the forest would ravage the body, making it difficult for the authorities to detect the murder.

He hadn't been convinced his subterfuge would work and was haunted by fear of discovery. He saw Hazzard's face in every passing stranger and in the *ao 'ala'apapa*, the "circus-train" cloud formations, so common in Hawai'i's evening skies. He jumped at every knock on the door or passing policeman. Yet, gradually, his fears subsided.

Days passed before the *Hawai'i Tribune Harald* reported that hikers had found Hazzard's body in the remote cabin. It had been ravaged by *pua'a*, and the coroner had called it a suicide.

Although he didn't realize it at the time, Koa came to understand that the first sparks of his life's mission were born in the crucible of penetrating guilt and self-loathing caused by Hazzard's death. That death drove him into the U.S. Army. Officer Candidate School and Special Forces training made him into a man. Stints in Afghanistan and Somalia taught him about the world outside Hawai'i. The death of Jerry, his closest friend, had been the final turning point.

Unlike Ikaika, Koa's crimes were secret even from his family. But Koa hadn't escaped the guilt, which ultimately drove him to become a cop and devote his life to exacting justice. Fear and guilt, he imagined, accounted for the difference between brothers. He was terrified of getting caught and facing society's wrath, and he suffered penetrating guilt prompting the need to make recompense for what he'd done. Ikaika feared nothing and felt no remorse.

"So, my cop brother has come to gloat," Ikaika hissed when the guard brought him into the room. Ikaika, a big man, well over six feet, had the hard face of a convict and a sea of prison ink. Tattooed with black, genealogical, geometric bands spiraling around his neck and down his arms, he looked old beyond his years. Telegraphing attitude, Ikaika's eyes shocked Koa, exuding a strange, demented anger as he paced the small room, turning frequently to glare at Koa. Koa wondered if his brother was sick or if jail had further warped his twisted mind.

Koa never understood what had gone wrong with Ikaika. Eight years apart, they'd both grown up in a shack on the hill overlooking Laupāhoehoe on the northern coast of the Big Island. Koa's father, a humble sugar plantation worker, and his mother, a native healer of local renown, presided over a poor but close-knit family. Except for

Ikaika. He'd lived in a world steeped in cruelty and violence. Barely halfway through grade school, Ikaika beat up another kid, breaking his jaw and putting out one of his eyes. With time and punishment, Ikaika only got worse. His white-hot temper and swift left hook enabled him to break records for schoolyard fights and later barroom brawls. Ruggedly handsome and physically powerful, true to the meaning of his name, Ikaika had left a trail of broken hearts and *hāpai*, or pregnant girls. Graduating to car theft and drug dealing, stints in juvie, and later prison, only made him more violent.

"You think I want to see you like this?" Koa responded.

"Sure you do, big brother. You and that asshole Moyan got me locked up." Ikaika referred to Hardy Moyan, his hard-assed parole officer. Ikaika clenched and unclenched his fists while he prowled the room.

"I opposed Moyan's pulling your parole. *Maopopo 'iā 'oē*, you know that."

"Bullshit!" Ikaika screamed, turning to face Koa. He leaned forward like he might lunge across the table that separated them. "You like seeing me locked in a cage." Ikaika's spittle sprayed Koa's face, but he didn't back away.

"*'A'ole*, not true," Koa responded in a calm voice. "You were in the courtroom. You heard me plead for your release."

"Yeah, yeah, sure you did. All mouth. Only lies."

The previous year, Ikaika, on parole after a burglary conviction, got himself mixed up in a child sex ring. After a complicated investigation, Koa ultimately arrested his brother but fought against parole revocation—to no avail. Hardy Moyan, his brother's parole officer, despised Ikaika, telling the parole commissioners that he was "a mean, nasty bastard with no moral code, a violent streak, and an uncontrolled temper." Ikaika's involvement in the sex ring hadn't helped. He wound up sentenced to a minimum of four more years behind bars. Worse yet, Hawai'i had contracted with a corporate prison company to house its convicts in Arizona.

Looking at Ikaika, Koa thought of a split screen. On the left half, Koa saw his handsome baby brother cradled in his mother's arms, waiving some household object and cooing with delight. On the right-hand side, he saw Ikaika, his knuckles bruised and face bloodied with a malicious snarl, after beating some classmate to a pulp. Koa couldn't reconcile the two halves of the screen nor comprehend the tortured route that led from one to the other.

Ikaika refused to acknowledge that Koa had fought to keep his brother out of prison. Instead, Ikaika blamed Koa for all his problems, and Koa wasn't going to convince him otherwise, so Koa changed the subject. "How was the trip back here from Arizona?"

"A goddamn joyride, sittin' in the last fuckin' row in cuffs with the motherfuckin' tourists starin' at me. Just like one of 'em paradise posters."

Koa had promised himself not to rise to his brother's bait, but Ikaika's self-pity rubbed his nerves raw. Koa displayed self-restraint when he was on the job, but when it came to family, he found it difficult to control his emotions. He wanted to say, "You've got only yourself to blame, little brother," but instead asked, "When are you scheduled to testify?" His brother had been blackmailed into helping a criminal gang prostitute runaway children and had been returned to the Big Island to testify at the trial of one of the gang's leaders.

"No ask me. They don't tell me shit."

That, Koa thought, had the ring of truth. "I asked, 'cause Māmā's coming in to see you."

At the mention of his mother, Ikaika's face softened, and his whole body relaxed like someone had pulled a plug letting the tension drain out. Māmā, something of a mystic, had defended and protected Ikaika no matter how outrageous his conduct, and she alone had the ability to reach through his convict shell to his core.

"When?" Ikaika asked.

"Your sister is driving her in from Laupāhoehoe as we speak."

Ikaika, who'd been pacing the room like a caged animal, slumped into the chair across the table from Koa.

Koa, responding to the change in demeanor, softened his tone. "So, *pehea*, how are you doing, little brother?"

"Shitty. Being locked in a cage ain't a fuckin' picnic. Every damn day is the same. Time don't move much."

"At least you look fit."

"Yeah, well, workin' out is as good as it gets in da slammah, an' you gotta bulk up or else the other cons screw you over."

Koa understood how that worked. "You want something to eat? Something different than prison crap. There's a Mickey Dee's down the block. I could get you a burger and fries."

"Sure. A triple cheeseburger, an' maybe you could score a couple lines of snow. Be good to get high."

Koa just shook his head. Why, he wondered, did he bother? Leaving to get the food, a sense of sadness rushed over him. Something had happened to Ikaika growing up and prison had turned him ever more bitter and violent. Koa had seen it in other criminals, but witnessing it in his own family depressed him.

When he returned with the food, his sister, Alana, was standing outside the interrogation room, looking distressed. In physical appearance, Koa's baby sister took after their mother, short of stature with a roundish face, flawless golden-brown skin, long black hair, and inquisitive black eyes. She lived with their mother, worked as a part-time social worker, and shared her mother's passion for native medicine. Unlike their mother, she couldn't tolerate Ikaika, largely because of the pain he caused Māmā. After taking a drag on her cigarette, she said, "Māmā's inside with Ikaika."

"You're not going to visit him?"

She scowled. "Spend time with my bastard brother. No way. The cops should never have brought him back here. Māmā's going to be upset for weeks."

Koa understood. Ikaika's violent behavior had ripped fissures like earthquakes in his family. Mauloa, Koa's middle brother, had given up on Ikaika and hadn't visited him in years. His sister, Alana, spoke to Ikaika only when it couldn't be avoided. As the oldest Kāne male, Koa tried to maintain a relationship, but every effort ended in acrimony. He'd once talked his fisherman friend, Hook Hao, into giving Ikaika a job on Hook's commercial fishing vessel, the *Kaʻupu*, the albatross.

"So, you like me be one swab on a stinkin' boat?" Ikaika had mocked.

"It pays okay and Hook's good to his people," Koa responded.

The job had lasted four days before Hook fired Ikaika for assaulting another crewman. Somehow, that, too, was Koa's fault.

When Koa entered the interrogation room, he found Ikaika sitting beside his mother. She had her hand on his arm, while he pleaded with her. ". . . It's hard, Māmā. It's hard being in a cell." In a deeper, sharper voice, he turned on Koa, hate blazing in his eyes. "And my big-shot brother does nothing to get me out."

Koa had seen and heard it all before. For Ikaika, truth was not the truth. Something in his psyche required him to blame Koa for every tragedy that befell him.

Fortunately, or unfortunately, Māpuana knew her youngest son's nature. "*ʻAʻole*, my *keiki*, it is not Koa's fault you are in jail. It is the result of your own actions." Only Māpuana could speak the truth without provoking Ikaika, but her words still went unheeded.

Koa pushed the McDonald's bag across the table, and Ikaika ate like he'd been starved half his life. When he finished the triple cheeseburger and three orders of fries, Māpuana produced a container of *haupia*, and Ikaika wolfed down a dozen of the sweet coconut cream custard squares. Koa knew only Māpuana's presence prevented Ikaika from complaining about the absence of the cocaine he'd requested. Although the thought dishonored his sense of family, Koa secretly felt glad that Ikaika would soon testify and be on a plane back to Arizona.

* * *

When he returned to the command center, a news report on a TV caught Koa's eye, and he stopped to watch. A short woman with brown hair and tears in her eyes stood on the street with the Kona-Wili school in the distant background. Firemen still pumped water onto the south end of the building and clouds of steam and yellow smoke still billowed upward.

The banner across the bottom of the screen read: "Mica Osbourne, missing child's mother." The woman, her hair frazzled and her face contorted with grief, barely controlled herself. "They should never have built a school on top of a volcanic fault. They killed my baby girl. The government killed my baby girl, and they can't even find her body." The image shifted to a picture of her child, a beautiful little girl with bright black eyes and dark hair in pigtails, tied with pink bows.

Images of the dead and injured kids flashed through Koa's head. For a moment, he was back inside the classroom, nauseated by the smell of sulfur dioxide and choking on the yellow smoke. Once again, he held the little girl he'd rescued. And the little boy. He saw the dead kids lying in the pouring rain, so real he might have reached out to touch them. The slideshow from hell. He'd seen horrible sights in Afghanistan and Somalia, visions he'd suppressed only after a thousand sleepless nights, but he'd never forget the night just past.

As a detective, Koa worked to create a bond with the victims of the crimes he investigated. He retraced their paths, walked in their shoes, breathed the air they breathed, and tried to think the way they thought. It fostered his empathy, powered his pursuit of justice, and made him a good detective. His empathy for the KonaWili kids needed no battery, no jump starter. Their innocence powered his fury at the adults who'd put them in harm's way.

And it had been foreseeable. The super-thick concrete meant the builders knew of the risk, and they couldn't have acted alone. Planners, architects, and inspectors must have visited the site. They must have seen the concrete and asked questions. Koa couldn't imagine what would possess a whole cadre of professionals to put schoolkids at risk. It wasn't negligence, not with those concrete walls. It was deliberate. Greed motivated people to take extraordinary risks, but he couldn't imagine a conspiracy of avarice reckless enough to endanger a school full of children. Some more sinister evil lurked behind the KonaWili disaster. And the faces of those poor kids would haunt him long after he cornered the culprits.

The image of Mica Osbourne's little girl stuck in Koa's mind. He tried to imagine a parent's grief at the loss of a child. How would he feel if it were his child? Maybe a child he'd have with Nālani, his girlfriend. The idea was too awful to contemplate.

He and Nālani had been living together for three years, and, after he'd suffered several failed romances, she brought him profound joy. Still, there were strains in their relationship. Both had been working crazy hours. He'd had a series of tough cases, and *Pele's* eruptions at the summit and in Puna had doubled Nālani's normal workload as a national park ranger. They hadn't had a weekend off in over two months, but their last break had been spectacular. They'd driven to Hōlualoa to celebrate *tūtū's* eightieth birthday.

Nālani's grandmother had raised nineteen children and knew more about parenting than Dr. Spock. As all too often happens among poor Hawaiian children, Nālani came into the world as the illegitimate daughter of a seventeen-year-old meth addict and an older lowlife who disappeared into the prison system. *Tūtū* saved Nālani and taught her to excel in school, college, graduate school, and as a biology researcher before she returned to the Big Island. Koa had first seen her at a fundraiser and been smitten.

Fourteen of *tūtū's* charges came to honor their surrogate mother's eightieth. Nālani wasn't surprised that her younger half-sister, who lived on Maui and had been in and out of drug programs, wasn't there. The party had been a lovefest with *'ahi* poke, *kālua* pork, *poi*, fish *laulau*, squid *lū'au*, and a dozen *haole* dishes. *Tūtū* had more energy than most of her "children" and spent time with each of them individually, learning about their lives and dispensing wisdom. If there were saints in heaven, Koa figured *tūtū* would ultimately claim her place.

On the drive back to Volcano, Koa had asked Nālani about her private conversation with *tūtū*. Nālani put him off and that only made him more curious. They were nearly back to their little cottage before Nālani said, "She told me not to let you get away."

"She's a *wahine akamai*, a brilliant woman," he quipped, and they both burst out laughing.

Recollections of their last outing reminded Koa that they hadn't talked in many hours. He'd texted her a couple of times during his long afternoon and endless night at KonaWili, but there hadn't been time to talk. He called. "Good morning, my *ipo*," he greeted her with his favorite Hawaiian endearment.

"God, you sound exhausted. Are you okay?"

"One of the longest and most painful nights of my life."

"It's as bad as they say on TV?"

"Worse. I can't get the images of those kids out of my head. And it didn't have to happen."

He heard her sharp intake of breath. "What do you mean?"

He told her about the concrete.

"My God, Koa, they killed those kids."

"Yeah. The builder killed those kids and he didn't act alone."

"I'm so sorry, Koa." She paused and a long silence followed. "Where are you?"

"Back at headquarters." He told her about his visit with Ikaika, describing the hostility in Ikaika's eyes. She, like Alana, wanted little to do with Ikaika, who resented her place in Koa's life and missed no opportunity to express his dislike.

"*Pilikia hoʻi kau a lohe mai,*" she said. Serious trouble indeed.

Little did he know how serious.

CHAPTER FIVE

THAT THE BUILDERS concealed a volcanic vent beneath an elementary school profoundly shocked Koa. He needed to warn the mayor and the governor before word leaked, triggering a political frenzy. Every parent of a school-aged child would clamor for heads to roll. But before sounding the alarm, Koa wanted to confront Hank Boyle, owner of Boyle Construction, shown on the plans as the general contractor for the KonaWili school. Boyle must have abandoned the original plans in favor of the massive walls, flooring, and fire door sealing off the classroom at the south end of the building. Koa needed to know why.

When Koa wanted the lowdown on someone, he turned to Detective Piki. Piki, the most junior of his detectives, looked younger than his age, especially with his crew cut, and bubbled with energy and enthusiasm—in Koa's experience, too much enthusiasm. Still, Piki displayed hacker-level skill at mining information from public and law enforcement databases. After some digging, Piki found a picture and generated a profile of the sixty-four-year-old contractor.

Boyle's father had raked in a fortune from land development in the 1950s and '60s before starting Boyle Construction to build homes in subdivisions he'd created. A classic double dip. Hank Boyle inherited the business and parlayed Boyle Construction into

one of the largest government contractors in the state. A major contributor to Democratic political candidates, he lived in a mansion
outside the tiny, historic mountainside community of Hōlualoa,
south of Kona. Ironically, not too far from Nālani's *tūtū*.

Koa and Piki took Route 180 south past coffee farms, funky little
art galleries, and Hōlualoa's historic, pink Kona Hotel, infamous for
its bathroom perched all by itself at the end of a long, elevated walkway overlooking Kona and the Pacific. They turned onto a private
road, climbed the side of Mauna Loa volcano to a stately white co-
lonial mansion, and parked next to a pickup truck emblazoned with
the Boyle Construction logo. Six wide steps led to a portico graced
with white columns. Piki rang the bell but got no response.

Music blared from inside the house—a radio or perhaps a television—but a second and then a third ring brought no response. Koa
walked along the porch peering through the windows. Lights blazed
inside, and at first, he saw nothing out of the ordinary. Then the
view through the second window to the left of the front door
stopped him cold. He'd get no answers from Hank Boyle, whose
lifeless body dangled at the end of an electrical cord.

They broke the door down and rushed into the house. Boyle hung
like a crippled puppet in the center of a small office. Koa checked for
a pulse, but Boyle would never again need medical help. Koa then
stopped to study the scene. His own criminal experience informed
his penetrating eye. Having staged a fake suicide and fooled the
cops, he was uniquely qualified to spot the inconsistencies in a crime
scene, compulsively suspicious, and paranoid about being misled.
And recently, he'd begun snapping cell phone pictures. Ronnie
Woo, the police photographer, would shoot the official pictures, but
Koa liked having his own pics.

He worked the process in phases. His first impression of a crime
scene frequently proved critical, and he'd learned to let his mind

absorb every detail. He searched for telltale signs, inconsistencies, something out of place, anything that didn't belong, what should have been present but wasn't. Later, he would reassess his early impressions in light of crime scene photos, forensics, witness statements, and any other evidence. Finally, when he had a suspect, he'd repeat the process, making sure the pixels came together to form a coherent picture.

Koa slowly cataloged the scene in his mind—an old wooden desk, a straight-back chair, file cabinets, bookcases, and a floor lamp. An empty glass. A half-empty bottle of Glenlivet single malt whiskey on the desk. A section of brown electrical cord sliced from a floor lamp, leaving neatly chopped ends. Koa looked around for a cutting tool but saw none. Odd. The chair—surprisingly still upright—stood where a man hanging himself might have kicked it away. Koa looked from the chair to the body and back again.

Boyle—matching the picture Piki had turned up—hung on a brown electrical cord from a twisted ceiling fixture, his neck stretched and body naked, save for a pair of boxer shorts. His arms hung limply at his sides with fingers straight and nails undamaged. He hadn't tried to save himself, an oddity in hanging cases. Unlike most hangings where the victim dies gasping for air, Boyle's mouth remained closed. Petechiae—tiny red blotches—covered his face.

Suicide held tenth place as a cause of death in the U.S. People aged forty-five to sixty-four accounted for the majority of suicide victims, and men killed themselves four times more often than women. Firearms led suffocation, mostly by hanging, as the most common method. Suicidal men often mustered their courage with alcohol. And Boyle certainly had a motive to do himself in. He'd built an elementary school over a volcanic vent, triggering the deaths of fourteen children and four teachers. To a less perceptive cop, the scene showed all the earmarks of an open and shut suicide.

To the man who'd successfully faked Hazzard's suicide, the discrepancies in the Boyle hanging radiated like a heat lamp—the body hung too high off the floor. A man standing on a chair to hang himself inevitably ends up with his feet dangling below the height of the chair seat. Boyle's feet hung a good two inches above the height of the chair seat. Humans harbored a powerful instinct to live, and most suicides made a last-ditch attempt to save themselves, but Boyle's straight fingers and unbroken fingernails meant he'd made no effort to tear the electrical wire from his neck. And while Koa knew red pinpoints of petechiae commonly appeared in hanging suicides, there shouldn't be any on the face. In a full-suspension hanging, the noose tightens above the victim's heart. Blood pressure in the head drops and gravity drains the blood down from the face. Petechiae might be present elsewhere on the body, but not on the face. Koa had little doubt Boyle had been unconscious, maybe even dead, before someone staged a fake suicide.

Piki, who'd been on the phone calling for a crime scene team, peered into the office from behind Koa. "Looks like a classic suicide by hanging."

Although tremendously energetic, Piki too often jumped to quick conclusions. Koa tried, without much success, to slow him down, but he ran like a battery-operated toy with only one speed. "It's not," Koa responded. "Don't go in that room or touch the body until we get a crime scene team in here." Always conscious of training his detectives, Koa turned to face his younger colleague. "Now stand here and figure out why it's not a suicide."

Slowly, Piki took in the scene. "It doesn't look like he tried to save himself," the young detective said hesitantly.

"What else?" Koa demanded.

"He's awful high off the floor."

"Now you're thinking," Koa rewarded his young colleague.

First, the discovery of the strange concrete structures under the school building and now the murder of its general contractor left Koa with a mess on his hands—an understatement by any measure. The lack of a competent medical examiner to confirm his suspicions only made matters worse. Hawai'i County employed no qualified ME. Shizuo Hiro, a seventy-eight-year-old Japanese obstetrician, doubled as the county coroner. Appointed only because of his status as a mayoral crony, Shizuo played poker with the mayor's gang, losing large sums on absurd bets. A millstone around Koa's neck, he impeded every criminal investigation requiring even semi-sophisticated medical analysis. Koa couldn't imagine relying on Shizuo in such a high-stakes crime with national publicity.

If Chief Lannua were on-island, he'd tell Koa, as he had so often in the past, to suck it up and deal with Shizuo. But the chief wasn't around, so Koa, having reached his limit with the incompetent quack, took matters into his own hands. He called Mayor Tanaka, explained the discovery of the construction anomalies at the school, and stunned the mayor by reporting the murder of Hank Boyle.

"I'm going to call the governor's office and ask him to assign the Honolulu ME to this investigation," Koa announced.

"Shizuo can handle it. Besides, I don't like asking Māhoe for help," the mayor responded.

"No, Shizuo can't handle it," Koa said. "He'll screw it up and embarrass both you and the governor. You got the national press all over this disaster, and it's only going to get worse with Boyle's murder. You really want CNN's Walker McKenzie interviewing Shizuo?"

That stopped the mayor. An uncomfortably long pause followed before Tanaka replied, "Damnit." Another pause. "Okay, Detective. But I'll call the damn governor."

While Koa waited for the Honolulu ME to arrive, the crime scene team went over the Boyle mansion like watchmakers. Piki canvassed neighbors. Ronnie Woo, a young Chinese photographer who wielded his Nikon like a weapon, photographed the scene, using a yardstick to show Boyle's feet were twenty-three inches off the floor. The seat of the chair stood barely twenty inches high. Diminutive Georgina Pau and hulking Chip Baxter, evidence technicians, affectionately known to police insiders as Mini and Maxi, dusted for prints and searched for bloodstains and other evidence.

Having endured years of Shizuo's incompetent forensics, Koa had mastered a few tricks of the ME's trade. He carried a digital thermometer and took the hanging man's temperature. Guessing the air-conditioned room temperature to be in the mid-seventies—substantially less than normal body temperature—Koa applied the old forensic standard: a corpse cools at the rate of about 1.5 degrees an hour. With a body temperature of 89 degrees, Koa figured Boyle had been dead about six hours. His estimate seemed consistent with the stiffening of the corpse. He put the time of death at roughly four in the morning or seventeen hours after the first news reports of the KonaWili school disaster. Despite his seat-of-the-pants medical exam, Koa left the body hanging so the Honolulu ME could make her own assessment.

Slipping on a pair of latex gloves, Koa opened the nearest file cabinet. He found the files organized into categories—residential, commercial, and government—with the governmental grouping further subdivided by building type. In the section for school buildings, he found a gap where the KonaWili file should have been. And if the empty space didn't arouse suspicions enough, a loose label in the bottom of the drawer for "KonaWili School" confirmed a missing file. Its absence solidified the connection between Boyle's death and the KonaWili school disaster.

"Looks like he had some help."

Koa turned toward the doorway at the sound of a woman's voice. Anne Ka'au, the fiftyish Honolulu medical examiner, stared intently at the corpse. Dressed in jeans and a light blue blouse, Kaʻau had a long angular face with inquisitive black eyes behind wire-rim glasses.

"You sure got here quickly," he said.

"I was already on-island, visiting my daughter." Kaʻau had a nationwide reputation as a top-flight professional, lecturing regularly at leading university forensics programs. Koa watched her register every aspect of the scene like a walking digital camera. He wasn't surprised she shared his initial impression of the crime scene.

"*Mahalo* for leaving the scene intact for me," she said, extracting a camera from her kit and taking her own photographs. Then she checked temperature and lividity. When they cut the body down, she examined every centimeter of the deceased's skin, including the inside of his mouth and between his toes, as well as the electrical cord, closely observing its cut ends and knots.

While she worked, she questioned Koa. "The governor told me this phony suicide might be connected to the KonaWili disaster but didn't give me any details. What's the deal?"

Koa explained the strange concrete structures in the school and ID'd Boyle as the general contractor. Then he told her about the missing file.

"My God," she exclaimed, "they must have uncovered the volcanic vent during construction and tried to cover it up. They put those poor kids at risk. That's criminal."

"Dead on," he agreed.

Leaving her to work her forensic magic, Koa toured Boyle's mansion. Autographed photographs of NFL football players dotted the forty-foot living room. A commercial kitchen, a huge wood-paneled dining room, a small movie theater, a billiard room with a professional pool table, a library, three bathrooms, and Boyle's office occupied the first floor. The luxurious house showed that Boyle had raked in a fortune as a contractor. Why, Koa wondered, would such a wealthy man risk it all by hiding a deadly threat under a grade school?

Boyle apparently lived alone. Koa found no signs of a spouse or other companion. Oddly, the lights blazed all over the ground floor, and the sixty-inch television in the living room flickered with an old movie rerun. A violent explosion on the big screen caught Koa's eye, and he stopped to watch part of *Krakatoa, East of Java,* before switching the TV off. Had, he wondered, Boyle really been watching a volcano movie?

Upstairs, he found Boyle's bedroom. Once again, he sensed something out of place and stopped to examine the scene. Boyle's clothes—a pair of jeans and a Hawaiian shirt—lay discarded on a chair in the corner of the room. Boyle's flip-flops lay on the floor half under the chair. A tangled top sheet covered only part of the unmade bed. One pillow remained on the bed while another lay discarded on the floor. As he peered at the bed, Koa saw two faint, but distinct, reddish-brown smudges. From dirty shoes, maybe? Smudges, he wondered, left by an assailant kneeling on the bed?

He tried to imagine the sequence of events. Boyle undresses and goes to bed in his boxers. He's restless, throws off the pillow, gets up, leaves the sheets tangled, goes downstairs, pours himself a farewell drink, and hangs himself. A plausible scenario. A killer, he knew, might have staged such a sequence, but only as an illusion.

More likely, he thought, the killer snuck into the bedroom, suffocated the sleeping Boyle with a pillow, tossed the pillow aside, and carried the dead man down to his study to be strung up. The killer had turned the lights and TV on to give the impression Boyle had been awake. He wondered if they'd find Boyle's fingerprints on the Glenlivet bottle. Koa called downstairs to his team, telling them to treat the bedroom as a secondary crime scene.

Turning down a hallway, he studied Boyle's framed memorabilia. A UH sheepskin, a fraternity certificate, and decades-old pictures.

Like Koa, Boyle attended the University of Hawai'i Mānoa campus in Honolulu. He'd graduated in 1975, long before Koa, but unlike Koa, Boyle belonged to one of the few UH fraternities. He'd been a Tau Kappa Epsilon frat boy. Studying the photos on the wall next to the certificates, Koa spotted a youthful Boyle in picture after picture with his fraternity brothers. Koa thought he recognized one or two besides Boyle, but the young faces and long hair made it hard to be sure.

A TKE fraternity connection, Koa thought, made sense. Only a tiny percentage of twenty thousand students at the UH Mānoa campus joined social fraternities, but for those who did, the frats offered a well-known route to political and economic power in the state. Three governors, both U.S. senators, dozens of state legislators, and hundreds of the state's business elite wore TKE pins. Boyle had started polishing his political connections as a freshman in college.

In the bathroom, Koa opened the medicine cabinet. Prescription medicines often yielded up clues, and Koa discovered a full-scale pharmacy—more than forty orange and green pill bottles. Boyle's prescription drugs spoke volumes. Half-empty bottles of Prozac, Zoloft, Lexapro, Paxil, Tofranil, Anafranil, and Marplan told the tale of a man suffering from depression and anxiety. From the variety of drugs and the dates on the labels, Boyle obviously suffered from a severe and long-standing disorder. For all his wealth, Koa realized, Hank Boyle had been an unhappy man. Koa made a note of the doctor's name—Dr. Teddy Patrone with a Kona telephone number.

Nothing else upstairs shed light on Boyle's murder, so Koa went back to check on the Honolulu ME and the crime scene team. He found Georgina, one of the crime scene techs, using a portable vacuum with a special filter box to collect trace evidence. He waved to her. A short, slight woman with prematurely gray hair, she was compulsively thorough with a wicked sense of humor. To escape the noise of the vacuum, he led Anne Ka'au, the ME, into the hallway to ask what she thought of the scene.

"It's not a suicide. Body temperature, lividity, and degree of rigor mortis put the TOD at about four o'clock this morning. It's pretty hard to string up a conscious, able-bodied man, so he was probably unconscious, or more likely, already dead. I didn't find any wounds or needle marks, so I'd guess the killer suffocated him. That would explain the petechiae on the face."

Koa smiled inwardly, pleased she'd agreed with his own conclusions and thrilled to be working with a real ME. Georgina finished vacuuming so Koa stepped back into Boyle's study and gave her an inquiring look.

"Boyle wiped his fingerprints off the whiskey bottle and the glass, so we wouldn't know who did it," she said with a grin.

Koa, an old hand at crime scene humor, rewarded her with a chuckle. It served as further confirmation Boyle hadn't killed himself. "What else?"

"He also hid the tool he used to cut the electrical cord. It's not here and Chip hasn't found it anywhere else in the house."

At that moment, Chip Baxter, the other crime scene tech, came down from upstairs. A big man with a round face and a thick shock of black hair, he was Georgina's opposite in almost every way, except he, too, loved crime scene jokes. "Body fluids on the discarded pillow—a good deal more than you'd normally find—and what looks like lava particles on the sheet. Funny, 'cause I went through Boyle's closet. If the man had dirty shoes, he tossed them before he snuffed his own lights."

Koa wanted something to tie a perp to the crime scene. "You recover any suspicious prints or anything with the perp's DNA?"

"Nada," Georgina responded. "It's too clean. The killer must have worn gloves and a stocking, or something over his head. Otherwise, there'd be loose hairs, especially given the time he spent setting up the phony hanging."

An amateur had staged the fake suicide, cutting the electrical cord without leaving the cutting tool, wiping his prints off the liquor glass, and hanging the body too high. The smudges on the bed probably came from the killer's shoes.

Koa focused on the big picture. With Boyle's murder, he still needed someone who knew what went down on the school construction site. Whatever had happened, it wasn't pretty, and Boyle had almost certainly died to keep it secret.

*   *   *

Late in the afternoon, CNN's Walker McKenzie called wanting an update on the case. Koa began to put him off when the TV journalist shocked him. "I hear the contractor committed suicide."

McKenzie enjoyed incredible sources. Koa hated dealing with the press, but McKenzie was a pro, and it made no sense to alienate him, especially over something soon to be in the papers. "I can confirm we found him hanged."

"A suicide or just staged that way?"

Koa paused, thinking how to play it. It might be useful, he concluded, to let the killer know he hadn't fooled the police. "We're calling it a suspicious death, at least until we conclude our investigation."

"Thanks, Detective."

After the reporter hung up, Koa wondered what he'd set in motion. Boyle, he felt sure, died because of KonaWili. The death had been faked to look like a suicide to deceive the police. A news story reporting that the police regarded the death as suspicious would make the killer nervous. Nervous killers make mistakes. At least he hoped this killer would screw up.

Later that night, Koa had second thoughts, not about his conversation with Walker McKenzie, but about the crime scene itself. That Boyle's death hadn't been a suicide had been obvious to him and to Anne Ka'au. He'd known almost immediately and so had Anne. Could the killer, he wondered, have been so sloppy, so incompetent?

Hanging the body too high, taking the tool used to cut the electrical cord, wiping prints from the liquor bottle and the glass—maybe the killer panicked—but other aspects of the scene reflected thought. The killer left no fingerprints, no trace evidence, no DNA. If the killer smothered Boyle in bed, then the killer likely turned on the television and the downstairs lights. It was almost as though the killer deliberately staged the suicide to make it look phony.

Why would the killer do that? Maybe to send a message. But what message? And to whom?

CHAPTER SIX

Koa assembled his brain trust—Basa, Piki, and Zeke Brown, the Hawai'i County prosecutor. Zeke, a Tom Hanks look-alike with a decade and a half less wear, held one of the most powerful positions on the Big Island. He sat behind his huge wooden desk with his trademark black buffalo hide Lucchese boots on one of the pull-out extensions. A sports jacket hung behind the door for serious court work, but as usual, Zeke wore jeans and a *paniolo* shirt. He had an easy, friendly way with voters, who didn't seem to mind his frequent profanity. The others in the room saw nothing friendly in his piercing black eyes when Koa described the concrete structures under the school and the faked suicide of its builder.

"You're telling me the builder knew about a volcanic vent and nevertheless built the school?" Zeke asked in his abnormally loud voice.

"There's no other explanation for the fire door and the six-foot-thick walls," Koa responded. "And a lot of people besides the builder had to know, including the architect and the building inspectors."

"Christ, that's reckless endangerment and adds up to murder." Zeke pounded his desk, which had absorbed numerous blows over his six terms as county prosecutor.

"And somebody killed Boyle to keep him from talking," Koa continued.

"Makes me want to check out Samantha's school," Basa, who had two children, Samantha and Jason, in Hilo schools, added.

Koa, no stranger to Basa's family, knew both Samantha and Jason and saw the concern in Basa's eyes. "You and every other parent," he said.

"In a way," Piki said, "it's worse than Columbine, Sandy Hook, or Parkland." He referred to three of the worst school shootings in U.S. history. "I mean, in those cases, disturbed kids killed their classmates. Here the people who were supposed to protect kids put them in mortal danger."

Zeke steered the meeting back to its purpose. "So how do we proceed?"

"We need," Koa laid out his plan, "to learn everything we can about the KonaWili school—who owned the land, who selected and approved the site, who designed the school, who besides Boyle built it, who served as a watchdog during construction, and who inspected the final building. We need to understand the players, their backgrounds, their motivations, and the ugly choices they made."

"What should I do?" Piki, ever eager, asked.

"Piki, you hit the internet. Get everything you can on the school and everyone involved in siting, planning, and building it. Basa, you go collect all the county planning, inspection, and other public records."

"And I'll," Zeke said, "trace the ownership and get the property records."

"Great. We'll meet back here this afternoon," Koa said.

On the way down the hall, Piki, his eyes wide, turned to Koa. "Are those real Lucchese boots . . . I mean, like John Wayne real?"

Koa laughed. "Yeah, there's nothing phony about Zeke."

*   *   *

After completing their searches, they had twenty-five names span-
ning four key areas. First, the present and former owners of the
school property. Second, the land planning officials who zoned the
site. Third, the DOE officials who authorized and accepted the
completed school. And finally, the construction group, consisting of
architects, contractors, and subcontractors.

Zeke addressed the property issues. "The land around the
KonaWili school originally belonged to one of Hawai'i's original big
five landowners, who then sold it off to two ranchers. In the 1960s
during one of Hawai'i's cyclical land development booms, the ranchers sold the property to the Paradise Land Company, but Paradise
failed to develop it. In 2004, Paradise sold several thousand acres to
Hualālai Hui, a partnership planning to build hundreds of homes,
a recreation center, and a shopping plaza."

"Hualālai Hui sold the land for the school?" Koa asked.

"Yeah," Zeke responded. "The development plan called for public
facilities, and in 2006, Hualālai Hui sold the KonaWili school parcel to the state at a premium price as the site for the future elementary school."

"Who owes Hualālai Hui?" Piki asked.

"Damn good question," Zeke responded. "State records identify
two Big Island personalities—Howard Gommes and Cheryl
Makela—as the owners, but most of these land deals have sub-*huis*
with silent partners."

"What do the records show about the share of ownership?" Koa
asked.

"Gommes 60 percent and Makela 40 percent, but like I said,
they've probably got silent partners."

"I've seen Gommes on TV. He's all over the tube." Piki's eyes glowed.

"Yeah," Zeke responded, not sharing Piki's enthusiasm. "He's a big swinging dick with a local Hawai'i-based *Apprentice*-type reality TV show. Made his money in shady real estate deals on the Big Island and Maui where he developed several large residential subdivisions and a half-dozen major hotel projects."

"And the other owner, this Cheryl person?" Basa asked.

"Ahh," Zeke sighed, "Cheryl Makela, the Teflon lady. She's buddy-buddy with Mayor George Tanaka, who appointed her director of the county planning department before her retirement."

"Teflon lady?" Piki asked.

"Yeah," Zeke responded. "She's rumored to have more conflicts than Hawai'i has beaches, but nobody's ever made anything stick."

"She approved the KonaWili development while serving as director of planning even though she owned a share of the development?" Basa asked with raised eyebrows.

"Yes, indeed," Zeke acknowledged.

"More than a little conflict of interest there," Piki added.

"Government in Hawai'i is rife with conflicts," Zeke said with a disapproving shake of his head.

Koa turned to Basa. "What did you find in the county files?"

"Francine Na'auao, the director of the Department of Education, approved the selection of the school site."

"I got a whole lot of stuff off the internet about her," Piki interjected. "She's been the DOE director for ages and ages. I mean like more than a decade. And she's close to Governor Bobbie Māhoe."

"Then," Basa resumed, "the DOE hired Arthur T. Witherspoon to be the architect and Boyle Construction to be the builder. The school cost nine point nine million dollars and took eleven months to complete."

Koa knew the Witherspoon name. One of the most sought-after architects in Hilo, he'd designed Hilo's new government center and numerous other local public buildings. "So," Koa summarized, "we've got the four key players in the KonaWili disaster: Gommes, Makela, Na'auao, and Boyle—developer, planning director, DOE head, and general contractor."

Piki again spoke up. "Boyle may not be the only key player on the construction side. According to one press story, Boyle hired a guy named Tony Pwalú to do the excavation and grading for the project. I figured as excavator, he'd know about the volcanic vent."

"Nice catch," Koa said. "He might be a good place to start. We could get some background before we move up to the central actors." Koa always liked to start with lower-level people before working his way up to the big *kahunas*. "Piki, you got an address for this Pwalú guy?"

"Sure do."

Zeke nodded his agreement. "I like starting with Pwalú. Then what?"

"Witherspoon," Koa responded. "As the architect, he must have visited the site both before and during construction. Then Makela and Gommes."

"What about Na'auao?" Zeke asked.

"She's in Honolulu and outside my jurisdiction, so I'm going to need your help to get to her and other DOE people."

"I'll start working on it," Zeke responded. "We have a plan?"

They all nodded in agreement, and the meeting broke up.

* * *

With Tony Pwalú's address in hand, Koa and Basa drove across the island and up the slope of Mauna Loa.

"This KonaWili thing gives me stomach acid," Basa said. "I mean the accident last year with those teenagers gettin' scalded in a steam vent over in the national park was bad enough, but this. This was deliberate. Boyle put those poor kids in danger. Makes me worry if Samantha's safe in school." The KonaWili disaster enraged the police sergeant, and he'd come to Koa's office begging for a major role in the investigation.

"I don't get it. What kind of sicko puts kids on top of a volcano?" Basa asked.

"Not just one sicko," Koa replied. "It wasn't the work of a single person or even two. The KonaWili disaster was a group effort, a conspiracy."

"You mean some group of wackos sitting around a table, like Wall Street executives, planned this fiasco?"

"Not necessarily. Doesn't have to happen in one big meeting. Could have been a series of one-on-ones."

"Jesus," Basa swore.

"And why?" Koa added. "That's the most important question. Why would a group of professionals put kids at risk?"

Koa looked over at Basa, noticing a camera fastened to his uniform. "You wearing a body cam?"

"Yeah. The department's running a pilot program. It's really just a souped-up GoPro. You know, those little action cams the sports guys wear."

"Sure, Nālani got me one for Christmas. I've been fooling around with it. Shot some on our walks through the national park. Took some neat videos of the steam vents around Halema'uma'u crater before *Pele* closed the park in May."

"Cool. I got one for my kids. They shot some funny stuff at the playground an' around the house. Jason hams it up like a professional clown."

"How's the body cam different from a GoPro?" Koa asked.

"A bunch of ways, but the biggest are battery life and access. These VieVu things have a twelve-hour battery life, a hell of a lot more than a GoPro, and the wearer can't access the pictures."

"So, no selfies?"

Basa laughed. "Ugly cops don't make great selfies."

"Speak for yourself."

They rounded a curve and approached a ramshackle farm at the end of a long, rutted lane. An old farmhouse with a dozen additions tacked on hadn't seen a coat of paint in thirty years. A rusted bulldozer along with other construction equipment in various states of disrepair littered the property. "Looks like a graveyard for dozers." Basa shook his head.

When the two policemen climbed out of their vehicle, twenty children, most in dusty shorts and some still in diapers, came running to greet them. Koa spotted more faces peering from the doors and windows of the farmhouse, sheds, and other makeshift structures.

Squatting on his haunches, Basa ruffled the hair of a couple of the young boys and let them touch the decorations on his uniform. Basa enjoyed a natural way with kids. His empathy underlined Basa's outrage at the KonaWili disaster and his determination to help Koa track those responsible. After a minute, a young Micronesian girl, probably no more than four years old, perched on Basa's knee with her arm around his neck. The scene reminded Koa of the way his Army buddies in Afghanistan treated village kids to chocolates, except in the war zone you worried about kids carrying explosives.

The handsome, dark-skinned kids, many with curly black hair, belonged to a miniature Micronesian community. Under the Compact of Free Association between the United States and Micronesia, the U.S. secured continued military access to the Micronesian islands—where it once tested nuclear weapons. The peoples of those islands won unrestricted access to the U.S. and the full array of its educational, medical, and social services. As a result, thousands of Micronesians flocked to Hawaiʻi. Unfortunately, the federal government picked up only a small portion of the cost of complying with the pact, straining Hawaiʻi's social service budget. Resentment and discrimination oppressed this new underclass. Like many immigrant groups, they hung together, a pattern reinforced by the powerful family ties traditionally binding not just blood relatives but all Micronesian islanders.

The kids scattered when an old man, plainly an elder of the group, approached. Basa stood, and Koa extended his hand, identified himself, and asked for Tony Pwalú.

"He much sick," the old man responded, motioning them toward the farmhouse. Once inside the man led them down a hallway past several small bedrooms with multiple bunk beds and sleeping mats blanketing the floors. Koa didn't have to resort to higher math to know more than a hundred people lived in this mountainside community.

At the end of the hall, they emerged onto a decaying *lānai* overlooking a small farm pond where naked children swam. "Tony Pwalú," their guide said, pointing to an emaciated man sitting in a rocking chair at the end of the veranda. Although Piki's research put Pwalú in his fifties, this gaunt, withered skeleton looked more like a frail eighty. Some terrible disease, probably cancer, had ravaged his body.

"Tony Pwalú?" Koa asked as he sat down on a stool facing Tony. The man nodded and turned to look at Koa. Tony's bony arms stuck out of an ill-fitting tee shirt and a small crucifix on a steel chain hung around his turkey-like neck. He'd lost his hair, and his face bore a shrunken, hollowed-out look, but his black eyes shined sharp, under nonexistent eyebrows. Perhaps his illness hadn't dulled his brain.

Koa introduced himself and Basa before turning to the point of their visit. "You worked on the KonaWili school project?"

The man nodded. "This terrible thing. Those poor children. It didn't have to be that way," Tony said in a hoarse, halting whisper.

Koa's mind raced at the words—"it didn't have to be that way." Tony knew something. Koa didn't like tape-recording interviews. People frequently refused to talk with the machine running, and even if they did speak, they became guarded. But Tony didn't have long to live, and Koa wanted to capture his words before he passed. He started to pull out his cell phone but then thought of Basa's body cam. He looked inquiringly at Basa, who nodded. "Tell me about KonaWili."

"I never tell anyone," Tony responded with an effort in a raspy voice.

"You can tell me," Koa replied.

Tony stared at Koa for a long time, his coal-black eyes searching Koa's face, before finally saying, "I keep secret for Hank."

"You mean Hank Boyle?"

The man coughed and took a moment to recover. "Yes. Hank good to me. Much work Hank give me."

"Tell me about the secret."

"*Pele's* secret."

Koa leaned forward to reinforce his connection with the frail man. "Tell me about *Pele's* secret."

"Hank give me work on school. I dig hole, move rocks. Find much yellow powder. Bad smells."

Yellow powder meant sulfur, and in Hawai'i, sulfur deposits meant volcanic activity, but Koa needed to be sure. He and Nālani had often visited the sulfur banks at Hawai'i Volcanoes National Park, so Koa knew exactly what to ask. "Bad smells?"

"Yeah, like rotten eggs and matches . . . burned matches."

Rotten eggs smells meant hydrogen sulfide and a burned match smell meant sulfur dioxide. "And the ground—rocks or clay?"

"Some rocks, but much red and brown clay."

Koa had the clincher. *Pele's* hydrogen sulfide fumes ultimately became sulfuric acid breaking down lava rocks into clay of distinctive red and brown iron oxides. Sulfur, sulfur dioxide, hydrogen sulfide, sulfuric acid, and iron oxides—all *Pele's* trademarks. Tony Pwalú had found a volcanic vent while preparing the KonaWili site. Now Koa needed to know why the discovery hadn't stopped the project. It was one thing to build an elementary school atop a fault on a volcano dormant for two hundred years. It was quite another to build the same school over a known volcanic vent—one actively producing sulfur gases.

"What did you do?"

"I tell Hank."

Koa leaned even closer to Tony, and their eyes locked. "And what did Hank Boyle do?"

Tony hesitated, and Koa thought he might clam up, but Tony wanted to tell his story before he died. "Hank showed the lady."

What woman had visited the construction site? Someone from the DOE? "What lady?" Koa demanded.

Tony shook his head and spoke so softly Koa could barely hear. "Some . . . lady from Honolulu."

Koa wondered if this dying man knew more. "Then what happened?"

Tony raised a bony hand to his neck to finger his crucifix. "Hank tell me. I keep secret, I get big bonus."

"And you got a bonus?"

Tony spread his emaciated arms. "Bonus buy this farm."

"And what did Hank Boyle do?"

"He build school."

Stark as a super moon in a cloudless night sky, Tony had discov-ered the vent, and Boyle had charged ahead oblivious to the risk. Tony Pwalú must have seen the condemnation in Koa's eyes. He reacted by looking down at his emaciated hands now folded in his lap and said almost inaudibly, "I sinned. I sorry."

"Not as sorry as the parents of those children," Koa said.

When Tony looked up, the man fought back tears. "It was *Pele's* revenge."

"*Pele's* revenge?" Koa asked.

"My . . . my grandson, he died at KonaWili." The old man choked and barely got the words out.

Maybe, Koa thought, there were worse things than dying of cancer.

CHAPTER SEVEN

An urgent call blasted over the police radio as Koa and Basa drove along the rain-slick Māmalahoa Highway past the KonaWili property toward Hilo. An unruly crowd of angry parents demonstrating near the KonaWili school had busted through the police cordon. Patrolmen, desperate for reinforcements, fought to regain control.

Crowd control wasn't Koa's job, but the school remained a crime scene. The building had killed, and Koa didn't want it to claim any more lives. He spun the car around, flipped on the emergency lights, and headed for the crippled structure.

Basa grabbed the radio to marshal more police units, only to find most units in Kona, more than seven miles away in heavy traffic. "It's up to us," Basa warned Koa. "We're seven to ten minutes ahead of most other units." Koa pushed the accelerator to the floor.

At the school, Koa's heart rate spiked. Conditions had worsened since the first night. Although the rain had slackened, the steel roof at the south end of the building had curled upward like the lid of an open sardine can, and chunks of the front wall lay scattered. An eerie rumbling like a runaway freight train filled the air. Thick yellowish gas billowed into the sky. Hundreds of angry demonstrators already through the thin police cordon moved up the hill toward

the crippled building. Half a dozen policemen, hopelessly outnum-
bered, struggled to restrain the demonstrators, while desperate parents, crazed by the loss of their children, goaded the crowd forward.
TV cameras recorded the chaos.

Pele's unearthly rumblings failed to drown out the chanting
of the crowd—"We want answers . . . we want *answers*." The demonstrators fell silent for several beats before continuing: "The
DOE killed our *keiki* . . . The DOE *killed* our *keiki*." Then the
chants repeated.

Koa and Basa raced up behind the crowd. Signaling to another
police car to follow, Koa cut off the road, bumped over the curb, and
swung across rough ground around the crowd before heading
straight into the gap between the demonstrators and the smoking
hulk of the broken school. He stopped—emergency lights flashing—and the second cop car did likewise, creating a barricade between the crowd and the school.

Koa, bullhorn in hand, and Basa faced the crowd, their backs to
their vehicles and the school beyond. The patrolmen from the other
car joined them. Waiting for the next pause in the chanting, Koa
triggered the bullhorn—"You'll get answers. You'll get answers, but
everyone needs to move back. Move back. It's dangerous." The
crowd quieted and stopped moving. Koa repeated his message, and
the demonstrators retreated a couple of steps. Then someone yelled,
"We want answers *now*!" and the crowd surged forward as it took
up the new chant, "We want answers *now*! We want answers *now*!"

"Shotguns?" a cop from the other car asked.

"*No!*" Basa yelled. "Just stand tall." Koa continued to face the
crowd with the bullhorn. "This is no way to mourn your children,"
his amplified voice barreled over the crowd. "There's a volcanic vent
under this building. It's dangerous! Move back! *Move back!* We
don't want anyone else to get hurt."

A woman in the front row of the crowd stared at him with tears streaming down her face. Koa recognized Mica Osbourne's face from TV as the mother of the missing child. "Please, Mrs. Osbourne," he boomed over the hailer, returning her stare and hoping his use of her name would reinforce his message. "*Please move back. Don't let anyone else get hurt.*"

He locked eyes with the grieving mother for a long moment before repeating his plea. "This is no way to honor your children." The stalemate lasted several more seconds before Mica Osbourne turned, pushing back through the crowd. Slowly, others began to follow. Koa breathed a sigh of relief.

At that moment, an explosion ripped through the shell of the school. A wave of debris hit the vehicles behind him and showered those in the closest row of demonstrators. One man fell to the ground. Screams shot through the crowd as the group turned *en masse* and ran. The vehicles shielded the cops from serious injury. They had saved the demonstrators.

* * *

Koa's cell phone rang while he and Basa drove back to Hilo. He looked at the screen and recognized the number, county prosecutor Zeke Brown. He answered, and Zeke spoke slowly and softly, a rarity for the prosecutor. "Koa, your brother, Ikaika, collapsed in the Hilo lockup."

"Is he okay?"

"He's alive but unconscious. The medics put him on an air ambulance to Queen's Medical in Honolulu."

"What happened?"

"The doctors say it's some kind of seizure."

"Jesus." The news stunned Koa. He'd been sitting in the interrogation room with Ikaika less than twenty-four hours ago, and his brutal, foulmouthed brother had been healthy. Hell, he'd been weight-lifting in the joint and developed the physique of a professional bodybuilder. "How'd it happen?" Koa asked.

"The video shows he just stumbled and keeled over."

Koa wondered why Ikaika had faltered. Ikaika, a tough bastard, was always eager to take on all comers in a barroom brawl or jailhouse rumble. Koa had seen him, bruised and battered with a black eye and a cut lip after one of his fights, but the other guy lingered in the hospital. Maybe, Ikaika had gotten into a jailhouse scrap with some tougher inmate who'd knifed him. Starting a jailhouse melee fit his brother's style.

Still, Koa felt an unexpected surge of concern. Not long ago he'd been hoping Ikaika would testify and go back to his cage. Now he wanted to see his brother. With the school disaster relief at a critical stage, the investigation just starting, and the police chief off-island, Koa couldn't go to O'ahu, at least not right away. Still, someone from the family had to go. He thought about calling Mauloa, their middle brother, but he had disowned Ikaika years ago. He'd have to call his sister, Alana. It'd be a tough sell. She'd given up on Ikaika, refusing even to talk to him, but in the end, Koa knew, she'd listen to him and reluctantly agree. A combination of respect for her older brother and pressure from Māmā would overcome her resistance.

He called Alana, and three hours later, made his way to Hilo airport, parked in the lot across from the terminal, and walked through the rain under turbulent gray clouds. He'd come to see his sister Alana off to be with his stricken youngest brother. Flashing his credentials, he made his way past security. Alana surprised him by showing up with his mother. He should've guessed Māpuana would insist on going to see Ikaika. No one cared more for Ikaika. She'd been there for Ikaika throughout his violent adolescence and beyond, making excuses for him and crying each time the authorities hauled him off to prison. She'd just recovered from a near-fatal bout of pneumonia, and at sixty-eight, the trip would take its toll on her.

The two women peppered Koa with questions while they waited for the flight. What had happened to Ikaika? Had he been attacked in jail? How badly was he hurt? Why did prison officials move him to Oʻahu? Koa told them what little he knew—that Ikaika blacked out in the local jail while waiting to testify in a criminal trial. He hadn't regained consciousness, and local medics had ordered him airlifted him to Queen's Medical Center, the best hospital in the islands. His vital signs remained strong, but he hadn't awakened from some sort of coma.

His mother took Koa's hand, holding it painfully tight. "You must pray for him," she said. "*E pule i kēia manawa.* Now is the time for prayer."

Koa acknowledged Māpuana's request, but she didn't release his hand. "And you must see your brother. Soon. He needs you."

He nodded, but inside he asked himself when Ikaika had ever needed anyone.

Finally, the gate agent announced the flight, and Koa walked his family to the jetway. He worried as much about Māpuana as Ikaika. Visiting her son in the hospital would be tough on her. Then he wondered if he'd ever see his brother again.

CHAPTER EIGHT

FIFTEEN MINUTES LATER, Koa stood at his office window, watching the rain come down, and worrying about his brother.

"The mayor wants an update on KonaWili," Piki announced.

Koa sighed. The young detective, shifting from one foot to the other in the doorway, hadn't brought good news. Koa hated dealing with politicians. Most of the time, Chief Lannua dealt with the mayor and the county council, shielding Koa from politics. Politicians always had an agenda—intrigue, punishing perceived enemies, outmaneuvering the opposition, winning the next election—but never about justice. Koa felt out of place in the political world, but physicians still had the chief in a California hospital, preparing him for gallbladder surgery, and the mayor wouldn't wait.

Koa grew more anxious when he found Watanabe and Inaba with the mayor. They'd worked themselves into a state of agitation. "This whole fucked-up situation is out of control," the mayor announced. Short in stature and powerfully built, Tanaka wielded authority like the Army lieutenant colonel he'd once been. Koa could almost see the silver oak leaves on his shoulders. Yet, he looked tired, and an unusually prominent five o'clock shadow darkened his face. "The press is running wild, printing crap like 'criminally negligent,' and that's one of the nicer things. Parents are screaming for blood and

Na'auao's head. The governor called me earlier and wants to take control of the investigation. And then there's Cheryl Makela, God help us. The conservatives on the county council wanted her arrested. It's a goddamn mess. And the timing shits. We got an election coming up."

"We need," Tomi Watanabe, the small ferret-like man who served as the mayor's press aide, interjected, "to call this KonaWili thing an unavoidable accident—an act of God—a disaster no one could control." Koa couldn't help watching the ugly black mole on Watanabe's right cheek jump around as the spin doctor carried on in a shrill voice. He and Koa crossed swords every time the weasel stuck his nose into police business. He'd even tried to get the department to fix DUI and speeding tickets for his friends and threatened to retaliate by cutting the police technology budget when Koa intervened. Neither liked the other.

"Can you sell that?" Ben Inaba, the mayor's top political advisor, asked. Inaba had the polish that Watanabe lacked—carefully tailored clothes, a soft but authoritative voice, and an intuitive ability to ask just the right question.

"We can sell anything if we say it loud enough and often enough," Watanabe responded. "We make our own reality." As a press jockey, he knew what he wanted the public to believe and never let the facts get in the way.

"Then we need to put out a statement saying no one in government knew anything about a volcanic vent on that property," Inaba said. More thoughtful and less abrasive than Watanabe, Koa viewed him as smarter and therefore distrusted him even more.

"Agreed," the press aide responded. "And we need to get it out fast. A full-scale media blast—newspapers, TV, radio, and social media."

Koa held his tongue, but when the mayor turned to him, he could no longer stay silent. "Remember the old military adage—never make a crisis worse. You say nobody in government knew, and it comes out they did. Then you're fried. Better to say nothing."

Watanabe glowered at him. "You don't know what you're talking about."

Koa kept cool and responded calmly. "Higher-ups in government knew, and the facts are going to come out."

Watanabe jumped at him like a rabid rat. "How'd they know?"

"First, the contractors knew about volcanic activity and tried to cover it up. And the contractor showed the vent to someone from Honolulu, probably a DOE official. So, the government has a problem—"

"That's news to me, Detective," the mayor interjected.

"I just learned that fact, sir. The contractor used concrete—thousands of cubic yards of it—to cover up the vent. Cement costs money. That money didn't come out of thin air. Somebody, most likely someone in the DOE, approved a big bill for several hundred thousand dollars."

"That doesn't mean they knew about the vent," Watanabe responded.

Koa wasn't about to be bullied by the former newspaper reporter. "Then explain to me how a government employee approves a big-ticket bill for thousands of yards of concrete without knowing what it's for or why it's needed."

"You're guessing," Watanabe accused.

There was no convincing Watanabe, but Koa could see from Inaba's face that he understood. "Moreover, as I told Mayor Tanaka, somebody killed Hank Boyle, the general contractor—"

"I hear he hanged himself," Watanabe interrupted. "Probably felt guilty 'cause his school snuffed a bunch of first-graders."

Watanabe's callous attitude appalled Koa. "That's what the killer wanted you to think," Koa said. "And it doesn't explain why his KonaWili file went missing."

Watanabe wouldn't give up. "That's just your opinion."

"It's backed up by the ME's opinion," Koa responded.

"Shizuo's opinion?" Watanabe said. "That's not worth a pair of twos."

"As a matter of fact, we brought in Anne Ka'au, the Honolulu ME. She called it murder, not suicide. There's no doubt."

"Jesus, we're screwed," Inaba said.

Watanabe pointed a bony finger straight at Koa. "Not if the police call it an act of God and halt their investigation. They can treat the Boyle thing as a separate matter."

Koa locked eyes with Watanabe. The man was a viper—as black as the mole on his face. "That's not going to happen," Koa said calmly.

"Maybe we need a new chief detective," Watanabe threatened.

"That's enough, Tomi," Mayor Tanaka ordered. "We'll sit tight until this thing sorts itself out."

Mayor Tanaka turned to Koa. "Listen, Detective, you're the lead on this investigation. This thing happened in my county, and I'm not about to let the governor snatch control to protect his sorry ass. You and the county prosecutor coordinate with the state AG, but we're going to control the investigation. You understand?"

Tanaka's orders surprised Koa. Given the state control of the education system, he'd expected the governor to take over the investigation. Seeing the determination in Tanaka's eyes, Koa realized he hadn't fully appreciated the antipathy between the mayor and the governor. Tanaka obviously planned to use the investigation to embarrass his rival. "Yes, sir. I understand," Koa responded even though he wasn't sure he did.

"You need to clamp a lid on this thing before it blows. I'm looking to you to get to the bottom of it. Fast. You understand me, Detective?"

"Yes, sir," Koa responded.

"And one more thing, Detective." The mayor's dark eyes bored into Koa. "You don't talk to reporters. Watanabe will handle the press."

"Yes, sir."

Koa left the mayor's office with mixed feelings. He wanted Chief Lannua back to deal with the obnoxious political animals in the mayor's office. But mostly, he felt intense time pressure. He had a window to investigate, but he wasn't naïve. Political pressure would rise, like the steam clouds from the crippled school, and unless he got to the bottom of this complex conspiracy, there'd be volcanic political fireworks.

CHAPTER NINE

DESPITE TWO TRIPS to the KonaWili school, Koa hadn't mastered the crime scene. He'd focused on the rescue operations, checking out the building with the robot, and turning back the mob of angry citizens. The stormy weather hadn't helped. He needed a feel for the land purchased by the Hualālai Hui development. He worked best when he could absorb the feel of a crime scene in context. And he needed an expert guide, like Richard Tatum, the USGS volcanologist, who'd briefed the governor and mayor. He called the geologist.

"Richard, I'm taking a police chopper for a look around Kona-Wili. Any chance you can come along and bring any old maps or photos from the USGS files?"

Tatum proved eager. "I'm in. Just tell me when."

When they met at the Hilo airport to board the police chopper, Tatum had a gleam in his eye. "I've got a surprise for you." He patted the leather carrying case he'd brought with him.

Koa, tired of surprises, asked, "What?"

"Wait until we get our boots on the mountain."

From the air, Koa studied the western slope of Hualālai, an 8,271-foot volcano. The KonaWili development formed a triangle with its apex about 5000 feet above sea level and its base along Māmalahoa Highway at 2000 feet. A line of cinder cones marked the southern boundary and a barren lava flow the northern edge. The dead school, still emitting nasty yellow smoke, sat near the top of the development.

Tatum pointed to the cinder cones lined up and down the Hualālai slope to the south. "See that line of cinder cones? They mark the northwest rift zone, where gravity cracked the side of the volcano allowing lava to vent before reaching the summit."

Dozens of cinder cones, blackish chocolate brown hillocks, ran in a narrow zigzag pattern. "Each cone represents an eruption?" Koa asked.

"That's right," Tatum responded. "Geologists figure Hualālai is about 300,000 years old and has become a late-stage volcano. Eruptions from the top built the large shield shape of the mountain. Then, the eruptions shifted to those cinder cones—like pumice pimples on the side of the mountain."

Koa turned to the other side of the chopper and pointed to the sweeping band of ebony lava extending from just above the apex of the triangle down its northern border to the sea. "That's the 1801 flow?"

"That's part of it," Tatum responded "That's the *Ka'ūpūlehu* flow, but 1801 is just an approximate date. We've found twenty-three historical references to eruptions with dates ranging from 1774 to 1811—might even have been multiple eruptions during that period. We chose 1800–01 as a proxy date based on geologic testing."

"And the other part of the 1801 flow?"

Tatum pointed farther down the slope to bands of rust and black lava extending from the bottom southwest corner of the triangle to Keāhole airport on the coast. "There's the other portion of the 1801 eruption, called the *Hu'ehu'e* flow—the part that did the most damage."

"Damage?" Koa asked.

"Yeah. Covered *Pāʻaiea*, one of King Kamehameha's most valuable fish ponds. Historical accounts say the pond was three miles long and half a mile wide. Its loss marked a true disaster for the early Hawaiians."

"Wow, that's a lot bigger than the ponds at Mauna Lani."

"Yeah, and there's a legend about the *Huʻehuʻe* flow. Old native storytellers say King Kamehameha stopped the lava by throwing a lock of his hair into the river of burning rock."

"Too bad he wasn't around to save the KonaWili kids."

"Yeah," Tatum agreed.

"So KonaWili wasn't the first Hualālai disaster," Koa mused.

"And it won't be the last." Tatum pointed to the town of Kona, sitting south of the *Huʻehuʻe* lava flow. "Almost forty thousand people live in a high threat eruption zone."

"If there's an eruption, would it really reach all the way down to Kona?"

"It could," Tatum responded. "You have to understand, Hualālai extends many miles out to sea. Kona is on the slope of the volcano, not the bottom. And Hualālai is one of the highest threat volcanoes in the United States."

"I heard you say that the other day. How can it be such a high threat when Kīlauea, on the southeast side of the island, is actually erupting?"

Tatum grimaced. "Good question. The USGS bases volcano threats on risk to populations, and there are a lot more people at risk from Hualālai than from Kīlauea. Sure, Kīlauea is erupting now, but it's burning forest, a few hundred homes in lower Puna, and altering the seacoast. It's hard on the people affected, but at worst, only a couple thousand people, some rural roads, and beautiful landscapes are in danger. And, because of the topography, those affected have had plenty of notice. That might not be the case if Hualālai blows.

With the mountain's steep sides, lava could inundate Kona in a couple of hours. We've been warning people about Hualālai for years, but it mostly falls on deaf ears."

"Weird."

"Yeah. People don't put enough credence in things that happened a long time ago. It's just like the big tsunami in Japan. There were tsunami markers way inland warning people not to build close to the coast, but people forgot and built the Fukushima nuclear plant right on the water."

Koa took in the area between the line of cinder cones to the south and the lava flow to the north. Once all farmland, only a few old farm buildings, fences, and water tanks remained where the developers hadn't replaced them with subdivision streets and houses. Tatum pointed to a building—more of a shack than a house—just outside the top of the triangle. "Can you get the pilot to set us down someplace close to that shack?"

Koa looked quizzically at the volcanologist, but Tatum, not ready to give up his secret, only smiled. The pilot landed the helicopter, and the two men walked out to the top of a small rise where they could look out over the triangular development site. The school near the apex of the triangle was as far as possible away from the Māmalahoa Highway, which bounded the lower side of the development.

"Odd place for a school," Tatum said. "Don't they usually put schools near major roads for convenience and safety? You know, like in case of a fire or other emergency."

"Dead-on," Koa responded. "It's only one of the many oddities surrounding KonaWili."

"You asked me"—Tatum held up his case—"to dig out any old maps and photographs of Hualālai." Tatum opened his portfolio and extracted a single sheet of paper. "I've got some maps, but they won't tell you anything you don't already know. But this"—he handed Koa a sheet of paper—"I found stuck in with some other papers. I made a copy for you."

Koa peered at the paper—a handwritten letter, dated forty years earlier, addressed to the head geologist at the Kīlauea volcano observatory. Squinting to decipher the tiny handwriting, Koa read the long rambling letter—its contents somewhat disjointed—describing a steaming vent on the side of Hualālai Mountain and asking the USGS to check it out. It was signed "The *Pueo*." Koa looked up at Tatum. "The owl?" he translated from the Hawaiian.

"Yeah. The owl."

"Sounds like a nutcase."

"That's what the geologists thought forty years ago 'cause they never followed up. Just stuck the letter in a file."

"But you think there's something to it?"

"Two weeks ago, I would've laughed, but KonaWili proved there's a fumarole down there." Tatum used a geologist term for a volcanic vent and pointed at the smoke rising from the destroyed school. "After I found this letter, I started asking around, trying to identify this owl guy and find out whether he's still alive."

"And?"

"A friend of a friend—a guy who's into the aging hippie community—said there's a guy who calls himself 'the owl.' Says he's a recluse, a former flower child who burned out on drugs during the seventies. He's been living in a shack up here for the past fifty years. Want to see if he'll talk to us?"

Koa saw no downside. "Sure, why not."

They followed a short trail toward a decrepit building that once served as an overnight cabin for hunters. Someone had repaired the walls with discarded chunks of plywood and particleboard. The roof, a mess of rusted tin, patches of wood, and strips of tar paper, looked sure to leak in a good rainstorm. An old man with a belly-length, untrimmed gray beard—he had to be at least seventy-five—sat on the *lānai* in a chair with one busted rocker. Wearing dirty brown overalls, he smelled like he hadn't bathed in quite a while.

The island harbored a whole cadre of aging hippies left over from the free-loving era. Most of them hung out in the Kaʻū and Puna districts growing Puna butter and Kona gold—marijuana—the island's largest cash crop. Koa had busted many of them and knew their type. But this man with his long unkempt hair, pockmarked face, and tattered clothing lived like a poor cousin of those marijuana barons.

"*Aloha*," Koa said as he approached the sagging porch.

"What's *the man* doing on my mountain?"

Koa hid his surprise that the old-timer had pegged him as a cop. Maybe the old codger had more on the ball than first appeared. "We wanna ask you about a letter you wrote to the U.S. Geological Survey a long time ago."

The old man looked up. "Took your sweet time getting here."

Koa concealed his astonishment. They'd found their man, and he actually remembered the letter he'd written forty years earlier. "You must be Pueo."

"Got dat right. Come siddown, yeah." Pueo pointed to a three-legged stool.

Koa took the stool while Tatum tested the strength of the porch railing before leaning against it.

"You here about *ka wahine ʻai honua*, yeah?" The earth-eating woman—along with the tree-eating woman and the stone-eating woman—was among the many traditional descriptions of *Pele*.

"Yeah, we're here about *Pele*," Koa agreed.

"The old fire god, she owns dis mountain. She got her friends and her enemies, yeah." Like many locals, Pueo added a "yeah" to the end of his sentences, probably to be sure you were still listening.

"How so?"

"You know, back in the good old days the Hawaiians had this big fishpond down there." Pueo pointed toward the edge of the ocean. "Belonged to their big chief, yeah."

Koa nodded.

"One day a haggard old lady with glassy white hair comes a hobblin' down dis mountain. Hungry, she goes a beggin' for some fish. The *konohiki*, or overseer, he tells the old witch to get lost. On her way home, a kindhearted fisherman, he gives her some fish. She all grateful an' tells him to hang a piece of *kapa* cloth on the corner of his house, yeah?

"Further up dis mountain—" Pueo pointed over his shoulder up the hill—"the old witch, she stops in a little village, where two young girls, they're roastin' some breadfruit. They see hunger in the old woman's eyes an' give her a piece of their breadfruit. She grateful an' tells them to put a piece of *kapa* cloth on their house. You following me?"

Koa, being drawn into the tale, nodded. Pueo, like many old islanders, had a gift for talking story.

"That night a great fire—dis avalanche of rock and burning lava—comes a bustin' down the mountain, engulfs the village, and buries the fish pond. By the time people realize dis old beggar was Madame *Pele*, it was one whole boatload of time too late. The fire and brimstone, it spares the houses of the generous fisherman and the young girls, but everybody else gets their shit baked. The old fire god, she like that, she got her friends and her enemies, yeah."

Silence hung heavy in the mountain air for a time. Despite his faith in modern science, the Hawaiian in Koa loved the old legends. He couldn't help wondering, at least for a few moments, who had offended *Pele*. Certainly not the innocent children who'd died at KonaWili. Finally, he said, "Tell us about the steam vent."

"Which one?"

"There's more than one steam vent up here?" Koa asked.

"Yeah. There's one farther up the mountain." Pueo hooked a thumb over his shoulder to indicate the direction of the summit. "And then there's the one that popped the kiddie school. Quite a show with all 'em flashin' lights. Better than a fuckin' Grateful Dead concert."

Pueo didn't have much empathy for the dead kids. "Tell us about that one."

"It don't go splish splash too often—jus' every couple a dozen or so years after we get one of those motherfuckin' Kona storms and the angry gods they dump a boatload of rain on my mountain."

"But you've seen steam from that vent?"

"*Luahine moe.*"

"Old woman who sleeps and snores?"

"Yeah, man. *Pele* sleeps and she snores. Most of the time the vent's asleep. But I've seen 'er vent leakin' a little trickle of steam and, yeah, I've seen it steaming like Old Faithful, 'cept it smells like shit."

"When?"

"Maybe two or three times since I come here in '72 and before dem developers covered it up. Da buggah stopped steaming after they dumped all the rock and shit down the hole."

"Damn," Tatum interjected. "Trying to seal a volcanic vent is beyond stupid. Just causes the pressure to build up until you get an explosive release."

It was even worse than Koa feared. If Pueo was to be believed, the developers had deliberately filled the vent to choke it off, creating a ticking time bomb just waiting to explode. "When'd they cover it up?"

"First, the cowboys put a fence around it to keep the stupid cows from gettin' roasted—"

"The old ranchers knew about the vent?"

"Sure as shit, yeah. Fenced it off way back."

Koa wondered if the ranchers disclosed the existence of the fuma-role when Paradise bought the property or if Paradise told Gommes and Makela. He guessed not. Why would Gommes buy into a vol-canic problem? But then again, Koa thought, a sharp operator like Gommes might have used the existence of the fumarole to bargain for a better price. Either way, the buyers learned of the existence of the vent. Pueo's recollection made that clear. And rather than dis-close the hazard, the Hualālai Hui developers bulldozed it over.

"When?" Koa asked. "When did the developers bulldoze the site?"

"Just before the surveyors showed up to mark out all 'em streets. Yeah, man, the developer, he brings in a dozer to fill up the sucker with rocks and dirt."

Koa wanted to pin the time frame down. He guessed the Hualālai Hui had hired a heavy machinery contractor to do the job. Most real estate developers didn't own construction equipment. They rented what they needed, and only a few outfits on the island rented heavy equipment. Koa planned to have Piki check those companies. "You're talking about 2006. How long before the surveyors showed up on-site?"

"Yeah, man, sounds about right," Pueo responded.

That wasn't good enough. Koa wanted a better date. "How long before the surveyors arrived?"

"Maybe a couple of weeks . . . yeah, about that."

If there'd been a volcanic vent down there, and it popped off ev-ery fifteen or twenty years, why hadn't the USGS known about it? Koa turned to Tatum. "Doesn't the USGS monitor Hualālai?"

"Yeah, we do, all the time," Tatum responded. "Better today than in the seventies and eighties, but we watch for magma movements."

"So how come you didn't detect these vents?"

"We use seismographs to monitor earthquakes, GPS to measure ground movement, and satellite imagery to search for temperature changes, but none of those methods would pick up an isolated steam vent, especially if it only rarely erupted."

Koa outlined the timeline in his head. Gommes's Hualālai Hui covered up the vent before selling the land to the state. The state hired Boyle to build the school, and Tony Pwalú graded the site, scraping away enough rock to reveal hidden yellow sulfur powder. Tony told Hank Boyle, who showed it to "the lady from Honolulu." The school project should have died. But no. Somehow Boyle got money to buy over a thousand yards of concrete and forged ahead with construction. They thought they'd fooled *Pele*, but the old fire witch never tolerated interference for long.

All the important players in the chain of title had known about the fumarole, and none of them raised the alarm. Why? Why would they knowingly put grade-school children at risk? Money? Could it just be pure greed? The Hualālai Hui stood to make tens of millions of dollars on the subdivision. But could greed alone—even big-time greed—motivate a whole group of people to expose children to the risk of being burned alive? Maybe, but Koa's instincts told him something more sinister must be at work.

CHAPTER TEN

BACK IN HIS office, Koa answered his sister's call. His brother had fainted, but Koa first thought of his mother. "How's Māpuana?"

"She's fine. It's our brother Ikaika we have to worry about. The doctors did some kind of scan and say he's got a brain tumor. It's really serious, Koa. I'm here with the doctor now. He wants to perform surgery tomorrow."

A brain tumor? Surgery? The news stunned Koa. After a pause, he said, "Can you put the doctor on the phone?"

A moment later. "This is Dr. Carlton." The doctor's deep baritone voice reached across 213 miles from the hospital in Honolulu.

"Tell me about my brother."

"Your brother has a pilocytic astrocytoma in the cerebrum."

After years of listening to pathologists, Koa hated medical jargon. "Excuse me, Doctor, but I need you to speak English."

"Oh, sorry, your brother has a large tumor, or maybe two tumors, in the frontal lobe of his brain. This type of tumor typically occurs in children and grows very slowly. It's rare, but not unheard of, in adults. In children, it is typically benign, meaning non-cancerous, but your brother's tumor shows some evidence of malignancy."

Koa wanted to be sure he understood. "You're saying my brother has brain cancer, and the tumor may have been there for years?"

"That's partially correct. I can't tell you for sure when the tumor developed, but he's most likely had it since childhood. And we won't know if the tumor is malignant until we remove it."

Koa thought of his brother lying in a hospital bed with a brain tumor and wondered if he'd ever see Ikaika again. He suddenly recalled his baby brother, maybe an eighteen-month-old, playing on the *lānai* of his family home. Ikaika had been such an inquisitive and fearless baby, venturing down the steps and crawling off into the yard. Koa's mental image morphed into an ugly picture of his brother drunk after a bar fight. Ikaika had lashed out at him so often and caused so much pain, their connection had atrophied. But now Koa couldn't bear to lose his brother. Funny how a moment of tragedy pulled estranged brothers together. "What are his chances?"

"Actually, pretty good. These types of tumors are well contained and good candidates for surgical resection. Based on the MRI scans we've done, we should be able to remove it. The extent of surgical resection is the best indicator of long-term survival."

"Resection?" Koa asked.

"In simple terms, if we can cut out the entire tumor, then your brother will have excellent odds for long-term survival."

Good long-term news, but the short term concerned Koa more. "And the survival rate for this kind of surgery?"

"We've made lots of advances in the last few years. With advanced imaging and computer-guided surgery, patients come through the surgery amazingly well."

Koa had a lot to absorb all at once. "And this needs to be done right away?"

"Yes. Any brain tumor increases intracranial pressure and can damage other parts of the brain. That's why your brother blacked out."

"What's the recovery time?"

"Typically, about eight to twelve weeks, but it varies depending on the person and the surgery."

Koa knew the state paid for routine medical care of prison inmates but wasn't sure about complex surgery. "I've one last question, Dr. Carlton. I'll bet there's a hefty price tag on this kind of surgery."

"Oh, don't worry about the cost. The Supreme Court interprets the Eighth Amendment to require the same level of medical treatment for prisoners as other citizens receive. The state of Hawai'i will pay for your brother's care."

After putting down the phone, Koa walked to the window. Rain splattered against the glass, and gray clouds hung low over Hilo Bay. Was it ever, he wondered, going to stop raining in sunny Hawai'i? His brother in a coma with a brain tumor, a tumor he'd had since childhood. Scenes flickered through Koa's mind like comic-book pictures: his brother's angry face, his shouting irrational taunts, his sudden bouts of violence. He thought of Ikaika's schoolyard fights, his first car theft, his first stint in prison. The pain in his mother's face as clear as if it all happened yesterday. He flashed back on all the times he'd tried to get through to his brother. The visits to his prison, helping Ikaika get jobs, bailing him out when he got in fights, the excuses. And Ikaika always blaming Koa.

One particular scene stuck in Koa's mind. Ikaika must have been seven or eight. Koa had found him in the forest preparing to butcher the neighbor's cat. When Koa challenged him to stop, Ikaika had turned on him. He'd seen a demented light in Ikaika's eyes, and his brother had stepped forward swinging his knife at Koa. Only at the last second had Ikaika halted. "I hate you," Ikaika said. "Hate . . . You understand, big brother." An hour later, Ikaika had strolled through the house, announced he was going fishing, and left as if nothing untoward had happened.

Koa had thought of Ikaika as a bad seed, like eight-year-old Rhoda Penmark in Maxwell Anderson's movie. He'd viewed Ikaika as evil to the core, but he now saw the glimmer of a different cause. Maybe Ikaika had been sick. Maybe his violent acts had a medical explanation. Koa wondered if any of the doctors he knew could shed light on that possibility.

Brain surgery! They were going to cut open his brother's head. Would Ikaika be the same person? Then Koa caught himself. Ikaika's future wasn't the question. If he didn't survive the doctor's knives, he'd have no future.

CHAPTER ELEVEN

KOA, RESPONDING TO Piki's urgent call, reached Reed's Island, one of Hilo's toniest areas, at 6:30 a.m. Small mansions occupied large lots on the tree-lined street. Driveways harbored Mercedes, BMWs, Lexus sedans, and a Tesla or two. Neighborhood children went to private schools like HPA—Hawai'i Preparatory Academy—in Waimea or Punahou in Honolulu. Hilo's one percent.

Koa parked behind two other police vehicles, lights flashing, outside 7 Ka'iulani Place. The front door of the white clapboard-style house stood wide open. The elegant setting made the bloodied body of Arthur T. Witherspoon, the architect who'd designed the KonaWili school, all the more startling.

Koa knelt beside the body. Witherspoon, dressed in linen slacks, a silk shirt, and expensive loafers, had been shot twice in the chest at close range. One bullet was still lodged in his body, but the other had gone through, splattering the man's blood over the foyer.

Witherspoon had fallen backward and lay with his eyes open seemingly fixed on the crystal chandelier above. Koa took note of the man's gold chain, wedding band, and platinum Rolex watch. Inside Witherspoon's pants pocket Koa found several keys on a sterling silver ring and a leather wallet with several $20 bills. Plainly, not a robbery. A Hawai'i driver's license confirmed the man's identity.

He checked around the body for shell casings but found none. Koa tried to imagine what the architect saw just before the bullets ripped into him. Most likely the eyes of an assassin. The killing had the earmarks of a professional hit.

Koa experienced a wave of guilt. After the Boyle killing, he should have warned Witherspoon or put him under police protection. Koa had become a cop to assuage his guilt over killing Hazzard and his part in the death of Jerry, his Army buddy, who'd died from a bullet meant for Koa. Yet he couldn't escape guilt. When cops screwed up, people died. Witherspoon might have been partly responsible for the KonaWili disaster, but his death still weighed on Koa. He sighed. *'O ka mea ua hala, ua hala ia*, what is gone is gone. His guilt never solved a homicide.

Turning to look out the front door, Koa peered down the concrete path from the stoop to the roadway and noticed a puddle halfway between the house and the street. Walking back over the lawn to avoid disturbing evidence, he found two places where wet footprints hadn't dried, leaving impressions—heavy thick treads—on the concrete. Hiking boots? Not the kind of shoes worn by cops. Knowing the prints would dry up before the police photographer arrived, he knelt and snapped cell phone shots of each print.

Koa returned to the house where Piki advised him that Mrs. Witherspoon had gone upstairs to change out of her nightclothes. While he waited, Koa examined the living room and the adjoining dining room. He wanted to know more about Arthur Witherspoon. Seeing how a person lived—what things occupied special places—often yielded insights into personality. If you couldn't get inside a dead man's mind, you could still study his man-cave.

The house had a warm, lived-in feeling. Tasteful and expensively furnished, the rooms appeared orderly, but not obsessively neat. Architectural photographs and drawings of churches decorated the

dining room walls. One in particular, a color photograph of a cathedral with two massive, but different, spires rising to enormous
heights caught Koa's attention. Another picture showed the front of
a church with a giant circular window between two towering spires.
As he studied the spires in the two photos, he realized they belonged
to the same church.

At that moment, Mrs. Witherspoon entered the dining room,
dressed in jeans and a green pullover. A tall woman in her early sixties,
she moved with an easy grace. Her face even in distress without
makeup remained unwrinkled and unblemished. Koa imagined that
she'd been stunning in her prime. Gesturing to the other photographs
on the dining room walls, he asked, "They're all the same church?"

"Yes, the Cathedral of Our Lady of Chartres—Arthur's favorite
building." Her eyes teared, and her voice choked. "We went there on
our honeymoon." She reached out to straighten one of the pictures.
"And planned to go back next year for our thirty-eighth wedding
anniversary." She began to cry again and reached for a tissue.

He waited before asking, "If you're up to it, I need to ask you
some questions."

"Alright, but I need to sit down." She led him back to the living
room and sank onto the couch. Koa pulled a chair close to her. He
kept his voice gentle. "I'm sorry for your loss." Words failed when
people confronted death. Most people took it better if you simply
acknowledged their loss. She sat stone-faced for what seemed an
eternity before beginning to regain her composure.

"Mrs. Witherspoon, you need to tell us what happened." She stared
blankly—her mind lost in faraway spaces—and didn't seem to hear.

His words, more forceful this time, brought her back, and her
eyes focused. She swept a lock of hair away from her face and looked
at him through tear-filled eyes.

"What . . . what do you want?"

"Tell us what happened."

She pulled a tissue from the pocket and dried her eyes. "He ... he got up early. He always does. I'd just woken up when I heard the doorbell. He went to answer it. I heard him say something, and then ... and then I heard two gunshots close together." She started crying again, repeatedly dabbing her eyes. "I ran to the foyer, and ... and it was *awful*. Blood all over the place." She began to lose control.

He paused, giving her time. "What did he say?"

"I just ..." She choked on the words. "... Just heard his voice, not the actual words."

"Did you see anybody?"

She shook her head. "No, I was in the bedroom upstairs when it happened."

"Tell me about your husband, his work, his habits."

"He's an architect."

"Yes."

"He runs his own firm here in Hilo." Not uncommon in such situations, she used the present tense. "He has lots of clients and works day and night."

"Have you noticed anything unusual recently?"

"No—" Then she caught herself. "Well, he's been upset since that awful KonaWili school thing."

"Why? You didn't have a child at KonaWili, did you?"

"No, no, but the daughter of our closest friends died there. Karen's death devastated Arthur. Really upset him." She paused to blow her nose.

"Anything more than sympathy for a friend's loss?"

She started to say something and then stopped.

"You need to help us, Mrs. Witherspoon. Tell us anything you know."

She sighed heavily. "Arthur said he felt guilty about the terrible accident."

Witherspoon might have been upset about a friend's loss, but Koa focused on the word "guilty." "Any reason why your husband would feel guilty?"

"He said he'd done his best, but it hadn't been enough."

Had he been referring to the unsuccessful effort to choke the vent off? It made sense. As the project architect, Witherspoon would have inspected the site during construction. He couldn't have missed the extra concrete. And his words suggested he'd, in fact, designed the massive—but ultimately unsuccessful—concrete cap over the volcanic vent.

"He'd done his best. What did he mean?"

"He didn't say, but I took him to mean the design of the school. I told him not to be silly. It wasn't his fault."

But it was Witherspoon's fault, Koa thought. He should have stopped the project or at least blown the whistle on it. Why he hadn't remained a mystery. Why would a respected, successful architect like Witherspoon—a man who'd designed many public buildings in Hilo—keep quiet about a potential threat to grade-school children?

Thinking the answer might be somewhere in the architect's files, Koa asked, "Where is your husband's office?"

"On the corner of Puʻuʻeo and Waiānuenue. On the second floor."

Koa pictured the filing cabinet in Boyle's home office—the one with the missing KonaWili file. If Boyle's killer took the file, then Witherspoon's killer might have taken his files, too. Koa called Basa to request a check on Witherspoon's office.

Turning back to Mrs. Witherspoon, Koa asked, "Did your husband have a partner or an assistant?"

"Not really. He mostly worked alone. Sometimes on big jobs, he hired a young woman to make copies and deliver plans, but it wasn't a regular thing."

"What's her name?"

Mrs. Witherspoon looked down at her hands. "Sally . . . Sally Meacham or something like that."

"Do you have an address or telephone number?"

"It's probably somewhere in Arthur's records."

Koa sensed an evasion. She couldn't recall—or more likely didn't want to remember—the name and address of her husband's assistant. He considered pursuing it but decided to find Sally and get the story from her.

"Did he receive any threats?"

"Heavens no. Arthur didn't have enemies."

As he walked back to his Explorer, Basa called. Witherspoon's office had been ransacked. Koa drove across town, leaving the SUV, its lights flashing, on Pu'u'eo street, and climbed to the architect's second-floor office. Filing cabinets hung open, files and architectural drawings lay strewn about the floor, desk drawers pulled out.

Witherspoon's death and this break-in at his office had to be connected. Whoever killed Witherspoon had searched for something—like the KonaWili plans. But as Koa looked around, the complete destruction of the office struck him as odd. Unlike Boyle's place where a single file had gone missing, Witherspoon's office resembled the aftermath of a tropical cyclone. If the murderer wanted the KonaWili files, why tear up the place?

Koa took a fresh look around the office. Every file had been ripped out of its place and dumped on the floor. Papers were strewn everywhere. Every drawer opened and its contents scattered. Several drawers had been removed from their slots and turned upside down. Supplies littered the floor. An air-conditioning vent had been ripped from the ceiling. No architect would store files in a ventilation duct. The more he studied the mess, the more he thought the thief left empty-handed. Witherspoon had hidden something—something so incriminating he'd been murdered to keep it secret.

CHAPTER TWELVE

PULU 'ELO I ka ua o ka ho'oilo—drenched by winter's rain—grief filled Kona. The distraught Kona community held a memorial service for its lost children at the United Christian Church. More than a thousand people mobbed the historic house of worship, spilling out onto the lawn and even into the street. Thirteen poster-sized pictures of the dead children bordered in thick black frames lined the walkway leading to the sanctuary. The fourteenth poster had a double black frame around the picture of Mica Osbourne's daughter, the one child whose body hadn't been—and probably never would be—recovered. Photos of the dead teachers, one on each corner, guarded the ends of the rows. *Leis* of *maile* and *'okika*, orchids, draped every portrait, and mourners brought more flowers until the façade of the church became a single mass of blossoms.

Koa and Nālani came with fourteen *leis*, one for each of the fallen children. Koa attended out of genuine sadness for the victims and the community's loss. With the investigation only secondary in his mind, he mingled with the mourners and listened for anything that might shed light on the tragedy. He sensed a seething rage bubbling just below the surface underlining the community's shared loss. People came to honor the dead, but Koa felt a powerful groundswell of outrage rising like a rogue wave directed at the officials who'd let this disaster happen. When that wave broke, it would affect the power brokers in Hilo and as far away as Honolulu.

Governor Bobbie Māhoe and Mayor Tanaka vied to deliver the most compelling eulogies, with each man focusing individually on the uniqueness of each of the fourteen children and calling upon the community to support the parents, grandparents, siblings, and friends who'd never forget their loss.

After the service each official held a private reception for the wounded families, taking time to console each of the relatives. The governor visited the children at Kona Community Hospital while Mayor Tanaka did the same for the children hospitalized in Hilo. Although both men kept the press at bay for most of the day, Mayor Tanaka held a late afternoon press conference, while the governor returned to Honolulu.

Hawai'i mayor Tanaka, flanked by his ever-present aides—Ben Inaba and Tomi Watanabe—told the world that Chief Detective Koa Kāne, one of Hawai'i's most experienced detectives, would command the investigation. "We will get to the bottom of this tragedy," he promised. "And we will hold anyone who let this tragedy happen responsible."

*   *   *

Immediately after the mayor's press conference, Koa returned to the Kona side of the island. He'd arranged an early evening meeting with Howard Gommes at his home in Kūki'o, an enclave of multimillion-dollar estates. A security guard at the guardhouse directed him to Gommes's residence. Gommes, the Donald Trump of Hawai'i developers, came across as brash, controversial, politically connected, phenomenally wealthy, and quite the showman. Working on his third wife, a showbiz model, he'd grown up the scion of a wealthy family and supposedly quadrupled his already enormous inherited wealth. Allegations of fraud and sharp practices swirled around him, but none of the numerous lawsuits against him had changed his behavior.

As soon as Koa stepped out of his car, a servant opened the front door and ushered the detective through the palatial, if gaudily decorated, house to a sundeck beside a sparkling infinity pool. The sun, dropping majestically toward the Pacific, blazed in a riot of red and yellow bands. A cool ocean breeze blew in from the *moana*, the sea. Despite Gommes's wealth, Koa found the developer in typical Hawaiian attire—a tee shirt, shorts, and sandals—sitting beside the pool, sipping iced tea. Broad-shouldered with muscled arms, huge hands, and bleached white hair, Gommes topped six-two and weighed a good two-twenty. Sunspots on his face and arms suggested extended hours in the sun, most likely on Kūkiʻo's world-class, members-only golf course. His laser-like onyx eyes radiated an intimidating power.

A pair of giant Rottweilers lay on the patio near their master. One remained still, staring malevolently at Koa, while the other lifted its head and growled. Gommes barked, "Quiet, Dante," but the black beast continued to growl until Gommes whacked it with a riding crop. The animal cringed and whimpered, but still bared its teeth.

"Someday I'll get that *Metzgerhund* to mind his manners."

"*Metzgerhund*?" Koa asked, staying well clear of the dogs.

"Butcher's dogs. Dante and Virgil from Dante's *Devine Comedy*." Gommes smiled, but there was no warmth in the expression.

How appropriate, Koa thought, trying to remember which level of hell was reserved for those with Gommes's avarice.

The man didn't bother to get up or shake hands, but instead, waved Koa to a chair across a glass-top table. Pointing to a sweating pitcher atop a silver tray, Gommes said, "Help yourself to an iced tea. Damned shame about those kids. Terrible accident. Knocked the hell out of property values."

Koa felt a surge of anger at the man's callousness. How could he think of profits when thirteen little bodies lay on cold slabs in the Kona morgue and one child remained missing? But ever the professional, Koa controlled himself. "Tell me about your Hualālai development."

"One sweet piece of real estate—or at least it was before this fiasco. Three thousand five hundred acres of prime land on the outskirts of Kailua-Kona, one of the fastest-growing communities in the state. Not far from the new community college. Great views from most of the lots. I've had my eye on that property for years."

"You bought it in 2004?"

"That's right. Those Paradise assholes got overextended, and we cut a sweetheart deal."

"Whose *we?*"

"I own 60 percent of the *hui* and Cheryl Makela owns the rest."

Koa frowned, showing his disapproval at the pat answer. "I know what the land records show; I'm asking who the real owners are."

"I hold my 60 percent in my real estate development company. I can't say how Cheryl holds her interest."

Koa didn't believe Gommes's bullshit for a moment. Hawai'i law required property owners to be registered, but the registration system had huge holes. Silent partnerships, often called sub-*huis*, permitted politicians to own hidden interests in land subject to their development decisions. "She's got silent partners in a sub-*hui*, doesn't she?"

Howard spread his arms. "That would be news to me."

Koa wanted to ruffle this man's too-cool feathers. "Did you know Hank Boyle?"

"Of course. He's been the general contractor on a bunch of my projects. Damn shame he took his own life."

"When did you last see him?"

"About a month ago at some dumb fundraiser. He seemed happy as a clam."

Gommes was full of shit. The anti-depressant medicine bottles in Hank Boyle's bathroom said Boyle hadn't been "as happy as a clam" in decades. Gommes's glib answer made Koa more determined to get under the developer's skin. "You know why anyone would murder Boyle?"

"Murder him?" Gommes bellowed. "I heard he snuffed his own lights."

"Well, you heard wrong. The murderer staged the scene to make it look like a suicide."

"Is that so?"

Gommes seemed surprised, but the man was hard to read and Koa couldn't tell whether his reaction was genuine—or faked like Boyle's suicide. In either case, Boyle's death didn't seem to faze Gommes. Koa switched directions. "How about Witherspoon? You know him?"

"Yeah, I know Spooner. A really fine architect. Designed lots of local buildings."

"You use him on your projects?"

"Sometimes."

Gommes's tone triggered Koa's antenna. "You have a problem with Witherspoon?"

"Not really. We had a couple of fee disputes and I quit using him. It wasn't a big deal."

Gommes said it softly, but Gommes plainly harbored animosity toward Witherspoon.

"But he designed the KonaWili school."

"On the DOE's dime."

Witherspoon's name got under Gommes's skin. No doubt about it. Koa tried again. "You and Spooner have some kind of falling-out?"

"*No!*" Gommes replied, and then as if to catch himself, he tried to smooth his harsh tone away. "We just disagreed and drifted apart."

Something had happened between Gommes and Witherspoon. Koa would have Piki check it out, but in the meantime, he shifted tacks. "Can you tell me how the particular site was chosen for the KonaWili elementary school?"

"Simple. We hired a planning firm, one specializing in laying out communities. They told us we needed an elementary school and recommended its placement."

The man's answers were way too facile. It couldn't be so simple. It defied probabilities that some independent firm had randomly selected the fumarole site out of 3,500 acres on which to build an elementary school. Besides, as Koa had seen on his aerial recon of the KonaWili development, the school was oddly placed. Gommes had buried the KonaWili school at the most remote point in the whole subdivision rendering fire and police access difficult. Koa, tired of playing games, got tough. "When did you learn about the volcanic vent?"

"When the school blew up."

"You knew before then."

"You're out of your mind. You think I'd buy a property if I knew it harbored a volcanic vent?" Gommes's temper now flared. "Do you know how much money I stand to lose? Ten of millions." He shouted, "*Tens of millions.* I'm not an idiot."

Koa smiled inwardly. He'd broken through Gommes's reserve and provoked anger. Strong emotion—almost any strong emotion—inhibited thought and made people careless or even reckless. Things came out unfiltered. Koa decided to add more heat. "Maybe you didn't know about the vent when you bought the property, but you learned about it shortly thereafter."

Gommes's face grew red and hostility flared in his eyes. "That's a damn serious allegation. You have a basis?"

Koa watched Gommes's eyes. "Yeah, I do. The fumarole emitted steam a bunch of times over the years—"

"Jesus." Gommes hit the table so hard the iced tea pitcher jumped, crashed to the flagstones, and shattered. The two Rottweilers jumped to their feet and began barking. "Shut up, you damned *Metzgerhunds*," Gommes screamed and whacked the nearest dog with his crop. The dog yelped and both retreated. "You mean those Paradise fuckers screwed me?"

Koa hid his disgust at Gommes's violence toward the dogs and increased the pressure. "Maybe. Months after you bought the property and just before the surveyors showed up, a bulldozer shoved a bunch of dirt and rock into that vent, concealing it from view."

"What?" he roared. But something in Gommes's eyes told Koa it was an act, the kind of overwrought performance that so famously marked Gommes's public persona.

"I ask you again, when did you learn about the fumarole?"

"I told you." He slammed his fist down on the table, hard, and this time the glass top cracked. "When the goddamn school blew up." This time both Dante and Virgil cringed and moved well out of range of Gommes's whip.

Koa left with a new assignment for Piki—a forensic biopsy on the Gommes-Witherspoon relationship. Gommes had probably stiffed Witherspoon on his fees, provoking a disagreement, but there might be more, and Koa wanted to understand it.

He called Piki and explained what he wanted, and then asked about the search for bulldozer records. He'd hoped that Piki had found paperwork linking the dozer to Gommes. It would be sweet to confront the smug developer with evidence he couldn't refute, but Piki had yet to score. "Get on it," Koa said, and then softened his rebuke, "as quickly as you can."

CHAPTER THIRTEEN

As KOA AND Basa drove north on the Belt Road toward Cheryl Makela's farm, Basa handed Koa his cell phone. "Take a look at this Tony Pwalú video. I had one of the techs download it from my body cam."

Koa watched the video twice. On the third pass, he turned the volume up and put the phone close to his ear. Then he turned to Basa. "When we interviewed Pwalú, how'd he describe the woman from Honolulu?"

"He didn't."

Koa rewound the recording, turned the volume to max, and pressed the phone to Basa's ear.

"I'll be damned," Basa said. "I never heard him say '*haole* lady.'"

"Neither did I, but you can hear it on the tape. Your souped-up GoPro's got good ears."

"Thought you'd be impressed."

Koa had been thinking about body cams. "You don't tell people they're being recorded, do you?"

"Nope. The public can see the camera on my uniform, so people are on notice. Some police departments have put out public notices or press releases about body cams. If anyone asks, I tell 'em it's on."

Makela lived in a plantation house, raising horses on a thousand-acre farm outside the tiny town of Pepeʻekeo on the northern coast of the Big Island. In Hawaiʻi, land and political power were intimately interwoven, and Cheryl made her bones weaving that fine fabric. Pikiʻs research revealed that, while in law school, Makela had hitched her star to the Democratic Party then flexing its muscle throughout the islands. While the party's rhetoric called for the breakup of the huge, mostly Republican landholdings, the political reality was different. Democratic politicians at all levels of Hawaiian government became partners in *huis*—syndicates and partnerships. The *huis* developed Hawaiʻi's resorts, malls, and office complexes during the great postwar building boom.

Nowhere was this symbiotic relationship more finely honed than in the state's land planning offices. Investigative journalists wrote volumes about land deals where the directors and commissioners of the various planning agencies reaped untold profits. And Cheryl Makela represented the *huis* and the developers, all the while spinning the "revolving door" in and out of county government positions—always cutting a piece of the cake for herself. A piece heaped with frosting. The woman who attended UH law school on a full scholarship had become rich enough to retire on her thousand-acre horse farm.

Over the years, she greased the way with large campaign contributions and strong political connections with Mayor Tanaka. He'd first named her to the planning commission, then she'd become deputy director, and finally director of the Hawaiʻi County planning department. Bribery and conflict of interest allegations swirled like a typhoon around her, but nothing stuck to the Teflon woman.

Makela came out of the stables when Basa pulled up alongside her restored plantation house. Now in her seventies, still with a shapely athletic figure, she wore sleek black riding boots, jodhpurs, and a collared show shirt. A mane of thick white hair tumbled from beneath her traditional black riding hat. She turned to say something to a stable boy before addressing her guests.

"Good afternoon, Detectives. Welcome to Makela Stables."

Although he'd met her before, Koa introduced himself and Sergeant Basa. "Thank you for agreeing to see us," he added, taking in the stables, the dressage arena set up for eventing, and the thoroughbred horses in the pastures beyond. It cost a fortune just to maintain the place. County planners, at least those in land development deals, plainly lived better than police detectives.

"Let's talk in the garden," she suggested, leading them through a gate in a white picket fence into a flower garden with orchids, ginger, and heliconia plants in full bloom. Miniature iron horses dotted the pathways. They each took one of the heavy wrought-iron lawn chairs set around a small table beside a bubbling water fountain. With a touch of bravado, she removed her riding helmet and placed it on the table before shaking out her white hair. She was an attractive woman, but with her bright blue-green eyes and angelic face, she must, Koa thought, have been a knockout in her younger years.

"You're here about the awful accident at KonaWili."

"Yes," Koa responded.

"I never imagined anything like it could happen. Those poor children," she said.

"And their parents," Basa interjected, obviously thinking of his own kids.

"Yes, I suppose it's the worst thing ever to happen to a parent," she responded.

Her sympathy seemed stilted to Koa, but he'd learned a long time ago people displayed highly individualized reactions to tragedy. And with no children, this woman would be less likely to look at the disaster from a parent's point of view. "Tell us about the approval process."

"The developers planned a big community with several hundred homes. As part of the approval process for any large development, the county negotiates land for public facilities like a police subdivision, a firehouse, and an elementary school."

"The government purchases those sites?"

She ran her fingers through her hair, straightening strands displaced by the riding helmet. "Yes, of course. We don't use the zoning process to extort developers."

Why not? Koa thought. The developers stand to make a fortune. Why shouldn't they pay for the required public services? But he hadn't come to argue that point, so he moved on. "Who selected the KonaWili parcel for the school?"

"Well, the developer proposed the site, and the county approved it."

"Was it inspected?"

She gave a disinterested shrug. "I suppose so. I mean, some of my junior staff worked with the developers on the subdivision layout. They might've visited the site."

Koa knew from Zeke that few, if any, county personnel had land planning skills, but the notion that the county would approve a school building without a formal site review surprised Koa.

"Aren't site visits a normal part of the approval process?"

"Not necessarily. Mostly the staff examines the plans for conformity with the zoning codes."

"Did you ever visit the site?"

She hesitated, and he saw a tiny quiver in her lips, the first crack in her façade. "I went up at the top of the property once, but just for an overview."

"When you bought into the Hualālai Hui?"

Her eyes went wide for just a fraction of a second. She hadn't expected him to know about her interest in the land. "Yes, about then."

He wanted to pin down where she had gone and what she had seen. "Exactly where did you go?"

"Just to the top. There's an overlook off the road near the top where you can get a good view of the whole property. We just spent a couple of minutes getting the big picture."

"Who's *we*?" he asked.

"Just me and the broker for Paradise Land Company, the former owners."

"Did you see the fence?"

She fidgeted with her hands. "There were lots of fences. It was a ranch for a long time."

"I meant the one around the volcanic vent. From your viewing point, it wouldn't have been too far."

Her face lost its color and her eyes narrowed. "What are you suggesting? I never knew about a volcanic vent on the property. I never would have invested—"

"I simply asked if you saw the fence."

"No."

Koa knew he'd gotten to her. Her reaction was too sharp, and he thought maybe she, like Gommes, had known about the vent. "You invested quite a lot of money in the Hualālai Hui, didn't you?"

"It's a large property, and I've owned lots of real estate over the years."

"According to public records, you and your partner—Gommes's real estate development outfit—bought the property for forty million dollars. Do I have that right?"

"Yes."

"And you put up 40 percent?"

"I own 40 percent."

Zeke Brown had described how real estate sharks played the development game. Many public officials, especially those in a position to grant the necessary zoning and building approvals, "bought" into land development deals at big discounts. So Makela's glib answer didn't deceive Koa. "You know that's not what I asked. Did you put up 40 percent of the money or did your partner buy you a carried interest?"

She shifted in her chair and ran her fingers through her hair again. "That's none of your business."

Her body language provided all the response he needed. The developer had given her a disproportionate share to ensure he got his land use and building permits. Koa wondered how much of a discount, but he also wanted to know who else the developers had bribed. "Were there sub-*hui*s in that deal?"

"That's none of your business."

"Oh, it's definitely my business. Ranchers fenced off that volcanic vent years ago, and the developers subsequently covered it up twice—first before the surveyors arrived and again while the school was under construction. I'm here to find out who knew about the volcanic vent when you bought the property and when you approved it as an elementary school site."

As he spoke, the blood drained from her face, turning her skin as white as one of her fence posts. "Well, you won't learn any more from me." She stood and turned back toward the stables leaving her riding helmet on the table. "I'm sure you can find your own way out."

"Wow," Basa exclaimed as they walked back to Koa's Explorer. "She's sure got a poker up her ass."

"She's been the queen of dirty real estate deals since the late 1970s, and she's suddenly confronting a multimillion-dollar deal gone sour, not just financially, but politically and criminally. She's never before been in a position where she might have to name names."

"You really think she has silent partners in a sub-*hui*?"

"I'd bet my next year's salary on it."

"Then it's gonna start raining horseshit."

"That's what I'm hoping, that we've started a fire in the stables."

Koa's cell rang, and he stared at the screen. It was his sister calling from Honolulu. She had promised to get back to him as soon as his brother came out of the operating room, and he'd expected to hear from her hours ago. He answered, fearing the delay wasn't good news.

Alana sounded greatly relieved. "The surgery took fourteen hours, but it's done, and the doctors say they got all of the tumors."

Koa, who had been holding his breath, felt himself relax. "That's great news. How is Ikaika?"

"He's unconscious in the ICU, but the nurses say he should be awake sometime during the next few hours."

"How are you and Māmā holding up?"

"I was scared, Koa, really scared for him, but Māmā's doing fine. I've never seen her so calm around doctors. She's been in all the meetings and never once challenged the *haole* doctors. It's like she's always known something was wrong with Ikaika and suddenly discovered the secret. It's strange. Not at all like her."

"She's always believed in him even when the rest of us gave up."

"You're right. She felt something the rest of us never did."

After Koa thanked his sister and hung up, he turned back to Basa. "You ever follow up with your brother up at West Hawai'i Concrete?"

"Yeah. He'll talk to us. Says we'll be interested. Real interested."

*   *   *

When Koa arrived home that evening, Nālani failed to greet him at the door as was her custom. His heartbeat quickened and he felt a ripple of fear. As a police officer, he and those close to him lived with a level of danger beyond that of most people. Having recently come from two murder scenes, he was already tense, and with no sign of Nālani, his unease became palpable. "Nālani," he called out.

"Here," she answered before emerging from the kitchen with a handful of ginger root from their garden. "I was out back. Didn't hear you drive in." Coming forward, she kissed him, her arms outstretched to avoid touching him with her dirty hands. Relief surged through him.

"We saw you on TV. The super circulated the news clip," she said, referring to her boss at the national park. "Everybody was talking about the way you faced the crowd down."

"We were lucky no one got seriously hurt," he responded.

"You mean that crowd was lucky you were there," she replied.

Later, over dinner, he told her about Pueo. "He's a strange old codger with a beard longer than Santa Claus, living like a hermit on that mountain, lost in the past. Going on about the Grateful Dead, and I'll bet he's never even heard of Madonna. Hawai'i has some of the strangest dudes."

"'I will get by . . . I will survive.'" Nālani, something of a rock and roll buff, rattled off a few bars of the Grateful Dead's hit single.

Koa shook his head in awe. "You're amazing."

"My wasted tween years . . . listening to Jerry Garcia's brand of rock while my friends were into Madonna and George Michael. The other girls thought I was nuts . . . and maybe I was."

"That's my Nālani, always independent-minded," he said taking her in his arms with a smile. "It's one of the things I love about you."

"I hope there are other things," she said with the mischievous smile that had first attracted him.

"Oh, there are," he said, pressing his lips to hers.

CHAPTER FOURTEEN

KOA AND BASA turned off the Māmalahoa Highway a few miles south of Kamuela. Giant cinder cones dotted the landscape with Mauna Kea rising 14,000 feet to the east. Sunshine had returned to the Big Island, and brisk trade winds sent puffy white clouds skittering across a blue sky. Closer to the road, the silos and conveyor belts of West Hawai'i Concrete stood out against a mountain backdrop. Trucks kicked up dust trails as they hauled crushed stone from a nearby quarry. At least a dozen concrete mixers dotted the yard around the concrete company's headquarters building.

"How long has your brother been doing concrete?" Koa asked.

"Since the '80s," Basa responded. "He tried to get me into the business, but I turned him down. Big mistake. He makes a hell of a lot more than I do."

"There's money in concrete?" Koa asked.

"Not for the slobs who lay the stuff, but the drivers do okay, and the managers make good money, especially with all the construction activity on this side of the island. And West Hawai'i Concrete dominates the business on the west side. My brother does alright."

When they drove through the gate, the ground turned from the rusty red of oxidized lava to the white of concrete dust, and the glare from the reflected sun intensified tenfold. They parked and got out.

The trade winds caught them in a swirl of concrete dust, blinding them and coating them with fine white powder. They'd be cleaning shit out of their hair for a week. At least, Koa thought, it didn't have the taste or smell of rotten eggs like the KonaWili site.

Koa stopped just inside the admin building, letting his eyes adjust from the blinding glare outside to the fluorescent office lighting. He looked to Basa. White dust coated the sergeant's face, and Koa guessed he too must look like a ghost.

"Arsenio!" The deep voice boomed across the confined space. A taller and heavier carbon copy of the barrel-chested police sergeant came around the counter to bear-hug his brother. Dressed in jeans and a company logo shirt, the older Basa topped six-three and weighed over two hundred pounds, but it was all muscle. Although Basa's brother was a good ten percent taller and bigger than his little brother, the resemblance was uncanny.

Basa hated his given name. Cops used it at their peril, but family, Koa guessed, got a pass. Slapping his brother hard on the back, Sergeant Basa turned to Koa. "This hairy caveman is my older brother, Osvaldo." Koa barely suppressed a laugh; Arsenio had wrought his brotherly revenge on Osvaldo.

"Just call me Ozzy," the older Basa said, leading them around the customer counter into a small room with a conference table. "You're here about that horrific disaster down at KonaWili." It was a statement, not a question. "Let me get the paperwork."

"Osvaldo?" Koa asked with a raised eyebrow after Ozzy left the room. Basa just spread his arms and shrugged. "What can I say? Parents!"

"You got your body cam running?"

"No. I turn it off for family."

Ozzy returned with a sheaf of papers. "You want to know about the concrete orders for the school?"

"Orders ... plural?" Koa asked.

"Yeah," Ozzy responded. "Unusual for a government contract, but that job had two separate orders." Ozzy pulled papers from his stack. "This first one is pretty straightforward. On big government contracts, we typically get about three months' notice, 'cause the contractor wants the materials ready. Delays on these government jobs cost big bucks."

Koa pulled the order across the table and studied it. Boyle Construction had ordered hundreds of cubic yards of concrete to be delivered in stages—foundation, foundation walls, main floor, main building walls, sidewalks, and miscellaneous finishing. The order appeared to cover the entire job and bore the number of the DOE-approved construction contract. Dozens of delivery tickets, some dirty or crumpled from having been countersigned on the job, were clipped to the order, showing the deliveries as the job progressed. Finally, the file contained a series of invoices requesting payment and vouchers reflecting the dates and amounts of payment.

Koa looked up at Ozzy. "This all seems pro forma."

Ozzy nodded. "It is. That's typical of the way these government contracts work."

"What about the other order?"

"Strange, that one. Never seen anything like it on a government deal, and I've been doing this job for more than twenty-five years."

"What happened?"

"Hank Boyle comes in here just after they start grading the site and wants an emergency delivery—twenty-five hundred cubic yards of concrete. You know how many trucks that is?"

"A truck holds nine yards. Isn't that where the expression 'the whole nine yards' comes from?"

"Very good. You want a job?"

"No thanks," Koa responded, wiping some of the concrete dust from his face.

"Boyle wants two-hundred-eighty truckloads of concrete, like yesterday."

"And you guys delivered?"

"Yeah, we delivered, but we jacked the price up by 50 percent. We brought in all the temporary drivers and layers we could find and still had guys working eighteen-hour shifts. Ran thirty trucks a day for ten days."

"Jesus." Koa had seen the six-foot walls at KonaWili, but he still asked the question. "Where'd they put all that concrete?"

"I wasn't out at the site, but my guys said they were pouring some kind of concrete bunker under the school."

Koa wanted more. "Can we talk to one of the drivers who was out there?"

"Sure." Ozzy picked up a telephone from a table in the corner of the room, dialed, and asked, "Is Keao around?" He waited a moment before saying, "Send him in here."

A couple of minutes later, a huge Hawaiian man, dressed in cement-covered coveralls, stepped into the room. "Keao," Ozzy introduced the driver, "this is my brother Arsenio and Detective Kāne. They want to know about the rush job down at KonaWili."

Though Keao looked to be all of two-hundred-fifty pounds, he was taller than Ozzy and his massive shoulders and arms bulged with muscle. A match, Koa thought, for my fisherman friend, Hook Hao. Keao pulled a chair from the end of the table. One of those plastic bucket chairs with metal legs. The chair legs bowed outward, and creaked under Keao's weight, but held. Keao ran a hand through his hair, sending a shower of concrete dust onto the table and the floor. "Crazy fuckin' job."

"*Aloha*, Keao," Koa began. "Tell us what you saw out there."

"Crazy fuckin' job," Keao repeated. "Started out fillin' a goddamn hole, 'cept it wouldn't fill. Took seventy trucks even with all the accelerators."

"Accelerators?"

"Chemicals. Makes the concrete harden faster."

Koa did the math. "You poured more than six hundred cubic yards of concrete into a hole?"

"Yeah, 'cept your 'rithmetic is screwed up. It was six-hundred-thirty yards."

"Got it," Koa conceded. "But you filled the hole?"

"Yeah. We filled the damn hole."

"And then?" Koa prodded.

"Then we poured the bunker."

"Bunker?"

"Yeah. A big cube with floor, walls, and top six feet thick, like one of the damn military ammo bunkers up at Pōhakuloa."

There it was, stark as a movie in Technicolor. Tony Pwalú uncovered the volcanic vent. Hank Boyle filled it with concrete and covered it with a bunker. What had Tatum said: "Trying to seal a volcanic vent is beyond stupid. Just causes the pressure to build up until you get an explosive release." Boyle created a ticking time bomb just waiting for rainwater to flash into steam under millions of pounds of pressure. Six-hundred-thirty cubic yards of concrete might be a big cork in the neck of the volcanic bottle, but it didn't stand a chance against *Pele—ka wahine 'ai pōhaku*, the stone-eating woman.

Koa stared at Keao. "You ever ask Boyle's people what they were doing?"

"Yeah, once."

"And?" Koa prompted.

"The foreman told me to mind my own business and get the fuckin' concrete poured."

"Ever see a building inspector at the site?"

Keao laughed. "Sure. When Zak showed up, Boyle's guys gave him a six-pack and a fifty. He signed off and crawled back in his hole. He's a joke."

Koa pulled the papers for the rush job across the table and focused on the government order number. Unlike the first set of documents, this one said: "Change Order No. 1" followed by the
original contract number. Koa had seen the original contract, but no
change order. "I didn't know there was a change order."

"Had to be a change order," Ozzy responded. "Otherwise we
don't get paid."

"You have a copy?" Koa asked.

"I don't, but the accounting department will. The gov gets a special rate, but we've got all kinds of contractors in here blathering
on about how the state sponsors their jobs, trying to get the government rate. We have a simple rule: no state contract, no state
discount."

"Can you get me a copy?"

"Sure." Ozzy left the room and came back a few minutes later. He
handed Koa a copy of an official state document. The DOE change
order for "environmental improvements" increased the contract
price for the school from nine-point-nine million dollars to eleven
million dollars. It bore the signature of Francine Na'auao, head of
the DOE. Environmental improvements, Koa thought, like sealing
up a volcanic vent. Still, the numbers puzzled Koa. "The rush concrete job didn't cost a million-one, did it?" he asked.

"Hell no," Ozzy responded. "With the surcharge and overtime, it
barely topped four hundred thousand."

The concrete had cost roughly a third of the $1,100,000 autho-
rized by the change order. What, Koa wondered, about the remaining $700,000? Bribes? But to whom? Gommes stood to make tens
of millions from the project. So too did Makela, who supposedly
owned 40 percent. They had incentive enough. Boyle? Had he been
bribed? Probably. Why else would a contractor knowingly cover up
a volcanic vent? What about Na'auao? Had some of that money

found its way back to her? Or Witherspoon? Or were there other silent partners who had extracted a toll for participating in the conspiracy? They—whoever they were—killed fourteen children and four teachers. Koa intended to chase them, every one of them, to the ends of the earth.

CHAPTER FIFTEEN

RAIN AND FOG returned that night and continued into the following morning, making the road slippery and the visibility poor. "Where'd this shitty weather come from?" Basa asked. "Kona's supposed to be sunny."

"It's a Kona front, weather coming in from the west. We're getting more western storms. Must be global warming," Koa responded.

"Hope it doesn't start the damn vent spewing again," Basa said.

Koa, too, worried about another volcanic blowup on Hualālai, one that might be even worse than the one that had killed the kids. "From your lips to God's ears."

"Hey," Basa suddenly caught on, "you're worried about more than just the school, aren't you?"

"Yeah, you heard Tatum. Kona's at risk if Hualālai blows."

"Jesus, that would be awful." Basa paused. "Didn't he say we'd have some warning?"

"Yeah. I hope he knows what he's talking about."

"Me, too." Basa paused, wiping the condensation off the inside of the windshield before changing the subject. "We're gonna get soaked, and for what? Talking to this doctor is gonna be a colossal waste of time."

Basa probably had it right. Koa viewed getting anything useful from Patrone as a long shot, but dozens of prescription pill bottles in Boyle's medicine cabinet bearing Dr. Patrone's name meant Boyle had suffered serious depression. The trip would be worth getting soaked if Dr. Patrone could shed some light on Boyle's mental condition.

When they arrived at their destination, rain pelted them before they got to the door. They took the stairs to the second floor and walked down a hall, their wet shoes squeaking, to a door marked, "Dr. Patrone, M.D., Mental Health and Psychiatric Services."

Finding the door locked, Koa followed the instructions posted on the glass and called the doctor's number. After a few seconds, a tall, thin man opened the door and introduced himself as Dr. Patrone. Koa judged the psychiatrist to be north of eighty years old, and the years hadn't been kind. His straggly white hair hung to his hunched shoulders, and framed a heavily scarred face, likely from too much Pacific sun. He let them into a tiny office just large enough to hold a couch, a chair, a small desk, and a steel filing cabinet. A larger-than-life poster of bodybuilder Mickey Hargitay, Mr. Universe 1955, seemed way out of place.

"Can't afford a receptionist," Dr. Patrone apologized in a soft, girlish voice. He gestured toward a tiny couch, too small for both policemen, so Koa stood against the wall. The atmosphere felt claustrophobic, and Koa doubted the good doctor treated many clients. He plainly paid little rent.

"We're here about Hank Boyle," Koa began. "He was your patient?"

The doctor frowned. "Did something happen to him?"

"Yes, Doc, I'm afraid he's dead."

"Oh, my God . . . oh, my God." Dr. Patrone's eyes widened, and tears gathered in his eyes.

The emotional physician in his ice-cube-sized office under the watchful gaze of Mr. Universe did nothing to heighten Koa's low regard for doctors. "He was your patient?" Koa repeated.

Patrone hesitated, took a tissue from his desk, and blew his nose. "Well, yes."

"From the number of antidepressants you prescribed, Boyle seems to have had some nervous or anxiety disorder?"

Patrone evaded the question. "How'd he die?"

"We found him hanged and are investigating the circumstances. Was he—"

"Oh, my God." Patrone went limp and slumped into his chair with his face in his hands.

Koa found the doc's reaction bizarre. Most medics, even psychiatrists, dealt all too often with death. To Koa, Patrone's reaction signaled more than a doctor-patient relationship. "He was your friend?" Koa asked.

The doctor seemed not to have heard. "He was your friend?" Koa repeated.

Patrone looked up, his face stricken with grief, tears in his eyes, and nodded. "Yes, a dear, dear friend."

Koa waited, giving the shrink time to recover. "We need to know about his recent condition, his state of mind."

Patrone pulled another tissue from the box and dried his eyes. "I . . . I can't. I just can't. There's a doctor-patient privilege."

"Hank Boyle is dead under suspicious circumstances. We need—"

Patrone shook his head. "The privilege survives his death."

Koa knew the law and remained undeterred in seeking answers. "Did he have any relatives who survived him?" Koa demanded.

"No. None I know about."

"Then who are you protecting, Doc?"

"I can't. I just can't—"

Koa moved closer to the physician, invading his space and leaning close until their faces were no more than six inches apart. "He was your friend. Don't you care what happened to him?"

The doctor stared at Koa for several seconds. "Talk to Gene." The doctor spoke so softly, Koa barely heard.

"Who's Gene?"

"Gene Forret, Hank's friend. He lives down at the Sunset Villa condos."

Recognizing he wasn't going to get what he needed from Patrone and now more curious than ever about Boyle, Koa said, "Don't go anywhere. We'll likely need to see you again."

He led Basa back through the rain to the Explorer in search of Gene Forret.

"That quack is one weird dude!" Basa exclaimed. "Not like any doctor I know. Acted more like a bereaved spouse than a shrink, and he's damn sure hiding something."

Koa nodded in agreement. In his years on the street, Basa had developed uncanny instincts for unusual personalities, of which the Big Island had more than its share. "Yeah. I'm getting strange vibes about Hank Boyle. He's coming across as an untold tale."

"You think Boyle and the doctor were more than friends?" Basa asked.

"Don't you?"

"Yeah."

They found the Sunset Villa condos, hidden behind cascades of rain-drenched red bougainvillea flowers not far off the south Kona waterfront. A woman in the office pointed them to Gene Forret's unit, and they trudged through the rain, still falling with thunderous force. A sixty-something bodybuilder with long gray hair and a beard, dressed only in dusty green shorts, responded suspiciously to their knock, opening the door only a few inches. His hard, well-muscled body reflected regular workouts, but tattoos covered his chest, and a gold hoop hung from his nose. He spotted Basa's uniform and said, "Cops. What do you want?"

"I'm Chief Detective Kāne. It's about your friend Hank Boyle," Koa responded.

"He's dead." Guarding the door, Forret gave no sign of inviting them inside.

"We're aware of his death," Koa responded. "Dr. Patrone suggested we chat with you."

Forret's expression changed at the mention of Patrone's name, and he stepped back, letting the two officers into his one-bedroom apartment. Life-sized, bodybuilding posters—Arnold Schwarzenegger, Dexter Jackson, Bob Paris, Tony Atlas, and others—dominated the walls of the living-dining-kitchen area, and a massage table sat where the architect had envisioned a dining table.

"You a fitness trainer?" Basa asked.

"Yeah, and a freelance masseur."

Koa wondered if this aging hippie held a massage license. Koa didn't see one hanging on the walls. The two policemen sat on folding chairs around a large mat spread in the center of the living room floor. Forret dropped into a lotus position in the center of the mat. Koa noticed a diamond stud on his left ear. It weighed at least two carats and glinted like the real thing. He hadn't paid for the earring with his massage business. "How well did you know Hank Boyle?"

"He finally committed suicide."

Koa jumped on the word "finally." "He attempted suicide before?"

"Yeah, that's how we first hooked up."

Koa had missed a turn somewhere. "I don't understand."

"Patrone treated him after he attempted suicide back in college. The quack and I were together back then, and he introduced me to Hank. He was really fucked up, coming off some kind of weird episode."

"You met at UH?"

"I didn't go to college, but Patrone introduced me to Hank back then. We've been together ever since."

"Tell me about this weird episode?"

Forret shook his head. "It's a mystery, a forty-year-old mystery."

"Meaning?"

"Something happened to Hank Boyle during his senior year at UH. Something terrible, involving a woman, and it changed his life. That much I know. The rest—" Forret spread his arms—"only the gods, and maybe old Doc Patrone, know."

"What year was this?"

"Mid-1970s. We were all still living the 1960s hippie life chronicled by Tom Wolfe in *The Electric Kool-Aid Acid Test*. You remember those days, don't you? Ken Kesey and the Merry Pranksters ridin' across the country in a painted school bus named Further. You know, free love, sex, and LSD, all in search of intersubjectivity."

Although Koa had once read the book, he wasn't a Tom Wolfe fan. "Boyle had a bad trip?"

Forret shook his head slowly, the way people do when they're replaying memories in their head. "I've had some bad trips but not like Hank Boyle. I don't know what drove him into a lifelong depression, but it was a hell of a lot worse than acid, much darker and more dangerous."

"You know any of his friends?"

"Maybe a couple, but as you can see, Hank lived two lives, and I was never part of his other life."

"The name Witherspoon mean anything to you? Arthur Witherspoon?"

"I've heard the name, but never met the man. Like I said, Hank didn't introduce me to his straight friends."

"What about Gommes? Howard Gommes?"

"The developer? Sure, Hank worked for him. Talked about him from time to time. Described him as one nasty son of a bitch, but rich as Midas, and tough as lava chewing gum."

"Boyle and Gommes have a run-in?"

"On every job. Boyle would come back from meeting with Gommes all chewed up. Gommes is a screamer, yelling, banging his fist, making threats, acting like he owned Hank, or had some kind of hold over him, but Hank always took his jobs. Made good money, too."

"When did you last see Boyle?"

"We had dinner together down at the beach the evening before he killed himself."

"Anything unusual happen?"

"Yeah, Hank was bummed out about the school thing up at KonaWili."

"What'd he say about it?"

"That it shouldn't have happened. He just kept saying over and over: 'It shouldn't have happened . . . it shouldn't have happened.'"

"He say why?"

"Naw, just it shouldn't have happened."

"Where were you the rest of that night?"

"Here. All night by myself."

Koa hadn't expected to learn much from Boyle's psychiatrist, but Gene Forret had given him a lot to think about. Koa had pegged Gommes as an arrogant prick with a mean streak, but Forret made him out to be more sinister with "some kind of hold" over Hank Boyle. Gommes, Koa thought, must treat people the way he treated his butcher's dogs.

CHAPTER SIXTEEN

As they neared the KonaWili school on their way back to Hilo, strange streaks of light off to the right of the highway cut through the water-soaked sky. Basa opened his passenger-side window, and, despite the drumbeat of the rain, a violent whooshing noise filled the air.

"My God," Basa exclaimed, "the school is blowing up."

When Koa turned into the subdivision, they saw a giant geyser of smoke and ash shooting into the gray sky, creating an ominous blanket of darkness. TV trucks, cameramen, and a few rain-soaked demonstrators stared. None ventured too close. *Pele's* violence kept everyone at a distance.

A new eruption of superheated gases blasted through the school. *Pele's* fury lifted the steel roof entirely off the building, casting it aside like so much tinfoil. The front wall exploded. Massive chunks of concrete—some twice the size of an SUV—flew about like children's toys. In the center of it all, steam and ash fountained fifteen hundred feet into the air. Even from a quarter-mile away, the noise overpowered all other sounds, and heat turned faces red. Fine gray ash filtered out of the sky like dirty snow.

"My God," Basa exclaimed. "I've never seen anything like it."

"If there had been kids in that school tonight—"

"We'd have hundreds of fatalities," Basa finished Koa's sentence. "People should be thanking their lucky stars *Pele* gave us a preview."

"But they won't," Koa responded. "You thought people were riled up. Just wait 'til these images go viral. Parents will go ballistic."

"I suppose you're right. And Gommes won't be selling houses in the KonaWili subdivision anytime soon. Wonder how much money he's lost on this project?"

"The forty million purchase price for starters."

Basa whistled.

* * *

It was late when Koa arrived back in Hilo. He'd been running at full tilt since the school blew up and needed a break. He called Nālani, suggesting they make dinner together. Cooking with her by his side always had a calming effect on him. He then rang Hook Hao, his fisherman friend, and ten minutes later, Koa parked at Wailoa Harbor, where he crossed the quay and boarded Hook's commercial fishing vessel, named *Ka'upu*, Hawaiian for albatross.

"*Aloha*, my friend," Hook said, as he stepped from the wheelhouse, dressed in a tee shirt, bearing the Suisan Fish Market logo, cutoff shorts, and his ever-present, size sixteen black rubber boots. A giant of a man, he'd spent his whole life around the Hilo docks and wielded a gaff like an extension of his arm. Hook knew all the dirty secrets worth knowing on the island's waterfronts. Ever since Koa helped Hook's son out of a jam, the big fisherman had been a valuable source of information for Koa. Along the way, they'd become fast friends.

Koa reciprocated with an *aloha*, and the two men chatted awhile, before Koa asked, "What's in the fish locker tonight?"

"Depends on what you're offering," Hook responded.

Koa pulled out two hefty Cuban cigars. "What is a pair of these worth?" He dangled the two Montecristo Edmundos playfully.

"Ahh," Hook sighed with delight before breaking into a broad smile. "You like *ʻōpakapaka*?" It was a rhetorical question. Blue snapper fresh from the ocean was one of the island's delicacies. They exchanged prizes, and Koa headed for home to share his "catch" with Nālani.

On the infrequent occasions when they both had time, he and Nālani loved to whip up special meals. Favoring the savory, he made a wicked *nori*-wrapped *ʻahi* and delicious vegetable risottos. Nālani specialized in sweets. Friends begged for her to-die-for *tarte tatin*. Koa and Nālani, both covered in aprons, enjoying a good Russian River chardonnay, swapped stories, laughed, and occasionally kissed as they reveled in foodie heaven. The prospect of *ʻōpakapaka* with a ginger crust only added to their happy mood. More relaxed than he'd been in weeks, Koa managed to put KonaWili out of his mind. Then the doorbell rang.

Koa opened the door to find Walker McKenzie. The reporter, dressed in jeans and his signature white shirt with rolled-up sleeves, might have just stepped from behind the newsroom cameras.

Annoyed by the interruption—especially from a reporter—he wanted to shut the door, but Nālani came up behind him and recognized TV's famous "Mr. Disaster."

"Walker McKenzie!" Nālani beamed. "What a treat." She pushed the screen open.

"Hello, Nālani, it's a pleasure to meet you." McKenzie, who somehow knew Nālani's name, gave her his trademark on-air grin, and Nālani nearly swooned.

"Please, come in," she offered, and McKenzie stepped inside before Koa could intervene. "Have a seat." Always gracious, Nālani added, "Can I get you something? Maybe a glass of wine?"

"That would be nice," McKenzie said, taking a seat and looking around the cozy cottage. "Nice place."

Remembering the mayor's warning—"You don't talk to reporters. Watanabe will handle the press"—Koa cut McKenzie off before he started asking questions. "I don't have any new information on the KonaWili situation."

McKenzie repeated the grin. "Actually, I'm not here about KonaWili."

Nālani poured a glass of chardonnay for the reporter. He took it and sipped. "Russian River," he identified the wine, nodding his approval.

McKenzie had piqued Koa's curiosity. "If not KonaWili, what brings you to Volcano?"

The reporter swirled the wine in his glass and took another sip. "We're doing a human-interest story on you."

Koa didn't like the sound of that. "On me?"

"Yes. The sugar mill worker's son from Laupāhoehoe graduates from the prestigious Kamehameha schools, plays football for the UH Rainbow Warriors, serves his country in the 5th Special Forces in Afghanistan and Somalia, joins the police force, and rises to the rank of chief detective. Our viewers around the world will be charmed."

The idea repulsed Koa. Deeply suspicious of the press, he stayed in the background even when the mayor hadn't warned him to stay away from reporters. Let the politicians have the limelight. He appreciated the reporter's next suggestion even less.

"Your brother's history only makes the story more fascinating."

Koa felt his heart rate jump. He hated having his own face plastered across the TV, but dragging the family name through the mud yet again because of his brother's crimes was intolerable. "I want no part of this," Koa responded hotly, moving toward the door to show the reporter out.

Walker McKenzie hadn't become a national news celebrity by failing to anticipate the reactions of his subjects. "We don't need your approval," he said, "and we could do this story without your cooperation, but there's an angle you might find interesting."

Koa stopped. "What's that?" he asked, making no attempt to hide his skepticism.

"I've been working on a story about the personality changes in veterans from Iraq and Afghanistan who suffered brain injuries. Medical experts tell me frontal lobe injuries frequently trigger significant personality shifts, typically making people more impulsive and aggressive."

Koa thought he saw where the reporter was heading, and, if he had it right, the idea intrigued him. He returned to the chair opposite McKenzie.

McKenzie continued with a glint in his eye. "I sent one of my gophers to Arizona to interview Ikaika. That's when I learned he'd been brought back here and fainted. I had someone check Queen's Medical in Honolulu and discovered he's had surgery for a frontal lobe brain tumor."

McKenzie enjoyed phenomenal sources, Koa thought, wondering how the man had gained access to Ikaika's medical information. Koa knew he should be furious but held his temper to hear what the reporter had to say.

"If you work with us on our human-interest story, I'll put you in touch with some serious medical experts, people on the cutting edge of brain research. At a minimum, they may help your family cope with Ikaika's surgery and recovery, and there is a possibility they could help you build a case your brother's brain tumor is at least partially responsible for his criminal conduct. They might even help you structure a case for parole."

Koa felt a flash of hope spark through his brain so strongly he shivered. Ikaika paroled and in control of his behavior would be a family dream come true, a triple rainbow for his mother. He remembered Dr. Carlton's words: "I can't tell you when the tumor developed, but he's most likely had at least a small tumor since childhood." Could a brain tumor have triggered, or at least exacerbated, Ikaika's criminality? Koa would never know if he didn't explore the question. He sat for several moments before speaking. "And what do you get out of this?"

"That's simple. I get what I live for, covering interesting stories. I get your cooperation on the personal biography, and, if the experts can help your brother, CNN gets an exclusive on that story, too."

Koa had to admire the reporter's straightforward approach. He offered invaluable access to experts—something out of Koa's reach—and McKenzie only wanted to do his job. An exchange Koa himself might have proposed. Still, he hesitated. The mayor would fire him if he learned of an alliance between Koa and Walker McKenzie, and a puff piece about his chief detective would upstage and annoy Police Chief Lannua. Other detectives might even be jealous.

Nālani, sensing his uncertainty, intervened. "Koa doesn't have to decide tonight, does he?"

Bless her, Koa thought, she's given me time to think.

"Of course not," McKenzie responded. "Take some time and call me if you have questions." He handed Koa a card and thanked Nālani for the wine.

After McKenzie left, Koa and Nālani talked long into the night. The decision tortured Koa, pitting his deep-seated distrust of the press and his concern about the effect on his role as chief detective against his familial ties, and, as the oldest Kāne male, those ties weighed heavily.

"Māpuana would want you to do what you could for Ikaika," Nālani stated the obvious.

"But what if nothing comes of it? I'll look like a publicity hound. It'll piss off the chief and undercut my leadership of the detectives."

"Sure, there are risks," Nālani conceded, "but you have to weigh them against the possibility of putting your family back together."

In the end, Nālani recalled an old Hawaiian proverb, and it turned the tide of his thinking. *'O ke keiki he loaʻa i ka moe, ʻo ka pōkiʻi ʻaʻole*—one can produce a child by sleeping with a mate, but he cannot produce a younger brother. Brothers were brothers, and regardless of Ikaika's crimes, blood ties required Koa to do what he could. His mother would expect no less. Old Hawaiians said, *hoʻi hou i ka mole*—return to the taproot.

The following morning, Koa accepted McKenzie's proposal.

CHAPTER SEVENTEEN

"You've been rattling cages, my friend." Zeke Brown greeted Koa with a grin. From anyone else, it might have been a rebuke, but Zeke delighted in investigating politicians. He held an old-fashioned view of government service. To him, government employees worked for the people who elected them, not the other way around. He hated politicians who augmented their compensation at the public trough. His credo was simple: If you weren't willing to work for your public salary, you shouldn't take the job.

Koa wasn't surprised Zeke knew of his visit to Cheryl Makela. Zeke's tentacles extended into every aspect of county government. "You heard?"

"Have I heard?" Zeke chuckled. "That weasel press jockey in the mayor's office screamed at me before I told him to stick it up his ass. You're not the most popular boy in town."

In provoking Cheryl Makela, Koa hoped to stimulate a reaction. He'd intended to stir the pot and see what scum floated to the top. But he hadn't expected to excite the big shots in the mayor's office. "What'd you tell him?"

"That you were helping me with a grand jury investigation."

"You've convened a grand jury?"

"Sure. The public expects me to investigate the KonaWili disaster. "And besides—" Zeke grinned—"I've been looking for an excuse to put Cheryl Makela under oath for a decade. She's the queen bee of our rotten political land-use game."

Koa nodded. "Based on what she refused to answer, you've got plenty to work with."

"Let me guess." Zeke cupped his hands like two bowls. Hefting one hand, he said, "She refused to say how much money she put into the Hualālai Hui and how much was carried by Gommes." Lifting the other hand, he added, "She refused to admit to sub-*hui*s or identify the participants."

"Were you eavesdropping?"

"No." Zeke smiled. "But I'd have been disappointed if you hadn't asked, and I knew she wouldn't answer."

For the umpteenth time since he'd made chief detective, Koa thanked the gods for the protection Zeke Brown afforded him. He was the longest-serving elected public official in the county. He'd prosecuted mayors and police chiefs. Nobody crossed Zeke Brown. And his intercessions had saved Koa's job more than once.

"You're going to put her in front of a grand jury?"

"Yeah," Zeke responded, "but not yet. I want you to dump some more *kiawe* wood in the *imu* before we roast this pig."

"Let me fill you in on my latest discovery."

Zeke pounded his desk when Koa described his visit to West Hawai'i Concrete and the discovery of the change order.

"That certainly puts the spotlight on the DOE," Zeke responded. "I've been on the horn to the state attorney general. The governor is pissed at Tanaka. He wants the state AG to run the KonaWili investigation, but the Big Island police have jurisdiction and, politically, the governor won't spend the capital to overrule the mayor."

"I get the jurisdiction angle, but why does Tanaka want to keep this lava ball? You'd think he'd be happy to dump it off on the state."

Zeke put on his schoolmarm's face and asked, "Why do you think?"

"I don't know, Zeke, I'd like to think it's politics. You know, Tanaka trying to blame the governor, and Māhoe laying it off on Tanaka, but my gut tells me Tanaka's got skin in the game. I'd guess he's protecting Makela."

Zeke nodded. "Māhoe and Tanaka hate each other, so it could be politics. On the other hand, like you, I'm betting Makela is dirty."

"And if she's dirty, could she be the mayor's bag lady?" Koa asked.

"That would explain why Tanaka wants to keep the investigation and why Māhoe is hot to take control."

Koa nodded. "Fucking politicians." He hesitated. "Present company excluded."

"No offense taken," Zeke said. "All this political maneuvering does have some advantages."

"Like what?"

"The state AG seems to think Na'auao might have something to say about Makela and suggested that you interview our DOE chief."

Koa had been wondering how he was going to get to the state-level officials who'd approved the KonaWili site, executed the construction contract, and signed off on the change order. Still, the suggestion, coming from the state AG, bothered him. "Is somebody trying to manipulate the investigation?"

"Maybe, but we still need to hear what Na'auao has to say."

"Agreed. What should I focus on?"

"The location, the price, and the change order. If you look at the subdivision plot, the location of that school up at the top of the property is damned odd. Then, the state paid a premium price—on a per-square-foot-basis almost 40 percent more than the statewide average. And this change order is downright wacky. I mean, does anyone really think Witherspoon forgot to design in the standard environmental improvements? He wasn't senile. The discovery of *Pele*'s volcanic vent was the only environmental change. And, of course, you'll need to hear what she has to say about Makela." Zeke grinned like a wolf, contemplating dinner.

*   *   *

Koa prepared for his interview with Francine Na'auao throughout the forty-five-minute plane ride to O'ahu. Na'auao had run the DOE for nearly a decade. In a state known for its poorly performing public schools and a controversial public education structure—Hawai'i had the only statewide single district public school system in the nation—her longevity marked Na'auao as a consummate political insider. Making matters worse, as a protégée of Governor Māhoe, Koa had to handle her with kid gloves. He was nevertheless determined to dig beneath the surface. Na'auao had approved the change order, increasing the cost of the school building by more than 11 percent. She couldn't have done so without a reason. But what reason could she possibly give? Surely, she wouldn't admit to covering up a volcanic vent.

A detective from the Honolulu police picked him up at the airport and drove him to Queen's Medical Center. He'd allowed extra time to visit his brother in the hospital and found his way to the ICU. He stood just outside his brother's cubicle. He'd seen dozens of crime victims in hospital emergency rooms, but it still shocked him to see Ikaika, his head covered in bandages and hooked up to more inputs, outputs, IVs, and monitors than a computer motherboard. Their mother, Māpuana, sat with her left hand on Ikaika's left arm, whispering a traditional Hawaiian health prayer. *Mai ka piko o ke poʻo a ka poli o ka wāwae, a loaʻa mai nā kihi ʻehā o ke kino.*

Although unskilled in the art of the *kahuna lāʻau lapaʻau*, the traditional Hawaiian healer, Koa knew that the left, or feminine, side represented the inner body. Māpuana was passing her inner strength to Ikaika to replace the *mana*, his personal power, that the tumors had drained from him. Māpuana had also placed *ti* leaves, *ʻōlena*, and other healing plants on Ikaika's bed. Such materials were surely prohibited in the ICU, but Koa doubted that the staff had the fortitude to confront his mother.

While Koa stood watching, his sister, Alana, came up behind him. "Ikaika looks so helpless like that."

It was probably the nicest thing she'd said about Ikaika in a decade. Koa turned to face his sister, taking in the deep purple circles under her eyes, and putting his arms around her. Her hug was so tight, it conveyed her desperation. "How long has he been out like that?" Koa asked.

"Since the surgery. The nurses keep saying he'll wake up, but it hasn't happened."

Māpuana heard them talking and looked up. "Koa, my *keiki*, come sit." She patted the chair next to her, the one Alana had been using, but Koa moved to the other side of the bed and took Ikaika's limp hand in his own. Looking down, he saw only the baby brother he'd tickled and taught to play hide-and-seek. All of the acrimony between them faded into the background, and he said, "Hang in there, tough guy. We're rooting for you."

Across the bed, Māpuana struggled to her feet, her left hand still on Ikaika's arm. "The *haole* doctors say he will be better, maybe not so possessed by angry spirits. I pray the gods to make it so."

"I hope so," he responded.

"You must help make it so."

He felt helpless in the face of her plea. "What can I do? I'm not a doctor. I have no special skill for healing."

"Ikaika comes from a good root, but *'uhane 'ino*, demons, have possessed him. All of us have done bad things . . . things we regret . . .."

Their eyes locked and Koa suddenly wondered if his mother somehow knew of his confrontation with Hazzard. Logic told him it was impossible, but his mother possessed mystical powers beyond his understanding. The thought sent a chill through him.

Then she continued, ". . . but the *'uhane 'ino* have caused Ikaika to do many, many bad things. They have possessed him and hidden the goodness inside. I know this in my *na'au*, the depths of my soul. *'Ike aku, 'ike mai, kōkua aku kōkua mai; pēlā ihola ka nohona 'ohana . . .* family life requires mutual help. You must forgive the pain Ikaika has caused, and find a way to help him . . . to put your family back together . . . for my sake . . . for your ancestors. That too I know in my *na'au*."

He thought about telling her of his conversation with Walker McKenzie, but it was too speculative. They stood like that for a long time, both holding Ikaika's hands—Koa hoping his brother survived, while his mother continued her prayerful *oli*, her chants.

*   *   *

Koa excused himself, left the hospital, and walked across Punchbowl Street to the Queen Lili'uokalani Building that housed the Department of Education. His thoughts turned to the KonaWili children. What physiological toll would the disaster inflict on them? Having survived trauma in a supposedly safe place, would they ever feel secure? He wondered if *Pele's* wrath would turn some to violence or criminal behavior.

Na'auao made him wait nearly forty-five minutes. Her cold reception surprised him only because the state AG had encouraged Zeke to arrange the interview. Once an attractive woman, the years hadn't been kind to Na'auao. Her stony face looked brittle, like pieces might chip off, and her once black hair had thinned and turned gray. Still, she radiated an intimidating frigidity. He couldn't imagine working for this woman, the "Iron Lady" of the DOE.

He began by thanking her for the meeting.

"Get to the point, Detective. I've got a school system to run."

He got to the point. "Did you have an interest in the Hualālai Hui?"

She glared at him with undisguised malice. "I wasn't a partner in that *hui*."

That didn't answer the question. "Did you have any financial interest, Mrs. Na'auao?"

"I told you I wasn't a partner," she said, clipping her words.

"That doesn't answer my question. Were you a participant in any *sub-hui*?"

"No."

Why had she danced around his questions? If she really didn't have a financial interest, why not just say so? "Do you know who had undisclosed financial interests in the Hualālai Hui project?"

"No one's said there were undisclosed financial interests."

She was playing games with him. "I'll rephrase the question. Do you know of any undisclosed interests?"

She stared at him for several seconds before letting out a long sigh. "My husband was offered an interest but turned it down. We don't invest in school projects."

Koa felt a jolt of electricity. The developer had offered undisclosed interests to entice public officials. "Who approached your husband?"

She hesitated. Finally, with another sigh, she said, "Cheryl Makela."

"How much did she offer?"

"It never got that far."

Gommes had partnered with Makela, and she'd tried to bribe a government official whose approvals were needed to make things happen. Zeke would be thrilled.

"Do you know of any other undisclosed interests?"

"I assume shares were offered to planning officials, but I've no direct knowledge."

"Why do you assume that?"

She looked at him like a teacher chastising a stupid child. "Because I've heard the same rumors you've heard. The state's land-use system is notoriously corrupt, although there's rarely been any proof."

"Who selected the KonaWili school site?"

"Let me tell you how this works. My former deputy Joanie Pupuka, head of facilities, handled all the school acquisition and construction issues. In the case of KonaWili, the developer offered the site, and the Hawai'i County planning department approved it. The DOE accepted the planning department recommendation."

"Didn't the DOE do any environmental survey of the site?"

"The DOE hired land surveyors, not environmental people, to review the site. For environmental issues, we rely on county planning people. The Hawai'i County planning department prepared an environmental report on KonaWili, and we accepted it."

"Were you aware the site is quite far from the main roads with limited access in the event of an emergency?"

"We look to the county planning people for that sort of thing."

"Would it surprise you if the Hawai'i County planning office never visited the site?"

"Officially, yes. Unofficially, it wouldn't have mattered. No one in that department was competent to perform an environmental survey. They just relied on the developer."

"So why didn't the DOE check the environmental suitability of the site?"

"We supervise two hundred ninety-one public schools. We don't have time or money to inspect every site, let alone look into local environmental matters."

Koa wasn't surprised she laid responsibility off on the Hawai'i County planning department, but the DOE hadn't been completely hands-off. He checked his notes to find Tony Pwalú's exact words: Hank showed "some *haole* lady from Honolulu." Koa considered how he'd phrase his question. Boyle and Witherspoon had been murdered. Tony Pwalú might not have long to live, but Koa didn't want to get him killed.

"I have information," he began, "that a DOE employee visited the site during the early phases of construction. Do you know who that might have been?"

"That would be unusual. We rely on the county building inspectors to check on construction. If anyone from this office visited the KonaWili site, it would have been Joanie Pupuka."

He looked her directly in the eye. "You didn't visit the site?"

She stared straight back. "No."

Changing tacks, he asked, "How come the DOE paid a premium price—some 40 percent over the average—for the land?"

"I didn't like the price, but the developer wouldn't budge. It was sufficiently out of line so I asked the board. The board approved the price."

"Couldn't you have acquired the site using the state's power of eminent domain?"

Her lips tightened and she scowled. "Sure, but that process takes years."

She had an answer for everything, so he went for the jugular. "Tell me about the one-point-one-million-dollar change order."

She looked at him quizzically. "What change order?"

He concealed his surprise. She'd signed the change order, so he hadn't expected her answer. "The change order for one-point-one million in environmental improvements."

"That's news to me."

He pulled the document from the folder he'd brought with him and slid it across the table to her. She stared at the document for a long, long time. "Where did you get this?"

"That doesn't matter. It bears your signature. What basis did you have to sign it?"

She picked it up to examine the signature. "I didn't. My office uses Signoscript machines. This looks like a machine signature. Joanie had signing authority."

"You're telling me you didn't authorize this change order?"

"That's exactly what I'm telling you."

"Did you know about the change order?"

"No."

"Is that the KonaWili file?" He pointed to a thick folder on her desk.

"Yes." She pushed the documents toward him. He leafed through the file without finding the change order. "The basic contract is here, but no change order."

"Like I said, I knew nothing about any change order."

"The change order is for environmental improvements. What environmental improvements would have been needed at KonaWili?"

"None, so far as I know."

"Did anyone ever tell you there was a volcanic vent under that school?"

"No."

"Would you be surprised to learn that the contractor knew about the vent and filled it with concrete?"

"It would shock the hell out of me."

The interview was turning out to be a bust. He'd learned Makela had offered Na'auao's husband an interest in the development, but not much else. He needed to interview Joanie Pupuka. "I'd like to talk to Ms. Pupuka."

"Good luck. She died in a car crash three months ago."

Shit. He'd run up against a wall. Well, almost. He had one further avenue to pursue.

Koa left Francine Na'auao's office and walked several blocks past the capitol into Honolulu's Chinatown. He stopped in the mouth of an alley, checking to make sure he hadn't been followed, before ducking down the alley and around a corner to a small Thai curry house. It was far enough from the DOE headquarters so he, and more importantly, his luncheon guest, wouldn't be observed by the wrong people. Inside, the rich smell of southeast Asian spices assaulted him. He made his way past the lunch crowd to a booth in the back corner, screened from the main part of the eatery.

"*Aloha*, Koa," Christina Waters greeted him. In her late-thirties with blond hair, blue eyes, and a cherubic face, she wore a conservative light blue dress. He studied the pale smooth skin of her face. His fingers and lips had once touched every facet of that face.

"*Aloha*," he replied, sliding into the booth opposite her.

"You're looking good," she said with a genuine smile.

"You, too, Christina." They'd been an item years ago but parted friends when she'd left the Big Island for a state-level job. His current girlfriend, Nālani, wouldn't be thrilled he was with an old flame, but he had good reason, and Nālani didn't need to know.

Her face darkened. "Such a tragedy at KonaWili."

"Unimaginable, Christina. I never thought I'd see anything like it."

"I hear you risked your life to save some of those kids."

"Yeah, well, we didn't save enough. Fourteen kids and four teachers died. And all because of a conspiracy among reckless people."

"You've got a mess with the investigation."

"Yeah, and Na'auao didn't help."

"Your meeting with *he'e* didn't go so well?"

"The *octopus*? Is that what you call her?" Koa asked.

"Only behind her back. She's smart as hell and her tentacles reach everywhere."

"Funny, because she laid the fault off on Joanie Pupuka and the Hilo planning office."

Christina frowned. "Poor Joanie. A terrible accident. Reminds me how fragile life is." She pushed a menu across the table to him. "Order us some curry like old times, and then I'll tell you about life in the DOE."

He ordered soft shrimp spring rolls, octopus with red chilies, chicken say-ta, fish cakes, and green curry with beef. His memory of Christina's favorites surprised him.

"I can't believe she laid it off on Joanie."

"Why?" he asked.

"You have to understand that Na'auao controls everything in the department with an iron fist. That's how she's maintained control for so long."

"You're saying, it's unlikely Joanie signed a change order without Na'auao's knowledge?"

"Flat out impossible. Joanie didn't order paperclips without Na'auao's blessing. Let me show you something." She pulled a thick sheaf of papers from her bag. "This is the DOE capital budget for the fiscal year when we built KonaWili. These things are guarded like the crown jewels." She flipped to a page flagged with a sticky. "Here's the breakdown on KonaWili."

Koa scanned several pages. They showed an extensive breakdown of the acquisition and construction costs for the school building. Following the various categories for the initial contract, a separate breakdown categorized the change order—additional grading, reinforcing rods, concrete, sealants, etcetera.

"That's Naʻauao's bible," Christina said. "She goes over the updated version of that document four times a year. The review takes a full week. She makes her subordinates justify every single line item, and she often revises authorizations or dumps whole projects. There's no way a one-point-one-million-dollar change order escaped her attention. No way."

Koa looked back at the breakdown for the change order. The largest entry read "miscellaneous" and accounted for $600,000. Looking back up at Christina, he asked, "Any idea what's buried in miscellaneous?"

"I saw that entry. It's weird. Look through the rest of the capital budget; you won't find many miscellaneous entries and none even a fraction so large. Naʻauao hates undefined categories. She'd burn my ass if I'd put something like that in the budget."

Koa nodded. He had already guessed the six-hundred-thousand-dollar entry hid bribes or other shady payments.

"Can I keep this document?"

"Yes. But you didn't get it from me. If she found out I gave you that document, I'd be *persona non grata* throughout the Hawaiian government."

"She's that powerful?"

"You have no idea."

"You said Naʻauao controls everything in the department with an iron fist. Does that alone explain why she's run the department for so many years?"

Christina looked at him for a long time. He sensed her indecision before she finally said, "I shouldn't be telling you this stuff."

"Fourteen kids died, Christina. They deserve justice."

"Okay, I'll tell you, but I'll deny it if anyone ever asks. Na'auao's got some hold over the governor. Maybe it's some campaign finance irregularity. Maybe it's something else. I don't know the details."

"How do you know about this?"

"One Saturday I was entering her office when I heard her talking to the governor on the phone. She threatened him. I quietly backed away and left the building. I never want her to find out I overheard part of that conversation."

"That's it? That's all you heard?"

"More than I wanted to hear."

Koa left first to make sure no one would discover their meeting. On the way back to the Big Island, he reviewed the bidding. Na'auao had lied. She'd known about and approved the change order. What other lies had she told? About an investment in the KonaWili development? About visiting the school site? About knowing of the volcanic vent? The KonaWili conspiracy was expanding like an *'o'opu hue*, pufferfish, and, like the puffer, it held deadly poisons.

CHAPTER EIGHTEEN

KOA WAS CONVINCED that Witherspoon's office had been ransacked in an unsuccessful effort to find something the man had hidden. He called Mrs. Witherspoon, hoping she might shed light on the secret. She agreed to meet but warned she'd have only a few minutes. She greeted him dressed in a frilly pink blouse and sleek red silk skirt. A gold chain with a diamond pendant around her neck completed the picture of a woman far from mourning. She invited him in, but he sensed no warmth.

"Tell me what you need. I have a luncheon engagement."

Koa pressed her for any clue as to where Arthur might have hidden a treasured secret.

"There's nothing," she responded all too easily with a bored tone, giving Koa the impression she hadn't tried. Yes, she searched their bank safe deposit box—"it's just jewelry and some old papers." Yes, she reviewed everything in Arthur's home office, but—"he didn't spend much time there, and I didn't find anything." They'd stored some old things in the attic, but layers of dust confirmed no one had been up there in years.

He tried to question her about Arthur's friends, but she displayed little interest in her deceased husband. Koa concluded Arthur had been a man with many clients, few friends, and none who mattered to his wife. "We had no social life," she said with obvious regret. "Arthur worked from dawn to dusk. I urged him to hire assistants, but he resisted. He didn't trust assistants."

"But he had an assistant for big jobs," Koa responded.

"Well, yes, some kid," she said, "more of a step-and-fetch-it clerk than an assistant. She made copies, delivered plans to the printers and to clients, made coffee, things like that."

"What's her name?"

"Sally something... I don't know."

Koa recalled seeing Sally Medea's name on papers in Arthur's office. Medea, he'd thought at the time, like the name of the Euripides play *Medea* he'd seen during his days at UH.

"Sally Medea?"

Mrs. Witherspoon shook her head. "I wouldn't know."

"Do you know where I might find her?"

That elicited another shake of the head. "Are we done? I really do have an engagement."

In failing to find what he sought, Koa gained a troubling insight. The Witherspoons' relationship had been sterile, a marriage long since dried up, like an unwatered garden. That cast Arthur's death in a new light and made him think Sarah Witherspoon should be a suspect.

At Koa's request, Sergeant Basa located Sally Medea, Arthur Witherspoon's "step-and-fetch-it" assistant. Koa called her. A single mother with a young son, she suggested he come to her apartment.

He found the complex quite upscale—not at all what he expected. Sally, dressed in a long skirt and matching blue silk blouse, looked to be in her late-thirties. With luxurious long brunette hair and a full figure, she exuded subtle sexuality along with a cheerful open face and an easy smile. Her large green eyes sparkled with a captivating intensity. She led him through a lavishly furnished apartment to her kitchen. Someone with a decorator's eye had

selected a stylish combination of modern leather and steel furnish-
ings, painted the walls in lively contrasting colors, and picked out
attractive artwork. He knew without asking that Arthur Witherspoon had selected the framed pictures and architectural drawings
of cathedrals on the walls.

In her kitchen, appointed with the latest premium appliances
from Wolf, LG, and Miele, Sally pointed him toward a seat at a
glass-top table and offered him coffee. A skilled glass artist had
etched intricate architectural drawings of the circular windows of
Gothic cathedrals into the glass tabletop. Much time and effort, he
realized, had gone into the details of this apartment.

He watched Sally set out cups and pour coffee. When she brought
the coffee to him, tears pooled in her huge green eyes. "Such a beautiful man. I can't believe he's gone."

This woman was more than a part-time clerk. Although Koa
pegged her as Witherspoon's mistress, he started with the information
he'd been given. "You worked part-time for Arthur Witherspoon?"

The tears seemed to evaporate, and the beginnings of a smile at
the corners of Sally's full lips suggested he already knew better.
"You've been talking to Mrs. Witherspoon."

"And I take it, I've been incorrectly informed?"

With unapologetic directness, she said, "Arthur and I were partners."

"Professionally?"

"Professionally and personally. Arthur's marriage died a long time
ago. He wouldn't divorce her, but their relationship became as
empty as an abandoned warehouse."

The personal relationship didn't surprise him, not after seeing her
apartment, and her view of Arthur's marriage shed light on Mrs.
Witherspoon's reactions. She too knew her marriage had died on
the vine. Yet, Sally's reference to a professional relationship surprised
him. "Are you an architect?"

"I have the training, but not the license. I prepared drawings for Arthur's projects. He always signed off on them, but we worked as a team."

"Tell me about Arthur."

"A brilliant architect with a passion for detail but born into the wrong century."

"Really?"

"Do you believe in reincarnation?"

"No, not really."

Sally talked with her hands and her eyes in addition to her voice, giving authenticity to her animated manner. "I didn't—until I met Arthur. Once upon a time, like maybe the fifteenth century, he died before completing the cathedral of his dreams. He wanted nothing more than to go back and finish that church."

"Strange."

"A bit, but a wonderful man." She tilted her head. "I loved Arthur deeply."

He took a swig of coffee. It was strong, the way he liked it. "You worked together on the KonaWili school?"

"He drew plans for the school, but he didn't talk about it. And . . ." She stopped to gather her thoughts. "While I usually helped on public buildings, he wouldn't let me close to the KonaWili project."

It made sense, Koa mused. Arthur must have known about the vent and kept the knowledge from his mistress to protect her. Still, he wondered if she was trying to shield herself. "Why?" He asked more sharply than he intended.

"I didn't know at the time but I now suspect he was trying to protect me."

"From what?"

"The controversy and the risk."

"What controversy?"

She sighed, a long mournful sound. "I don't know the details, but just after Boyle started preparing the KonaWili site, he and Arthur had an argument. Boyle wanted Arthur to do something, and Arthur got really upset. I heard him yelling, and Arthur never raised his voice."

"Yelling about what?"

"I heard only one word—'never,' like a primal scream before Arthur slammed the phone down. It was a handset, and he broke it. And violence wasn't Arthur's style."

"Did he ever explain what Boyle wanted?"

"No, he was agitated, but he wouldn't talk about it. He left the apartment. I think he went for a walk or a drive. I'm not sure, but when he came back, he looked awful, like he'd been beaten down and totally demoralized. A shell of his former self."

"Did he explain?"

"Not really. He just described himself as a slave to the past. At first, I thought he meant architecture—how we're still creating buildings with Roman and Greek columns—but later I understood he meant something deeply personal."

Koa could see Arthur Witherspoon opening his soul with this woman. Something welcoming, profoundly emphatic, lit her face and infected her green eyes. Witherspoon must have found her a good listener. "Did he explain what he meant?"

"He repeated the phrase about being a slave in relation to my situation. I love my son, and I wouldn't give him up for the world, but getting pregnant when I did was stupid. Arthur said we were both slaves to the past, but in my case, something good had come of it. Maybe I was reading it through my own lens, but I took him to be saying nothing good had come of his past."

"Did you ask him about his past?"

"Sure. We talked about architecture. He was fascinated with the intricate rose windows of Gothic cathedrals. Every year he traveled to see a different cathedral with a rose window—the cathedrals in Prague, Reims, Notre Dame in Paris, and his favorite, the cathedral at Chartres."

With his roots firmly planted on the Big Island, Koa didn't share Witherspoon's fascination with European cathedrals and prodded her to refocus on the trouble in the man's past. "You know what made him a slave to his past?"

"No. As intimately as I knew Arthur, he never shared that part of his life."

Koa turned to his primary interest. "At about the time Arthur died, someone tore his office apart searching for something. I don't think they found it. Do you have any idea what he might have hidden?"

"Could it have anything to do with Howard Gommes?"

He hadn't expected her question, and his interest flared. "Why Gommes?"

"Arthur had his private demons, but he wasn't secretive with clients, except Gommes. Whenever Gommes called, Arthur retreated to his office and closed the door. In all our time together, Arthur got annoyed with me just once—when I accidentally walked in on one of his conversations with Gommes."

"Any idea why?"

"I never understood, and after Arthur vented on me, I never asked."

"And he wasn't like that with anyone else?"

"No, most of the time he worked with an open door."

Gommes had acted strangely at the mention of Witherspoon's name. "How often did Arthur talk to Gommes?"

"Whenever Gommes called him. Arthur never sought him out."

"So how often did Gommes call?"

"Hardly ever, until last year. Then Gommes called, maybe three or four times."

"Was this while Arthur was working on the KonaWili elementary school?"

"Yes, about then."

"But you have no idea what they talked about?"

She shook her head.

"Suppose," Koa asked, "Arthur wanted to hide something sensitive. Any idea where he'd put it?"

She ran a hand through her hair. "Gee, that's tough. It wouldn't be in a usual place, like a bank vault. It'd be in one of his buildings and cleverly concealed. A man who designs Gothic cathedrals in his mind could create lots of hiding places."

"So where should I look?"

She paused to think. "I don't know. Let me think about it. Maybe I can come up with some ideas."

When Sally walked him back to the front door, he looked into the dining room and saw a great Hawai'i state seal painted on the wall. He stopped to stare at the emblem originally adopted as the insignia of the Republic of Hawai'i in 1894. "That's not your usual dining room decoration," he remarked.

"Arthur's work. One of Arthur's first commissions. For the renovation of the East Hawai'i Cultural Center."

Koa knew the building well. "The old police station, long before my time."

"Yes," she responded, "police station and courthouse. Arthur supervised the restoration, including the restoration of the great seal mosaic in the foyer. It occupied a special place in his pantheon."

"Why?"

"I think the great seal reminded him of one of his precious rose windows."

As they reached the door, Sally gripped his arm. "Detective." Her voice became hard, and her eyes blazed with intensity. He sensed strength and passion he'd not seen before. "I want to find the people who killed Arthur. I'll do *anything* to bring them to justice."

CHAPTER NINETEEN

DETECTIVE PIKI POPPED into Koa's office. "We found a gun. Could be the Witherspoon murder weapon."

Although extraordinarily industrious, Piki's quick mind frequently leaped canyons in two bounds. Koa demanded details laid out in logical order. "Who found a gun? Where? And what makes you think it's linked to the Witherspoon killing?"

"The gun fell out of an airport trash container. One of the sanitation workers says it smelled like it'd recently been fired. And they emptied the bin last week, so someone chucked it this week. Timing's right for the Witherspoon shooting."

Piki might, Koa realized, be on to something. "What make and model?"

"Beretta M9A1."

Koa whistled. The Beretta M9A1, an updated version of the 9 mm combat pistol used by the U.S. armed forces since 1990, was also widely carried by police and other law enforcement personnel. It wasn't a cheap street gun, and Koa found it odd that one would be discarded.

"Serial number?"

"Gone. Ground off, but Cap Roberts in tech support is working on it. Says a professional did it, but he may be able to bring the number back."

Koa had judged the Witherspoon killing to be a professional hit and professionals used untraceable guns. "Where's the trash truck?"

"Don't know."

"Find it and impound it before they dump its contents."

"Why?" Piki asked, looking confused.

"The shell casings. If the killer discarded the gun, he probably tossed the casings. Get a move on."

Koa, now infected with Piki's enthusiasm, walked downstairs to Cap's laboratory. Sixty-year-old Cap Roberts was a serious scientist with a wide knowledge of forensic procedures dealing with everything from fingerprints to guns. At six-foot-six, he'd been a star on the UH Rainbow Warriors basketball team and could still handle a basketball like a Globetrotter. He now spent much of his free time teaching the game to Hilo high school students, both men and women.

Cap had just subjected the gun to a powerful magnetic field and sprayed the area where the serial number had been obliterated with tiny magnetic particles suspended in oil. "I typically use the magnaflux test first because it's non-destructive, but it doesn't work a lot of the time," Cap explained. He subjected the gun to high-frequency vibrations, hoping the magnetic particles would line up with the compressed metal beneath the serial numbers stamped into the gun. Unfortunately, the test failed to produce a readable serial number.

Cap removed the gun from the vibrator and cleaned away the oil. "There's one thing I can tell you. It's a military weapon."

"How can you tell without the serial number?" Koa asked.

Cap flipped the weapon over and pointed to the markings on the slide: U.S. 9mm M9A1 Beretta U.S.A. "It's definitely a military weapon."

"What's next?" Koa asked.

"I'm going to use hydrochloric acid to see if I can raise the serial number."

"Good. Let me know if you get anything. Also, test fire the weapon and do a comparison with the slug the Honolulu ME took out of Witherspoon's body."

"You think I wasn't going to do that?"

"Sorry, Cap. Just being anal."

Back in his office, Koa put the pieces together. A military weapon—most likely stolen from an Army storage facility. Hawai'i hosted several military reservations, but none closer than the U.S. Army Pōhakuloa Training Area. Koa figured his friend Jerry Zeigler, the commander of the military police detachment at Pōhakuloa, would know if weapons had gone AWOL.

Koa had worked often with the ferret-faced military police first lieutenant during previous cases and joint Army-county disaster recovery operations. Although Jerry was a good deal younger, they had a lot in common, including their humble beginnings and their love of sports—*heihei wa'a*, outrigger canoe racing, for Koa; and ice hockey for Jerry, who grew up in rural South Dakota. Ice hockey had left its mark on Zeigler, giving his crooked nose a distinctive left twist after several unsuccessful repair jobs.

"Hello, Jerry, how's life in the saddle?" The Pōhakuloa Training Area, the largest U.S. military installation in the Pacific, occupied 109,000 acres in the mile-high saddle between Mauna Kea and Mauna Loa, the two 14,000-foot mountains that made up the bulk of the island.

"Fine," Zeigler responded, "but somehow I'm guessing you're about to make it worse."

"You missing any guns?"

Zeigler hesitated, and Koa sensed he'd hit a nerve.

"Why do you ask?"

"We just found a U.S. Army Beretta M9A1 in a trash bin out at Hilo airport. Any chance you're missing one?"

"You got a serial number?"

"Not yet. Cap Roberts in technical support is working on it."

Another long pause followed before Zeigler said, "We need to meet. I can't talk about this over the phone."

Zeigler's response puzzled Koa, but he agreed to meet at the Pōhakuloa compound. Koa drove up the Saddle Road until the dense vegetation gave way to a mile-high plateau where ancient lava flows from Mauna Kea and Mauna Loa overlapped each other. Zeigler had a pass ready for him at the gate to the military compound, and the MP officer, dressed in desert camos, greeted him at the door to the military police building. He took Koa to a conference room with audiovisual equipment already set up.

"Sorry to make you come out here," Zeigler apologized, "but what I'm about to tell you is classified. I have authority to share with local law enforcement, but I've got to ask you to maintain confidentiality. Okay?"

"I'm okay with confidentiality. What've you got?"

"The Army suffered a series of small-scale weapons thefts—a few guns here and a few there—but it adds up and it appears to be coordinated."

"You've had thefts here at Pōhakuloa?" Koa asked.

"Yeah. Here, Fort Sill, Fort Benning, and a half-dozen other installations, but let me give you some background."

"Okay," Koa agreed.

"The inspector general first discovered a series of thefts from Bagram military base in Afghanistan. The CID guys investigated and isolated the thefts to a group of potential culprits but couldn't make the case. All were quartermaster types, and all were reassigned to different bases. That was supposed to be the end of it."

"But it wasn't?"

"Nope. Isolated thefts started popping up, and when the CID boys reviewed the records, they discovered a connection. Each of the new thefts occurred in a supply depot where one of the suspected guys from Afghanistan got reassigned."

"And you've got one of the culprits here?"

"Supply Sergeant Ralph Leffler."

Koa's cell phone rang, and he answered Cap Roberts's call. "I've got plain news, good news, and bad news," Cap began.

"Give me the news."

"It's the Witherspoon murder weapon. A solid ballistics match."

Koa had a sinking feeling. "And the bad news is no serial number?"

"Correct. I couldn't raise the whole number, but I did get four digits. That's the good news."

"Read 'em off."

Koa jotted them down as Cap spoke. "Eight, four, nine, zero, in that order. Those numbers are in the middle of the sequence—not the first number and not the last."

"Thanks, Cap. I guess that makes you a partial genius."

"Aren't you the clown."

After ringing off, Koa turned to face Zeigler. "The M9A1 was used in a recent homicide. We've got a partial serial number." He passed the note with the numbers to Zeigler, who compared it to the serial numbers on the missing handguns.

"Got it. These numbers match one of our stolen guns. What are the odds of a four-number match?"

Koa struggled to recall his college statistics course. "I think it's one in ten thousand, but the fact the gun was stolen here and found here must up the odds."

"Okay. But doesn't finding it in an airport trash bin suggest it was dumped by someone leaving the island who couldn't risk walking it through TSA security? That wouldn't be Leffler's because he's still here," Zeigler questioned.

"Good point, but the killer acts like a pro. A pro would most likely get a gun locally, and a pro leaving the island wouldn't dump the gun at the airport, not with a thousand other places to lose it. On the other hand, a pro might dump it at the airport to mislead us into thinking he's left the island."

Zeigler paused, and Koa could almost see his mind working. "Let's make this a little more complicated." He stood up, retreated to the door, and killed the lights.

The room went dark before Zeigler turned on a projector, and a large face filled the screen. "That's Leffler. He's twenty-six and one angry man. Born and raised in Naoma, West Virginia. Worked in the coal mines at sixteen and lost his father and most of his friends in the 2010 Upper Branch coal mine explosion. Quit being a miner and joined the Army so he could kill people. I'm not kidding."

Koa studied the big oval face with deep-set eyes atop a thick, football center's neck. The man had a nasty scar across his right cheek—the kind you get in a knife fight. Koa wondered if he was looking into the eyes of the man who sold the gun to Witherspoon's killer.

"And the Army," Zeigler continued, "trained him to kill like a pro. Ranger school, Q course, demolitions training, expert marksman, proficient in hand-to-hand combat, you name it."

Koa himself had graduated from the Q course, Army slang for the Special Forces qualification course, one of the mentally and physically toughest training courses in the world. "Special Forces?"

"No. The Army docs didn't like his psych profile. Only made him angrier."

"Jesus, so he's a psycho, and he's here because the Army thinks, but couldn't prove, he stole weapons in Afghanistan?"

"Yeah, that and brutality concerns."

Koa felt his eyebrows go up. "Brutality concerns?"

"Yeah, four Afghan rape-murders occurred in his assigned area. Nobody proved anything, but the crimes stopped when he transferred back here."

Koa looked at the wall-sized picture of Leffler in a different light. He'd been thinking of the man as a possible source of the purloined murder weapon. Now he viewed Leffler as a possible candidate for the murder itself. "Could he be our killer?"

"Wouldn't rule it out," Zeigler responded.

"Where was he about five thirty on Thursday morning?"

"We don't know. We've had him under episodic surveillance, but he's a hard man to tail, especially with the limited manpower we've got up here."

"You have surveillance logs?"

"Yeah. We've only been at it a couple weeks, and like I said, it's spotty. I made a copy for you." Zeigler passed a few sheets of paper to Koa. "And we've got some photos."

Zeigler clicked and the projected image changed to a picture of Leffler with a Chinese woman. "That's his current girlfriend. He's been with her at least five times in the last two weeks."

"Name?"

"Linda Huang. Taiwanese. They usually meet in a bar or go to her apartment. The address is in the log." Zeigler brought up a new picture of Leffler, sitting alone at one end of a bar.

Koa recognized the place from the old Wurlitzer jukebox in the background. "That's the Monarch bar. Pretty sleazy place."

"He hangs there some nights."

The next several images showed Leffler driving, with Linda Huang on the Hilo street, and others of Leffler at the Monarch. Zeigler shut the projector off before Koa realized the significance of the last picture.

"Put the last picture up again."

Zeigler turned the projector back on. The picture showed Leffler sitting at a corner table in the Monarch with a man. Not any man, but Tomi Watanabe, the mayor's press aide. Koa couldn't miss the distinctive black mole on the spin doctor's cheek.

What the hell could Watanabe be doing with Sergeant Ralph Leffler? How had the two of them hooked up, and why was the mayor's press aide in one of Hilo's sleaziest joints with a rogue Army sergeant? Koa thought of a possible connection. Drake, the barkeep at the Monarch, was just the sort of douchebag you might visit if you were looking for a gun—or a killer.

"The man with Leffler in that picture." Koa pointed to the screen. "You know who he is?"

"No. Never seen him before."

"That's Tomi Watanabe, the mayor's press aide. What business would Leffler have with him?"

Zeigler looked quizzical. "Beats me."

On his drive back to the office, Koa's sister, Alana, called. "I'm scared, Koa. I'm really scared."

"What's the matter, Alana?"

"It's Ikaika. He hasn't regained consciousness. The doctors aren't saying much, but they're concerned. I can tell. Māmā's with him. She won't leave the ICU." Her words came tumbling out.

"Slow down, Alana. What have the doctors told you?"

"Not much. Just that sometimes people come back slowly, but it's been a long time. We can't lose him, Koa. Māmā would die."

"Can I talk to the doctor?"

"He's not here right now, but I'll have him call you."

"Okay, Alana. Keep me posted." Ringing off, Koa felt his heart sink. He'd been elated when Alana had reported the surgery successful, but now things didn't look so good. He felt palpable concern for

Ikaika. Despite past animosities, he desperately wanted his brother to survive.

Back in his office, Koa found Piki covered in filth from head to toe and smelling like last week's rotten meat.

"You smell like shit," Koa greeted his younger colleague, his mind still focused on the call from Alana.

"Do you know how long it takes to comb through twenty cubic yards of garbage?" Piki asked, his face red and his grungy shirt wet with sweat.

Koa laughed half-heartedly. "At five minutes a cubic foot that would be forty-five hours. You must have had help. What do the other guys smell like?"

"It's not so damned funny when you're half-buried in the nasty shit people throw away."

"You find the casings?"

Piki held up an evidence bag with two shell casings. "Nine-by-nineteen NATO parabellum cartridge casings. Definitely military."

"From the gun in the trash?"

"Cap says the hammer strikes match."

"Fingerprints?"

"A partial, not enough to run through the FBI's IAFIS, but probably enough if we catch the perp."

"Anything else?"

"Yeah. What do I get for spending a day crawling through grimy, smelly, shitty garbage?"

Koa grinned. "A free shower in the lockup because they're not letting you in the police gym smelling like that."

Piki groaned. "Thanks for nothing."

"You should've used a metal detector. Would have been a lot faster."

Piki smacked his forehead with a hand. "Oh, shit. Why didn't I think of that?"

CHAPTER TWENTY

WITH THE CHIEF out of town and his status as the head of the KonaWili investigation, Koa got trapped into unwanted social obligations. Ben Inaba, the mayor's political consultant, invited Koa to the surprise birthday party for state senator George Kenoi, a long-standing buddy of Mayor Tanaka. Koa despised political events and tried to beg off, but Inaba told him to show up. "The mayor wants you there."

Unlike Koa, Nālani expressed delight at the invitation. She dressed in a clingy, bright-red dress and wore the Niʻihau shell *lei* Koa had given her on the anniversary of their first date. She looked ravishing, and Koa felt a swelling of pride in escorting her to the event.

For Koa, the location provided the only redeeming grace. Mayor Tanaka threw the party at the East Hawaiʻi Cultural Council building, also known as the "old police station." Built in 1932, it once housed the district court and police station, where Koa's predecessor many times removed served as captain of detectives. Slated for demolition after the police department moved out in 1969, the East Hawaiʻi Cultural Council rescued the building in 1979 and successfully applied to list it on the National Register of Historic Places.

Witherspoon honchoed the renovation. His design preserved and restored the leaded glass top to the double front doors, the decorated ventilation openings, the four columned central front porches, and the great seal of the Territory of Hawaiʻi embedded in the lobby floor. Koa always felt a certain pride when he entered the old police station and walked across the great seal, so perfectly restored under Witherspoon's direction.

Originally designed by the College of Arms in London in 1842 as the seal of the Republic of Hawaiʻi, the wording changed in 1900 when Hawaiʻi became a territory of the United States, and again in 1959 when Hawaiʻi became the fiftieth state, but its imagery remained unchanged. King Kamehameha and Lady Liberty still supported the shield-bearing *Ka Hae Hawaiʻi*, the state flag, and the *puloʻuloʻu*, a *tabu* ball, pierced by a black stick. And the legend on the twelve-foot seal still read "*Ua Mau Ke Ea O Ka ʻĀina I Ka Pono*," roughly translated as *the life of the land is perpetuated in righteousness*.

Koa and Nālani admired the seal as they entered the building. Then Koa, who'd memorized the floor plan of the original structure, led Nālani to the left front corner. "We're standing in the captain of detectives' old office," he said with a flourish. "The sheriff occupied the opposite corner, and the only judge in town presided over a courtroom upstairs."

She laughed, enjoying his trip down history lane. "It's a far cry from the way things are today."

"You've got that right."

"You think it was simpler back then?" she asked.

"People haven't changed much, but there are more of them, and they have more powerful tools to make mischief. Where a bad guy typically hurt only a few people back then, one fraudster can rip off thousands today."

He led her into the crowd of guests. On his way to the cash bar to get a glass of wine for Nālani and a beer for himself, he caught a glimpse of Sarah Witherspoon. He supposed she and Arthur had been invited because of the architect's connection with the building but thought it odd for the grieving widow to be at a festive gathering so soon after her husband's murder—and her dress gave no hint of mourning.

At the bar, he requested a chardonnay for Nālani and a Paniolo Pale Ale for himself. As he was paying for the drinks, he felt a presence at his elbow. He turned to look down at Watanabe, the mayor's press aide. "So, Detective, you stepped in horse manure."

Koa sized up the little weasel. He undoubtedly referred to Koa's visit to Cheryl Makela's horse farm. As Zeke had already told him, she'd complained to the mayor. Koa found it surprising that anyone in the mayor's office would care. Or, had someone in the county front office partnered with the horse lady? Or, perhaps, had an economic interest in the KonaWili development?

"Somebody stepped in something far worse at KonaWili," Koa responded.

"It's really too bad about the kids, but nobody can predict Mother Nature. The tsunami at Laupāhoehoe proved that."

Watanabe referred to the disastrous tsunami on April Fools' Day, 1946, that struck a school building in Koa's hometown, killing twenty students and four teachers. The press aide, still trying to present KonaWili as a random act of God, had found a precedent. But Koa wasn't buying.

"In 1946, they had no warning. KonaWili is different."

"Really?" Watanabe said, raising his eyebrows in mock surprise.

"Yeah, prior notice and two murders make the events different as day and night." Koa turned his back on the weasel, picked up Nālani's wine and his beer, and went to find his girlfriend.

"Who was that?" Nālani asked as he passed the wine glass to her.

"Tomi Watanabe, the mayor's press aide. He's a snake, the lowest of the low, and among politicians that's dredging the bottom of the harbor."

"What did he want?"

"He wants me to drop the KonaWili investigation. Dismiss it as an unavoidable act of God, like the Laupāhoehoe tsunami."

Her mouth came open in amazement. "You're kidding!"

"No. He's hiding something he doesn't want me to find."

At that moment, Koa caught sight of Mayor Tanaka, and they locked eyes. The mayor inclined his head, signaling he wanted to chat. Koa led Nālani across the room and introduced her to the mayor. "Ahh, why does the National Park Service employ all the most beautiful women?"

Nālani thanked him for the compliment, and Koa marveled at the mayor's political savvy. He might be a political hack, but he knew how to win votes. With apologies to Nālani, the mayor drew Koa aside.

"You've seen the public outrage in the press?"

Koa immediately sensed the direction of the conversation. The KonaWili disaster put the mayor under enormous pressure with an election coming up. Shit, as usual, would flow downhill. "Yes, I've seen the press, Mayor."

"This KonaWili disaster has blown the lid off discontent with the public schools. And these murders only made things worse. The public wants scalps."

The mayor had to be worried about his own political future. "Yes, sir. I understand."

"The status quo isn't acceptable." The mayor's eyes turned hard. "You need to arrest someone for these murders. You understand me?"

Koa saw no point in explaining he couldn't just arrest someone off the street. The mayor well knew that already, and Koa understood the message—get on the stick and save the mayor's electoral bacon. He answered simply, "I understand."

"That's good, 'cause you're either on the team or you're not," the mayor added before turning away.

Koa found Nālani amidst the crowd and slipped his arm around her. "Goddamn politicians," he whispered. "Those assholes drive me crazy. Come on, let's get out of here." He heard the anger in his own voice but made no effort to restrain it.

She gripped his hand hard. "We can't leave yet," she whispered, "not 'til they make speeches and cut the cake."

She was right, but still, it galled him. The damn pols made him feel cheap. They represented the grimy underside of his job, and he resented it. Koa still seethed when an amplified voice announced, "The honorable Bobbie Māhoe, governor of the great state of Hawai'i." Heads turned toward the front doors.

Koa hadn't expected to see the governor but realized it made sense. Senator George Kenoi, the birthday boy, chaired the powerful state education committee. The KonaWili disaster had roiled the whole education establishment, and the governor would have to implement changes. He undoubtedly needed all the support he could gather.

The governor's entourage held the real surprise. Governor Bobbie Māhoe entered the room with Francine Na'auao, the embattled DOE head. She wore a sleek black silk gown and held herself like royalty. Her presence at the governor's side represented a powerful public endorsement. That the governor stood behind his appointee wouldn't be lost on the other politicians in the room. Nor would it go unnoticed by the press. But the governor, like all politicians, had a finely honed sense of self-preservation, and his support for the DOE head made no sense. It would cost the governor dearly among voters with school-age children.

Koa remembered Christina's words—"Na'auao's got some hold over the governor. Maybe it's some kind of campaign finance irregularity. Maybe it's something else." Although Māhoe had accumulated a huge campaign war chest, Koa had been skeptical of Christina's vague allegations, and Zeke hadn't yet found evidence of illegal contributions. Still, how else could he explain the governor's behavior?

Koa watched the handsome governor sweep around the room, shaking hands, telling jokes, and slapping friends on the back. A pol in his element. As Māhoe moved from one group to another, he stopped to chat with Howard Gommes. Almost the whole Kona-Wili cast of characters had turned out for the senator's birthday. Only Cheryl Makela was missing. Koa wasn't surprised Māhoe and Gommes knew each other—both were public figures—and, given Māhoe's pro-development platform, Gommes was undoubtedly a big contributor to the governor's campaign.

As the governor and Gommes ended their chat and drifted apart, Mayor Tanaka, followed by his aides, slid into the group surrounding Gommes. With a half-smile, Koa realized that Māhoe and Tanaka were avoiding each other. When Māhoe moved right, Tanaka moved left. Koa admired the skill with which the two political rivals shunned each other, like similar magnets repelling one another. The tension in their dance mirrored their fight over control of the investigation, leaving Koa a pawn in a political game he didn't yet understand.

Koa moved closer, discretely trying to catch a snippet of the mayor's conversation with Gommes. Although he caught the word "KonaWili," he lost the rest of the sentence. Still, from the tone, he could tell the mayor was agitated. Koa caught phrases . . . "Goddamn it, Howard . . . fucking mess . . . out of control . . . Hank and Spooner . . ." in the mayor's distinctive military voice. Witherspoon's nickname rolled easily off Tanaka's tongue.

Koa tried to assess what he'd heard. Tanaka had railed against the KonaWili mess just as he had previously complained to Koa. Nothing new there, and no surprise that the mayor would bitch to the developer. Yet, the mayor's tone and his causal use of Weatherspoon's nickname bothered Koa. He'd wondered if the mayor wanted control of the investigation simply to protect Makela, but now, he thought, maybe the mayor might be in even deeper.

Nālani put her hand on his arm and leaned close. "There's a starstruck woman in the room," she whispered.

"I have that effect on you?" he quipped.

"Of course." She grinned mischievously. "But I was thinking of Sarah Witherspoon."

Koa snapped around to stare at the woman. Sarah Witherspoon and Ben Inaba, the mayor's political aide, had their heads together, and Koa didn't need his girlfriend to know the couple was engrossed in each other.

Nālani gripped his arm. "Don't be so obvious," she hissed. Koa's mind shifted into high gear as he turned away. He'd assumed Arthur Witherspoon had distanced himself from his wife before Arthur got personal with Sally Medea, but now it looked like both parties had wandered. He needed to look at Sarah Witherspoon as a suspect. That was the problem with assumptions. He'd assumed Witherspoon's death had been related to the KonaWili school, but maybe the murder arose out of jealousy and lust. Most murder victims died at the hands of friends or relatives, frequently spouses. According to Sally Medea, Arthur wouldn't divorce his wife, but maybe she'd found a permanent way to end the relationship. But what about the break-in at Witherspoon's office? Could that, he asked himself, have been a diversion? It seemed unlikely.

Trumpets blared and the room fell silent. All heads turned toward the stage where the mayor stepped to a podium to begin the birthday speeches for Senator Kenoi. Koa barely heard a word. His mind raced through the tangle of new relationships. The mayor's warning . . . Governor Māhoe and Francine Naʻauao . . . Mayor

Tanaka and Gommes . . . Sarah Witherspoon and the mayor's aide . . .
what did it all mean?

Suddenly, the mayor himself had become a player in the investigation he'd chosen Koa to lead. Sure, Tanaka sought to embarrass
the governor by blaming the DOE, and Māhoe would undoubtedly
be happy to cast a political rival in a bad light by going after Makela.
Just the kind of gutter politics Koa hated. But what if one or the
other had ulterior motives, like a hidden investment in KonaWili?

CHAPTER TWENTY-ONE

KOA HAD A history with Drake, the Monarch's owner-barkeep. In his late fifties with stringy yellow-gray hair, Drake presided over one of the sleaziest bars in town in cutoff jeans and a ratty black, beer-stained tee shirt. Serving mostly stevedores, dockhands, and down-and-out fishermen, he somehow managed to stay open despite dozens of health department citations.

Even though Drake had cleaned up his act after his last run-in with the police, the joint remained a health inspector's nightmare. Last time, Koa's threat to bring in the health inspectors forced Drake to cooperate, but the same ploy wasn't going to work again. Mere threats wouldn't make Drake fess up to illegal gun sales or running an agency for hired killers.

Koa sent Bane, an undercover cop, into the Monarch. Bane, like other patrons, dressed in work clothes. An ugly, but artificial, scar on his neck concealed a tiny microphone and transmitter. For the first couple of nights, the undercover cop sat alone at the bar sipping beer and engaging Drake in chitchat. Presenting himself as a deckhand off a fishing vessel operating out of Hilo harbor, Bane talked fish, bitched about the prices of *'ahi*, and whined about the UH Rainbow Warriors football team. He tipped well, but not outrageously.

On Bane's third night in the Monarch, Koa sat in an unmarked car up the street listening to Bane's transmitter. After a couple of beers and more chatter with Drake, Bane laid a Grant, a $50 bill featuring the face of the 18th U.S. president, on the bar. Koa listened intently as the conversation turned critical.

"I'm looking for a dude who can sell me a piece, preferably a nine, without a legend."

A pause followed before Koa heard Drake's raspy voice. "Whatchu want it foah, my man?"

"I'm going on a cruise carrying some shit, and I gotta have some protection, you get me?"

"You got the bread?"

Koa heard rustling noises as Bane gave Drake a brief look at the wad in his pocket.

"What's in it foah me, my man?"

Koa grinned. They'd guessed right. Drake served as a middleman for illegal gun sales, and he'd bought Bane's story, like a marlin hitting a ten-inch lure.

"A couple of Grants." Bane made the deal worthwhile for Drake without offering enough to make him suspicious.

"Hang foah a while, okay, my man?"

Bane sipped beer, and Koa waited.

Half an hour later, Koa heard the scrape of a bar stool and a deep gruff voice. "I hear you're lookin' for somethin'?"

According to Zeigler, Leffler had a deep, gruff voice, but Koa listened carefully for Bane's next words.

"Might be." Bane sounded cautious. Koa jabbed his fist in the air. The word "might" identified the contact as Leffler; any other word signaled somebody else.

"Let's take a walk back to the john," the gruff voice suggested.

Now came the tricky part, but they'd anticipated it. Leffler wasn't going to risk selling stolen guns to a cop. Koa heard the john door close.

"Lose the shirt," Leffler ordered.

There was a pause before Leffler said, "That's some fuckin' scar."

"Knife fight," Bane said. "The other dude went to the hospital."

"Okay," Leffler said, "turn around." Unintelligible noises. "Now the pants."

Koa heard the rustling of clothing and a clank, like a belt buckle hitting the floor. "Satisfied?" Bane asked.

Koa tensed as he heard a grunt. Then Leffler asked, "What kind of shit you movin'?"

"How do I know you ain't a cop?" Bane asked.

Koa heard sounds he couldn't identify before Leffler said, "You ever see a cop carrying one of these?"

A pause. Then Bane said, "Nice. That's what I'm lookin' to buy."

Koa felt a rush of excitement. Leffler carried a 9 mm Beretta with a filed-down serial number. Just possessing such a weapon was a felony. Things were moving fast—much faster than Koa had anticipated. He grabbed the radio mike and called for backup with a silent approach.

The bar sounds increased as someone opened the john door. "We're busy, man. Shut the fuckin' door. Use the girls' if you got to pee," Leffler growled in a loud voice. The bar noises receded.

"I asked you what kind of shit you're movin'?"

"Butter." Bane used Hawaiian street slang for marijuana. "But the buyer's a newbie an' I ain't sure I kin trust him." Bane spun out his cover story.

"Ought not to do business with people you don't trust," Leffler said.

"You got that right. But a dude's gotta make money where he can."

Leffler still wasn't ready to do business. "Why a nine?"

Koa and Bane had predicted this question. "The Army taught me to use a nine, so it feels right. Ya know what I mean?"

"Where'd you serve?"

They'd picked a place where Leffler had never been stationed and where none of his buddies likely ever served. "The ceremonial guard at Fort Meyer, Virginia."

"Fuckin' pansies."

"Yeah, well, I bailed as soon as I could."

"It'll cost you three grand."

Leffler asked for more than five times the cost of the comparable civilian model from a legitimate dealer. The price was steep even for an untraceable, stolen Beretta. Bane wasn't spending his own money, and the police were going to get it back when they arrested the son of a bitch, but Bane didn't want his eagerness to queer the deal. "Can't ya give me a break . . . say twenty-five hundred?"

Leffler knew a hungry pigeon and had no incentive to bargain. "Three grand."

"Okay." Koa held his breath as he heard more sounds, which he assumed involved counting out thirty one-hundred-dollar bills. Then the bar noise increased as one of them opened the john door. A few moments passed. Bane spoke in hushed tones. "Thanks, Drake. Here's your bread. Good doing business with you."

"Any time, my man, any time," Drake responded.

Moments later, Bane walked out of the bar. After making sure Bane was alone, Koa flashed his lights. The cop climbed into the passenger seat and placed a U.S. Army 9 mm Beretta with a filed-down serial number into an evidence bag.

Satisfied they had the goods on Leffler, Koa wanted to get the cuffs on the man, but not inside the Monarch. With a killing machine like Leffler, Koa couldn't risk possible collateral damage in a barroom confrontation. They'd wait until Leffler called it a night.

With an unmarked car and two patrol officers at his disposal, Koa parked two policemen in front. He placed one officer against the wall on the hinge-side of the bar's front door, where he'd be out of sight behind any patron exiting the Monarch. He positioned the last uniformed officer in the bushes on the other side of the door. Koa had the front door covered but figured a pro like Leffler would sneak out the back. If Leffler came out this back door, they'd have to wait until he stepped outside and closed the door. Otherwise, he could duck back inside and create a possible hostage situation inside the bar.

A streetlight at the end of the alley provided only dim illumination. Koa spotted two hiding places. He positioned Bane behind a trash container to the right of the bar's back door. Koa stood in the shadow of ventilation equipment for the building across the alley. Both men checked their weapons. Once in position, they waited.

An hour passed. All remained quiet, and it seemed as if Leffler would never call it quits when Koa heard a creak from the back door. Koa drew his Glock. Leffler peered out checking for danger. A cautious man even after several beers. Leffler stepped into the alley, and the bar door closed behind him. Perfect.

Koa, his Glock pointed at Leffler's chest, stepped out of the shadows. "Police. Hands up, Mr. Leffler." Bane moved from behind the trash container, his Glock also out and pointed at Leffler.

Leffler stopped, hesitated, looked from Koa to Bane, and slowly raised his hands.

"Face the wall," Koa ordered.

Leffler turned.

"Hands above your head, flat on the wall. Feet spread. Do it, Leffler."

Leffler turned, put his hands high on the wall, and spread his legs. Koa signaled to Bane, who holstered his gun, grabbed his cuffs, and approached Leffler without blocking Koa's line of fire.

When Bane stepped behind Leffler, the man whirled on one foot, slamming his free leg into Bane's left knee, toppling him to the ground. In the same instant, Leffler threw a knife at Koa. Koa caught the glint of metal coming straight at his head and ducked. As he did so, his gun hand dropped. He felt the knife slice through his hair missing his head by less than a centimeter. Behind him, the knife pierced the metal ventilation duct with a loud thunk.

By the time Koa recovered and brought his gun back up, Leffler was twenty feet down the alley, bobbing and weaving, to avoid getting shot. Koa aimed and fired, but Leffler juked right and Koa's shot missed. Adopting a shooter stance with a two-handed grip, Koa aimed carefully at the fleeing suspect. Just as he began to squeeze the trigger, a woman crossed the mouth of the alley. Shit. He couldn't risk hitting a civilian. Leffler made it to the end of the alley and disappeared around the corner. Koa turned to check Bane.

"Go after him," Bane yelled as he hobbled to his feet.

Koa raced after Leffler, but by the time he reached the mouth of the alley, the Army supply sergeant had disappeared. Koa alerted the police duty officer, directed dispatch to muster reinforcements, and broadcast an ABP for Leffler. Then he walked back to Bane, who was in obvious pain. "Son of a bitch," Bane swore as he rubbed his bruised knee and brushed the dirt from his pants.

Within minutes, emergency vehicles and policemen flooded the area—Sergeant Basa in the lead. "Be damned careful. He's a trained killer, armed, and as dangerous as they come," Koa warned.

Koa now put the second part of his Leffler plan into operation. With Zeigler's surveillance records showing Leffler a frequent nighttime visitor to his girlfriend's apartment, Zeke Brown had obtained a search warrant for Linda Huang's place. The woman, a recent immigrant from Taiwan, lived legally in the U.S.

Figuring Leffler was too smart to risk returning to his girlfriend's place, Koa executed the warrant. Koa and Bane, flanking either side of the door, knocked loudly and announced themselves as police officers. Linda Huang opened the door. A small woman with long black hair and tiny eyes, she offered no resistance while the two detectives combed through the one-bedroom rental. Bane searched the living room and tiny kitchen. Koa headed for the bedroom closet where he found a pair of jungle combat boots and a large safe.

Leading Linda Huang into the bedroom, he pointed to the safe. "Can you open it?"

"*Bù.*" She spread her arms, palms upward, and shrugged.

Again, he pointed to the safe. "Who installed it?"

"Him put," she responded.

"Leffler?"

"*Shi.*"

Koa called Benny Kuhio, his go-to lock and key man. While he waited for Benny, Koa called an interpreter to help him question Linda Huang. She told them she'd met Leffler at the Monarch, and they'd been living off and on together for the past month. A week after he moved in, Leffler installed the safe in her apartment, but never gave her access. She confirmed Leffler had been with her the night before the Witherspoon shooting, but left at 4:30 a.m.—just an hour before Witherspoon had been killed less than a mile and a half away. And, he'd been wearing jungle combat boots. "Him always wear boots," she told the interpreter in Chinese.

Just when they'd finished interviewing Linda Huang, Sergeant Basa called with bad news. Leffler had disappeared like the Hawaiian mists. They agreed to distribute Leffler's picture to the entire force. Koa also asked Basa to alert the airlines and post lookouts at each of the island's three commercial airports.

Benny drilled the safe three times to get it open. Koa put on plastic gloves before removing eight packages wrapped in oilcloth; each held a stolen 9 mm Beretta M9A1 handgun bearing U.S. military markings, but none had visible serial numbers. The police would hold the weapons until they could capture and try Leffler, but Jerry Zeigler would eventually get the Army's property back

Next Koa removed a thick envelope containing four bundles of U.S. currency—crisp new hundred-dollar bills banded in straps with mustard-colored bands. Koa knew from previous bank robbery cases the mustard-colored bands meant ten thousand dollar bundles. Where, he wondered, had Leffler gotten forty thousand dollars? A payoff for killing Arthur Witherspoon?

The picture from Zeigler's slide show flashed into his mind: Leffler sitting in the corner of the Monarch with Tomi Watanabe. Maybe Watanabe had hired Leffler to kill Witherspoon. But why? Watanabe played no part in the county planning process and had nothing to do with public schools. Could, Koa wondered, the mayor's spin doctor have been a secret partner in the Hualālai Hui?

The last item in the safe—a piece of paper folded in thirds, like a letter—shot Koa's Watanabe theory to hell. He unfolded the top third of the paper to find four names. The first two names—Hank Boyle and Arthur Witherspoon had been lined through. Koa felt a rush—he'd found Leffler's hit list. The third name was Cheryl Makela. The fourth name—Tomi Watanabe—was a shocker, but it seemed to let Watanabe out as a suspect.

As he focused on the name, Koa noticed two question marks and the word "confirm" following Watanabe's name. Was Watanabe a target or not?

Koa then unfolded the rest of the paper, revealing a fifth name—one that hit him like a rogue wave—Detective Koa Kāne. He, himself, was on Leffler's hit list! Someone desperately wanted to stop the investigation of the KonaWili school disaster. But who would plan to kill the contractor, the architect, the planning director, the mayor's press aide, and the investigating detective? And what awful secret were they hiding?

CHAPTER TWENTY-TWO

MICA OSBOURNE'S FACE filled half the TV screen. Her daughter's picture—a darling little girl in a pink dress with a pink ribbon in her hair and a teddy bear in her arms—appeared opposite. The grieving mother's red eyes and haggard appearance haunted viewers. Koa couldn't imagine the depth of her despair. "The Education Department is supposed to protect our children. Instead, they took my beautiful daughter, my beautiful little angel. How could they . . ." Her voice broke . . . "How could they build a school over a volcanic vent?" The picture changed to an aerial view of the wrecked school with the roof ripped off, the walls collapsed, and clouds of steam and noxious gas billowing upward in a mushroom cloud.

The TV switched back to the original mother-daughter split screen, and Mica Osbourne resumed speaking. "They've known about volcanic risks on Hualālai for decades, yet the DOE put an elementary school on top of it. They murdered my daughter, my beautiful baby daughter. We as parents—as the people of Hawai'i—must hold them accountable . . . *accountable*!"

Mica Osbourne's tortured face disappeared, and the announcer reported Mica Osbourne, together with other parents, had filed a multimillion-dollar lawsuit against the Department of Education, its senior leadership, and everyone else involved in the planning and construction of the school. Koa saw Mica Osbourne as a powerful spokesperson for the parents of school-age children throughout the state. The death of her child transformed this ordinary mother into the face of tragedy. Powered by her anguish, public outrage reached a crescendo. Parents called for inspections of their local schools. The state legislators fell all over themselves talking about the importance of school safety. All the while, the rising wave of public anger grew stronger.

Every day the newspapers carried more complaints about unsafe conditions in public schools. On Kauaʻi, a survey reported 10 percent of the school-age population afraid to attend classes for fear of violence. The roof of Waimea High School on Kauaʻi leaked allowing black mold to grow in its classrooms. A salmonella outbreak hit students at Maui High School due to unsanitary conditions in its cafeteria. Administrators let racial tensions at Kealakehe High School on the Big Island escalate to the point of open warfare. Students described Cooper High School on Oʻahu as a "cinderblock oven" without air conditioning. Teachers, students, and their parents blamed every fault in every school building on the State Department of Education.

No one felt the fire of public condemnation more than Francine Naʻauao, the head of the DOE. The *Honolulu Star Advertiser* and other newspapers questioned Naʻauao's leadership. She'd been in the job for more than a decade, and like any administrator with a giant workload—the DOE oversaw two hundred ninety-one schools with nearly one hundred eighty thousand students—she'd accumulated a long list of enemies. They had their *pahi hahau*, their knives, out.

Unnamed sources alleged Naʻauao spent more time on personal investments than running the department while others leaked more dirt. The department had fallen more than a year behind on school safety inspections with the Honolulu Fire Department citing one school three times for the same fire code violation. The press reported Naʻauao's spending of more than twenty thousand dollars in taxpayer money on a lavish outing for the top officials in the DOE. The allegations went on and on.

While public pressure escalated exponentially, politicians did what they always do; they formed a committee: a special investigating group with a broad mandate to "investigate the KonaWili disaster and all other reported safety problems within the state's public schools." Letters and emails poured into the committee's offices, and soon its members faced months of legwork and public hearings.

Francine Naʻauao might have fared better but for the investigative journalists at the *Honolulu Star Advertiser*. The *Star Advertiser* and its predecessor, the *Star Bulletin*, had a history of game-changing articles, stretching back to its opposition to the internment of Japanese citizens during World War II. The first of its DOE exposés asserted that Boyle Construction had known about a volcanic fumarole beneath the building. A statement from Tony Pwalú described how he'd uncovered the vent and reported it to the general contractor. The article never closed the loop by establishing Boyle had informed the DOE, but the reporters wrote the article so the public would assume so. Tony apparently hadn't told the reporters, as he had Koa, that Boyle "showed the *haole* lady from Honolulu." Or maybe the reporters were saving Tony's bombshell for another blockbuster story.

The second *Star* article described Francine Naʻauao as a close friend of Cheryl Makela, who owned a big part of the residential development surrounding the school. Since Makela approved the zoning for the school, it was guilt by association. The story went on to allege Naʻauao signed a $1,100,000 change order, funding the concrete barriers erected to hide the volcanic fumarole. Seeking to rebut the charges, the DOE released a statement saying the project architect recommended the change order for environmental improvements. The press carried the DOE statement, but it did little to curb the fury. Journalists had chosen their target and would attack until they'd hounded Na'auao out of office.

While Na'auao may have thought it couldn't get worse, the third and last installment reported that the DOE had lost, or more likely destroyed, important KonaWili files, including the official copy of the change order. Unnamed sources described trash bags full of shredded paper on the executive floor. In the face of these allegations, the department's assurance it knew of no document destruction fell on deaf ears. The public wanted a summary execution, and the *Star Advertiser*, happy to oblige, printed a scathing editorial, calling upon Na'auao to resign.

The newspapers exposés, particularly the *Star Advertiser's* editorial, forced Governor Māhoe to respond. Koa watched the TV coverage of Māhoe's statement. The governor again expressed his dismay at the KonaWili disaster and reiterated his condolences to those who'd lost loved ones. He then addressed allegations of misconduct at the DOE. "The Hawai'i police are conducting a comprehensive investigation. The investigators are following every lead and will leave no stone unturned."

Looking squarely into the camera, he continued, "Based on a no-holds-barred investigation by the criminal authorities, those responsible for this disaster will be brought to justice. And if any member of my administration is guilty of malfeasance, or even neglect, they will be gone from public service."

Pausing slightly and appearing to appraise his audience, Māhoe made a plea for patience. "Unfortunately, malicious rumors attributed to unnamed sources and isolated facts taken out of context have created a distorted picture. That is not fair to those in public service nor to the good citizens of this great state. Accordingly, I ask citizens to be patient and await the outcome of the criminal investigation. The authorities will deal harshly with any and all wrongdoers, but we will be fair-minded and act on established facts, not irresponsible and incomplete disclosures by unnamed and disgruntled publicity seekers."

Māhoe gave a strong speech, but Koa thought the governor should have fired, or at least suspended, Francine Naʻauao. Her agency authorized a school to be built atop a volcanic vent. That was fact. Her agency approved a bizarre change order. That was fact. Her agency lost vital and relevant records. That was fact. Fourteen children and two teachers had died.

The warden of the federal reformatory at El Reno, Oklahoma, had given Harry S. Truman, Koa's favorite president, a desk placard, reading: "The buck stops here." To Koa, Truman's wisdom seemed apt—the buck should stop on Naʻauao desk. Naʻauao had to have some powerful hold over the governor for him to have expended so much political capital for her.

CHAPTER TWENTY-THREE

AFTER HIS SISTER reported that Ikaika hadn't reawakened from surgery, Koa called her almost every hour. Again and again, the news was the same—Ikaika hadn't recovered consciousness. Then slowly, late in the afternoon of the second day, the tide began to turn. First, Ikaika moved his hands, then he opened his eyes, and most encouragingly, began to respond to voices. Initial tests showed his reactions to be slow, but normal. The news got better and better. Five hours later they moved him out of the ICU. Ikaika had survived the surgery. Now they'd have to see how much of the old Ikaika the surgeons had excised along with the tumor.

* * *

Koa had no leads on Leffler's whereabouts. He shared the bad news with Zeigler, only to get an even more distressing report. Leffler had stolen more than twenty handguns, M16A2 assault rifles, and most troubling of all, a DesertTech SRS A-1 military sniper rifle. They'd recovered only a small portion of his arsenal. Leffler might have sold the other weapons, but Koa feared he faced a heavily armed fugitive.

Koa asked Sergeant Basa to assign officers to guard both Cheryl Makela and Tomi Watanabe, the next two names on Leffler's hit list.

He knew he'd have to talk to each of them but needed to make sure Leffler didn't get to them first.

He took Leffler's jungle combat boots to Cap Roberts to see if he could match them to the prints found outside the Witherspoon residence. Cap took an impression from one boot, photographed it, and put it side by side with the photo of the wet footprints outside Witherspoon's house.

"As you can see," Cap explained, "they match. Made by Wellco, a style called hot weather gen II jungle boots. It's a military boot."

"Great," Koa said, "your match reduces the pool of suspects to about twenty thousand soldiers stationed in Hawai'i."

"Hold on." Cap picked up Leffler's left boot and held it upside down. A deep notch cut through the ribbing at the base of the heal. "That's field damage; the boots didn't come that way." Cap pointed to a matching gap on a picture of the impression from the sidewalk. "That match gives us a near positive identification and puts Leffler at the Witherspoon house on the morning of the killing."

"Better than that," Koa said, "it puts him there between four and six that morning."

Cap looked puzzled. "How'd you get the time frame?"

"It didn't rain that night. The puddle on the walkway came from the automatic watering system—clock activated in the front yard at four o'clock every fifth day."

"Nice."

Koa wanted more. "Yeah, but we don't have anything other than the hit list to tie Leffler to the Boyle murder."

"Not so sure about that," Cap said. "Remember those dirt marks on the sheets?"

"Yeah."

"It's lava dust."

Koa responded with a frown. "The whole island's made of lava."

"Yeah, but not all lava is the same. I sent samples to the police crime lab in Honolulu. They used a microspectrophotometer. It measures the technical qualities of color. They also checked the chemical composition."

"Micro-whatever. That's a mouthful. So?"

"There's explosive residue mixed in with the lava dust."

"Like might be found up at the Pōhakuloa Army Training Area?" Koa asked.

"You got it. I had one of my boys take a run-up to the Army firing range."

A touch of excitement crept into Koa's voice. "You got a match?"

"Yeah, I got a match, a near-perfect match."

Koa slapped the technician on the back. "I owe you a six-pack of Bikini Blonde Ale."

Cap's grin rewarded Koa.

They got much the same result when they compared Leffler's fingerprints, lifted off the hit list with the partial fingerprint found on one of the shell casings. Cap had created two separate images at a resolution of five hundred pixels per inch—one of the partial print from the casing and the other from Leffler's actual print.

"There are," Cap explained, "three levels of print comparison—patterns, minutia points, and pore/ridge contours. The FBI IAFIS system uses only patterns and minutia points. With that system, I get an 80 percent likelihood of a match on these two prints."

Koa groaned. "A defense lawyer will have a field day with a four-out-of-five chance."

"Right," Cap responded, changing the screen to show two more detailed images of the same prints. "But if I compare images at one thousand pixels per inch, I can compare pores and ridge contours, yielding many more matching points. I put the likelihood Leffler left the partial print on the casings to 99.8 percent."

Koa let out a deep breath. "That's more like it."

"In essence," Cap concluded, "there's only one chance in five thousand someone else left the print on the casing."

Koa bettered those odds. "Yeah, but combining the fingerprint and the damaged bootprint with the circumstantial evidence like his access to the military weapons, the sale of a similar weapon to Bane, his girlfriend's testimony putting him alone in Hilo just before the shooting, and the list with Boyle's and Witherspoon's names crossed off, I like our chances of a first-degree murder conviction."

Although they didn't have him in custody, they'd identified the killer. Forty thousand dollars in crisp new hundreds said someone had hired him. Koa now wanted to know who. He guessed Leffler wouldn't be talking anytime soon, so his only leads were the picture of Leffler and Tomi Watanabe at the Monarch bar and the forty thousand dollars. The picture wasn't proof Watanabe hired Leffler, and his name on the hit list made it unlikely, but the mayor's press aide still had some serious explaining to do.

CHAPTER TWENTY-FOUR

WHEN KOA RETURNED to his office, he found Sally Medea waiting for him. His hopes of finding Witherspoon's secret soared at the sight of her. "You figure out what Arthur hid?"

"No, but I've been thinking. No matter which way I look at it, I keep coming back to a rose window. The rose windows of medieval churches captivated Arthur. He visited the great cathedrals in Europe and marveled at their rose windows. He drew dozens of architectural plans for rose windows."

"I'm not sure I follow. What do rose windows have to do with anything? Are there any buildings with rose windows in Hilo?"

She shook her head. "No, that's what troubles me. There's no building with a cathedral-like rose window in Hilo or anywhere on the Big Island. Yet, I just know if Arthur hid something, it'd be near a rose window. It's driving me nuts."

"Keep trying," he encouraged her.

"Are you making any progress in finding Arthur's killer?"

"Yeah. An Army sergeant named Leffler pulled the trigger, but he's a hired killer. I'm still trying to figure out who hired him."

"The man who arranged Arthur's death deserves to die," she said with a vehemence that surprised Koa.

"Hawai'i doesn't have the death penalty, but he'll go to prison for life."

"That's not good enough. Premeditated murderers should get the Biblical treatment—An eye for an eye."

Koa knew the death penalty affected mostly the poor with bad lawyers, and that wasn't right, but still, murder for hire deserved more than life in prison.

He thought about Sally after she left. She must have been deeply in love with Arthur Witherspoon, and he with her. Yet Witherspoon hadn't shared his deepest secrets with her. She hadn't participated in designing the KonaWili school. She knew nothing of the extra concrete and little about his conversations with Boyle or Gommes. Nor did she know where he'd hidden his secret. Rose windows, she'd said, but there were no rose windows on the Big Island. After puzzling on it for a while, he set it aside.

His sister called from Honolulu. Ikaika, now fully conscious, seemed to be doing well. "He's happier than I've ever seen him. He's actually glad to have us around," Alana reported.

"That's wonderful."

"He wants to see you. He asks about you all the time. When are you coming?"

Koa felt yanked in conflicting directions. The chief was still away, and the case had heated up with a host of new leads. Having discovered Makela's name on Leffler's hit list, he needed to re-interview her. He had to confront Watanabe. They had to track down Leffler and investigate Na'auao's hold over the governor. Yet, he felt an urgency to get to Honolulu and spend time with his brother. He'd been the one to arrest Ikaika, saving his life in the process. That event had momentarily renewed a troubled connection with his estranged brother at least until Ikaika blamed him for his subsequent parole revocation.

And now Ikaika might have a new lease on life, maybe even a new attitude toward his family. Koa also had to explore Walker McKenzie's offer to arrange access to medical experts. Perhaps having been an instrument of Ikaika's incarceration, he could help set him free again. Was he dreaming? Probably so.

"Koa, are you there?"

His sister's voice broke his reverie. "I need to make some calls, then I'll come see Ikaika. I'll call you with the details."

"Come soon, Koa."

Koa left police headquarters and walked to a block of 1920s storefronts not far from the county offices. Climbing the rickety steps to Alexia Sheppard's office. He found her in her sun-streaked, plant-filled office working at her laptop. He sat down in one of the easy chairs opposite her desk and waited for her to look up. An attractive woman in her late thirties with luxurious long black hair, tied back in a loose ponytail, she was the daughter of one of Hilo's most well-known lawyers and philanthropists. Her father had set her up in a law practice before his death, and she'd made a name for herself with a powerful courtroom presence and a magical way of connecting with juries. Koa knew many a male opponent who had underestimated her skill only to pay the price.

Concentration lined her round face and furrows wrinkled her forehead as she worked her way through some legal problem. He spent the time watching Alibi, her big black cat, cleaning himself atop a pile of books on the shelf next to her desk. Alexia and Alibi were inseparable, and some judges even allowed the black beast into their courtrooms.

"Hello." Her voice—one of her most treasured assets—floated like the soothing timbre of a fine-tuned musical instrument.

"Got a few minutes to talk about your least favorite recidivist client?" She'd represented his youngest brother through his many court appearances, all at Koa's expense.

"Ikaika?"

"Yes." He told her about Ikaika's seizure, tumor, and surgery. Then he laid out Walker McKenzie's idea about building a case for parole.

She looked dubious. "It's never been done here in Hawai'i, at least not to my knowledge."

"Does that mean it can't be done?"

"Well, when he's served the minimum term set by the parole board, he's entitled to a parole hearing. We could present the health issue then, but it would require medical experts. I've got no idea how the parole board would react. It's uncharted territory in violent felony cases."

"Remind me about Ikaika's minimum term."

"Because of his extensive criminal record, the board set his minimum at six years. He's served two, so he's eligible in another four."

Koa felt discouraged. "He has to wait four more years before he gets a chance at parole?"

"That would be the standard approach, but the board reviews inmates at administrative hearings from time to time and has the power to reduce a prisoner's minimum sentence. I've heard of it, but it's never happened in any of my cases, and it would be an uphill battle in your brother's situation."

"But it's possible? There's a chance?" he asked.

"Sure, there's a legal basis in the regulations."

"What would I have to do to get this process started?"

"You'd have to line up medical experts, and they'd have to be prepared to deal with his entire criminal history, including his juvenile record."

"I have his juvenile record."

"But you're not supposed to have it, and it would be a crime for you to disclose it to anyone else without Ikaika's written permission," she warned.

"Okay, so I'll get his permission."

"You'll need his permission to disclose his medical records, too."

"Can you prepare the forms?"

"Sure, but don't get your hopes up. This is not going to be easy."

On the way down the stairs from her office, Koa called Walker McKenzie, who had arranged for two renowned neurosurgeons to examine Ikaika. Having fulfilled his part of the bargain, McKenzie was hot to tape an interview with Koa. They arranged to meet in Honolulu after Koa's session with the doctors. He feared McKenzie's Koa Kāne human interest story would irrevocably change his life, but his loyalty to his disloyal brother left him no choice.

CHAPTER TWENTY-FIVE

THE TUG OF WAR between duty and family troubled Koa on the flight to Honolulu. He remembered the first time he'd stood on the rocks above the ocean dared by a friend to make his first high dive. He was about to take a greater plunge into the unknown pool of public notoriety. The thought of personal publicity didn't sit well, but he could hear his ancestors calling. Then his mother's voice rang in his ears—"You must forgive the pain Ikaika has caused, and find a way to help him . . . to put your family back together . . . for my sake . . . for your ancestors. That too I know in my *nu'au*." His wayward, black-sheep brother needed him, and he could not deny the obligation.

Memories from Ikaika's troubled life flickered in a continuous loop. The recollection of a treasured fishing rod was among the most disturbing. Koa had been fifteen when Uncle Pau, a friend of his father, had given Koa a fiberglass fishing rod with a genuine reel. The three of them, Koa, his father, and Uncle Pau, fished from a *wa'a*, a canoe outside one of the reefs just east of Laupāhoehoe Point. Koa remembered the trips as a magical time, with Uncle Pau regaling them with stories of King Kamehameha's visits to Laupāhoehoe, a regular stopping point since ancient times on the well-traveled canoe route from Hāwī to Hilo.

On one such adventure, Koa had hooked an *aʻu*, a broadbill swordfish, one of Hawaiʻi's most prized sport fish. It wasn't a grander, a fish weighing over a 1000 pounds, but it was a tremendous haul for a fifteen-year-old, and he'd spent the better part of an hour working the line before he finally landed the big fish. Koa bragged about his triumph for weeks, and the fishing pole became his most treasured possession. He named the pole *makau*—fish hook.

Despite, or maybe because of, Koa's pride in his fishing pole, Ikaika repeatedly threw things at it and warned he would break it in half. Koa never dreamed his brother would actually make good on his threat, yet Ikaika did just that. One day, Koa walked into their house to find Ikaika holding the precious pole. With a malevolent gleam in his eyes, he snapped it in two, hurling the pieces to the floor. Koa confronted his brother and a fight ensued during which Ikaika laughed hysterically. Koa would never forget his brother's glee at his cruel act or the sound of his chortling. For the first time in Koa's life, he'd come face-to-face with pure malice. A harbinger of things to come.

His mother, Māpuana, said Ikaika would grow out of it, but she'd been wrong. As he grew older and stronger, Ikaika, which meant *strong* in his native Hawaiian, became a fierce bully, terrorizing other kids in school. Ikaika had his first of many run-ins with the juvenile justice system when, at age twelve, he stole a bicycle from a local shop. By the time he reached eighteen, he'd become an experienced criminal. Joyriding turned into auto theft, and glue-sniffing morphed into marijuana and cocaine. Not unlike many Hawaiian men, by age thirty-four, Ikaika had been in and out of jail more times than he could count, having spent nearly a fourth of his adult life behind bars.

The toll on the family was horrendous. Each member reacted differently as the stress from Ikaika's misconduct ricocheted throughout the family and ultimately reflected back on Ikaika himself. Māpuana forgave Ikaika his every failing and pressed her other three children to do likewise. But neither his middle brother, Mauloa, nor his sister, Alana, shared their mother's compassion. Alana, who lived with Māpuana, reacted angrily, often screaming at Ikaika whenever he caused his mother pain. Mauloa simply withdrew and hadn't spoken to Ikaika in years. The varied reactions within Koa's family turned in a vicious circle, only amplifying Māpuana's pain.

Koa tried, visiting his brother in prison, lending him money, and helping him find jobs. Ikaika never repaid or thanked Koa and blamed Koa for every reversal. Their relationship soured.

What had Alana said? "He wants to see you." Koa couldn't remember the last time his youngest brother wanted to see him. Had brain surgery really made Ikaika less hostile? Was it just a temporary reaction to survival? Or had surgery caused a real change in personality? Koa would know soon enough.

He went straight from the airport to the hospital—to the special ward for prisoners and those locked up for psychiatric reasons. The old, ugly, gray wing of the hospital seemed more like a jail than a medical facility. Koa found his brother sitting up in bed, his head bandaged with wires connecting him to all variety of monitors. Ikaika appeared calm, even relaxed. When had he ever seen his kid brother relaxed?

"Hey, big brah." The warmth in Ikaika's simple greeting gave the words special meaning. The hostility so often filling his eyes had disappeared, replaced by calm, or passivity.

"Hello, little brother, how are you feeling?"

A shadow of a grin flashed across Ikaika's face. "Like they cut a fuckin' hole in my head."

The tiny grin struck Koa like a thunderbolt—he hadn't seen his brother smile in years. He tried to think of the last time he'd seen

Ikaika smile. Maybe when Māpuana had given Ikaika a toy tractor for his eighth birthday? "You need medicine?"

"Nah." Ikaika nodded toward a machine. "That crazy thing feeds me dope every few minutes. It's a damn fine candy man." Another tiny smile.

Koa felt a surge of affection toward his brother unlike any he'd experienced in a long time. "Tell me what happened. Why'd you black out?"

"I had a seizure in the jailhouse. I remember a weird dizzy feeling—the room spinning 'round like a top—then bang. Somebody pulled the plug, and the power went dark. I guess the paramedics tried to revive me. I don't know. I woke up here, and they told me they'd removed a brain tumor."

"What have they told you about the tumor?"

"The doc cut the suckers out, got two tumors. That's supposed to be good. I might actually live a while longer."

Ikaika's recognition of vulnerability surprised Koa. "That's great."

"The tumors were right here." Ikaika pointed to his forehead.

"Have the medics told you what to expect?"

"A little. They told me I might have different feelings, like a personality shift or some shit like that." Ikaika paused. "Maybe not a bad thing, huh?"

Ikaika's mild self-deprecation stunned Koa. The old Ikaika would never in a lifetime have said anything like that. "Like what?"

"Dunno. Right now I'm mostly screwed up in the head."

"Confused?"

"Yeah. It's like I don't know how I got in prison. I mean, I know what I did, but I don't understand why. It's all jumbled up in my head."

Koa's spirits soared. The calmness, the half-smile, the self-deprecation—all good signs. He started to discuss the future and the possibility of parole with Ikaika, but a nurse came in to take Ikaika's vitals. She looked at Koa for a moment before saying, "You must be the hero brother."

Her words took Koa aback. "*The hero brother?* Where'd you get that idea?"

"From him." She pointed to Ikaika. "Told me you saved his life."

Standing out in the hall while the nurse worked, Koa wondered what had happened to the old Ikaika. He wasn't sorry to lose the mean brute he'd known for thirty-five years, but the transformation left him feeling strange, like the ground had shifted under his feet. His brother blamed him for destroying his life by sending him back to prison, and now, Ikaika was telling the nurse Koa had saved his life. The change was disorienting.

When the nurse left, Koa took a seat beside his brother's hospital bed. Alexia Sheppard had warned against exaggerating the chances of parole. Koa didn't want to create false expectations, but he needed to secure Ikaika's cooperation. He explained the possibility, emphasizing the risks. He wasn't yet ready to reveal his agreement with Walker McKenzie, so he said he had a line on some medical experts.

His brother listened intently without interrupting. Yet another new behavior. When Koa finished, Ikaika had a thoughtful, but serious expression. "You know, big brother, I've made a lot of enemies over the years, like that prick Moyan." Ikaika referred to his parole officer. "You really think the parole board is going to give me another chance?"

"It's a long shot," Koa conceded, "but what have you got to lose? I mean, all they can do is say 'no' in which case you're no worse off."

"Okay, whatever you say, big brother."

Koa couldn't quite believe Ikaika's new attitude, but he knew how to test it. The old Ikaika, imagining some evil conspiracy, objected to any communication between Alexia Sheppard, his lawyer, and

Koa. Koa took a deep breath before saying, "I've talked this over with Alexia Sheppard—"

He provoked no outburst—no reaction at all—and continued toward the next potentially explosive hurdle—Ikaika's paranoia about access to his criminal history. "She says the medical experts will need both your criminal history and your medical records."

Koa saw a flicker of something—maybe anger—in Ikaika's eyes. "They want to pick me apart like some lab rat?"

Koa paused, absorbing this subtle throwback to the old Ikaika. "They need to understand whether the tumors affected your behavior."

The tantrum Koa's words would have provoked before the surgery never materialized. Instead, Ikaika sat silently, staring at him. Koa couldn't read his brother's passivity, so he asked, "Are you following me?"

"Yeah, big bro, I'm following you."

"I've brought the consents if you're ready to sign."

"And you think I ought to do this?"

Extraordinary. Ikaika asking him for advice. That had never happened before. "Yeah, Ikaika, I think you should do this. As I said, you've nothing to lose by trying."

Ikaika stared off into space, and Koa wondered what he was thinking. Then it struck him. His brother was thinking, actually thinking and not just reacting like the old Ikaika. Finally, his brother spoke. "I guess felons don't have much privacy worth protecting, do they?"

What could Koa say? "No, not much."

"Okay, let's do it," Ikaika finally concluded.

Koa called for a nurse, who witnessed Ikaika's signature. They wrapped up, and when Koa was on the way out the door to meet with the experts Walker McKenzie had lined up, Ikaika stopped him. "Koa."

"Yeah, Ikaika?"

"*Mahalo.*"

That word nearly brought tears to Koa's eyes. In thirty-four years, his brother had never thanked him for anything.

*   *   *

Koa met Dr. Carlton in his office, and Ikaika's neurosurgeon led Koa into a conference room where he introduced Drs. Reinhardt and Kepler. "I don't know who's pulling the strings for you, Detective," Dr. Carlton said, "but you've lined up two of the country's leading brain experts." Koa shook hands and thanked the doctors for taking the time to meet with him.

The three doctors could not have been more unalike. Dr. Carlton, a small wiry man with close-cropped blond hair and piercing blue eyes, had hands like a concert pianist with long, strong fingers. A surgeon's hands. Images of those deft fingers inside Ikaika's skull, illuminated by the bright lights above an operating table, flashed through Koa's mind.

Koa couldn't imagine Dr. Kepler, a redheaded Irishman with a neatly trimmed beard, in an operating room. With sparkling green eyes and an impish smile, he seemed better suited to an Irish pub than the lecture hall of the California medical school where he usually held forth. Still, he exuded warmth, and Koa took an instant liking to the man.

Dr. Reinhardt, a tall Brooklyn New Yorker with a narrow face, wearing a yarmulke, was the most reserved. And he, unlike the others, wore a dark suit and tie. Koa sensed he felt out of place and wondered if he had come only as a favor to Walker McKenzie.

Dr. Carlton took the lead. "I've shared Ikaika's scans and the surgical findings with my colleagues, so they know we found two

separate pilocytic astrocytomas in the orbitofrontal cortex. The biopsy results showed variably textured glioma matrix with Rosenthal
fibers and eosinophilic granular bodies and indicators of increased
proliferative activity." The doctor stopped and looked at Koa. "In
plain English, these tumors grow quite slowly—so slowly they likely
developed in childhood. They are rare in adults—about one per
four million people—and were just beginning to show signs of developing malignancy."

"What interests me," Dr. Kepler intervened, standing up and moving to a computer monitor attached to the wall, "is the location of
the two tumors—" he placed a finger on the X-ray, inside the forehead just above Ikaika's eyes—"located right here behind the eye
sockets. Numerous studies show this part of the brain plays a role in
decision-making, especially in balancing reward and punishment."

As Dr. Kepler spoke, Koa watched the doctor's animated face and
the laugh lines around his eyes. He appeared to be in his fifties and
utterly absorbed in his specialty.

"Studies suggest trauma to the orbitofrontal cortex can impair a
patient's ability to anticipate the consequences of antisocial behavior."

"Does that mean," Koa asked, "that these tumors caused my
brother's sociopathic behavior?"

"That's not a meaningful question," Dr. Reinhardt intervened in
a deep voice with a stereotypical Brooklyn accent. "Let me explain.
If you had an impulse to hit me with your fist, a normal brain would
evaluate the likely positive rewards and negative punishments. No
medical expert could responsibly assert that a tumor caused your
impulse to use your fist, but a tumor could impair your ability to
assess the consequences of acting on that impulse."

"What's interesting about your brother's case," Dr. Kepler reas-
serted himself, "is these tumors have existed for a long time—
probably since childhood. Children become socialized and adults

learn to balance and rebalance rewards and punishments as they accumulate experience. If the balancing function is impaired throughout a lifetime, it could plausibly lead to sociopathic behavior—what one researcher labeled 'acquired sociopathy.'"

"Is that what happened to my brother?"

"It's theoretically possible," Dr. Reinhardt responded, "but we have almost no clinical experience with long-term cases. All of the recent advances in our understanding come from battlefield injuries."

That didn't sound promising. "You wouldn't be able to say the tumors contributed to my brother's behavioral problems?" Koa asked.

"I'm telling you the odds aren't good," Dr. Reinhardt responded clinically. "We can study his medical and criminal history, and maybe, just maybe, find markers to support the conclusion you want, but it will more likely be inconclusive."

"Are you willing to give it a try?" Koa asked.

"I understand that your brother was involved with a child sex ring. Is that correct?" Dr. Reinhardt asked.

It wasn't a friendly question. Koa wasn't sure where the medic was going, but he didn't like the direction. "Yes, that's correct, but he wasn't prosecuted."

Dr. Reinhardt shook his head and began to collect his papers. "I'm sorry, but I really don't have time for this project." He pushed his chair back from the table, rose to his feet, and left the conference room.

Koa looked quizzically at Dr. Kepler.

"You'll have to forgive him. His daughter was raped. He's understandably sensitive about sex crimes."

CHAPTER TWENTY-SIX

THE CONFERENCE ROOM remained deathly quiet for what seemed like an eternity after Dr. Reinhardt left. Koa felt bitterly disappointed. He turned to Dr. Kepler. "What about you? Are you willing to see what you can do to help my brother?"

"Most definitely," Dr. Kepler responded. "For me, this is a unique opportunity to study a brain with long-standing damage, but I don't want to get your hopes up. Dr. Reinhardt is correct that the results will most likely be inconclusive."

Koa cringed. This neurologist viewed his brother as a bizarre case study, like a one-legged rat in a laboratory cage. He knew what his brother would think. Ikaika would be angry and offended. He'd tell this doctor to go to hell.

Yet, there existed a small chance the doctor could help. Koa wondered if he should have another discussion with his brother but decided against it. He handed Dr. Kepler a thick file. "This has my brother's whole criminal history, including psychiatric reports from various prison doctors. The file also contains a consent for access to his criminal and medical records."

Dr. Kepler took the file. "I'll also need more tests—including some interactive brain scans—as well as interviews with your brother."

"The prison authorities won't release Ikaika for the additional brain scans," Dr. Carlton inserted himself, "but I can arrange for them to be done here while your brother recuperates."

"Thank you," Koa responded. "You know I can't pay you for your work."

"Don't worry," Dr. Kepler responded. "A pilocytic astrocytoma occurs in one in four million adults—very few of those are in the orbitofrontal cortex—and I've found no medical record of an adult patient with two such tumors. Your brother presents a unique medical anomaly, and it will be a privilege to study him."

There it was again, laid right out on the table for everyone to see. Ikaika the guinea pig—the lab rat—for this brain-shrink to examine. Koa hid his annoyance and chose to focus on the slim possibility of success.

"Before we break," Dr. Kepler said, "I have a question. As a child, did your brother ever have seizures?"

The question triggered a vague recollection. "I think so," Koa said, "but my mother would know for sure. She's in Ikaika's room. Let me bring her in here."

Koa found Māpuana, led her into the conference room, and introduced her to Dr. Kepler. Koa didn't want to get her hopes up, and he most certainly didn't want Dr. Kepler to repeat his guinea pig speech, so Koa said only that Dr. Kepler wanted to help Ikaika.

"Mrs. Kāne," the doctor began, "did your youngest son have seizures as a child?"

Koa saw the suspicion in his mother's eyes. Old-school Hawaiian, instinctively wary of *haoles*, especially doctors, she said, "What for? Why do you want to know?"

Dr. Kepler, too, noticed Māpuana's wariness. "We are trying to help your son, trying to determine how long your son had his tumors. Brain tumors frequently cause seizures, and if Ikaika had seizures as a child, the tumors could have affected him from a young age."

"Oh," Māpuana responded, "and why is that important?"

She guarded her son, protecting any information about him against misuse. Koa saw no choice but to tell her about the parole possibility, but he warned the odds against success were long.

Māpuana looked at Dr. Kepler in a whole new light and became a font of information. "Yes, Ikaika had problems around age four. He would just stare off into space and sometimes his body would go limp. He dropped things."

"Absence seizures?" Dr. Kepler asked.

"Yes, that is what the *haole* doctor called them."

"And he prescribed medicine?"

"Yes... dep... a... something," Māpuana struggled to remember. "I'm not sure."

"Depakote?"

"Yes... that was it."

Dr. Kepler nodded. "This is going to be most interesting."

*　　*　　*

Koa did not return directly to the Big Island but instead went to the KITV studios on King Street in Honolulu's Chinatown to fulfill his commitment to Walker McKenzie, who had arranged to use its studio facilities. McKenzie, in his ever-present white shirt with rolled-up sleeves, interviewed Koa for three hours, filming as the discussion progressed. They began with Koa's childhood, living with two brothers and a sister in a shack with no indoor plumbing alongside the dying cane fields on the Hāmākua coast. They talked about his father's death in a sugar mill accident, and how his mother, a native healer in the tiny village of Laupāhoehoe, had insisted he get a good education. He didn't mention his confrontation with Anthony Hazzard—that he'd killed the man—or that he'd covered up the crime. He told McKenzie about his years at the Kamehameha schools for children of Hawaiian heritage. "I'd be poor, unemployed, and in jail, if it hadn't been for Māmā," Koa admitted.

McKenzie then turned to his military service with the Army's elite 5th Special Forces Group. "I thought I grew up poor until I got to Afghanistan," Koa said. "In Hawai'i, we had no money, but we had land and gardens. We grew our own food year-round and caught fish. We didn't eat steak, but we never starved like the villagers I saw in Afghanistan."

"Tell me about Somalia. You were in Mogadishu during the *Black Hawk Down* episode, weren't you?" McKenzie asked.

"The worst day of my life. The politicians put us in an impossible situation with inadequate resources and bad intelligence. I lost two good men. It was touch and go for the rest of us. I hope the powers in Washington learned never to commit American lives without backing our guys up, but I doubt the politicians are that smart."

"Any other reflections on that experience?"

"Many, but one changed my whole perspective on life. Somalia was full of fanatics, wild men with no regard for human life. You couldn't talk to them. You could only shoot them before they shot you. That experience taught me to reject fanatics—all fanatics of whatever stripe—including those in Hawai'i who would turn the clock back to the old monarchy."

They talked about Koa's role as a police officer and some of his more notorious cases before McKenzie turned to the most sensitive topic on his agenda. "Koa, you have a brother in prison." McKenzie summarized Ikaika's long history of violence and incarceration. "How have you dealt with that as a police officer?"

"It's been difficult. People look at my family and see two brothers—the cop and the criminal." Once again, Koa omitted that he—like Ikaika—had committed a serious crime or that he—unlike Ikaika—had gotten away without prosecution. "People don't understand. My superiors and colleagues in the police department didn't understand. I couldn't control my brother, and he blamed me for his problems."

"Your brother blamed you. Why?"

"I don't know, Walker. I've often puzzled over it. My brother has been disruptive since childhood, and I have wondered whether there wasn't some medical or psychological reason for his behavior."

"You risked your life to arrest him, didn't you?"

"There's always a risk when a police officer goes into an unknown situation, but I focused on saving his life, not arresting him."

"How did you do it?"

"Actually, he did it. He picked the right moment to turn on his criminal friends, and we took advantage of his actions."

"You've just come from visiting him. How's he doing?"

"As you know, Walker, he had a seizure in prison caused by a brain tumor. I visited him in the hospital after his surgery, and he's doing well. In almost every way, it was the best visit I've ever had with my little brother."

CHAPTER TWENTY-SEVEN

A DOUBLE RAINBOW over the mountains welcomed Koa when he stepped off the plane in Hilo. Then he turned his cell phone on, and all hell broke loose. Police Chief S. H. Lannua was back in town from his gallbladder surgery and on a warpath. He had Koa on the carpet in his office less than an hour later. Lannua, a tall, patrician man with black hair and hard black eyes, traced his roots back to one of the missionary families who arrived in Hawai'i in the 1820s.

"What have you done, Detective?"

"Chief, I've been in Honolulu with my brother. I have no idea what's going on."

"Last night, TV4 ran an exposé, accusing Cheryl Makela, the mayor's former planning director, of being partners with one of the mayor's top aides in the Hualālai Hui. The reporter painted her approval of the development as part of a bribery scheme."

"Okay. What does that have to do with me?"

"People in the mayor's office say you leaked the story."

The allegation stunned Koa. "That's preposterous. Who says that?"

"Watanabe. And he says you also leaked the story about the missing DOE documents. He says you've been spending a lot of time with the press, especially Walker McKenzie. Is that true?"

The chief had hit a sensitive topic. Koa knew he should own up to his deal with the reporter, but he hadn't leaked the Makela story and wasn't ready to tell the chief about possible parole for his brother. He ducked the question. "Watanabe is trying to hide something. He was in a bar with the killer, Army Sergeant Ralph Leffler."

Disbelief clouded the chief's face. "You have proof?"

"Yes. The Army guys got photos of the two of them together at one of the Monarch's back tables."

"Jesus. That sleazy dump down by the docks? What was Watanabe doing there?"

"I don't know, but the two of them were having a *tête-à-tête* at a corner table and from the expressions on their faces it didn't look social."

"Meeting about what?"

"I don't know, Chief. There's something fishy going on with Watanabe. On the one hand, he and Leffler had something going, and on the other hand, Watanabe's name is on Leffler's kill list."

"Jesus, have you told the mayor?"

"Not yet. I want to talk to Watanabe first. It's only fair to hear his story, and I haven't had time with this trip to Honolulu."

"What the hell were you doing in Honolulu?"

"I guess you haven't heard. After they brought my brother back here to testify at the Lono trial, he lost consciousness and was diagnosed with a brain tumor."

The chief's face softened for a moment. "God, Koa, I'm sorry. I didn't know."

"I don't advertise my family's issues. But Ikaika's okay, at least for the moment."

Then it was back to business. "So back to Makela. The mayor's really hot about the press story."

"You'd better be careful with that one, Chief."

"Why?"

"When I interviewed her, she refused to say whether she had sub-*hui* partners—suggesting she's got silent partners. And Zeke's planning to put her in front of a grand jury."

"Jesus Christ, this KonaWili thing is a serious mess." The chief paused as if thinking through the options. "Now that I'm back, I'll be taking the lead."

Koa had been around the chief long enough to recognize his ulterior motives—namely, to protect the mayor. "That's fine, Chief. I'll be glad to be out of the hot seat, but you should probably run it by the mayor."

"Why?"

"Because he issued some kind of executive order officially appointing me to lead the investigation."

"Why? You'd naturally head it up in my absence."

"The governor wanted to take control. He and Mayor Tanaka got into a pissing contest. The county prosecutor told Tanaka he could keep control with an executive order."

"Goddammit. I run this department."

"Absolutely, Chief. But you weren't here when the balloon went up at KonaWili. I didn't ask to be on the podium with the mayor, and he didn't give me a choice."

"Goddammit," the chief swore again. "The mayor wants a briefing."

"Okay, but I'd really like to keep the Watanabe thing under wraps 'til I talk to him."

"We'll have to see how it goes," the chief responded just before his assistant announced the mayor's aides had set up the conference call. They got on the speaker and waited for the mayor to join along with Inaba and Watanabe.

As soon as they identified themselves, Watanabe took the first shot. "What do you know about these goddamn leaks, Detective Kāne?"

Koa was about to deny leaking the story, but the mayor interrupted. "Let's not waste time on news leaks, Tomi. I want to hear
what progress we've made in wrapping up this investigation."

Koa's mind raced, planning his response. He found it trouble-
some to brief the mayor with Watanabe on the phone. He decided
on a short version, focusing on Leffler as Witherspoon's killer and
the prime suspect in Boyle's staged suicide. The question, he told the
mayor, was who had hired Leffler and why.

"The question," the mayor shot back, "is why haven't you arrested
Leffler? I told you, I wanted this investigation wrapped up."

Koa looked at the chief, wondering whether he really wanted to
retake control. That would put him, not Koa, in the mayor's gun
sights. But the chief's need to be at center stage got the better of
him. "Mayor," the chief began, "now that I'm back from the mainland, I'm sure you want me to take over the investigation?"

Silence.

Unable to conceal his surprise at the mayor's long pause, the chief
looked shaken.

"Well, Chief Lannua," the mayor finally responded, "no reflection
on your leadership of the police department, but I'm on record appointing Detective Kāne as the lead, and I'm loath to change pad-
dlers mid-race. Let's leave things as they are for now."

The mayor's words troubled Koa. The rebuke to the chief would
do his relationship with Lannua no good. But more worrisome, Koa
wondered once again if he was being set up. All Koa's instincts said
the mayor should have been happy to cede control to the governor.
Unless he was protecting someone. And now with the police chief
back, the mayor wasn't even following the chain of command. Koa
had a sinking feeling in the pit of his stomach.

The chief frowned, obviously unhappy. "That's fine, Mayor."

Koa, relieved the conference call was over, turned to leave the chief's office.

"Don't go yet. There's another thing, Detective."

Lannua appeared frustrated and about to lash out. Koa knew from experience where he was going. *Here we go again*, he thought.

"How many times have I told you to work with Shizuo Hiro? You took advantage of my absence to bring in the Honolulu ME. That was underhanded. Shizuo is hopping mad."

With some effort, Koa suppressed a smile to avoid launching the chief over the edge. "Sir, I cleared the decision with the mayor personally. He agreed Shizuo wasn't up to the task, especially with the national press involved."

The chief looked stunned. "The mayor agreed to sideline Shizuo?"

"Yes, sir." He wanted to add that it was probably because Shizuo hadn't lost enough money in his recent poker games with the mayor, but Koa held his tongue.

Koa left the chief's office with a big problem looming. He'd successfully avoided the chief's question about his dealings with Walker McKenzie, but they wouldn't stay private for long. If he didn't break the KonaWili case before McKenzie aired his personal interest story, he'd be sitting on the hot seat, accused of using the press for his own personal gain—and God only knew what else.

CHAPTER TWENTY-EIGHT

KOA HATED DEALING with politicians. He preferred real people who daily faced the frequent hardships and occasional joys of normal life. He understood how their minds worked and knew their vices. Politicians reigned like aliens from another planet, their lives padded with special prerogatives. They didn't stand in the DMV line to register their cars. They cut ahead of everybody else at the airport security barriers. They lacked experience with food stamps or uninsured medical bills. They followed hidden agendas and talked in political codes designed to deceive the uninitiated.

While politicians fell among Koa's least respected, their press agents fared worse. Too often, Koa had heard Watanabe assert that saying something loudly enough and often enough led people to believe even patently false statements. Koa detested few people in Hawai'i, but Tomi Watanabe made the grade. And Koa knew Watanabe reciprocated. Thus, he approached the prospect of interviewing Watanabe with extreme caution. He asked the county prosecutor to arrange the interview and sit it on it. Watanabe might blow Koa off, but he'd think twice before stonewalling Koa in Zeke's presence. *I 'a'a nō i ka lā o ka ikaika*—he can be daring until he meets someone stronger.

They met in Zeke's office. The cocky little press aide strutted in like a *nēnē*, a Hawaiian goose, and, like the beautifully feathered bird, Koa figured he was 60 percent fluff.

Watanabe stared accusingly at Koa. "I assume we're here to talk about the scandalous leaks to the press."

"No," Zeke informed him. "You're here to answer our questions in a murder investigation."

The man tensed. "Maybe I should retain a lawyer?"

"That's your choice, Mr. Watanabe," Zeke responded. "Hilo's a small town with a chummy bar. I can recommend someone if you'd like."

The message was subtle, but Watanabe wasn't stupid, and Koa sensed him evaluating the risk of a newspaper story about the mayor's press aide showing up at the prosecutor's office with a lawyer. "I think we can proceed. I have—"

Koa was sure that he'd been going to say, "nothing to hide," but the little snake apparently thought better of it. Protestations of innocence, Koa knew, often shielded guilt.

"Mr. Watanabe," Zeke asked, "do you have an economic interest in the Hualālai development around the KonaWili school?"

The man bristled. "No. Absolutely not."

"Do you know anyone who does?"

"I've heard that Howard Gommes owns it, but I've never seen any legal ownership documents."

"Anyone else?"

"Not that I know of."

"Have you heard of any other owners?"

"Wouldn't that be hearsay?" Watanabe tried playing lawyer.

Zeke wanted none of it. "Answer the question, Mr. Watanabe."

"No."

Zeke turned to Koa. "You want to take over."

Koa had planned his questions to give Watanabe every opportunity to make a false step. "Have you ever been to the Monarch bar?"

"That's the hole-in-the-wall dump down by the port?"

"That's the one."

Watanabe shook his head. "It's not my kind of place."

Koa disliked evasions, especially from this little weasel. "I asked you, Mr. Watanabe, if you've ever been there."

Watanabe stiffened. "I may have been. What's it to you?"

"When?"

"I don't remember."

Koa leaned forward invading Watanabe's personal space. "Maybe about three weeks ago. Does that refresh your recollection?"

Watanabe tried to look nonchalant. "Not really."

"Mr. Watanabe," Koa asked, "do you know Ralph Leffler?"

Watanabe's facial muscles twitched and the mole on his check bobbed before he answered. "I . . . I don't think so."

"I think you do, Mr. Watanabe. You met him in the Monarch bar about three weeks ago."

"I don't remember that," Watanabe snapped.

Koa laid a picture on the table—the photograph taken during Zeigler's surveillance of Leffler. It showed Leffler and Watanabe sitting at a corner table in the Monarch. Koa tapped Watanabe's image. "That *is* you, isn't it?"

Watanabe's face grew pale, making the black mole on his cheek more prominent. He stared at the photograph, obviously trying to think of a way out of the box he'd built for himself. His hands trembled. "Un-huh."

"What did you and Leffler talk about?"

"Uh . . . uh, a private matter."

Koa forced himself to chuckle. "Really. What private matter?"

"I . . . I don't want to discuss it."

Zeke started to speak, but Koa waved him off. "Let's see if I can guess. You found out Leffler killed people and had access to unregistered guns."

The blood drained from Watanabe's face and neck, leaving his skin with a yellowish tint. His trembling became a pronounced jitter.

Koa continued, "You wanted Boyle and Witherspoon eliminated so Leffler agreed to fake Boyle's suicide and execute Witherspoon, all for forty thousand dollars."

Watanabe opened his mouth to speak, but no words came out. After a second, he wiped his mouth with the back of his hand.

"We know Leffler did the killing, and we've recovered the forty thousand dollars."

"It . . . it . . ." Watanabe stuttered, then paused. Finally, he got the words out. "It . . . it didn't . . . didn't happen like . . . like that."

"Really?" Koa said, enjoying the man's distress. "Tell us how it did go down."

"He . . . he ca . . . call . . . called me," Watanabe stuttered before catching his breath. "He threatened to hurt me if I didn't meet him at the Monarch." The words came out in a torrent. "Otherwise I'd never go there. It's a nasty place." Watanabe took a deep breath, almost like gasping for air. "He told me he'd be alone at a corner table."

"And what happened at the corner table?" Koa demanded.

"He said he knew where I lived, and he'd kill me if I didn't get the KonaWili investigation shut down."

But for Leffler's hit list, Koa wouldn't have believed him. Koa's own name on the list meant someone wanted to stop the investigation at all costs. And the conditional threat to kill Watanabe could explain the question marks after his name on Leffler's list.

"Why didn't you report the threat to the police?"

Watanabe looked down at his hands, and his voice dropped to just above a whisper. "I was afraid. He's a big brute with a scary scar, and he had a gun." Watanabe looked up. "You have to believe me. That's what happened."

"And that's why you tried to stop my investigation?"

Watanabe nodded his head.

That wasn't enough for Koa. "I want to hear you say it."

Watanabe hesitated before admitting what he'd done. "Yes. That's why I tried to stop the investigation."

Zeke took over, asking the question Koa hesitated to ask. "And exactly what did you do to stop the investigation?"

"I called a friend at the governor's office, urging the state to take over, and I . . ." Watanabe's voice faltered.

"And you what?" Zeke demanded.

"I told Mayor Tanaka he should fire Detective Kāne, but he wouldn't hear of it."

"And," Zeke struck a hammer blow, "you falsely accused Koa of leaking information, didn't you?"

"Yes." Watanabe's voice was barely audible.

"In fact," Zeke struck again, "you leaked the KonaWili stories, didn't you?"

Watanabe bowed his head. "I . . . I did."

Koa looked at Watanabe, slumped in his chair, lost in the misery of his own making. Half the story made sense. Someone wanted to stop the investigation, and pressuring Watanabe, even threatening to kill him, offered a path to that end, but why put Watanabe on the hit list? Why actually kill him even if he failed to stop the investigation? What would be gained by his death? Koa was missing something.

"Mr. Watanabe," Koa began, but the man seemed lost in his own world. "Mr. Watanabe," he said louder and the press agent looked up. "Aside from stopping the police investigation, do you have any idea why anyone would want to kill you?"

Watanabe recoiled as though Koa had slapped him. With a ghost-like expression, he stammered, "Kill me . . . I . . . I don't know."

It was an odd reaction, and it reinforced Koa's belief that the man knew some secret worth killing to protect.

"You know something someone out there wants to keep secret. What is it?"

Watanabe shivered and his hands shook. "I have no secrets."

Watanabe's body language said *lie* but for the moment an impenetrable one.

*   *   *

Cheryl Makela didn't look pleased to see Koa. She answered his knock in jeans and a wrinkled white blouse, looking haggard with purplish bags under her eyes. Koa had never seen her without makeup and barely recognized her wrinkled face, splotched with sunspots. The KonaWili disaster had gotten to her. Maybe because it ruined her investment.

"I've nothing to say to you. And I don't appreciate having a police car down the road spying on me," she said in a nasty tone.

She started to close the door when he said, "I came to tell you your life may be in danger."

Her lips parted slightly, her eyes narrowed, and the corners of her mouth turned down. Fear, apprehension, or maybe disbelief—he couldn't tell. She stepped back, let the door swing open, turned, and disappeared into the house, implicitly inviting him to follow. He trailed her into a large, luxurious kitchen. Her hands shook as she poured herself coffee from a silver urn on the counter without offering him any.

Lovely lady. Then he told her about the threat to her life, hoping to shock her into providing more information. "We identified the man who killed Hank Boyle and Arthur Witherspoon. Those were the first two names on his kill list. You rated number three."

Her face turned as white as her hair, and she weaved unsteadily on her feet. Coffee slopped over the edge of her cup and splashed to the floor. "Shit," she said softly, looking down at the spill. For a moment, he feared she might faint, but she put her free hand on the counter to steady herself. Looking up, she stood staring, her eyes unfocused, looking through him into some unseen space. He'd hit her with news of a serious threat, hoping to get her to talk, but instead, he'd driven her mind to some distant recollection. He almost turned around to see whatever apparition attracted her attention, but restrained himself, knowing the vision had to be in her mind.

He expected her to ask the killer's identity, but instead, she asked, "Who . . . who else is on the list?" Not, *who is the killer*; not, *why would anyone be after me*; not, *oh my God, what can I do to protect myself*; but, *who else?* Why would the identity of the others be foremost in her mind?

"Tomi Watanabe—"

She gasped, and letting go of the counter, raised her free hand to her mouth. "Oh, my God!" Wavering on her feet, she dropped her coffee and began to collapse. Koa caught her as the coffee cup hit the floor, and shattered into a thousand pieces, splashing hot coffee everywhere. He lowered the unconscious woman to the ground and instructed the dispatcher to send an ambulance.

CHAPTER TWENTY-NINE

WHEN KOA RETURNED to the station, he found that Piki, who was off duty, had left a note. "Found a lead on the bulldozer rental. Jake's Machinery Rentals on Māmalahoa Highway. Handles a lot of big subdivision jobs. Their rental girl, Sandy, found the paperwork. Said Jake might remember something once he sees the invoice." Koa grinned. Now he might have evidence against Gommes. He grabbed Basa, and they headed for Jake's.

"I see you're still wearing the body cam. How's the test going?" Koa asked as they headed for the highway.

"Okay, I guess, but there are a bunch of problems."

"Like what?"

"Privacy issues for us officers, you know, like bathroom breaks, and for interviews with sensitive victims, like children or women in sexual assaults."

"Makes sense."

"Then there's access. Best practice seems to be for supervisors, not individual officers, to have access to the video; and battery life, that's a problem, too."

"It's gotta have better battery life than my GoPro. Nālani's been using it since the volcano's been acting up. One of the volcanologists took her down to Puna where the lava is pouring into the sea."

"You got new pics?"

"Do I have new pics!" Koa unlocked and handed Basa his iPhone. "The pictures of the laze rising in huge clouds along the ocean entry will blow you away." Koa used the local term for clouds of steam mixed with hydrochloric acid and tiny particles of glass created when lava mixed with seawater.

Basa watched the screen. "Wow. That's some video. Nālani should sell it to the *Star Advertiser* or one of the mainland papers. They'd pay big dollars for something like that."

"But it would violate park service regs."

"Too bad."

A half hour later, Koa and Basa pulled into the equipment yard at Jake's and found themselves surrounded by bulldozers, front-loaders, cherry pickers, and power shovels. The heavy equipment made Koa think of his childhood. As a kid, Koa had owned a hand-me-down Tonka front-loader, and later, he and his buddies had climbed all over a yellow dozer temporarily parked at a construction site down the road from his family home. One of the crew gave them a ride on the giant machine. Even now, he felt an urge to get up on one of the big bruisers and crank it up.

When they walked into the office, Sandy, the receptionist, had the paperwork waiting for them. Gommes Development Co., doing business as Hualālai Hui, had rented a Case crawler dozer along with an operator just two weeks before the surveyors began work on the KonaWili development. When Koa picked up the invoice, Sandy pointed toward her boss's door. "Jake remembers that rental."

Koa and Basa entered Jake Forrester's office, introduced themselves, and laid the invoice on his desk. Forrester, short, overweight, and graying, with a double chin below a friendly open face, barely glanced at the document before looking up at Koa. "I guess I'm not surprised to see you after that school thing."

The two officers pulled up chairs. "Why's that?" Koa asked.

"Strange business. Seemed odd at the time."

"How so?" Basa asked.

"Gommes's guy calls me up. His boss wants a dozer to cover up some garbage on this property he bought. I asked him how long he needed the rig, and he says a couple of hours. Well, I don't rent out a dozer, put it on a flatbed, and haul it twenty miles up the road for a two-hour stint. He shoulda known that. I mean, the dude's not a weekend warrior fixin' up his backyard. He's been around the development business for years."

"He said his boss wanted this. You mean Gommes?"

"Yeah, Howard Gommes. This dude, he's not some flunky. He's the big man's right-hand guy for construction."

"What's his name?"

"Ricky something or other. Name's on the invoice."

"Okay, so what happened?"

"I tell Ricky the minimum rental is five days, but I'll give him a break and make it three days, if he promises me the contract for the heavy gear when they start the real work. He says okay, and I send the flatbed up there with the dozer and Pete, one of my best operators."

"And?" Koa asked.

"The rig is back here at three o'clock the same afternoon. I asked Pete what happened. And he says he found twenty or thirty bags of garbage. Said it would have been a lot cheaper to throw them in the back of a pickup and drop them off down at the transfer station. But no, Ricky wants him to bulldoze the trash into a depression in the ground and cover it up with dirt and rocks. Pete follows orders, and Ricky tells him he can go home."

"How come you remember so much?" Basa asked.

"Well, it seemed weird at the time. I mean, the rental cost them fifteen hundred dollars for something a couple of kids with a pickup truck could have done in fifteen minutes. And Ricky stiffed me on the deal. He gave the main contract to a competitor. So, I remember alright."

Koa and Basa went to find Ricky. It wasn't hard. He'd scrawled his signature across the bottom of the dozer invoice, and Basa's quick call to the station turned up his address. He added little to what Jake described. Gommes had called him up, complained about a bunch of garbage on the property, and told him to rent a dozer and bury it. When he suggested removing it might be cheaper, Gommes insisted it be buried—"bury it deep and cover it up good." Ricky suspected Gommes had disposed of something in the trash and wanted it deep-sixed, but he was a good soldier and did as Gommes directed.

Koa and Basa drove to Kūkiʻo to see Gommes. To their surprise, the guard waved them through the exclusive community's tightly guarded gate without an identity check. At Gommes's place, he found four police cars and a police team, led by Roger Crane, one of the detectives out of the Kona police substation. Crane, a tall, handsome man with dark curly hair, was one of Koa's best detectives. Koa had a sinking feeling he'd find Gommes dead. Climbing out of his car, he asked Crane, "What's happening?"

"Gommes came home, got out of his car, and started toward the front door when somebody took a shot at him." Crane pointed to a bullet hole in the door.

"Gommes hit?" Basa asked.

"No. He says he stumbled just as the assailant fired. Damned lucky, too. Bullet went right through a solid wood door. Had to be a high-powered rifle."

"Where was the shooter?"

"Gommes says he saw a flash up there on that *puʻu*." Crane pointed to a small hill about twelve hundred yards up the mountainside. "I got some guys up there now."

Koa took in the hill and the distance, trying to picture the trajectory from the *puʻu*. He put himself behind the gun, mentally sighting through a scope, compensating for the sloping terrain, and the wind, which gusted from right to left across the line of fire, and then imagined adjusting for the distance. It was an impossibly tough shot, and he wondered if Leffler could really be that good. "You're kidding. That's a tough shot for a trained sniper with a DesertTech sniper rifle." Koa was thinking of the weapon Leffler had stolen.

"I'm guessing that's exactly what we've got—a trained sniper," Crane responded.

"Leffler," Koa muttered.

"What?"

"You must have seen the APB out on an Army sergeant named Leffler. He killed an architect in Hilo and is a suspect in Hank Boyle's death."

"Yeah, I remember. You think that's our guy?"

"Yeah. Tell your guys, he's a trained killer and as dangerous as they get."

Koa turned to examine the house—the Mercedes in the drive, the front of the building, and the door with the bullet hole three and a half feet from the bottom. He pictured Gommes getting out of the car, walking toward the house, and stumbling as the bullet zipped past him. The pieces didn't fit quite right. Turning back to Crane, Koa asked, "If Gommes was walking toward the house when he stumbled, how would he see a flash from the *puʻu* behind him?"

Crane pointed to the large glass window to the right of the front door. "Says he caught the reflection in the glass."

Koa moved toward the door and looked at the window. Sure enough, he could see the reflection of the *pu'u*. It could have gone down just as Gommes described. "Is Gommes inside?"

"Yeah, but be careful. You're not going to believe the mess inside."

"What mess?"

"Best see for yourself."

His curiosity piqued, Koa signaled to Basa and started toward the house. "Watch out for the dogs," Koa warned. "Gommes has two mean-looking Rottweilers. Calls them butcher's dogs."

Koa opened the front door and swore. Beside him, he felt Basa tense.

"Oh, God," Basa moaned.

Dante, one of the Rottweilers, lay dead on the marble foyer floor. The dog must have been up on his hindquarters, pawing the front door, when the shot caught it in the chest. Koa hadn't liked the snarling butcher's dog, but no animal deserved to die that way.

"The poor beast," Basa said, shaking his head at the Rottweiler.

They skirted the animal and found Gommes in his home office with the blinds drawn. Hunched over his desk, he wore a white silk shirt. His sport coat hung on the back of a second chair next to the desk. Gommes looked unnaturally pale even in the poor light. Not surprising, Koa thought, for a man who'd nearly been killed by a sniper. Gommes looked up as Koa entered his office. "Somebody just murdered my goddamn dog. Shot the beast through the fucking door." Virgil, Gommes's remaining Rottweiler, growled and bared his teeth. "Shut up, Virgil, you dumb mutt," Gommes screamed. The dog crawled under a table.

"Sorry about your dog, but the real question is why someone tried to kill you?" Koa said.

Gommes shrugged. "How the fuck should I know? An angry parent, maybe."

"Your school definitely created a lot of angry parents," Basa responded.

"Maybe it's because you tried to cover up the vent under the school," Koa said.

Gommes's face reddened and his mouth set hard. "That's bullshit. I already told you."

"You sent Ricky up to KonaWili with a bulldozer to cover up the fumarole." Koa held up a copy of the invoice.

Gommes stared at Koa. Their eyes locked in an exchange of hostile glares. Then Gommes looked away. "I sent him up there to bury some garbage."

"What? A handful of plastic garbage bags?"

"It was more than that," Gommes responded.

"Is that why you ordered Ricky to 'bury it deep and cover it up good'?"

Gommes shrugged again. "What difference does it make?"

Koa could hardly believe the words. It made a world of difference to those kids and their families. He was about to call Gommes on it but reversed direction. "It might explain why someone hired a trained sniper to kill you."

"That was a sniper?"

"It takes an expert shot to hit a man from twelve hundred yards, and it sounds like that bullet would have killed you if you hadn't stumbled. So, yeah, somebody hired a sniper to kill you. Want to tell me who doesn't want you to tell what really happened at KonaWili?"

"You can go now, Detective."

"If you don't level with me, the sniper is likely to try again."

Silence.

Koa thought about Leffler's hit list—Boyle, Witherspoon, Makela, Watanabe, and Koa himself—but not Gommes. If Leffler had attempted to kill Gommes—and given the difficulty of the twelve-hundred-yard shot, it had to be Leffler—then the sniper's instructions must have changed. Koa wondered why? And who gave those instructions?

He and Basa left, but Koa stopped in the doorway and turned to see Gommes cradling his head in his hands. The man knew who tried to kill him. He just wasn't going to tell.

CHAPTER THIRTY

KOA AND ALEXIA Sheppard flew to Los Angles, took a taxi to West 3rd Street and Willaman Drive, and walked up the pedestrian mall to Cedars-Sinai Medical Center. They rode the elevator to the eighth floor and entered the Johnnie L. Cochran Jr. Brain Tumor Center in the Department of Neurology, where a receptionist showed them to a conference room, offered them coffee, and informed them Dr. Kepler would join them shortly.

"Not your usual hospital waiting room routine," Alexia commented.

"God, I hope this works out," Koa responded.

Alexia frowned. "Don't get your hopes up. I told you it's a real long shot."

Dr. Kepler came in, as jaunty as ever, with a thick file under his arm. "Welcome to Cedars-Sinai. I'm Dr. Kepler." He extended his hand to Alexia. "You're Ikaika Kāne's attorney?"

"Yes. Alexia Sheppard."

"Good." Dr. Kepler sat down across the table from them. "Let me tell you what I've found, what I've concluded, and what I'd be prepared to say in a legal context. Then you can tell me what you need to package the information, assuming you think it is worthwhile going forward."

"Sounds perfect," Alexia responded, and Koa nodded his agreement.

"As a preface, let me say when I reduce this to writing, there will be a certain amount of medical jargon. I'm going to translate everything into plain English for you today."

Music to Koa's ears. "We'd appreciate that."

Kepler slid his résumé across the table. "My curriculum vitae. I won't bore you with the details. I've been recognized as an expert in more than twenty-five legal proceedings. You should have no trouble qualifying me."

Alexia glanced over the materials and looked up, satisfied with his credentials.

"Okay," Dr. Kepler began, "this breaks into five parts. First, Ikaika had two extremely slow-growing tumors located in the front part of his brain since childhood. That is established by the pathology of the tumors, his mother's recollection of absence seizures in early childhood, notes from the doctor who treated him back then, and prescriptions for Depakote, an anti-seizure medication.

"Second, neurological research, including a number of case studies, establishes that tumors located in this particular area of the brain affect behavior. In essence, when spurred to anger such a patient is unable to grasp the consequences of violating social norms and does not learn from punishment. These patterns are self-reinforcing and typically become more pronounced as the child and the tumor grow."

"It fits my brother's conduct," Koa acknowledged.

"Third, research in this area has accelerated a thousandfold because of extraordinary advances in brain imaging technology and the numerous brain-damaged patients coming from the Afghan and Iraqi wars. We now have electronic images actually showing the patterns of brain activity. In other words, historically, we only intuited the cause-and-effect relationship, while today we can see the abnormalities in electrical impulses within the brain.

"Fourth, I obtained interactive scans of Ikaika's brain, literally watching the electrical impulses at work while we subjected him to various stimuli. His tumors disrupted normal brain patterns, but with the removal of the tumors, his brain patterns are slowly returning to normal. Most importantly, his brain patterns after surgery were not consistent with the psychological profiles we would have expected based on examinations conducted during his periods of imprisonment."

"You're saying," Alexia asked, "you have scientific evidence his thinking is different today than it was in the past?"

"Essentially, that's correct."

"And the fifth point?" Koa asked.

"My expert opinion is that his brain tumors contributed substantially to Ikaika's antisocial behavior. It is also my opinion the removal of those tumors significantly reduces the risk of antisocial behavior in the future."

"That's pretty powerful stuff," Koa said. "Don't you agree, Alexia?"

"I do agree, if we could get it before the parole board."

Dr. Kepler looked quizzical. "I don't understand. I thought Ikaika was entitled to a parole hearing."

"He is, but under Hawai'i law, his right to such a hearing accrues when he has served his minimum sentence, and that won't be for another four years."

Dr. Kepler appeared crestfallen. "Isn't there some way to do it sooner?"

"Yes, but it's dicey," Alexia began. "Ikaika would have to request an earlier parole hearing, his prison counselor would have to submit a compellingly favorable report on his adjustment and conduct in prison, and an administrative board would have to approve."

"How can his prison counselor file a post-surgery report when he won't even be back in prison for several more weeks?" Koa asked.

"That's the point," Alexia emphasized. "We'd be asking the parole board to do something it normally wouldn't even consider."

Dr. Kepler wasn't ready to give up. "If I wrote a letter outlining my findings, could Ikaika submit it with his request for an earlier parole hearing?"

"Yes, and it might help."

"What else can we do?" Koa asked.

"Well," Alexia said, looking pensive, "I could talk informally to a member of the parole board and explain the special circumstances."

"And slip him a copy of my letter?" Dr. Kepler asked with a grin.

"That's a bit outside the rules." Alexia grinned back. "But I could probably do it."

"Looks like we have a plan," Koa said. He thanked Dr. Kepler, and he and Alexia headed home.

CHAPTER THIRTY-ONE

KOA HAD SERGEANT Basa pick up Drake, the Monarch bartender, and bring him to the Hilo police station. They left him sitting in an interrogation room for an hour before Koa walked in and sat down with Bane watching through a one-way mirror.

The skinny barkeep wore his work clothes, cutoff jeans, and a none-too-clean, black tee shirt. Koa wondered when he'd last washed his stringy yellowish-gray hair. His eyes had a cloudy, glazed-over look, reminding Koa, as he'd noticed once before, the man had untreated cataracts. "Hello, Drake."

"What's this 'ere about? I need to git down to the bar. It's nearly openin' time."

Koa ignored Drake's needs. He'd heard it all before. "Tell me about Leffler, the Army guy who's been coming into the Monarch."

"Don't know no Leffler, honest I don't."

That's where Drake always started. He didn't know nothing about nothing. Koa put an Army identification photograph of Leffler on the table. "This guy, tell me about him."

Drake picked up the photograph and held it a couple of inches from his face. "I seen him."

Koa knew from his past dealings that the bartender's elevator didn't stop on every floor. Talking to him required patience, a lot of patience. "Tell me about him, Drake."

"He's a guy. Comes into the bar a time or two. Drinks San Mi-guel. Had to git me a couple more cases when he started comin' in."

"What'd the two of you talk about?"

"Don't rightly remember."

"Bullshit."

"Hell, I got a lot a brahs hangin' in the bar. They talk story 'bout football, fishing, broads, music, the bitches they married, the damn tourists. Can't 'member all that shit."

"You remember talking guns with Leffler?"

Drake's eyebrows shot up. "I . . . I," he stuttered, "don't 'member talkin' no gun talk."

Tired of "don't 'member stuff," Koa signaled Bane who entered the room.

Drake had no trouble recognizing Bane. "Aw, shit."

"You remember Detective Sergeant Bane?"

"Ya're gonna hassle me, aren't ya?"

"You want to tell us about Leffler?"

Drake looked down at the table, then around the room, like he was searching for an open door. It took him several seconds to figure out he couldn't escape. "Okay, my man, okay," he said finally. "Lef-fler, he's bin in drinkin' an' talkin'. He's some kinda Army gun nut, yammerin' about Army pistols, ammo, M9s, SRS something 1s. Can't understand half that shit. It's jus' talk."

Koa and Bane exchanged looks. Leffler had stolen a DesertTech SRS A-1, almost certainly the sniper rifle he'd used to attempt to kill Gommes. "What else, Drake?"

"Shit, I can't 'member."

Time to jog this idiot's memory. Koa turned to Bane. "Play the tape."

Bane pulled a small MP3 player from his pocket and keyed the track of his conversation with Drake: "I'm looking for a dude who can sell me a piece, preferably a nine, without a legend . . . What ya want it for, my man? . . . I'm going on a cruise carrying some shit, and I need some protection, you got me? . . . You got the bread? . . . What's in it for me, my man? . . . A couple of Grants . . . Hang for a while, okay, my man?"

When Bane turned off the MP3 player, Drake sat with his mouth open gazing into space. It took him several moments to realize the recording had ended, and the two detectives were staring at him.

"Okay, okay, my man, the dude he showed me this gun, said it was an M9. Said he knowed where to git one if anybody was askin'."

"You handle this weapon, Drake?"

"Yeah, took me a look. Nevah held no gun like that 'fore."

"It didn't have a serial number, did it?"

"Ain't seen no number."

"And it said U.S. 9mm M9A1 Beretta U.S.A. on the slide, didn't it?"

"Reckon so."

"How many people looking for guns did you send to Leffler?"

Koa could see in Drake's face he didn't want to answer, but Koa had given the barkeep no choice. "A couple, I guess."

"Who?"

"I ain't no snitch."

Koa had just about reached his limit with this mental defective. "Conspiracy to sell stolen weapons is a felony, Drake."

That got Drake's attention. "The dude, he nevah said nothin' about stealin' nothin'."

Drake couldn't pick the winner in a one-horse race. "And where do you think he got a U.S. Army handgun with the serial number filed off?"

"Aw, shit. Ya gonna take me down, ain't ya?"

Under other circumstances, Koa could have felt sorry for Drake. He was dumb as a box of rocks. "I haven't decided yet. You want to tell me about Leffler's clients?"

"The Filipino dude."

"What Filipino dude?"

"Don't know 'is name. Works on one 'em freighters. Comes into the harbor sometimes."

Koa would have Bane check it out, but it didn't sound related to the KonaWili killings. "Who else, Drake?"

He pointed to Bane. "Jus' him."

Koa didn't believe Drake. "I find you been lying to me, I'll put you away. You'll be living in that contract prison in Arizona—"

Panic registered in Drake's dull eyes. "I swear it was jus' the two times."

Koa thought about what he was hearing. Maybe Drake was telling the truth and Koa was asking the wrong questions. He tried a different tact. "But Leffler met people at the bar, didn't he?"

They'd scared Drake so bad his hands shook. "Yeah, yeah, my man." Drake talked faster. "He met that slant-eyed townie. He come in all stiff, like he ain't nevah bin in a damn bar 'fore. I seen 'im once in the county building."

That sounded like Watanabe. "Anyone else?"

"Naw. Ain't got no memory."

Koa slid the Army surveillance photo of Leffler and Watanabe across to Drake. "Is this the townie?" Koa tapped Watanabe's picture.

"Yeah, that's 'im. They sat at the corner table. The townie, he wanted plum wine. Now, ya know, I ain't got none of that shit."

"You overhear them talking?"

"Naw. But they had their heads together foah a while. Talkin' some kinda serious shit."

Koa switched back to his previous line of questions. "What else did you and Leffler talk about?"

"Nothin'. Done told you all I kin 'member."

Koa pushed. "You're not thinking hard enough, Drake. What else did Leffler say?"

"Shit. Ain't got no memory."

"That's not good enough. I want to know what Leffler said, every last word. You got that?"

"Yeah, yeah. I hear ya."

"Now Detective Sergeant Bane and I are going to go outside to get a cup of coffee. While we're gone, you think, think hard about Leffler. We'll see what you remember when we get back." Koa laid a picture of a man in a jail cell on the table—a trick he'd used before. The picture helped some people focus their thinking, and Drake needed a whole lot of focusing. He and Bane got up and went out, closing the door behind them.

Outside, Bane said, "He's a dumb son of a bitch. I think you've got all you're going to get."

"Maybe," Koa responded, "but Drake's slow, and I'm not sure we've got it all yet."

They gave Drake fifteen minutes before returning to the interrogation room where they found Drake staring at the jail picture. "What else did you and Leffler talk about?"

Drake looked up from the picture. "Pig huntin'. Dude's bin shootin' 'em wild pigs."

Wild pigs, Koa thought, that's a bust, and he caught the thin I-told-you-so smile on Bane's face. Drake's intermission with the jail photograph had yielded zip. Then Koa felt a spark and turned back to look at Drake. "Where? Where'd he go wild pig hunting?"

"Mauna Kea."

Thousands of wild pigs—pests, tearing up native plants and doing environmental damage—roamed Hawai'i's forests. Hunters favored them as targets because everyone loved *kālua* pork from the *imu*. And a man on the run could feed himself on wild pig. "Where on Mauna Kea?"

"Some cabin off the jeep road on the east side. Some old dead guy, a pig hunter, he's buried up there."

Koa knew the area and the old dead guy. David Douglas, a bota-nist, not a pig hunter, had died on the mountain in 1832 under suspicious circumstances, giving the island one of its first modern murder mysteries. The island hadn't had a coroner back then, and Douglas's body had been salted to preserve it for the coroner on Oʻahu. "Off the Keanakolu Road, near the David Douglas grave?"

"Yeah, 'cept *mau ka.*"

A cabin *mau ka*, uphill, from the Keanakolu Road would offer a near-perfect hideaway for a fugitive on the run, especially one trained to survive in hostile conditions. It would probably be a bust, but Drake might just have told them where to find Sergeant Ralph Leffler. They needed to move quickly—they had a killer on the loose with a sniper rifle.

CHAPTER THIRTY-TWO

KOA AND LIEUTENANT Zeigler brainstormed ways to see if Leffler had hidden on the eastern slope of Mauna Kea. They considered airborne surveillance but concluded they'd be unlikely to identify Leffler from the air. "The only sure way is to go in boots-on-the-ground and stake out the place," Koa argued.

"The theft of military weapons is a federal crime. You want me to bring in the Bureau?"

Koa wasn't buying that option. He wanted Leffler on state murder charges and wasn't about to let the feds haul him off on gun-theft charges. "No. I want him for the Witherspoon killing, and I want him alive."

"I could send in a couple of experienced scouts," Zeigler suggested.

"Leffler will be on the lookout. You got men who could get in and out without being spotted?"

Zeigler didn't hesitate. "There's a pair of scout instructors here who could shave Leffler's butt, and he wouldn't know it."

"Can they get me close to Leffler?"

Zeigler looked skeptical. "You want to go in yourself?"

"Yeah. Leffler banged up one of my guys and tried to take me out. So, it's personal. I want the SOB, and I want him alive."

"You don't want much, do you?"

"You going to bitch or help?" Koa shot back.

"Okay. I'll set up a meet with my scouts."

"I'll be bringing Dr. Corwin with me."

"Who's Corwin?"

"He's a doctor, an expert who may be able to help us bring Leffler in alive. I'll explain when we meet."

Five of them, Koa, Zeigler, two scouts—Sergeant Rich Olson and Sergeant Newel Boggs—and Dr. Corwin met in a Quonset hut at the Pōhakuloa Training Area. Koa sized up the two scouts. Both men were in top physical shape and had the hard, watchful eyes of soldiers who'd lived close to danger for long periods of time. Olson, thirty-eight years old and a grizzled veteran of three tours in Iraq and two in Afghanistan, hailed from Alabama and spoke with a distinct southern accent. Boggs, younger than Olson, was black with curly black hair and a startling intensity. He, too, had been on his share of clandestine ops.

After introductions, Zeigler led them to a large-scale map of the eastern slope of Mauna Kea and handed out pictures of Sergeant Ralph Leffler.

"We have a lead putting Leffler somewhere in this area." Koa drew a circle with his finger around an area about 7500 feet above sea level between the Hakalau National Forest and the summit of Mauna Kea. "He could be in a cabin here." Koa tapped the map.

"How do y'all get in there?" Olson asked.

"The only civilized access is along Keanakolu Road here." Koa traced the road with his finger. "It's passable in a four-wheel-drive vehicle if it's not raining, but it's a bitch in the mud. Leffler, if he's up there, will be watching the road."

"You want to go in another way?" Boggs guessed.

"Yeah, from the summit. It's wild, volcanic country with only a few trails, but Leffler won't be expecting visitors from higher elevations."

Olson grinned. "Just my kind of Sunday walk in the park."

Boggs turned practical. "We'll be above the tree line 'til we get down to somewhere around 9,000 feet."

"Then we move," Olson suggested, "in the late afternoon and evening when the sun's setting in the west and the eastern slope is in deep shadow."

"Right." Zeigler spread a series of high-resolution satellite photos on the table. "We drop you here—" he pointed to a trailhead on the east side of the Mauna Kea summit—"and you work your way down the slope along this route." He traced a red line on the photo.

He pulled out another satellite photo—this one taken early in the morning when the sun was low in the eastern sky. "See the shadows. We chose this route because most of it won't be visible from Leffler's probable position. I've marked GPS waypoints."

"Fuckin' A," Boggs responded.

Olson moved to the next topic. "And if we find this dude?"

Koa had planned this part. "You get me into position where I can take a shot."

"You gonna take him out? No warning?"

"Yes and no. That's where Dr. Corwin comes in." Koa motioned to the doctor who'd been standing at the back of the group. Compared to the others, Corwin looked like a teenager—young enough to be Sergeant Olson's son. Koa patted Corwin on the shoulder. "Dr. Corwin is an anesthesiologist and a bit older than he looks."

Corwin placed a long black gun case on the table, unfastened the latches, and opened the lid. An odd-shaped gun with a long barrel extending back over the stock lay nestled in the case.

"What's that, Doc, a blowgun?" Boggs asked.

"Good guess," Corwin responded. "It's a CO_2-powered dart gun. It shoots chemical darts."

"A tranquilizer gun," Olson said, "but they don't work on humans."

"You're partly right," Corwin responded. "Neither the police nor the military use them on humans because you need to know the weight and muscle mass of the target in order to set the dosage. That's not practical in most situations, but I've reviewed Leffler's medical records and calculated the dosage."

"Don't those chemical things take time to work, especially in a man?"

"Some do, but others are fast-acting. You hit Leffler with one of these darts"—Corwin pointed to a package of darts at one end of the case—"and he'll be down in less than five seconds."

"What's the range of that thing?"

"In the hands of a marksman, it'll hit a four-inch circle at 150 yards 95 percent of the time."

Boggs was still doubtful. "Where do you aim?"

"Buttocks first, upper thighs second, biceps third. Not the head, neck, chest, or extremities. But you don't get a second shot. Takes too long to reload."

"Okay, Doc," Olson began, "are you the shooter?"

"No, I am," Koa responded.

Olson's thick black eyebrows shot up almost touching across his forehead. "You? Are you a shooter? You ever use a tranquilizer gun?"

"Did my time in Army Special Forces. Qualified expert on twenty different weapons," Koa responded. "With a little practice, I can handle Dr. Corwin's dart gun." Koa pointed to the cartridges in the gun case. "That's why we have a couple of hundred practice darts."

"And what if he spots us or you miss or he doesn't go down? I mean, you got a highly trained dude with a sniper rifle, M16 assault weapons, and God only knows how many handguns," Boggs said.

Based on his own military service, Koa guessed that Boggs wanted a shot at Leffler whom he almost certainly regarded as a disgrace to the armed forces. "I know who he is and how he's armed, and I want to take him alive."

"But just in case there's a problem," Zeigler interrupted, "you've got weapons release. We're not sending you on a suicide mission, but your orders are to get Koa into position, and let him take his shot. We want Leffler alive, if possible."

"What about backup?" Olson asked.

"Sergeant Basa will bring one team in from the Waimea side, and hold here on the Keanakolu Road"—Koa tapped the map—"just north of the active zone. Detective Sergeant Bane will lead a team from the Saddle Road and hold south of the active zone." Koa again marked the spot on the map. "They'll be in civilian clothes on ATVs. Although the forest service tries to discourage it, there's a lot of ATV activity in the area. They're unlikely to spook Leffler."

Boggs looked at Olson who nodded. "When do we jump off?"

"The three of you move out at five o'clock this afternoon and you jump off from the trailhead atop the mountain at six. You should have three hours before it gets too dark to move. If you're moving again at first light, you should be in the target area a little after dawn."

Olson turned to Koa. "Want to head out to the range?"

"You bet."

Koa practiced all afternoon until he had the feel of the tranquilizer gun and could put a dart inside a four-inch ring nineteen times out of twenty at 150 yards.

At 5:50 p.m., a military truck dropped Koa, Olson, and Boggs at the trailhead near the telescopes atop Mauna Kea. For Koa, it was familiar terrain. One of his first big murder cases had ended atop Mauna Kea. All were dressed in boots and civilian hiking gear with packs and weapons. Koa carried Dr. Corwin's dart gun in addition to his Glock. At 6:00, they began making their way down the mountain. Heavy mist blew in at the higher elevations so they didn't have to worry about being spotted and made excellent time down the gulches and ravines radiating from the summit of the 14,000-foot extinct volcano. At 9:15, they encamped for the night.

Koa's teams were in place before dawn broke over the ocean to the east. One group, led by Sergeant Basa, traversed the Mana Road from Waimea around the north side of the mountain to the Keanakolu Road. The other, under the command of Detective Sergeant Bane, picked up Lieutenant Zeigler and Dr. Corwin before driving in from the Saddle Road on the south side of Mauna Kea.

At 6:30 a.m., Koa, Olson, and Boggs were about two thousand yards from the cabin. They caught the faint smell of wood smoke in the air, and Koa's adrenalin ramped up. Someone occupied the cabin or camped nearby. Good chance it was Leffler. Olson broke off to circle around the cabin and approach from the back. Koa and Boggs moved cautiously, avoiding noise or abrupt movements, until just past 9:00 a.m. when they had eyes on the cabin. The smell of wood smoke had disappeared. They saw no one, and Koa's miniaturized infrared detector revealed no sign of life within the cabin.

A small, freshly chopped stack of wood outside the door suggested a recent visitor, who planned to return. They spent another hour getting into position, Koa in the forest about 75 yards from a stump used to chop wood and Boggs slightly uphill. Olson reported from his concealed position 150 yards behind the cabin. Then everyone waited—an hour, two hours, three hours.

Koa heard a rifle shot off to the northwest and estimated the distance at four thousand yards. Koa told everyone to hold position and wait. If Leffler was in the area, they might ultimately have to track him down, but it would be much easier to wait for him to return to the cabin.

At 1:15 p.m., Olson reported movement in the trees to the northwest of the cabin. Then Koa's infrared scanner detected a man-shaped heat source in the forest. It remained still for nearly ten minutes. Koa grew hopeful. Leffler would be cautious, whereas an ordinary hunter would have no reason to check out the cabin before approaching.

Olson then reported the man had retreated into the forest, and Koa's optimism faded. If it was Leffler, he'd seen something to arouse his suspicions. After another four minutes, the heat source reappeared. The man had stopped, reversed course, and headed back toward the cabin. Next, Olson had eyes on the man. It was Leffler. Then Koa saw Leffler emerge from the woods with a hunting rifle in one hand and a wild pig slung over his shoulder. He approached the cabin warily. Placing the pig on a tree stump, Leffler turned back to the cabin and went inside.

Koa instructed Basa and Bane to move their forces along the Keanakolu Road toward the cabin, and then adjusted his own position for the best shot toward the stump where the pig lay waiting to be butchered. Minutes ticked away. If Leffler came out of the cabin to butcher the wild pig, Koa would have a clean shot from fifty yards—well within the range of the dart gun.

"Something's going on," Boggs whispered over the radio. "Leffler's moving from one window to the other. He's checking. Something's made him nervous."

Shit. Koa couldn't believe they'd gotten this close only to blow it.

Leffler came out of the cabin with his rifle in hand. He moved into the forest toward Boggs. Koa tensed, figuring Boggs had blown his cover, but two small trees deprived Koa of a shot with the tranquilizer gun. Then Koa realized that Leffler wasn't looking at Boggs, but at something else in the forest.

Suddenly, Leffler raised his rifle to his shoulder and fired. Koa heard a grunt deep in the trees, and Leffler moved in that direction, about fifteen degrees west of Boggs's position. Five minutes elapsed before Leffler came out of the forest and headed back toward the cabin carrying a dead goat. Leffler put the goat next to the stump and again retreated to the cabin.

Basa reported being in position. Bane followed two minutes later.

They waited.

Leffler came out of the cabin carrying a large knife along with an M16 and headed toward the pig on the stump.

Boggs's voice sounded in Koa's earpiece. "I've got him in my gun sights if you don't take him down with Corwin's toy rifle."

Koa waited as Leffler parked his M16 against the stump and began to butcher the pig. At first, Koa had only a profile view, but as Leffler hacked away at the pig, he moved slowly around the stump, exposing his back. Leffler turned . . . turned . . . and swore. Maybe he'd cut himself. Koa had him in three-quarter profile, offering a decent, but not perfect, opportunity. Koa had only one shot. He had to make it count, so he held his breath and waited.

After half a minute, Leffler changed position, and Koa finally had the shot he wanted. With the rifle braced against his shoulder and his cheek against the stock, he sighted, let out half a breath, and slowly squeezed the trigger. The gun hissed. Leffler jumped as the dart hit his left buttock. A perfect strike. He lunged for his M16. His hand touched the weapon just before he sank to his knees. Then he was on the ground. Both Koa and Boggs rushed him with handguns drawn, but they needn't have bothered. Leffler was out cold. Koa checked his pulse. Slow and regular. Corwin had calculated the right dose. Koa handcuffed the rogue soldier.

"Show's over. Leffler's in custody outside the cabin," Koa reported over the radio net. Both Basa and Bane pulled up to the cabin a few minutes later. Koa sent them to inventory Leffler's stuff. They came out with a dozen pistols, several M-16 rifles, and a single Desert-Tech, SRS A-1 sniper rifle, along with several boxes of ammunition.

"That it?" Koa asked.

"Yeah," Basa responded. "Looks like we've recovered nearly everything the bastard stole from Pōhakuloa."

Dr. Corwin extracted the dart from the center of Leffler's left buttock, checked his vitals, and gave him an antidote for the knock-out drug.

"Too bad the Army ain't offering an expert badge for blowgun shooters." Olson grinned. "I'm sure you could use another shiny medal."

"I'm just sorry," Koa said turning to Corwin, "your darts don't contain truth serum. I'd love to get the truth from this bastard."

Corwin spread his arms in a helpless gesture. "Can't help you there. You'll have to talk to the CIA's medics, and from all their talk about torture, I'd guess their truth serum doesn't work too well."

CHAPTER THIRTY-THREE

KOA AND ALEXIA Sheppard shared plates of dim sum at the Chinese hole-in-the-wall in the 1920s strip that housed her law office. They ate shrimp, pork, and vegetable dumplings made the traditional way with sweet, sticky rice flour and salty fillings, Chinese barbecued pork, and buns filled with sweet bean paste. They finished, licked their fingers, and drank steaming cups of green tea before Koa turned to the business at hand. "So where do we stand?"

"There's going to be an administrative hearing at Hilo courthouse next week. I submitted Ikaika's request for a revision of his minimum sentence and attached Dr. Kepler's letter."

"Kepler's letter's great, isn't it?" Koa said. "Everything he promised and more."

"You're right. It's even better than the way he laid it out when we met in LA, and what he told us was powerful."

"Were you able to talk to any of the parole board members?"

She nodded. "In Honolulu, I dropped in on Benny Koi. He's a parole commissioner and an old friend. I refreshed him on Ikaika's story, gave him a copy of the letter, and told him what we were trying to do."

Koa leaned forward. "His reaction?"

She took a sip of her tea. "I've known Benny for a long time. He was pretty skeptical but promised to read Dr. Kepler's letter."

"What are our chances? And don't sugarcoat it."

"Not good. I'd give it one in ten of working. Better if we try again in a year. Ikaika's record cuts against him, and he hasn't served long enough. Not at all since his surgery."

"That bad, huh?"

"I'd give it even less of a chance if the governor and the legislature weren't trying to cut costs. The governor's experiment in closing Kūlani prison and moving prisoners to Arizona failed to save money. Instead, it's costing the state a fortune, and there's a lot of flak from families about having their jailed spouses and children far away. I hear they're planning to reopen Kūlani."

Koa hadn't heard that. "Really."

"The fact they're serious about cutting the prison population gives us a glimmer of hope. Still, it would take a leap of faith for the board to give Ikaika a parole hearing this early."

"Is there anything more we can do, Alexia?"

She gave him a mischievous grin. "I also stopped in to see our state senator Tommy Orfo. He used to be a buddy of my dad's, and he's a leading advocate of reducing the prison population and re-opening Kūlani. He might give another of the parole board members a call. Could help if it happens."

Koa wasn't happy about the prospects, but he understood the dif-ficulties and appreciated Alexia's efforts. "Thanks for everything you've done."

"Keep your fingers crossed, Koa. We'll know next week."

* * *

They took no chances with Leffler. He sat across the table from Koa, his legs in irons, and his hands chained to a bolt in the center of the table. An armed guard stood just outside the door.

Koa read him his Miranda rights two times and put them before Leffler in written form. The man hadn't asked for an attorney and had said nothing other than to ask for water.

Koa laid a cell phone on the table. They'd searched the cabin and Leffler's personal effects, finding nothing of interest except the guns and his cellphone, a prepaid model from Walmart. The phone's log showed calls to and from only one number—a number belonging to another prepaid cellphone. Koa had no way of knowing who carried the second cellphone. "This yours?"

"What if it is?" The scar across Leffler's right cheek, even uglier in person than in his photograph, moved when he talked.

"Who'd you call?"

"I ain't no rotten snitch."

"You're going down for the Witherspoon murder. You could help yourself by telling us who hired you."

"I said I ain't no snitch."

Koa tried another tact. "Where'd you get forty thousand dollars in new bills?"

Koa detected a quick flicker in Leffler's eyes. The man hadn't known they'd raided his girlfriend's apartment and opened the safe in her closet, but the knowledge didn't shake him.

Koa was considering his next move when the door opened and a policeman handed him a note. It read, "The mayor is on the phone."

Puzzled, Koa left the interrogation room to take the call. He wondered why the mayor was calling and doubted it'd be good news. After a moment, an assistant put Tanaka on the line.

"Detective Kāne?"

"Yes, Mayor."

"Congratulations, Detective. I hear you caught Witherspoon's killer, and the guy responsible for Boyle's death."

"Yes, sir. We have Leffler in custody."

"What's he saying?"

Why was the mayor taking such an active interest? "Nothing yet, sir. And I doubt he's going to talk, at least not until he's closer to looking at multiple life sentences."

"Well, it doesn't matter, Detective. You've solved the case. Damn fine detective work."

Koa felt a cold shiver run through him. The case wouldn't be solved until he learned who hired Leffler.

"It's an important step, Mayor, but we still don't know who hired Leffler or why."

"You've got your man, Detective. That's what counts. It'll satisfy this media clamor."

Suddenly, Koa understood. The mayor was shutting down the investigation. He didn't care who hired Leffler nor did he seem to care about the KonaWili part of the investigation. Then he remembered Watanabe's suggestion—he'd wanted to drop the KonaWili investigation and have the police "treat the Boyle thing as a separate matter." Koa thought the mayor had rejected the idea, but he'd been wrong.

"But, Mayor—" Koa started to protest, but the mayor cut him off.

"Damn fine detective work," the mayor repeated, "just the kind of action we needed to put a damper on bad publicity. I assume you'll be making a press announcement this afternoon or first thing in the morning."

Koa made one more try. "Mayor—"

But the telephone went dead in his hand. He had his marching orders.

The call shocked him. He hadn't expected the mayor to order an end to the investigation. Koa could think of only two reasons. Maybe the mayor himself was somehow involved—perhaps as an undisclosed investor in the KonaWili project. Or maybe he was trying to protect someone like Cheryl Makela.

Whatever the reason, Koa wasn't about to close the book on the case. He'd quit before he surrendered his integrity to a politician. But he'd have to be careful, and he'd have to talk to Zeke. They could get some cover and maybe buy a little time by putting out a press release announcing the arrest of Army Sergeant Leffler for the murder of Arthur Witherspoon.

CHAPTER THIRTY-FOUR

KOA WRACKED HIS brain. Five wealthy, successful people—Gommes, Makela, Boyle, Witherspoon, and Naʻauao—conspired to put elementary school kids at risk. Why? Koa had seen dozens of cases where money corrupted people, propelling them to awful deeds. He could see Gommes, and maybe Makela, doing almost anything for a buck, but the other three, that was hard to figure.

Koa could imagine Gommes hiring Leffler to cover up his crimes, but Leffler had tried to kill Gommes, nailing Dante, his Rottweiler, in the process. If Gommes hadn't hired Leffler, that left the others. Koa had a hard time believing either Makela or Naʻauao hired the rogue soldier. Koa had accused Watanabe of paying Leffler, but he didn't really believe Watanabe had the stomach for killing, and his name on Leffler's kill list made it unlikely. Too bad Leffler wasn't talking.

Koa found himself stumped, but he'd been there before and knew what he had to do. Go back to the beginning. Something besides KonaWili linked the five key players, six if he included Watanabe, and he had to find that thing. He called Piki and explained what he wanted. The young detective appeared an hour later, carrying a thick stack of internet printouts—every bio, news story, Facebook page, Instagram pic, LinkedIn reference, and website he'd been able to find about the six actors.

Together they separated the data into piles, one for each suspect, and began to construct a chart. Piki would have used a computer spreadsheet program, but Koa trusted the old-fashioned legal pads he'd taken from Zeke's office. Six columns with names across the top and various personal characteristics in rows down the page—birthplace, age, high school, college, profession, military service, political party, job history, etcetera.

They labored through the afternoon, but the chart led nowhere, yielding fewer similarities than Koa had hoped. Gommes, Boyle, Witherspoon, and Naʻauao were all about the same age—sixty-four, give or take a year—but Makela was seventy. Gommes, Boyle, and Naʻauao had graduated from UH in 1975, while Makela had finished up at UH earlier than the others before going on to earn her law degree there in 1975. Witherspoon had been an architecture student at the University of California at Berkeley, but strangely Piki could find no reference to his undergraduate education. As for Watanabe, he was only fifty-nine and hadn't gone to college. Only Boyle had been in the military. Boyle, Makela, and Naʻauao were Democrats, Gommes had switched parties twice, and Watanabe was an Independent. All except Naʻauao and Watanabe had worked in hotel and subdivision development. Koa stared at the pages, but no connection jumped out.

A little after six in the evening, Basa stuck his head into Koa's office. "You guys wanna join me for a beer?"

Frustrated with their lack of progress and needing a break, Koa agreed, and the three of them headed for the Hilo Burger Joint. Piki had a thing for Robyn, a hot young *haole* waitress, and the two of them bantered as they ordered. She brought bottles of Black Sand Porter and Bikini Blonde Ale for the cops and wiggled her ass for Piki when she retreated to the bar, making Basa chuckle. "That broad's got the hots for you."

"I wish. So far, it's all tease," Piki responded.

They clanked bottles together before Piki said, "I hear Leffler took out Gommes's dog."

Basa groaned. "Terrible to kill an animal like that. Bad as some murder scenes."

"You got pics on that fancy new body cam?"

"Not on the cam, but on my phone."

"Can I see?" Piki asked.

"The pictures aren't as pretty as your girlfriend," Basa teased, digging out his phone.

"Gimme a break," Piki responded.

Basa loaded the video and passed his phone to Piki. Both Koa and Basa saw a disgusted look cross Piki's face when the video showed poor Dante, the Rottweiler.

"Jesus," Piki exclaimed, "that's nasty." Still, he seemed fascinated, playing the video twice more. "Leffler's got to be a friggin' wizard to make that kind of a shot. I mean that's way more than a thousand yards."

Piki's comment reminded Koa of his own surprise that Leffler had come so close to killing Gommes. "Let me have a look at that video."

Piki handed the phone to Koa who started the video and watched the first few seconds before stopping. The camera's perspective gave Koa the feeling he'd been at an entirely different crime scene. At the time, he'd been focused on the window where Gommes had seen the reflection. "The camera gives me a wholly different feel than I got from being there."

"Yeah," Basa responded, "everyone in the evaluation group's been surprised by the point of view. The camera gives you a wide-angle, but it's not like being on the actual scene. And you get little sense of the distractions we face."

"Makes you wonder what some defense lawyer will make of body cam video when a case comes to trial," Koa mused.

"Your buddy Zeke, he's on the committee and he's worried about how the cams will affect trials. No doubt they'll help the department with training and reducing bad practices, but cameras don't always tell the truth."

Koa restarted the video at the point where he'd opened the front door to confront the carcass of the dog. After opening the door, he thought he'd moved quickly past the foyer, but in the video, the scene seemed frozen. Five, ten, fifteen, twenty seconds. He couldn't believe he'd stared at the slain animal for that long.

Then Basa's video showed Koa's back as he moved down the hallway into Gommes's office. Once in Gommes's study, Koa's attention had been fixed on Gommes, but the video captured a roomful of details—a credenza on the far side that Koa had never noticed, a colorful Persian carpet he barely recognized, and Gommes's sport coat hanging on the back of the chair next to his desk, the remaining Rottweiler's bared teeth, and other details.

When Basa moved deeper into the room, the video view shifted, now focusing on the meeting with Gommes. Koa watched his exchange with the wealthy developer, picking up a curl of the lip and the rapid blinking of Gommes's eyes that he'd missed during the actual questioning. He became fascinated with the differences between the pictures and his recollection, replaying the video four more times, cataloging the details he'd missed in confronting Gommes.

On his fourth pass through the video, a tiny detail caught his eye. He paused the playback and spread his fingers across the screen to enlarge the picture of Gommes's sport jacket. What had been a flicker of reflected light resolved itself into a gold lapel pin. Enlarging it still further, Koa saw a triangle, a skull with crossbones, and three white pearls atop a banner inscribed with the letters "TKE."

Gommes had been a TKE frat boy at UH. Koa remembered the TKE certificate and fraternity pictures he'd seen in Boyle's upstairs

hallway. And according to Boyle's friend Forret, something terrible—
"something a hell of a lot worse than acid, much darker and more
dangerous"—had happened to Boyle during his senior year as a
TKE member. Koa suddenly wondered about Witherspoon. He'd
gone to college somewhere, and Koa had a hunch where.

"C'mon," he said to Piki, "we're going back to the office."

"Tonight?" the young detective asked.

"You afraid of the dark? Or maybe you were gonna ask Robyn
out?" Koa responded.

From the look on Piki's face, Koa realized he'd guessed right. "Her
shift doesn't end for a while. You can come back later."

At police headquarters, Koa sent Piki back to the internet, while
he called Sally Medea, Witherspoon's partner and mistress. She answered on the second ring. Koa identified himself and came directly
to the point. "Where did Arthur Witherspoon attend college?"

"UH, Mānoa. Why do you ask?"

"It's not on his website, his Facebook page, or his LinkedIn profile."

She made a sound like a sigh. "Arthur never talked about his time
at UH. If anyone asked about his education, he talked about his
days in Berkeley."

"Why? What happened to him at UH?"

"I don't know. I asked him once, and he just said he didn't much
care for UH."

"Was he in a fraternity there?"

"What's this about?"

He didn't have an answer, so he said, "I'm just collecting information right now."

"I don't know anything about a fraternity. Like I said, he never
talked about UH."

"Thanks." He hung up and dialed Sarah Witherspoon's number.
She answered and informed him that she'd met her husband at a

fraternity party at UH—a Tau Kappa Epsilon party. Koa wanted more. "Did anything unusual happen to him at UH?"

"Like what?" she asked.

"A dispute, a fight, anything out of the ordinary?"

"I wouldn't know. He never talked about his days at UH."

"Why?"

"I wouldn't know."

Gommes, Makela, Boyle, Witherspoon, and Naʻauao had all been at UH at the same time, although Makela had been in law school, not college. Gommes, Boyle, and Witherspoon had been TKE fraternity brothers. Something bad had happened to Boyle, and Witherspoon had hidden his connection to UH. Koa's intuition told him to follow up on the TKE connection.

He called Piki into his office. "You've just won an all-expense-paid trip to Honolulu."

"Huh?"

"Go to the big city, dig around the 1975 newspaper morgues, check out the old-timers at UH, maybe one of the guys in security. Find out everything you can about this TKE connection involving Gommes, Boyle, and Witherspoon. And while you're at it, keep an eye out for any contact between them and Makela, who was in law school at the time."

"You want me to go tonight?"

"Yeah. You've got two hours before the last flight, and then you can get an early start in the morning. Robyn'll still be working the burger joint when you get back."

"You really know how to hurt a guy, don't you?" Piki said as he headed out.

Suddenly, another connection hit Koa like hardened cement. He loaded Facebook on his computer and checked. He could hardly believe his eyes. Mayor Tanaka, UH class of 1975, had been a member of the TKE fraternity. Right there in his campaign biography, big as life. In a flash, Koa understood the jurisdictional tug of war between Tanaka and Governor Māhoe over control of the investigation. Makela wasn't the only one the mayor was protecting. Koa had never imagined he'd be in such a jam, investigating the man who'd appointed him to conduct the inquiry and who'd just ordered him to end it.

CHAPTER THIRTY-FIVE

AT THREE THE next afternoon, Koa's cell phone rang, and the screen flashed Piki's name. Maybe he'd found out something about the TKE boys. "What's up?" Koa answered.

"I think I'm on to something, boss." Par for the course, Piki sounded excited.

Koa didn't like guessing games. "Don't make me guess."

"I started poking around the UH security department. There're mostly new guys, too young to remember the 1970s."

Piki relished describing his exploits step by step, and Koa could never be sure where things would end up. It made him impatient, and he made a come-on gesture with his fingers, even though he knew Piki couldn't see it.

"One of them put me on to an old-timer, guy named Hicky, who remembered a scandal back in the mid-'70s involving frat boys and some coed who committed suicide."

"Which fraternity?" Koa asked.

"Hicky wasn't sure but remembered a police investigation and a lot of concern by university bigwigs. One of the kids came from a family of big-time donors to the university."

"One of our development types?" Koa asked.

"Yeah. One Howard Gommes."

Koa whistled. "What else did you get from this Hicky guy?"

"Not much, but he remembered press coverage."

"You follow up?"

"Yeah, boss. I started with the university records, but I didn't find anything. After that, I hit the newspaper archives at the old *Star Bulletin*. I've been going through microfilm archives. It's slow as shit, but I found an article. The headline reads: 'Coroner Rules Student Death Suicide.'"

Koa didn't see the connection. "Is that all?"

"Bear with me, boss. The text doesn't add much to the headline, except for the name of the deceased, a coed named Kinnon." Piki paused. "Then I found another related news story. According to the second story—headlined 'Police Question UH Fraternity Boys in Woman's Death'—the police investigated the suspicious death of a pregnant coed. Unnamed sources reported the woman partied with the college fraternity crowd. She hanged herself after some kind of sex party. Police questioned several TKE fraternity brothers."

"What were their names?"

"The story doesn't say, but based on what Hicky said, I'm betting on Howard Gommes."

Koa turned it over in his mind. A coed's death ruled a suicide. Sort of like Hank Boyle's death. "Did you check the police file?"

"Funny thing. The police can't find the file. It shows up on the log of files transferred to the county records center, but no file."

"Shit." Old police files disappeared all the time, but the disappearance of this one might not be a coincidence. Koa thought for a moment. "What about the investigating officers? You check with them?"

"It was forty years ago, boss. They're all retired."

"You get names?"

"Yeah. The lead guy, a cop named Konane Kahaka, is quoted giving no comment in the second news article. He retired six years ago."

"You find him?"

"I got a phone number, but there's no answer."

Koa didn't believe in roadblocks. "You check out his address?"

"No. Not yet, and I'm going to have to stay over again if you want me to try running him down."

"What, you got a hot date in the big city?"

"I wish."

"I'll approve the expenses, just find this old cop. See if he remembers anything."

CHAPTER THIRTY-SIX

"YOU'VE GOT TO come to Honolulu." Piki spoke rapidly, and Koa's cell crackled with the young detective's excitement.

"What did you find?"

"Just get on a plane. You're not going to believe it."

"What is it?" Koa demanded.

"It's complicated. I can't do justice on the phone. You really need to be here."

Koa thought about ordering Piki back to the island but thought better of it. Even in his most uber-excited state, Piki wouldn't insist Koa come to Oʻahu unless he'd nailed something big. So, Koa flew to Honolulu, rented a car, and drove out to the address Piki had given him in Hawaiʻi Kai, east of Diamond Head.

He parked in front of a modest house in a working-class neighborhood. Someone had trimmed the yard and cut the grass, but the place needed a coat of paint. As he went up the walk, an older man—one Koa immediately pegged as a cop, or more likely a retired cop—opened the screen door.

"You must be Koa Kāne. I'm Konane Kahaka."

Konane, in his late sixties, had the olive-brown complexion and near-perfect white teeth of a pure-blooded Hawaiian. His hair, receding a bit, was still black and his eyes seemed to register every

detail, almost like a video camera. Konane might be too old to be
active, but Koa could see the former detective scanning him with
the alert eyes of an experienced cop. Now a retired detective, he'd
investigated the UH coed's suicide in the 1970s. They shook hands,
exchanging nods of mutual respect.

"Your young colleague's inside." He led Koa into the dining room
where Piki sat at a rickety round table. The room had a neat, but
shabby, quality. Koa guessed Konane lived alone. The place had the
retired-detective-living-alone quality Koa had seen when visiting
other men who had devoted their lives to routing out crooks, murderers, and rapists. "Have a seat."

Koa slid into a chair across the table from Piki.

"Want some coffee?" Konane asked.

Koa wanted a cup of java, but he also needed a moment alone
with Piki. "That would be great."

While Konane went into the kitchen, Koa turned to Piki. "What's
this all about?"

"Let him tell you. It's better that way."

Konane came back into the dining room with an old percolator,
dented from many years of service, and three ceramic mugs. He
poured each of them a cup of coffee. He obviously drank it black
because he offered them neither cream nor sugar.

"You investigated a coed's death in the '70s?" Koa asked to get the
conversation started.

"You know, there are some cases, they stay with you for years and
years. They come back to you at the strangest times, like long-lost
friends. You turn the evidence over and over in your head. You think
about them when you can't sleep and wonder what you missed.
Those cases drive you nuts."

Koa nodded. He had been haunted by cases and knew the truth
in Konane's words. "And this coed's death haunted your dreams?"

"Yeah." Konane scratched his chin. "MJK still haunts my dreams."

"Tell me about it."

Konane's eyes took on a faraway look, like he might be back at the crime scene. "She was in her bedroom hanging by an electrical cord from a light fixture, naked as the day she was born. From day one, the coroner thought she'd hung herself and ultimately ruled it suicide."

"But you didn't think so."

"No, it wasn't a suicide, not in my book, but I couldn't prove it, and the university wanted the case closed. Wanted it closed real bad, like somebody with serious juice was on their case. The coroner, well, we had a political hack back in those days."

Koa understood. Anyone who'd dealt with Shizuo Hori, Hawai'i County's miserable excuse for a coroner, understood an incompetent medical lightweight. "Tell me why it wasn't suicide?"

"She supposedly did it right after having sex. There were multiple semen stains on the sheets. Had to have been from more than one guy. We didn't have DNA back in those days."

Koa knew of cases where young women killed themselves after being raped. "Was she raped?"

Konane shook his head. "Not likely. According to her girlfriends, she was a wild one, dancing naked at parties, sleeping around, mini-orgies, into kinky sex. You could have opened a porn shop with the leather goods and sex toys we found in her apartment."

"What made you suspicious?"

"The crime scene." Konane scratched his chin again, making Koa wonder if he had a rash. "Let me show you something." Konane left the room and came back a minute later with a thick folder. Koa guessed he'd "borrowed" the police file when he left the force. That would explain why the police couldn't find it. Konane thumbed through the file, found the set of photographs, and handed them to Koa.

The first wide-angle shot showed a bedroom. Six small conical evidence markers sat on the ruffled, unmade king-size bed. Just to the right of the bed, a blond woman dangled naked on an electrical cord attached to a light fixture on the ceiling. The next series of pictures depicted stains next to the evidence markers on the sheet. Other shots showed a red vibrator on the bed, a negligée, and panties discarded on the floor. The last few pictures documented the position of the body relative to the bed. MJK's feet hung just below the level of the mattress no more than six inches from the edge of the bed.

"She supposedly stood on the bed, put the noose around her neck, and stepped off," Konane said with a touch of sarcasm.

Koa understood immediately. The human instinct for survival is so strong most suicide victims try to save themselves. "She could have stepped back on the bed and saved herself."

"Yep," Konane agreed.

"And look at this." He slid another picture across the table. It showed the electrical cord tied in four square knots to the frame of the light fixture. "She wasn't tall enough to reach the light fixture even from the bed, and there was nothing else in the apartment to stand on."

"You think she was dead before somebody strung her up?"

Another chin scratch. "Are you familiar with asphyxiophilia?"

"You mean autoerotic asphyxiation, where people cut off their own air supply to enhance sexual pleasure?"

"Yes and no. Autoerotic asphyxiation presupposes you're doing it to yourself. Some estimates back then suggested a thousand deaths a year, but autoerotic asphyxiation rarely killed women. No, I'm talking about a kind of sex play where one partner partially strangles the other for their mutual gratification."

"Okay."

"It's my theory that MJK and one or more of her partners were playing the erotic asphyxiation game, and got carried away. One of them choked her to death, probably while he was ejaculating. We found a ton of semen in her vagina. He and his buddies got scared and made it look like suicide. Even a good ME will tell you it's hard to distinguish erotic asphyxiation from suicide. And we didn't have a good ME. We had a hack."

Koa felt a tingle of excitement as he realized where Konane might be going. "You have evidence to support your theory?"

"Yep. Several things. First, I got conflicting statements. I know it ain't conclusive, but hear me out. First, this girl comes forward—volunteers, no less—that MJK suffered from depression. Suicidal, said she was going to kill herself. It was too slick. I mean, who volunteers that shit. Made me suspicious, so I—"

"This volunteer have a name?" Koa interrupted.

"Yeah, Frannie Kapule."

The name meant nothing to Koa. "Go on," Koa encouraged the old cop.

"Like I said, Frannie Kapule's testimony seemed too pat, like someone put her up to it, so I started checking around with other university women, and they told a different story. Said MJK was a real playgirl. What in my day we called a slut, but happy-go-lucky, the life of the party, free love, and all that crap. Several sources told me she slept around with a lot of guys. One girlfriend called MJK a 'gasper'—that's slang for someone who gets off on erotic asphyxiation. This girlfriend said she'd been in the room once when MJK's partner choked her almost to death and they laughed about it afterward."

"You said there were several things. There's more?"

"Yep. Strangulation marks on her neck. The coroner ruled them consistent with hanging. Bullshit."

Konane placed three autopsy photographs on the table. They were close-ups of MJK's neck from different angles—showing the deep purple ligature mark, higher on one side and lower on the other, where the electrical cord cut deeply into her neck. Less prominent, two quarter-sized dark blotches marked the front of the neck and a series of smaller bruises spread across the back of her neck.

Koa had seen similar bruising on victims who'd been choked to death. The marks weren't conclusive, but highly probative of manual strangulation and consistent with the possibility a sex partner on top of the woman had choked her. He noticed smaller red dots on the side of MJK's lower face, just at the border of the photograph. "Do you have a full facial shot?"

Konane shuffled through the file and produced another photograph. This one showed MJK's face. She'd been a beautiful young woman, but her naturally clear complexion showed numerous small red dots of petechiae, not dissimilar from those he'd seen on Hank Boyle's face.

Koa looked up into Konane's eyes. "The coroner called this a suicide?"

"Like I told you, the university wanted the case closed big-time, and the coroner was a dumb shit into keeping the right people happy."

Koa tried to absorb it. Even Shizuo would have called this one a homicide. "What about her parents?"

"Her dad died in Viet Nam, and the mother, a born-again zealot, disapproved of MJK's lifestyle. 'She got what she deserved,' that's a direct quote."

"Jesus." Koa took a deep breath. "You had a suspect?"

Konane snorted and scratched his chin. "Today you'd call them persons of interest. Never had enough to make them suspects."

"Them?"

"Four of them—rich, snotty frat boys, real jerks, from one of those UH fraternities."

"Tau Kappa Epsilon?" Koa prompted.

"That's it. I must be getting senile to have forgotten that handle."

"I doubt it," Koa responded. "I couldn't recall a forty-plus-year-old investigation half as well as you're doing."

"I had a witness, a guy in one of the apartments downstairs, who put the four of them in MJK's apartment less than an hour before we got the panicked call from her girlfriend. I brought all of them downtown. Took their written statements. Had 'em sign. They all had the same story—they'd all been out drinking at some strip club. All together, all night long. A fairy tale. Doctor Seuss from beginning to end, but I couldn't break it."

"Any witnesses see them at the club?"

"A bartender at the strip club backed up their alibi. Nasty little weasel with a big fat black facial mole. They probably paid him off, but shit, I couldn't prove it."

The word "mole" made Koa's synapses jump. "This weasel have a name?"

"Watanabe. He couldn't play poker worth a rat's ass, and I'd have busted his balls, except one of the strippers came forward. Said she'd been lap dancing for these four dudes just exactly when the hanging went down. A goddamn law student, no less."

Koa could hardly believe the way the pieces were falling together. "Cheryl Makela?"

Konane went bug-eyed for an instant. "Yeah, 'cept her stripper name was Babylips. I saw her onstage one night in nothing but a G-string. Great body. Guys chanting: 'Babylips . . . Babylips.' She must have raked in a fortune in tips. How'd you know?"

Well, well, well. Koa figured Makela wasn't the first female law student to augment her scholarship by working in a strip club. And

she'd made her bones with the rising TKE elite by lying to the police. No wonder she'd participated in more land development trans-
actions than all but the most notorious public officials. She'd been
lucky the bar examiners never got wind of her law school nightlife.

Koa wanted to get the rest of the story, so he ignored Konane's
question. "What about the guy in the apartment downstairs?"

"Funny you should ask. The son of a bitch changed his story. Said
he'd confused the days of the week or some such shit."

Koa jumped to the denouement. "Let me guess," Koa said. "The
frat boys were Gommes, Boyle, and Witherspoon."

Konane did a double-take. "How did you know?"

"And the fourth guy?"

Konane shook his head. "I don't know."

Koa couldn't hide his surprise. "You questioned him, but you
don't know his name?" The question came off more critically than
he intended.

"A redheaded kid. Gave his name as Abercrombie—Billy Abercrombie, and he had a Hawai'i driver's license—but later after the
coroner closed the case, and I went poking around, I couldn't find
him. No student by that name registered at UH for the semester,
and the driver's license was a phony. He snookered me." Konane
looked down at the table, embarrassed by his mistake.

It all fit together like a prize-winning Tonga canoeing team. One
of the four of them—Boyle, Gommes, Witherspoon, or the mysterious Abercrombie—had strangled MJK during a wild sexual orgy
in her apartment, and the four of them with the aid of Watanabe
and Makela had covered it up. No wonder they'd stuck together, like
Linus and his blanket, scratching each other's backs, for more than
four decades. Any one of them could have sunk the others with a
five-minute phone call to the state attorney general. But like an
Escher print, there was a huge uncertainty in the center of it all—
who was the red-headed Abercrombie?

Koa thanked the old detective. "You've no idea how much you've helped us. After all these years, we might even nail these fuckers. Pardon the pun. But we're going to need your help."

Konane's face lit up. "Whatever you need. Can't tell you how often I've dreamed of putting those arrogant pricks behind bars."

"We need to borrow the file. And we're probably going to need you to come to the Big Island and testify. Are you up to it?"

"Count me in. All the way," Konane said as he pushed the file across the table to Koa.

* * *

Koa was proud of Piki for his work in uncovering the long-hidden TKE secret, and he took Piki to a Japanese restaurant in Honolulu to celebrate. "What do you make of it?" Koa asked with a beer in hand.

"Well, one of the four of them is a killer, and since Boyle and Witherspoon are dead, it's got to be Gommes or this guy pretending to be Abercrombie."

"Why?" Koa challenged.

"Well, MJK's killer and Boyle's killer used the same MO, right down to the electrical cord, and the fact they weren't good at staging a suicide. That means the same killer must be responsible for both murders."

Koa took a sip of his beer. "I agree that the MJK and Boyle murders share the same MO, but in Boyle's case, we know Leffler was the killer."

"You're saying the person who hired Leffler knew about the MJK murder and told Leffler to stage a suicide with an electrical cord. Why would they do that?"

"Maybe to send a message."

"I'm sorry, Koa. I don't follow."

The waiter came by and Koa ordered *ʻahi*, sea urchin, giant clam, and eel. Piki, far less adventurous, stuck to California rolls.

Koa liked the young detective's honesty. Most police officers would nod and pretend to understand. Piki wanted to learn and wasn't afraid to let his ignorance show. "We got at least six people—Boyle, Witherspoon, Gommes, Makela, Watanabe, and Abercrombie—locked together for life. They all participated in covering up a murder. Any one of them could have destroyed the others. But they established an equilibrium. They scratched each other's backs. They passed their dirty deals around. They all profited, but each lived with the same ticking time bomb."

The light dawned in Piki's eyes. "Until KonaWili upset the balance."

"Exactly. Once the group lost its stability, each became fearful one of the others would spill the secret."

"Boyle and Witherspoon were the weak links?"

"Yeah. Boyle tried to commit suicide. I'm guessing it was right after MJK's death, and he remained depressed for the rest of his life. Witherspoon, who tried to erase UH and TKE from his life, must have been overwhelmed with guilt when his friend's daughter died at KonaWili."

"You think Boyle and Witherspoon got killed because of MJK and not because of KonaWili?"

"Not necessarily. MJK just explains why each of them got drawn into the KonaWili conspiracy and why each had a motive to kill anyone who threatened to bolt from the group."

"Then any one of them could have hired Leffler?"

"Why not?"

"I see two holes in your theory."

Koa liked the young detective's challenge. "What holes?"

"First, Makela and Watanabe weren't there for the MJK murder, and second, Boyle's killer struck just hours after the KonaWili disaster. There wasn't enough time for one of them to hire a killer."

"Good points," Koa conceded. "But who's to say Makela or Watanabe didn't learn about MJK's death? And any one of them could have hired Leffler in advance. We're talking about powerful people who typically plan ahead for contingencies, and they've had more than four decades to prepare."

"Jesus, Koa. That's ugly."

"Reality is ugly. I learned that in Afghanistan."

Their food came and they dug in. Koa mixed wasabi into his soy sauce and used chopsticks to dip his 'ahi before relishing the subtle flavor while keeping an eye on Piki. The young detective picked up a piece of California roll in his fingers. "You're not into sushi?" Koa asked.

"I like to know what I'm eating and don't understand that stuff."

"Give it a try," Koa responded offering Piki a piece of 'ahi. "Every adventure in life makes you a better detective."

Piki tried the 'ahi before he continued. "Our killer is one of four people—Gommes, Makela, Watanabe, or Abercrombie? And Makela's not likely because she was obviously afraid for her life when she learned about the hit list."

"I wouldn't rule Makela out. She must have known about Boyle and Witherspoon before I confronted her. She's brilliant, if devious, and must've thought about the MJK connection before I talked to her."

"Then we still have four suspects." Piki picked up another piece of California roll.

Koa had learned long ago to avoid getting trapped into a particular pattern of thinking by closing off avenues of inquiry too early in an investigation, and he saw Piki with his impetuous mind making just such a mistake. "Not necessarily. I said earlier either MJK or KonaWili could provide the motive, so you can't rule out Francine Na'auao. If we just looked at KonaWili in isolation, she'd be the most logical suspect."

"You thinking she might be the DOE lady from Honolulu who visited the site before she approved the change order?"

"Probably not." Koa finished his *'ahi* and started on the eel. "Tony Pwalú described the woman from Honolulu as a *haole*. Francine Na'auao's Hawaiian, but that doesn't mean she didn't know. My sources in the DOE tell me Na'auao had her fingers in everything. So even if she didn't make the trip herself, she knew about the fumarole."

"Could she have known what happened to MJK?"

"She was at UH when it happened, and the death of a coed would have been a pretty big deal on campus."

"Then we have five suspects."

Koa nodded, but thinking of Mayor Tanaka, he worried there might be a sixth suspect.

CHAPTER THIRTY-SEVEN

THE SHERIFF'S OFFICE typically served grand jury subpoenas, but Koa had personal reasons to deliver the summons to Cheryl Makela. The voyeuristic side of him wanted to see her face at the moment she recognized her predicament. Then, too, she might talk. People often felt compelled to explain themselves when silence served them best. Lastly, he and Zeke had devised a strategy for dealing with Ms. Makela, and he needed to plant the first seeds of misdirection.

Looking even more haggard than the last time, she frowned when she saw him. The public persona, the sophisticated makeup, and fancy riding clothes had disappeared. The heavy circles under her eyes evidenced stress, anxiety, and sleep deprivation.

"I have a subpoena for your appearance on Friday before a grand jury."

"About what?"

"The Hualālai Hui and KonaWili."

"I told you I won't answer your questions," she said, showing a spark of defiance.

"You'll have to tell that to the county prosecutor."

She started to say something but apparently thought better of it. "I'll have my lawyer talk to the prosecutor."

Hawai'i law restricts the access to grand jury proceedings to the grand jurors, prosecutors and their assistants, a legal counselor to the grand jury, the witness, and a court reporter. But Zeke Brown, the county prosecutor, wanted Koa's knowledge and insights available in the grand jury room and appointed Koa an assistant prosecutor.

The day before Makela's scheduled appearance, Zeke put retired Honolulu police detective Konane Kahaka before the grand jury. Under Zeke's skilled questioning, Konane walked the jurors through the 1975 MJK crime scene and explained his investigation. He told the jury how Boyle, Witherspoon, Gommes, and the mysterious Mr. Abercrombie—all suspects in the crime—presented the same alibi and emphasized the importance of Watanabe's and Makela's independent confirmation.

Koa whisked the retired detective in and out of Hilo so only those present in the grand jury and a few trusted police officers knew he'd testified. In that way, the trap they'd set for Makela remained secret. Time would tell whether she would come clean, refuse to answer all questions, or lie to preserve a secret hidden for more than forty years.

Not surprisingly, Ben Braff, Cheryl Makela's lawyer, called Zeke to ask for her testimony to be postponed. When Zeke refused, Braff argued Makela's appearance should be canceled because she'd assert her constitutional right to refuse to answer questions.

Unmoved, Zeke played hardball. "It's her right to decline to answer, but she is going to have to appear and do so in person."

Zeke left Makela with no alternative but to appear or face contempt of court. Frigid didn't capture the icy quality she projected when, having exhausted all pleas for escape, she showed up on Friday morning. Dressed in a dark gray pants suit, unadorned by jewelry, her mane of snowy white hair reinforced her haughty appearance. She wore makeup, but sparsely applied, just enough to conceal most of the effects of the weariness Koa still saw in her eyes.

Zeke left her attorney in the waiting area as he escorted her into the grand jury room. A guard at the door ensured the session wouldn't be interrupted. Makela sat rigidly in the witness chair, unaccustomed to the intense scrutiny of the grand jurors arrayed in a semicircle in the small amphitheater around her.

In front of a grand jury, Zeke Brown could put Rudolf Nureyev, the great Russian ballet dancer and choreographer, to shame. Intending to play on the human emotions experienced by people before such a panel, he set her up for a hard fall. He started with the usual name and address questions, which she answered.

Zeke guessed her attorney had instructed her to invoke her right not to answer as soon as he began to ask questions about either the Hualālai Hui or KonaWili. Zeke also knew that most witnesses are reluctant to invoke the Fifth Amendment because they think it evidences guilt. Playing on that fear, Zeke avoided KonaWili questions and instead asked about Makela's educational background. She saw no harm in talking about her education, and Zeke took her through her undergraduate education and then her legal education at UH law school.

Zeke slowly pulled her deeper into a sinkhole from which she wouldn't be able to extricate herself. First, he asked if she had known Howard Gommes during her time in law school, and she acknowledged that she had. Zeke then asked if she had known Arthur Witherspoon. Koa could see Makela's confusion and nervousness about the direction of the interrogation, but she acknowledged knowing Witherspoon. Zeke then asked, "While you were a law student at UH, were you ever questioned by the Honolulu police?"

Koa saw the look of surprise, and perhaps fear, on her face. She hesitated before making the worst mistake a witness can make. She lied. "No, why would I have been questioned by the police?"

Zeke then locked her into the lie. "Just so the grand jury is clear, Ms. Makela, is it your testimony you never gave a statement to the Honolulu police while you were a law student at UH?"

Having chosen her path, she straightened in her chair, looked the grand jurors in the eye, and said, "No. I was never questioned by the Honolulu police while I was a law student at UH."

With Makela now unequivocally on the record, Zeke dropped the bombshell. "Ms. Makela, have you ever been known by the nickname 'Babylips'?"

She turned white as new-fallen snow on Mauna Kea, then as red as the setting sun. "I . . . I . . . need to talk to my attorney," she stuttered.

"Okay, Ms. Makela," Zeke responded, "you may step outside the grand jury room and confer with your attorney, but you must return to these proceedings."

Her composure gone, she practically ran out the door. Ten minutes later, she was still conferring with Ben Braff when a sheriff informed her the grand jury awaited her return. Still visibly agitated, she again took her seat in front of the grand jurors.

Zeke repeated the still unanswered question. "Ms. Makela, have you ever been known by the nickname Babylips?"

"I respectfully decline to answer in reliance on my rights under the Fifth Amendment."

Zeke turned to the grand jury and spread his arms in a mocking gesture of helplessness. Then he asked, "Did you work at a strip club called the KitKat while you were in law school at UH?"

"I respectfully decline to answer in reliance on my rights under the Fifth Amendment."

After another mocking gesture to the grand jury, Zeke asked, "Did you tell Honolulu police detective Konane Kahaka you were with Gommes, Boyle, Witherspoon, and another man on the night of March 3, 1975? For your reference, Ms. Makela, that is the night a university coed named Mary Jane Kinnon was found hanged."

Makela's face betrayed her, and she stuttered, "I . . . I re . . . respect-fully decline to answer in reliance on my rights under the Fifth Amendment."

"Are you going to refuse to answer the rest of my questions today?"

"Yes."

"We will suspend these proceedings for the moment. You are free to leave the grand jury room, but you remain subject to recall."

Cheryl Makela heaved a sigh of relief as she left. Koa followed her out, watching her walk down the corridor toward the room where her attorney waited. She had almost reached the waiting area when two police officers stepped from a side hallway to confront her. "Ms. Makela, you are under arrest for perjury before the grand jury." One officer informed her of her rights while he placed her in handcuffs.

"I want my lawyer," she said more loudly than necessary.

"You can call your lawyer," the officer responded, "when you've been booked and admitted to the jail."

CHAPTER THIRTY-EIGHT

BEN BRAFF, MAKELA'S attorney, stormed into the meeting with Zeke and Koa. "Why have you arrested my client?"

"She lied to the grand jury. I'm charging her with perjury," Zeke responded coolly.

"What lie?" Braff demanded.

"I think you know," Zeke chided Braff, "but if not, ask your client."

Recognizing he wasn't getting anywhere with Zeke, Braff turned to his most immediate concern. "I want her out of jail. She's not a flight risk. Will you release her on her own recognizance?"

"No." Zeke shook his head. "And I'm going to ask the court to hold her in contempt."

"What?" Braff thundered. "What for?"

"For refusing to answer questions before the grand jury," Zeke responded coolly.

"You can't do that. She asserted her constitutional right to remain silent."

"True," Zeke conceded, "but she waived her Fifth Amendment rights by answering some questions and lying about her activities at UH before invoking her constitutional right. You know, Counselor, you can't use the privilege against self-incrimination as both a sword and a shield. Many courts have held, a witness may not answer some questions on a subject and then invoke the Fifth Amendment, leaving the jury 'prone to rely on a distorted view of the truth.' That is exactly what Makela did. She tried to deceive the grand jury by stating she hadn't been interviewed by the police in 1975 and then tried to invoke her right not to answer further questions. It's a classic case of waiver."

"Jesus," Braff responded, implicitly recognizing the merit in Zeke's argument and the potentially devastating weakness in his client's position. If she had waived her rights, then a court could lock her up for continuing contemptuous behavior until she answered all the prosecutor's questions.

Still, Braff had one argument left. "Even if she waived her rights with respect to whatever happened in Honolulu forty years ago, the prosecution of any crimes committed back then is barred by the statute of limitations and had nothing to do with the Hualālai Hui or KonaWili."

"Sorry, Counselor, but there is no statute of limitations on murder, and I am prepared to show the court an irrefutable connection between what happened in Honolulu and KonaWili."

"Jesus," Braff repeated himself. "What do you want from her?"

"Complete cooperation, and I want her to wear a wire in a conversation we'll set up with her coconspirators."

"No way. She won't do it," Braff responded.

Zeke remained unruffled. "Then we'll keep her in jail until she talks and prosecute her for the crimes she admits when she does talk."

"You're a hard man, Zeke Brown."

"Not at all," Zeke responded. "I just want to put an end to a conspiracy that's been going on for more than forty years."

"And if she cooperates? Are you prepared to offer her immunity?"

"That's going to depend on what she tells us, but she'll fare better if she helps us."

"You're not offering much."

"Talk to your client, Counselor," Zeke advised. "You have the weekend. We have an appointment with Judge Hatachi to argue our motion for contempt on Monday morning."

*　*　*

Koa had learned over the years that experienced defense lawyers understood the risks their clients faced and were expert in minimizing the bad consequences. And Ben Braff was as expert as they come. He called Zeke to set up another meeting on Saturday morning. Makela was ready to bargain.

The three of them—Zeke, Koa, and Braff—met in Zeke's conference room. Braff, a short intense man with bushy eyebrows over icy blue eyes, tried hard for immunity, but because of Makela's perjury, Zeke held all the bargaining chips. He refused to give much. In the end, he agreed to consider reduced charges if Makela cooperated. He also promised to describe her cooperation fully and fairly at sentencing if she was convicted.

Braff agreed to let his client tell her story, and Koa had her brought over from the cell block to the prosecutor's office. She came wearing a yellow jumpsuit and looking exhausted. Koa wasn't surprised that the haughty horse lady had found a night in the local lockup most disagreeable. As a cooperating witness, Zeke and Koa interviewed her rather than putting her back before the grand jury.

They began by questioning her about the events surrounding MJK's death in 1975. She admitted having worked part-time as an exotic dancer at the KitKat club performing stripteases and lap dances to help pay for law school, and she owned up to her stage name—Babylips. Although she'd been in a different part of the university, she had known Boyle, Witherspoon, and Gommes because they were frequent patrons at the KitKat.

Gommes, a big man on the undergraduate campus, hung out at the club, often treating groups of his friends to drinks and special dances. He'd taken a special liking to Makela and showered her with tips for performing for his friends. Boyle and Witherspoon had been regulars in his crowd.

Late one night—maybe about one thirty—in March 1975, Gommes showed up alone at the KitKat. In an agitated state, he'd taken Makela into one of the private rooms. He'd explained that, if anyone asked, he wanted her to say he, Boyle, Witherspoon, and Abercrombie had been together in the club from eight until after two a.m. He promised her five thousand dollars in cash if she agreed. She'd jumped at the offer.

"Tell us about Abercrombie," Zeke asked.

"I never met him. Gommes just told me to refer to him as 'a red-headed guy.'"

"Sitting here today," Zeke asked, "do you know anything more about Abercrombie?"

"No. Gommes just told me to say I danced and drank all night with the four of them and, if anyone asked about Abercrombie, to describe him as a redheaded guy."

"When Detective Konane Kahaka came around to the bar, you told him Boyle, Witherspoon, Gommes, and Abercrombie had been together in the club that night."

She looked down at her hands. "Yes."

"And it wasn't true, was it?"

Looking back up at him, she admitted, "No."

"Do you know why Gommes asked you to lie?"

"I didn't have any idea that night, and I still don't know for sure, but later after I heard about the girl, Mary Jane something or other, I suspected it had something to do with her death."

"And you still didn't tell the truth to the police?"

Makela's face had grown ashen in color, and she fidgeted with her hands. "No. I wanted the money."

"Did you later talk to Gommes or any of the others about what happened that night?"

"When Gommes gave me the money, he warned me something permanently bad would happen to me if I ever told anyone."

"He threatened you with bodily harm?"

"Yes. I was afraid of him. I still am."

"What about Watanabe? What was his role?"

"After Gommes talked to me that night at the KitKat, I saw him talking to Watanabe. I guessed Gommes got him to back up my alibi. The police detective later talked to Watanabe. That's all I know."

"Who killed Hank Boyle?" Koa blindsided her. He wanted to test his theory that Boyle's staged suicide had been intended as a message.

"Not me. And it scared the shit out of me. I mean, a hanging like that. Just like the UH coed. Someone warning us to keep our mouths shut."

He guessed right. "Gommes?"

"I have no idea, but he's a sadistic bastard and capable of anything, and I mean anything."

She said it with such venom, Koa sensed something personal between Gommes and Makela, but he let it go. They had a lot more to cover.

"Okay, Ms. Makela." Zeke took over. "How'd you get into the KonaWili development?"

"It was basically the same deal as always, going back to my first development. I was the go-between. Gommes gave me a share—sometimes 20 percent, sometimes more, but never as much as 50—and told me how to distribute it. I always got a piece, usually a few percent."

"You made no investment?" Zeke asked.

"No. I was never out of pocket."

"Who got the rest of what Gommes gave you?"

"Whoever had to sign off, usually planning people and politicians."

"And on KonaWili, who got a cut?"

"Gommes allocated 15 percent each to Watanabe and Na'auao. I got five and I spread the last five around to the building inspectors and other guys who had to sign off on things."

"Francine Na'auao at the DOE?" Koa asked, remembering how she'd announced she and her husband didn't invest in school projects.

"Yeah," Makela said, "Frannie's been getting a cut on Gommes's deals for twenty years."

"Fifteen percent of what?" Koa asked.

"Projections showed the project making seventy-five million in profits."

The amount stunned Koa. "Watanabe and Na'auao were going to get more than eleven million apiece?"

"If you believe it's all for them," Makela responded.

"What do you mean?" Zeke asked.

"Watanabe's a sneaky little shit. If you believe he keeps the whole 15 percent, you're a fool. He's somebody's bagman. Maybe the mayor. Maybe some of the council members. I don't know."

"How do you know he's a bagman?" Zeke roared.

"I don't know for a fact, but I'm not stupid, and I've been in state politics for forty years. I know how it works."

"And Na'auao?" Koa asked.

Makela's lip curled into a snarl. "Frannie's greed knows no bounds, and she's got half the politicians in the state by the balls, even the governor. I wouldn't expect her to do much sharing, not even crumbs."

The room was quiet for a long time. Koa knew what Zeke was thinking. Makela had copped to bribery of the worst sort, involving bagmen for senior county officials and possibly the governor. Zeke hated corruption of every kind and would be dying to prosecute the offenders. But the case depended on her word against Watanabe, and the little snake would lie through his teeth. It was also her word against Na'auao, one of the longest surviving politicians in the islands. The octopus would eat Makela alive.

Finally, Zeke asked, "Do you have any proof?"

Makela's attorney had been quiet throughout her confession. But now Braff held his hand in front of her to stop her from speaking and addressed Zeke. He'd obviously been waiting for this moment to spring his surprise on the county prosecutor. "If she gives you proof of the bribes to Watanabe and Na'auao, she gets immunity from prosecution."

Zeke stared at Braff for a long time, but they both recognized an offer too rich to resist. Sure, Makela could be prosecuted for perjury and bribery, but compared to the senior county officials and especially the all-powerful DOE head, she was a tiny fish in the smelly pond. And Zeke needed solid evidence to get to Na'auao.

"And just what might this proof be?" Zeke asked.

Ben had perked Zeke's interest, and he knew it. "If it's solid, she gets immunity from prosecution. She walks."

As a veteran prosecutor, Zeke had bargained with a lot of criminal defendants. He knew how to cut a deal without getting snookered. "She's got solid evidence, admissible in court, against both Watanabe and Na'auao?" Zeke asked.

Both Koa and Zeke caught Ben's hesitation and sensed a problem. Ben let out a long breath. "She's got admissible evidence against both of them. She can give you a lock on Watanabe. What she's got on Na'auao, well, it's complicated. Na'auao's smart and cautious. The bribes are camouflaged and paid through land swaps and intermediaries."

Zeke paused, but Ben had played his cards well. The idea of a rock-solid case against Watanabe and the prospect of going after senior county officials held great appeal. Still, he wanted more. "Your client gives us what she's got and wears wires in meetings with them if we ask her. She cooperates fully, including testimony at trial."

At the mention of testimony, Makela began to shake her head.

Undeterred, Zeke continued, "If her evidence is rock solid and she does all that, then she walks."

"I don't . . ." Makela's voice was shaky. "I don't want to testify. I can't sit there . . ." Her voice faltered.

Zeke's eyes burned into her. "You should have thought of that before you sold your soul to Gommes for five thousand dollars." Then he turned to her lawyer. "No testimony . . . no deal. We'll give you a few minutes to talk to your client."

Twenty minutes later they had a deal.

Makela's lawyer handed over two cassette recordings. "Makela started secretly recording her meetings with Watanabe and Na'auao over the last several years," he explained. "One of the tapes records meetings with Watanabe. The other contains Makela's conversations with Na'auao. Happy listening!"

CHAPTER THIRTY-NINE

THE AIR WAS crisp and breezy. Fleecy snow-white clouds spiraled across the intense blue sky. A perfect Volcano village morning for Nālani's big day. Koa beamed with pride as he climbed into his SUV and headed for the national park headquarters. Nālani's long hours and dedication since the unprecedented May 2018 Kīlauea eruption had singled her out for an exceptional honor.

Koa took his place in the sizeable crowd of park service employees, volunteers, and curious visitors gathered in a semicircle around Sally Kazaka, the diminutive park superintendent, who stood on a small platform with a microphone. Nālani, in her summer dress ranger uniform—flat-brimmed straw hat, dress trousers, and a short-sleeve shirt with her badge, National Park Service patch, and a tiny American flag pin—stood next to the superintendent. Koa smiled as he noted that she'd ditched the regulation brown shoes for her every-day hiking boots. Always ready for action. That was Nālani.

"*Aloha*," the superintendent began, turning to survey the guests. "I'm delighted we've a rather large crowd to honor park ranger Nālani Kahumana. As you know, Madame *Pele* shut down Hawai'i Volcanoes National Park in May 2018, but you may not appreciate that, rather than create time off, the eruption and closure only added to our workload. Ranger Kahumana spent hundreds of hours, many outside normal work schedules, identifying eruption sites, tracking lava flows, assessing hazards, and working with Hawai'i County personnel to help keep the public safe. It is a tribute to Nālani and her colleagues that no one died in this historic eruption, and, with one exception, the injuries were minor."

The superintendent paused, gathering her thoughts. "But Ranger Kahumana's extraordinary service didn't stop with the end of the eruption or the reopening of parts of the park. Sixty thousand earthquakes can do a lot of damage, and many critical areas of the park remain closed, including the Thurston Lava Tube, the Ka'u Desert Trail, and the Napau Trail. Ranger Kahumana has been a leader in our damage assessment, checking over a hundred miles of hiking trails, identifying hazards, and making sure that our annual million-plus visitors remain safe.

"For her outstanding service, I am proud to present Ranger Nālani Kahumana with the Andrew Clark Hecht Memorial Public Safety Achievement Award."

The audience erupted in applause, and Nālani thanked the superintendent.

Koa was among the first of many to congratulate his significant other and enjoyed basking in her reflected glory. Nālani deserved the award for her unrelenting drive to restore HVNP, but her real reward, he knew, was doing a job she loved.

As the crowd thinned and they were alone, she asked, "Have you heard from Alexia? Is the parole board going to give your brother a second chance?"

He marveled that, at this moment of personal accomplishment, she would think of Ikaika, who had always treated her like dirt, but that, too, was Nālani—intently focused on Koa and the people who mattered to him. "Not yet. Alexia promised to call as soon as she knows anything."

Koa kissed Nālani goodbye and was headed back to police head-quarters when the screen of his cell phone lit up with Alexia Shep-pard's name. The parole board hearing would happen later in the week, and Koa feared this call wouldn't bring good news. He an-swered. "Hi, Alexia, what's up?"

"Bad news, Koa. I've heard from Benny Koi. The parole board isn't going to revise your brother's minimum sentence, not for an-other year, and maybe not then. I'm sorry, Koa."

"Didn't he read Dr. Kepler's letter?"

"Yes, Koa, he read it and thought it impressive, but he says it's just too soon. They need to see how Ikaika interacts with the prison staff. Whether there's a real change in his behavior before they'll grant him a parole hearing."

"Shit."

She hesitated. "There's one more thing you should know, Koa."

"Yeah?"

"Hardy Moyan weighed in with the parole board, opposing any hearing. In fact, opposing any release until Ikaika's served his full term."

"That prick," Koa said angrily. He suddenly felt depressed. Alexia had warned him getting his brother a revised minimum sentence and a parole hearing would be a long shot, and he shouldn't get his hopes up. But after the fabulous report from Dr. Kepler, Koa had become optimistic. And if there were a valid medical explanation for his conduct, then Ikaika didn't belong in jail.

"Shit," he said again. "I guess. I'd really hoped it would happen."

"I know. I'm really sorry."

He sat in his office staring at the wall. After a while, he slammed his fist down on the desk. "Goddammit," he said aloud. He wanted to do something—anything—to reverse the decision. But what? He could call the members of the parole board, but there was no point, even if they took his call. The half dozen state legislators he knew well enough to ask would be unlikely to extend themselves for a felon with a long record. He racked his brain for another alternative but came up dry.

He knew he should turn his attention back to the KonaWili case to follow up on Cheryl Makela's confession and figure out how to get Watanabe and Naʻauao. And he needed to pressure Leffler, who still wouldn't talk. Yet, he had no enthusiasm, no energy, for any of it. Instead, he left the office and drove south, past the national park, slowing down where the earthquakes had cracked the road, past Pāhala, past Nāʻālehu, and down the South Point Road. At the southernmost point in the United States, he turned east along a nearly impassable track to the Green Sand Beach. He found the place deserted and climbed down into the broken crater to the secluded crescent beach with its tiny particles of olivine, a greenish volcanic glass giving the beach its name.

He'd been coming to this beach for years when the stresses of his job threatened to overwhelm him. He stripped on the beach and plunged into the ocean, swimming out through the gap the sea had cut in the side of the old cinder cone, feeling the pull of the ocean. He stroked dangerously far out.

While the waves rose and the ocean pulled at him, he heard his mother's voice running in a continuous loop: "You must forgive the pain Ikaika has caused, and find a way to help him . . . to put your family back together . . . for my sake . . . for your ancestors. That, too, I know in my *naʻau*." He swam until the muscles burned and his legs felt rubbery. But when he finally emerged, seawater dripping from his hair, he knew what he had to do.

He made the call sitting in the front seat of his Explorer. It took him several minutes to get through, but eventually, Walker McKenzie picked up the phone. Koa outlined his brother's parole situation.

He filled the reporter in on his meetings with Dr. Kepler and Alexia Sheppard's efforts to influence the parole board members. He told McKenzie he'd gotten advance word of the negative decision to be formalized in the next couple of days. Finally, he asked the question: Could McKenzie help change the expected result?

Koa understood the consequences of asking the reporter for help. If McKenzie helped, Koa would be deeply in his debt. McKenzie might not ask him to reciprocate for a long time, but one day the reporter would ask for a return favor—a big one—and Koa would be in no position to refuse. Still desperate to save his brother, he'd cross the repayment bridge when he got there.

To Koa's surprise, McKenzie said he'd get right on it and see what he could do. "I'll call you back as soon as I have something."

CHAPTER FORTY

KOA KNEW WHAT Zeke wanted to do, and it pissed him off. Watanabe had the ethics of a snake and deserved to be locked up in the ice house. The little asshole sat in the same seat Makela had occupied across the table from Koa and Zeke. "How much did Makela pay you on the KonaWili project?" Zeke demanded.

"I got no idea what you are talking about," the slimy press aide responded. Koa could see him struggling to appear relaxed, but beads of sweat on his forehead gave him away.

"Bullshit," Zeke roared. "Makela transferred a 15 percent interest in the project to you."

Koa saw the shock in Watanabe's face at the mention of 15 percent. The man's mouth opened before he could control himself and he almost said, "How—." Konane, the Honolulu detective, had pegged Watanabe. The man didn't have a poker face.

"Listen, mister," Zeke continued, "you come clean or I indict your ass and send you to the slammer."

"I don't—"

Zeke cut him off again. "You lunched with Makela at the Hilo Bay Café. She promised you a 15 percent interest in the KonaWili project. In exchange, you promised Howard Gommes he'd get all the approvals he needed for the development."

Koa saw the shock on Watanabe's face. It was as if Zeke had hit the little rat with a club. His eyes bulged. Sweat now ran down Watanabe's face. He shook like a palm frond in the trade winds. His mouth opened and closed, but no words came out. He knew, as did Koa, that only one person in the world could have told Zeke about the luncheon meeting. "That lying whore is trying to frame me."

"Be careful who you call a whore," Koa warned.

Watanabe's face flushed as he realized the import of Koa's remark. "You can't prove any of that shit," Watanabe responded hotly.

"Wanna bet," Zeke said, placing a small recorder on the table and hitting the playback button. Makela's voice filtered through the tinny speaker. "Hello, Tomi. How are things in the mayor's office."

"Hectic as usual. I'm working my ass off trying to keep everything under control," Watanabe said with arrogant self-importance.

"Howard has another deal for your principals. That KonaWili project."

"Oh, yeah."

"Howard gets all his approvals and your guys get the usual 15 percent, minus of course whatever they share with you."

"What's it worth?" Watanabe sounded eager.

"Howard projects the profit at seventy-five million. You can do the math."

"Very nice—"

Zeke punched the button ending the playback. "You didn't know Babylips recorded your sleazy little deal, did you?"

Watanabe trembled, nearly going into shock, at the mention of *Babylips*. "Oh, my God—"

"What'll it be, Mr. Watanabe, the truth or a prison cell?" Zeke demanded.

"I...I...I...won't...won't go...go to jail," Watanabe stuttered.

"Not if we get the whole truth, including your lies to the Honolulu police."

"*Masaka*—it can't be."

"Oh, yes it can be," Zeke responded. "Just like you really can go to jail."

"He'll cut my balls off." Watanabe's eyes grew shockingly wide. He appeared to be suffering a severe fever, giving his face a yellowish sheen beneath a layer of sweat.

"You should have thought of that before you climbed in bed with Gommes," Zeke said without mercy.

"No! You don't understand. You have to protect me. He'll kill me if I talk to you."

Neither Zeke nor Koa had expected Watanabe's terrified reaction. "Who'll kill you?"

"Gommes. You have to protect me. Give me a new identity or something?"

Koa thought of Gommes as a nasty blowhard, but Makela plainly feared him and now Watanabe acted flat-out terrified. "Yeah, we'll protect you from Gommes," Zeke assured Watanabe.

"How?" Watanabe demanded.

"With a police guard until we lock up Gommes," Zeke responded.

Watanabe sat pondering his options before he finally concluded he had no alternative. "What . . . what do you want to . . . to know?"

"Tell us about the KitKat."

"The KitKat?" Watanabe asked incredulously.

"Yes, the KitKat," Koa said with a hard edge in his voice.

"I tended bar there in the '70s."

"That's where you met Gommes?"

Watanabe's brow shot up and his eyes grew impossibly wider as he realized what Koa's questions meant. "Yeah, big-time spender, always surrounded by a bunch of loudmouth frat boys. Some nights he'd drop a couple thousand dollars on champagne and lap dances, except he got more than lap action if you know what I mean." Watanabe leered at the recollection. "But he tipped good—$150 or sometimes even $200."

"He asked you to talk to the police?"

"Yeah." Now into the tale, Watanabe found his voice. "One night he comes in all serious. Tells me he needs a favor and will make it worth my while. Says a couple of dumb cops are going to be checking his whereabouts, and he wants me to say he hung out in the club with his buddies, a kid named Spooner, a big guy named Boyle, and some red-head I ain't never seen. I asked him what's in it for me, and he says $2,500 and a ticket out of the KitKat. What the hell, it was a good deal."

"And you told the police a phony story?"

"Yeah. Some detective. I don't think he believed me, but after Babylips told him the same thing, he went away."

"And Gommes made good on his promise?"

"Oh, yeah. I got my money, and he got me a job at one of his development companies. Then I moved up to some political positions, a newspaper job, and then finally became press aide to the mayor."

"And he keeps asking for favors?"

"Yeah, well, he doesn't ask so nice. He pays good, but you don't cross Gommes. Bad things happen to guys who cross him."

"Like what?"

"When I worked for his development company, there was this guy. Gommes wanted him to do something, something illegal, and the guy told Gommes to go fuck himself. Next thing I heard, the police found the guy in an abandoned warehouse with a steel pipe jammed up his ass."

Zeke and Koa looked at each other. They were seeing the ugly side of Gommes. "Go on," Zeke ordered.

"Gommes used to come to me with his requests, but then he started sending Makela. Always the same deal—different numbers—but the same structure. He gets the land use and other approvals he wants and a percentage of the profits go into the trust fund."

"*The trust fund?*" Koa asked.

"Yeah. There's a lawyer here in Hilo who set up some kind of a trust fund. A percentage of the deal profits go into the trust fund, and the right people get paid."

"And who are the right people?" Zeke asked.

"I don't know. I get my piece, but I don't know how the other part gets distributed."

"Does the mayor get a cut?" Zeke asked with a hard edge in his voice.

Watanabe turned his palms up. "I could guess, but I don't know."

CHAPTER FORTY-ONE

WHEN SALLY MEDEA appeared in his office doorway, Koa could see the excitement on her face. "This is a surprise. What brings you here?"

"This." She held up a long roll of blueprints. "A lead on Arthur's hiding place."

Koa felt a tingle of anticipation and stood while she unrolled architectural drawings across his desk. "Where did you find these?"

"Hidden," she responded, "behind a loose panel in the alcove where he sometimes worked in the apartment."

Koa's optimism dimmed as he took in the tangle of lines. He couldn't make sense of the drawing nor read any of the notes, which appeared to be in a foreign language.

"What is it?"

She pointed to the large lettering across the top—CLAVIS. "It's Latin and it means 'key.'"

"Okay," he said.

"This is a top view, looking straight down." She pointed to a large five-pointed star with short, dotted lines across each of its points. "See the circle in the center of the star?" she said, running her finger around the circle.

"Yeah," he responded.

She pulled the sheet aside revealing a second page with a more complicated drawing. "This is a side view. This plug—" she pointed to a rectangle at the top of the drawing—"corresponds with the circle in the center of the top-down view."

"It's a locking mechanism." She pointed to a complex bundle of lines beneath the plug. Then he understood. The whole thing looked like a miniature bank vault in the center of a star with a locking mechanism near the top.

"Okay, I see it," he said. "It's like a lid on a canister with a combination lock."

"Exactly. And it's just the sort of contraption Arthur would imagine."

"So where is this mini-vault?"

"That's the problem. I don't know. From the drawings, I know the front or top of the device is flat, so it could be concealed in any wall, floor, or even a ceiling. I've been through our apartment, tapping on every wall, floor, and ceiling. It's not there."

"Where else might Arthur have put such a device?" Koa asked.

"Someplace where he could get to it, but not his house or office. Those places are too obvious, and Arthur never played obvious."

Koa wracked his brain. If it wasn't in his house, his office, or the apartment he shared with his mistress, where might it be? "Could it be in one of the buildings he designed?"

She nodded. "That's what I thought, but he designed dozens of buildings. I have no idea where to look."

"Let's think about this logically," he began. "It wouldn't be a private residence because he wouldn't have access."

"That makes sense." She fingered the edge of the drawing.

"Nor a private commercial space."

"Okay," she agreed.

"He'd have picked a nearby place. Let's say in Hilo." He paused. "How many public buildings did he design in Hilo?"

She thought for a minute. "The police station, the new court-house, the mayor's office, the government center, a couple of churches. Then there're the renovations of the old post office, the East Hawai'i Cultural Center . . ."

He stopped her. "Let me see the first blueprint again." She spread the drawing on his desk. He ran his hand across the blueprint, stopping at the star. He traced each of the dotted lines across the five points of the star. "What's with these lines?"

"I don't know," she admitted. "Normally a draftsman would draw dotted lines to show the connection between the thing in this drawing and the rest of the project, but I can't make sense of them."

Koa studied the lines and suddenly the picture snapped into focus. It made perfect sense. He took a ruler from his desk and extended each of the dotted lines until they formed a shield around the star—a shield with a flat top and a point at the bottom.

"The great seal of Hawai'i!" she exclaimed.

"Dead on!" Koa couldn't contain his excitement.

"The one in the foyer of the East Hawai'i Cultural Center?" she suggested.

"You bet. Right under the old police station. That's got to be it," Koa exclaimed.

"It's brilliant," Sally responded. "It's just the kind of place that would appeal to Arthur—history, mixed with symbolism, and cleverness."

They practically ran to Koa's police Explorer and sped across town to the East Hawai'i Cultural Center. Rushing into the building, they spooked the old Hawaiian docent who sat in her flowered *mu'umu'u* behind the information desk. "What are you doing?" she asked as Koa knelt on the floor at the center of the great seal.

He felt the center of the seal. He couldn't see any gap around the circle, but he could feel it with his fingertips. "There's a plug here."

"What are you doing?" the docent asked again, alarm evident in her voice.

Koa didn't know what Witherspoon had hidden, and he didn't want this woman gossiping about it. He turned to her and flashed his badge. "This is a police operation. You need to leave."

"I'll call *luna wahine,*" she responded.

"Fine," he responded. "Get your supervisor on the phone. Let me talk to her." Five minutes later, he ushered the docent out and placed a closed sign on the door.

He went back to the star in the center of the intricately fashioned mosaic seal. "How do I get the plug out?"

Sally consulted the drawings. "I think it's wedged or glued in. You'll have to pry it out."

Koa used his pocket knife around the edges of the small circle, working the blade into the nearly invisible circular crack. He worked the blade around once and then a second time until he saw the outline of the plug and dug the knife blade deeper. Slowly, a millimeter at a time, he pried the center of the star up until it popped loose. Using the flashlight app on his smartphone, he peered into the eight-inch round hole in the center of the great seal. The light reflected off the dial of a combination lock.

"Shit, there's a combination lock. I'll have to get a locksmith in here."

"Wait," Sally responded. After a moment, she said, "Try 12 . . . 12 . . . 12."

"Why?"

"It's the mathematical formula for the great rose window at the Cathedral Basilica of Our Lady of Chartres. The circular window surrounds a twelve-pointed star with Christ in the center. Twelve roundels display the Elders of the Apocalypse in an inner ring and twelve half-roundels show the dead emerging from their tombs with the angels blowing trumpets to summon them to the last judgment."

"Really?" he asked.

"Yes, really, and if Arthur was here, he'd quote Fredrik Macody Lund, one of the great historians of cathedral architecture: *Sacred architecture is not, as our time chooses to see it, a 'free' art, developed from 'feeling' and 'sentiment,' but it is an art strictly tied by and developed from the laws of geometry.* I know it sounds crazy, but I'm betting it will work. Give it a try."

Koa spun the dial and stopped at "12." Then back around past "12" to "12." And, finally, back to "12." He heard a click and pulled the tiny safe open. He'd opened Arthur Witherspoon's hiding place, where he found a single sheet of paper. He drew it out, unfolded it, and started reading:

> *"May the Lord forgive me for I have sinned."*

Sally gasped, but Koa kept reading:

> *"It has haunted me all my life, what we did that night, the six of us."*

Koa stopped reading and looked up at Sally Medea. *The six of us?* Mary Jane Kinnon and the four frat boys made five. Who was the other person?

He continued reading:

> *"I was high. We all were. The girls were naked, swapping partners, competing for the best climax, each goading the other on. Mary Jane was so beautiful, so sexy, so wild. He choked her. She was gasping, begging for it, playing a*

*deadly game. And then she wasn't breathing. Frannie tried
to revive her, but she was gone.*

*"We should have gone to the police, but we didn't.
Howard fixed the whole thing, the fake suicide, the lies, the
false witnesses. He got Frannie to lie. He paid Babylips and
that little Japanese bartender to say we were all at the
KitKat. I should never have gone along. The worst mistake
of my life. I was scared. We all were.*

*"Howard screamed at us. He wouldn't let some slut ruin
his life. He had money and knew how to fix it, how to set
up the alibi, how to get to the coroner, how to make
everyone believe Mary Jane committed suicide. Poor Mary
Jane. I didn't believe it would work, but it did.*

*"One lie begets another and another and another. After
that night, Howard owned us. We became his puppets,
richly rewarded pawns in his dirty deals, locked into a
lifelong trap. We faked Mary Jane's suicide, and I so often
contemplated my own, my escape. But I'm too much a
coward. No matter. It will come to a bad end, a terrible
tragedy, of that I am sure."*

"Arthur Witherspoon"

Koa thought he'd heard the whole story from Konane Kahaka, the
old Honolulu cop. He'd agreed with the old detective's educated
guesses about MJK's death, but Konane had ferreted out only part of
the story. There'd been six people at the orgy in Mary Jane's room, not
five. And Mary Jane hadn't been the only woman. Both Frannie and
Mary Jane had been engaged in sex— "each goading the other on."

"Frannie . . . Frannie." Koa turned the name over in his mind. If
Frannie had been in MJK's room that night, and Frannie Kapule

had approached Konane Kahaka, claiming MJK was depressed and suicidal, logic suggested the Frannie in the room was, in fact, Frannie Kapule. Because she'd been a participant in the faked suicide, she'd have had a motive to try to influence the police and the coroner to call the death a suicide. And Gommes, who was orchestrating the cover-up, would have wanted to keep the number of participants to a minimum.

But another Frannie played a central role in the KonaWili case. Although Koa knew her as Francine Naʻauao, Makela referred to Francine Naʻauao as Frannie. Was it possible that Frannie Naʻauao and Frannie Kapule were one and the same person? Francine Naʻauao was married. Maybe she'd been born Francine Kapule. Koa grabbed his cell and called Piki. The young detective answered on the second ring, and Koa explained what he wanted.

It didn't take long. Piki called back in less than ten minutes. Koa had guessed right. Francine Naʻauao and Frannie Kapule were one and the same. Francine Naʻauao had been in MJK's room the night she died. Christ. The whole KonaWili cast of characters had been in Mary Jane's room—Gommes, Witherspoon, Boyle, and Naʻauao, plus another man, the mysterious Abercrombie. And one of those men had strangled Mary Jane Kinnon. Which one?

Witherspoon's secret confession shed light on KonaWili. It explained why Gommes could exercise such power over the participants in the KonaWili disaster. In Witherspoon's words, "he owned us. We became his puppets." Still, Gommes must have pushed too hard. Witherspoon had spent a lifetime hiding his UH connection. Easy to see how he would have balked at covering up the death of schoolchildren at KonaWili, especially when the daughter of one of his closest friends died there.

Boyle, too, must have harbored a deep sense of guilt. According to his partner, he had suffered from depression since his days at UH, and Dr. Patrone had been treating him with anti-anxiety and anti-depressant medicines for forty years. After KonaWili, all the pills in the world wouldn't have been enough to salve his conscience.

Boyle or Witherspoon—maybe both of them—must have threatened to blow the lid off the conspiracy. And Leffler had killed them. But who'd ordered Leffler to pull the trigger? Gommes? That made no sense. A sniper—it had to be Leffler—tried to kill Gommes, missed, and instead killed Dante, his Rottweiler. Leffler's master must be Abercrombie, whoever he was?

CHAPTER FORTY-TWO

THE IDENTITY OF the one called Abercrombie haunted Koa. They knew little—only that Abercrombie hung out with the TKE crowd in 1975 and presented a phony driver's license to Detective Konane, who remembered him having fiery red hair. Makela and Watanabe never met him and described him as *a red-haired man* only because Gommes told them to do so.

Piki went through the records of every student member of TKE in 1975. He found no one with fiery red hair. Piki then expanded the search to TKE members from 1971 through 1976 on the theory Abercrombie might have been a pledge in 1975 or a graduate who still hung with his fraternity pals. Piki found several redheads, but according to Konane none of them had masqueraded as Abercrombie.

Piki took a pile of UH yearbooks up to Konane's house where the two of them spent two days going through the class picture of every undergraduate from 1971 through 1976. Still no Abercrombie. In frustration, one night when Nālani worked late at a national park function, Koa visited the Hilo Public Library and gathered up the UH yearbooks from the shelves. He couldn't imagine what he'd find after Piki and Konane had been through all the individual pictures, but he had to try.

He flipped through the pages covering student government. He skipped the black and white pictures, focusing on those in color, but found no red-haired man. He moved on to athletics. Nothing. Music groups. Nothing. The school newspaper. Nothing. Then he hit the drama department.

Scanning pictures of theatrical production, his eye hit upon a student with red hair. Koa hadn't been in the drama department, but he'd attended UH plays during his four years there. Judging from the stage, this show hadn't made the main stage of the Kennedy Theater. It looked like a late-night student production in the university's black box space.

He studied the red-haired actor. Was it possible that, in addition to a phony driver's license, Abercrombie wore a disguise? That could explain why Detective Konane Kahaka hadn't been able to identify Abercrombie among the TKE members. The photomontage identified the production as *The Red-Headed League* but failed to identify the actors.

Koa recognized *The Red-Headed League* as one of Sir Arthur Conan Doyle's Sherlock Holmes short stories. After becoming a detective, Koa had read every Sherlock Holmes story he could find and remembered Jabez Wilson, a flaming redheaded pawnbroker. Two crooks had concocted a menial, but well-paying, job for Jabez Wilson at the phony redheaded league in order to get him out of his pawnbroker's shop. While Jabez was away, the perps tunneled from Wilson's shop into a nearby bank to rob its vault. The story came to symbolize the proposition that things are not what they seem. That, Koa thought, was no joke.

The mysterious Abercrombie might have worn the wig to the police station in 1975 without undue risk of discovery. Now, Koa had his own Sherlock Holmes mystery—who was the Jabez Wilson wannabe who called himself Abercrombie?

He sent Piki back to Honolulu to search the drama department archives. The young detective spent two more days away from Robyn to no avail. The 1970s records of the UH Mānoa drama department had gone up in smoke in a 1980s fire, and no one could remember *The Red-Headed League*, let alone who had acted in it. Another dead end.

CHAPTER FORTY-THREE

THERE HAD TO be a way to identify Abercrombie. Of the original six people in MJK's room forty years before, Koa knew the identity of the three who were dead and two who were alive. He'd have to pry the identity of the last man from Na'auao or Gommes. But how?

Hard as steel nails, Gommes would be a tough man to break. Koa doubted he'd flinch even in the face of an indictment. And if it came to a trial, it would be his word against Makela's. Koa had little doubt Gommes's lawyers would make mincemeat of her. If Watanabe also testified against Gommes, he, too, would be a weak witness. Gommes's lawyers would have a field day with his long history of blatant lies to the press. Jurors would quickly see Watanabe's "truth" as more fiction than reality.

That left Na'auao. Koa had interviewed her in vain, but now they had Makela's story, her tapes of conversations with Na'auao, and the fact that Na'auao had been in MJK's room the night of her death. Koa spent hours listening to the Makela-Na'auao tapes, only to find them opaque and confusing. When Makela offered Na'auao a financial interest in the KonaWili development, Na'auao told her to arrange a land "swap" for a parcel owned by GRQ Partners. Zeke had yet to trace the ownership of GRQ, which according to Makela stood for "get rich quick." But even if Zeke could prove Na'auao owned all or part of the entity, it wouldn't be enough. He'd also have to prove the land swap a sham. Only then would he be able to make a bribery case stick. Koa wanted a faster way.

If Makela could entice Na'auao to a meeting, she might be able to provoke an admission—recorded if Makela wore a wire. Seeking to set up such a meeting, Zeke and Koa brought Makela in and explained what they wanted her to do. "We want you to call Na'auao and set up a meeting. Tell her you need to see her. You have information vital to her well-being, which you can't discuss on the phone. Tell her to meet you at the Honolulu Museum of Art. Tomorrow afternoon at three. We'll be listening and recording the call."

Both reluctant and nervous, Makela asked, "And if she balks?"

"Tell her it has to do with Mary Jane Kinnon," Koa instructed.

"Oh, God, that's the coed who hanged herself, isn't it?"

"Yeah, that's her."

"I have to do this to stay out of jail?" Makela asked.

"Yes, it was part of your immunity deal," Zeke responded.

Makela sat composing herself for several minutes before she picked up the phone and dialed Na'auao's home number. A voice on the other ended answered "*Aloha*" on the second ring.

"*Aloha*, Frannie, it's Cheryl," Makela began.

"Cheryl, I haven't heard from you in ages." Na'auao's voice sounded cool. Koa wondered if she was already distancing herself from Makela.

"It hasn't been so long, Frannie. We need to meet. I have something you need to hear."

"I don't know if that's such a good idea with everything that's . . . that's going on."

"It's pretty important. You'll want to hear what I have to say."

"You'll have to give me more if you want to meet," Na'auao responded.

"It's about Mary Jane Kinnon."

There was a long silence on the other end before Naʻauao responded with a single word—"Where?"

"The Honolulu Academy of Arts at—"

"No," Naʻauao interrupted. "Someplace outdoors, where we can take a private walk together." Naʻauao paused. "The Punchbowl cemetery, at the top of the steps. Tomorrow at three."

Makela looked at Koa. He didn't much like the meeting place. It was too big and open. Monitoring the conversation would be hard, but at least Naʻauao had agreed to a meeting. He nodded to Makela.

"Okay, see you there," Makela responded, and the line went dead.

The tenor of the call worried Koa. Naʻauao sounded suspicious even before Makela mentioned Mary Jane Kinnon, and the coed's name would spook the DOE chief. Koa worried she might not show for the meeting, and even if she did show up, she'd be wary. She might even check Makela for a wire.

The location of the meeting presented nearly insurmountable problems. The cemetery covered more than a hundred acres in a windswept crater above Honolulu. Its winding paths would enable Naʻauao to walk in unpredictable directions through wide-open spaces where it would be almost impossible for Koa to stay close and still remain undetected—especially since Naʻauao might recognize him. Worse, if the trade winds kicked up, the wind noise would likely make it impossible to hear their conversation. He'd need luck even with sophisticated surveillance equipment. Fortunately, with the meeting in Honolulu, Koa knew where to get help.

Years before, Koa had caught Joe Po engaged in illegal electronic surveillance, but Koa had given the former CIA electronics spook a break because his spying had helped break up a Ponzi scheme. A bad act for a good cause. Thereafter, Joe had helped Koa on a number of police operations. Identifying Joe as an odd guy was a bit like calling a platypus an unusual duck. Forty years old, Joe weighed 300 pounds, wore mismatched clothes, and exhibited a teenager's enthusiasm for Spider-Man, Han Solo, and James Bond. Weird and nostalgic, Joe knew his electronic spy gear and suffered an unfilled passion to play cops and robbers. He nearly always agreed to help the police and waived his usual fee. Koa called him and he agreed to help.

"Describe your informant, male or female, body type, and hair," Po said after Koa explained his predicament. When Koa described Makela's thick white hair, Po proposed just the ticket.

Koa, Piki, and Makela flew to Honolulu, rented a car, and drove to Spyland, Po's electronics shop. It took Po nearly an hour to fit tiny microphones, a recorder, and a transmitter into Makela's thick mane of white hair, but when he finished even her hairdresser couldn't have spotted his handwork.

"What if it's windy and my hair blows?" Makela asked nervously.

"Not to worry, My Lady," Po responded. "The Russian KGB couldn't find this little techno-marvel in a typhoon. It's got microphones the size of pinheads, and we'll have to cut some hair to get the equipment out when we're done."

"How do I turn it on?"

"Y'all don't. It's remote-controlled. Y'all just got to be your charming self. Forget the tech stuff. Y'all are wearin' genius-level equipment. Nobody's gonna find it no matter what happens. Uncle Po guarantees it."

"Okay, I'll try," she responded and snapped her head around, tossing her hair the way she'd done after removing her riding helmet the first time Koa visited her horse farm. It might have been a natural gesture or a small act of defiance. Koa couldn't tell.

"Koa controls the whole shebang with this." Po held up a small point-and-shoot camera. Turning to Koa, he said, "This here button activates the receiver-recorder. And this here dial adjusts the volume transmitted to your earpiece. The recorder in My Lady's hair records everything transmitted and the phony camera records everything received. That way, there's a backup."

He handed the camera to Koa and fitted him with a tiny, nearly invisible, flesh-colored earpiece. "Go ahead. Test the little sucker." Koa pressed the button while Po and Makela chatted and walked into the next room and back. It worked like a charm.

"Amazing!" Koa said as he weighed the little camera in his hand. "I don't suppose this gizmo takes pictures, does it?" Koa joked.

"Oh, it takes pictures," Po responded. "They just ain't very good." He shrugged. "Technology has its limits."

Koa didn't care about pictures. When Joe had first explained the equipment, Koa had focused on a different technological limitation—the transmitter's short range. Because of its extreme miniaturization, Po's gadget broadcast only about three hundred yards. Yet, the roughly circular cemetery extended over more than eight hundred yards with winding paths across wide-open spaces where any observer would be visible. Koa suspected Na'auao had chosen the Punchbowl for exactly that reason and wondered if she'd held other clandestine meetings there.

Koa wanted to hear their conversation firsthand so he could react if the need arose. He'd spent hours pondering how to stay close and be unobserved. Then he'd recalled the tactical advice given to him by Lieutenant Colonel Wallaby, one of his military mentors—"turn your weakness into your strength." That's when he hit upon his plan and spent hours making the arrangements.

Koa and Piki took Makela into Po's back room and once again went over the outlines of her script. At one o'clock, Koa stood up to leave. "Stay with Makela," he instructed Piki. "Make sure her taxi drives into the Punchbowl at five minutes before three. You park at the end of Pūowaina Drive outside the entrance to the cemetery and wait for my call."

"Where will you be?" Makela asked.

"I'll be there, but you won't see me. And don't look around for me. If Naʻauao thinks there's a watcher, she'll break off the meeting."

While Piki babysat Makela, Koa got busy with part two of his plan—picking up the van he'd hired, checking in with the Punchbowl security office, and parking on the roadway in the middle of the cemetery below the great semicircular monument to the American soldiers who'd sacrificed their lives for freedom. At two thirty, Koa, dressed in green coveralls, black work boots, and a baseball cap with a false beard with thick-rimmed sunglasses, opened the rear doors of the van. He unloaded a small two-wheeled pushcart and began filling it with flowers in special containers made to comply with cemetery regulations. The banners on the van, the logo on his cap, and the side panels of his little wheelbarrow read: PUNCHBOWL MEMORIAL FLOWERS, LTD, FTD

When Naʻauao arrived a few minutes later, Koa was placing a small bouquet of red roses before the grave of an eighteen-year-old sailor, who had died at Pearl Harbor on December 7, 1941. He watched through his sunglasses as Naʻauao climbed the steps of the memorial beneath the image of Columbia—representative of motherhood and liberty—carved into the semicircular granite wall of the cemetery's central memorial. Naʻauao surveyed the grounds looking for anything out of place. After straightening the flowers in front of the grave, Koa snapped a picture with his little camera, presumably so his boss, or perhaps the patron who'd ordered the flowers, could verify his handiwork.

At five before three, a yellow airport taxi entered the cemetery, came slowly up the drive, and deposited Makela at the foot of the memorial's steps. By the time she'd joined Naʻauao at the top of the steps, Koa had moved to the grave of an Army soldier killed during the Tet offensive in Viet Nam. Instead of taking a picture, he activated the transmitter hidden in Makela's hair and heard her voice loud and clear in his earpiece.

"*Aloha*. Thanks for coming, Frannie."

"You look haggard, like you've been through the wringer."

"Nice of you to notice," Makela said. "It's been a tough couple of weeks."

"Tell me about it," Na'auao responded in a throaty voice. "Let's take a walk."

The two women descended the steps and took a path out through the field of grave markers on the north side of the cemetery. Koa wheeled his flower cart across the grass between the markers and stopped at the grave of a Navy flyer shot down during the Battle of Midway. He was kneeling about a hundred yards from the two women when Na'auao asked, "Okay, Cheryl, what's this all about?"

"That policeman, Chief Detective Kāne, came around to see me. Scared me to death," Makela began.

"How?"

"He's asking questions about Mary Jane Kinnon."

"Who's Mary Jane Kinnon?" Na'auao asked.

"Jesus, Frannie, don't play dumb. She was your friend. He knows you talked to the police."

"Alright, I had a friend who committed suicide, so what?"

"He says it wasn't suicide. He accused me of lying to the police, telling them Gommes hung at the KitKat that night when he didn't."

"I hope you told him to go to hell."

"I did, but he seems to know a lot about what happened that night."

"Like what?"

"That one of the TKE brothers strangled Mary Jane and then staged the hanging."

"Why are you telling me this?"

"I think you know why."

The two women walked farther across the cemetery. Koa had already stayed too long at the airman's grave, so he wheeled his cart deeper into the cemetery and prepared flowers for another gravesite—this one of a Hawaiian soldier who'd died at Iwo Jima.

"I don't know what you're talking about," Na'auao insisted.

"The detective says you were there. You know who strangled Mary Jane."

"He's crazy," Na'auao snapped.

"I don't think so. The detective knows there were four men and another woman in that room. He knows about Abercrombie and his redheaded disguise."

"Oh, my God." Even at a distance, Koa saw Na'auao's hand fly to her mouth. She turned on her heel and ran toward her car, oblivious of the man placing flowers on the graves.

Koa could think of only one reason for Na'auao's abrupt departure. Everything had been going smoothly until Makela had revealed that Koa knew Abercrombie had used a redheaded disguise. Na'auao must have broken off the meeting to warn Abercrombie.

Koa pulled out his cell phone and called Piki. "Na'auao's coming out. I think she's going to warn Abercrombie. Tail her and keep me posted."

Koa packed up his flowers and hurried back to the van. He started it up and headed out of the cemetery. His cell rang as he passed the exit, and he answered Piki's call. "Yeah."

"She's headed downtown."

"Stay with her. I'm probably five minutes behind you."

Koa raced downtown pushing the flower delivery van as fast as he dared. Looking both ways, he ran the red light at 'Iolani Avenue. On the open line to Piki, he asked, "Where's Na'auao?"

"Turning on to Beretania. She's driving like a maniac."

Koa pictured the wide one-way street. It led past the state capitol, the governor's mansion, past shops and galleries, a public park, and then into Chinatown. Where could Naʻauao be going?

"She's just pulled into a no-parking zone in front of the capitol," Piki announced excitedly. "She's out of the car, hurrying into the building."

The capitol? Was Abercrombie now in the legislature? Koa ran another red light and peeled around the corner onto Beretania. Horns blared. Ahead he could see Piki getting out of the rental car in front of the capitol just as Naʻauao disappeared through the door into the capitol. "Go after her," Koa screamed into his cell. He roared down the street. Piki sprinted toward the steps.

Koa left the van at the curb and ran into the building, but, dressed as a flower delivery man, he lost a precious minute identifying himself and clearing security. Reaching the main hallway, he looked left and then right before spotting Piki far down the hall to his right. The young detective seemed to have lost his prey.

"She got into the elevator. I couldn't get there in time. I don't know whether she went up or down," Piki reported.

All the offices were upstairs with nothing below except the basement. Koa sent Piki to the basement while he checked the upper floors, moving from floor to floor, checking offices as best he could. He failed to locate Naʻauao. When he rejoined Piki, he learned Piki, too, had struck out. They went back to security. A police supervisor informed them that with the legislature in session, most of Hawaiʻi's lawmakers were in the building. Francine Naʻauao could have visited any of Hawaiʻi's 51 state representatives or 25 state senators. So close, Koa mused, and yet so far.

Tired and frustrated, Koa and Piki walked back to their vehicles, where two parking tickets added to their woes. At least the rental car and the van hadn't been towed.

CHAPTER FORTY-FOUR

NĀLANI HAD HER arms around Koa, trying to console him over his failure to get Ikaika a parole hearing. "You tried your best," she said.

"It's not right. If the tumors were responsible for Ikaika's actions, then he shouldn't be in jail."

Nālani squeezed him tight. "You don't know a hearing would have made a difference. A long shot, that's what Alexia said."

"Yeah, but I failed, and Ikaika will rot in prison for another year. Hell, if that asshole Moyan has his way, Ikaika will be behind bars for another four years. What a prick!"

"You should—"

The phone interrupted Nālani. Koa grabbed the phone, prepared to dismiss the caller, when he heard Walker McKenzie's voice. "It's all arranged. I've set up a meeting for you with Governor Māhoe at eight forty-five tomorrow morning. He knows you're going to make a plea for an early parole hearing for your brother. I think he'll be sympathetic."

Koa felt a sudden burst of elation. McKenzie had come through like a white knight, getting an immediate appointment with perhaps the only man alive who could order a parole hearing for Ikaika. A parole hearing didn't guarantee his brother's release, far from it. Alexia had said even if Ikaika got a hearing, the board would be unlikely to grant parole. Still, he now had a chance to free his brother.

"Are you there?" McKenzie asked.

"Yes, I'm here. Just surprised. Eight forty-five tomorrow. Where?"

"The governor is having an early breakfast with some Chinese officials in the Washington House. He'll meet you in his office there after the breakfast. You should be a little early."

"Okay. Any advice on how I should handle this?"

"Yeah. Three things. Use Dr. Kepler's letter, but tell him you've talked to your brother, and he's different since the surgery. Vouch for Ikaika. It will go a long way with Māhoe. And tell him about your mother, how devoted she is, and how hard it is for her to travel to Arizona. The governor's heard a lot of complaints about closing Kūlani. Put a human face, your mother's face, on the hardship Arizona presents. Finally, make it personal. He's a politician. He likes doing things for voters . . ." McKenzie paused, then added with a chuckle, "Especially when he knows he's going to get national press coverage."

Christ, Koa thought, McKenzie had promised the governor national press. Had he stacked the deck in Ikaika's favor? What, Koa wondered with a shiver, had he gotten himself into? "Thanks," he said. "I'll never be able to thank you enough."

"Don't thank me yet. Wait until we have your brother out of prison."

Koa put the phone down and sat in stunned silence. His mother's words rang in his ears: ". . . You will find a way to help him . . . That too I know in my *naʻau*."

"What was that all about?" Nālani asked.

"Walker McKenzie set up a meeting with the governor for me to argue for an early parole hearing for Ikaika."

"*Maikaʻi loa*, that's wonderful," Nālani exclaimed. "Māpuana will be thrilled."

"People are going to wonder how I arranged it. They might think it's a conflict of interest."

Nālani's face told a different story. "He's the governor. You're a citizen. You're within your rights to ask him."

He looked at Nālani, feeling a rush of emotion, and then pulled her into a long embrace. Of course, she was right; he had to make the plea for his brother. He owed it to his mother ... to his family ... to his ancestors ... and to himself as the *hiapo*, the oldest Kāne male.

Koa didn't sleep that night. Every time he closed his eyes a different vision assaulted him. A college coed hanging from an electrical cord. His brother walking out of prison as a free man. Leffler's ugly scarred face. Boyle's limp body hanging from a light fixture. Makela's weary face when she finally fessed up. His mother gleeful at the news of her son's release. The images just kept coming, and he couldn't turn them off.

All too soon the alarm rang, and he headed for Honolulu. He arrived at the Washington House a little before eight thirty and stood for a moment in front of the historic Greek Revival palace where the Committee of Safety had arrested Queen Liliʻuokalani on January 17, 1893, ending the Hawaiian monarchy. Thereafter, Washington House had served as the official residence of Hawaiʻi governors until 2008 when the state built a new official residence just behind the old one, and Washington House became a state museum where the governor still sometimes conducted business. Once inside, Koa waited less than ten minutes before being shown into the governor's office.

Koa took a quick glance around the room, beautifully paneled in native woods and hung with portraits of Hawaiʻi's governors. Then he directed his attention to the man who rose from behind the desk. Bobbie Māhoe, beaming like the politician he was, came across the room to extend his hand to Koa. Dressed in a casual Hawaiian shirt and slacks, the governor wore a *ti* leaf and green orchid *lei* that had become his trademark. "Hello, Detective, and congratulations on the apprehension of Leffler. That was first-class detective work."

"Thank you, sir."

"Have a seat." The governor waved to one of the chairs in front of his desk.

Koa sat down in a high-backed leather chair facing the governor's desk, immediately leaning forward to connect with the governor.

"Walker McKenzie told me a little about your brother," the governor began. "How's he doing?"

Koa seized the moment. "He's a changed man, Governor. The doctors removed two frontal lobe tumors he's had since childhood. Medical experts believe the tumors have affected his behavior since he was a kid. Dr. Kepler's letter explains their thinking." He handed the governor a copy of the letter. "I've talked to my brother, Governor. He's a different person. He's much more reflective. His hostility has disappeared along with his impulsiveness. I've known him all my life, and he's a new man. He deserves a second chance, a new lease on life."

The governor picked up Dr. Kepler's letter and began reading. Koa watched Māhoe scan the pages, wondering if anyone could really read that fast. When he finally looked up, the governor said, "Pretty impressive stuff."

"You know, sir, I'm a cop. I'm usually on the other side, urging the courts to put offenders away because they're a danger to the community. But if Dr. Kepler is right—and based on my personal interactions with my brother I think he is—Ikaika is not a danger to anyone."

"You make a good case. Anything else, Detective?"

"Just this, sir. I know you've heard a lot of complaints about the closing of Kūlani and the difficulties people have in visiting their loved ones in Arizona. That's been a real problem for my mother.

She's sixty-eight and it's hard for her to make the trip to Arizona.
She's always been close to my brother, and I know she wants to be
near him as he gets his life back in order."

The governor nodded. "I know that's a problem, and unfortunately this whole contract prison thing has been a financial disaster
for the state. That's why we're planning to reopen Kūlani."

The governor looked at his watch and stood up. Koa rose to his
feet. "I've got a meeting in the capitol, Detective. Mind walking
over there with me while you finish telling me about your brother."

"I'd be happy to."

The two of them walked out of the office and down the hall to
an elevator. The doors opened and the governor ushered Koa in.
Koa turned to face Māhoe. "I don't often make personal pleas, Governor, but our family would be enormously appreciative if you
could help my brother. I am personally convinced he no longer
belongs in prison."

"You make a strong case. I want to reread Dr. Kepler's letter and
discuss the issue with the attorney general. I promise you I'll give it
serious consideration."

When the elevator doors opened again, Koa found himself in the
basement of Washington House. "How long have you known
Walker McKenzie?" the governor asked.

"I met him the day of the KonaWili disaster. He put me on to
Dr. Kepler."

"Certainly a man of amazing sources."

"Absolutely," Koa responded.

A guard opened a steel door, and the governor led Koa into a long
tunnel. They walked along in silence for a couple of minutes before
arriving at another steel door and emerging in the basement of the
capitol building. The governor turned the corner, approached a
bank of elevators, and extended his hand.

Koa shook the governor's hand. "Thanks for taking the time to see me, Governor."

"Glad to do it. We just might find a way to expedite your brother's parole hearing." The two men separated, and the governor then stepped into the capitol building elevator, and the doors closed behind him.

Only then did Koa realize he was standing one floor below where Piki had last seen Francine Naʻauao just before she'd disappeared. They hadn't been able to find her in the capitol because she'd slipped into the tunnel to the Washington House and gone from there to the new governor's mansion to warn Governor Māhoe that Koa knew what happened to MJK in 1975.

Koa felt his face get red. He'd been snookered. He'd suddenly become beholden to the man at the center of the investigation. Christ, he'd worried that Mayor Tanaka had an ulterior motive in controlling the investigation, but it had never occurred to him that the governor wanted to take control in order to protect his own neck.

The governor must have had a good laugh when Walker McKenzie called him about Ikaika. And he'd grabbed the chance to put Koa in a compromising position. Māhoe would get free publicity to boot. No wonder the governor had been beaming when he met Koa. And now the other shoe would drop. Koa would pay a heavy price for his brother's chance at freedom.

CHAPTER FORTY-FIVE

KOA VACILLATED BETWEEN anger and depression all the way back to the Big Island. Furious at compromising himself, he felt like a dirty cop. Governor Māhoe would surely extract his price—termination of the KonaWili investigation and a whitewash. No justice for those children and their teachers. The thought drove Koa into fits of depression and rage.

The governor had boxed him in, and he knew it. He could stand up for his integrity and insist on pursuing the KonaWili investigation, but he'd probably get fired, and his brother would rot in prison for another four years. His mother might not even live to see her youngest son free. He turned it over and over in his mind. His integrity versus the possibility of his brother's freedom. He hated the trade, but he didn't have a choice. There didn't seem to be a way out. He'd screwed himself.

He didn't have long to wait. Chief Lannua called him to the chief's top-floor office less than thirty minutes after he walked back into police headquarters. "Have you heard?" Lannua waived an official-looking document and a press release. "The governor has issued an executive order putting the state attorney general in charge of the KonaWili investigation."

"And a press release?" Koa asked with a sinking feeling.

"Congratulating you on the capture of Leffler and terminating the KonaWili investigation. The Governor and the AG extend the profound thanks of the Hawaiian people for your extraordinary efforts. You're a hero, Detective."

Koa wanted to vomit. He wasn't a hero, but a traitor. A dirty cop, abandoning his duty and his integrity for a family benefit. It felt awful.

The chief handed the documents to Koa, and he read slowly feeling the pain of every word:

After an in-depth investigation by the Hawai'i County Police Department, the state attorney general announced the closure of the investigation into the KonaWili school disaster. After interviewing numerous witnesses and reviewing all the relevant documents, the Hawai'i County police and attorney general have concluded that this terrible disaster was an unfortunate act of God. No one in the County or State governments was aware of the potential risk to schoolchildren at KonaWili, and all normal and proper steps and precautions were taken in the location and construction of the school.

There was more—words about cooperation and expressions of condolence. The press release extolled the outstanding work of Chief Detective Koa Kāne, but Koa stopped reading. His life had become a sick joke. The goddamn politicians had their whitewash, and he'd stupidly handcuffed himself into a position where he could do nothing about it.

"What about the mayor?" Koa asked. "He's the one who appointed me."

"Tanaka's happy. For once, he's not fighting the governor."

Koa understood. Tanaka had kept control of the investigation to protect Makela, but she now had immunity. Maybe he'd also been protecting others, but now they too would be in the clear. Of course, Tanaka would be happy.

Koa thought about resigning, handing his badge and his gun to the chief, and walking out the door, but he couldn't even take that step. If he made waves, Ikaika would stay in jail. He'd fallen into shit up to his neck. Finally, he stood. "Thanks for letting me know, Chief."

He drove down to Lili'uokalani Gardens and walked across the causeway to Coconut Island in Hilo Bay, known to locals as Mokuola, island of life and a place of healing. According to legend, swimming three times around the island would cure all ills. For an instant, Koa considered diving in, but instead, he sat down on the seawall and stared out into the ocean. A cruise ship made its way into the inner harbor, but he didn't really see it. He'd violated his most sacred promise to himself—his promise never to sell his office. He removed his badge from his pocket and weighed it in his hand. He thought about throwing it into Hilo Bay but stopped himself. He had one last stop to make before he gave up his badge forever.

Koa entered Zeke's office and sank heavily into one of the prosecutor's chairs. Zeke must have known from the long look on Koa's face something heavy troubled the detective. "What is it, Koa?"

"I've screwed up, Zeke. I screwed up bad."

Zeke moved from behind his desk to sit across a small conference table from Koa. "It can't be all that terrible."

Koa slid a copy of the press release across the table.

Surprise registered on Zeke's face as he read the paper. "The AG put this out?" he asked incredulously. "With your approval?"

"No, Zeke, I had nothing to do with it. Well, almost nothing." Koa laid out the whole ugly story for Zeke, starting with his surveillance of Na'auao at the Pacific National Cemetery, her disappearance in the capitol building, his conclusion she visited a state representative or senator, his conversations with Walker McKenzie, the meeting with the governor, and his realization that Naʻauao had, in fact, gone to warn the governor. He ended by telling Zeke he'd wait until Ikaika got out of jail—if the governor did, in fact, intervene—and would then resign. "I can't be a dirty cop."

When he finished, a crooked little smile crept across Zeke's face. The expression annoyed Koa. "What's the smirk for?"

"It's fucking perfect," Zeke said.

Koa shook his head as though to clear away mental cobwebs. "Don't mess with me. This is the end for me."

"Not by a long shot, my friend. Don't you see what you've done? First, you've ID'd the last of the bastards in MJK's room that night. But more importantly, they think they're in the clear—that Kona-Wili is buried and it's business as usual. *Déjà vu* all over again, as Yogi Berra would say. We just have to figure some way to set them up. Maybe we can use Makela again."

"You have authority even though the AG has taken over?"

"Sure. The AG may control the police investigation, but I still have authority to prosecute crimes. Come on, Koa, put your mind to it. This is the endgame."

"I can't, Zeke. The mayor or the chief will have my head for bucking the governor, and . . . and I can't let my brother down."

"No problemo, my friend. Not on either count. The parole board meets tomorrow. The governor is either going to act or he's not, but we'll be over that hurdle by tomorrow night. And the mayor or the chief? I'll talk to the mayor and the chief when the time comes. In the meantime, remember, I appointed you an assistant prosecutor. That appointment still stands. You continue the investigation working for me."

"You're serious." Koa still couldn't quite believe what he heard.

"Damn straight, I'm serious. You need to get to work figuring out how to trap these bastards."

CHAPTER FORTY-SIX

THE PAROLE BOARD met the following morning at the Hilo court-house. They had a full docket of hearings, and it was three thirty before the commissioners got to the administrative questions, like applications for reduction of minimum sentence. Normally, the commissioners decided such matters without public input, but Alexia Sheppard had persuaded the board to let her present the case for Ikaika before they decided whether to reduce Ikaika's minimum sentence, allowing him the possibility of early parole.

When Koa arrived, only three of the five commissioners sat at the table, and they weren't the ones most likely to give Ikaika a sympathetic hearing. Worse yet, Hardy Moyan sat in the front row. The thirty-year-old parole officer, a short wiry man with a long sour face, had diamond-hard eyes behind horn-rimmed glasses. His reputation as one of the toughest—most would say meanest—of the island's parole staff preceded him.

Ikaika had scorned Moyan, stupidly calling him a stooge. Now, Moyan had a hard-on for Ikaika. Koa had tried to reason with Moyan but found him unyielding. Moyan regarded Ikaika as an incorrigible badass who needed to be locked up. Period. Full stop.

When Koa took a seat, Moyan noticed him and walked over to sit next to Koa. "I gotta give you credit, Mr. Chief Detective. You and your fancy lady lawyer cooked up a good one, but let me tell you, it ain't gonna work. Your brother, he's a real badass dude. That's what I'm gonna tell the commissioners. Hell, I already told 'em in writing, and I'm gonna tell 'em again. In fact, I'm gonna tell 'em every time your brother comes up for parole. That son of a bitch is gonna serve the maximum, every last minute."

Koa felt his muscles tighten and his jaw clench. He wanted to punch Moyan. The bastard didn't have an ounce of compassion. With enormous effort, Koa restrained himself. He could only hope the governor had worked his magic. If so, it wouldn't matter what Moyan said. And if the governor hadn't intervened, then Ikaika didn't stand a chance.

After finishing all the other matters, the chairman announced the commission would take up Ikaika Kāne's case. Ikaika's admin officer from the Arizona prison joined the proceedings by video conference. With everyone set, the chairman told Alexia Sheppard she'd have five minutes to present her evidence and argument in support of a revision of his minimum sentence.

Alexia was brilliant. She started by presenting medical records concerning Ikaika's collapse in jail, his diagnosis at Queen's Medical, his surgery, and Dr. Kepler's opinion that Ikaika's tumors had impaired his ability to conform to societal norms. With the removal of the tumors, Kepler expected him to behave differently. Alexia presented Māpuana's affidavit describing how Ikaika's behavior had changed since the surgery and followed with Koa's statement recounting the humor, the self-deprecation, and the new thoughtfulness in Ikaika's postoperative behavior. Alexia then went through the Commission's guidelines, arguing Ikaika met every condition for a reduction of his minimum sentence.

She took almost fifteen minutes, but the chairman let her finish before he called Hardy Moyan. Moyan described Ikaika as a violent recidivist with no moral code and no ability to distinguish between right and wrong. As Moyan spoke, Koa could see one of the commissioners nodding. Koa felt a sad, sinking feeling. It had been a long shot before Moyan poisoned the waters. Moyan had rendered it hopeless.

The telephone in the conference room rang before Moyan finished his tirade. Everyone paused while the parole board's administrative officer answered the phone, listened for almost a minute, and then whispered something in the chairman's ear. The chairman looked up with a surprised expression before announcing that the commissioners would take a ten-minute break.

During the break, Moyan approached Koa. "I told you I was going to nail the son of a bitch. You wasted your money on that fancy lady lawyer."

"Fuck off," Koa said softly before turning on his heels and walking across the room to chat with Alexia.

"You were brilliant," he told her, "but Moyan's queered the deal. There's no way now."

Alexia bore a forlorn expression. "I'm afraid I agree. Sorry."

Almost a half hour passed before the board chairman returned. The other commissioners remained absent. "We," the chairman announced, "have just received word from Governor Māhoe's office. The governor has commuted Ikaika Kāne's sentence. The papers are being faxed to the prison and the prison ward at Queen's Medical. He will be released from custody in the morning. Since he is now a free man and beyond our jurisdiction, there is no need to continue this hearing. I thank you for your participation."

A shocked expression distorted Hardy Moyan's face. Koa only wished he'd captured it on film. Koa embraced Alexia and rushed out to call his mother.

The governor had come through for him like gangbusters. An order of commutation was final and irrevocable. It made Ikaika a free man, and it also freed Koa to help Zeke put the governor in jail without fear his brother would stay in prison. Perhaps, he thought, he should feel beholden to the governor, but he didn't. The governor had helped cover up a murder, and he had almost certainly been on the take for years. He might even be a murderer. And he'd used Koa to shut down the investigation into the deaths of fourteen children and four teachers. Now he and Zeke were going to turn the tables.

Koa returned to his office with a light heart, like he himself had just been freed from prison. With his integrity in good stead, he felt like a whole person again and renewed his promise to himself never ever to sell out.

Refocusing on the investigation, Koa turned his mental spotlight on Gommes. According to Witherspoon's confession, Gommes had orchestrated the cover-up of MJK's murder. He'd dispatched Francine Na'auao, aka Frannie Kapule, to sell the cops the phony suicidal depression story and persuaded Makela and Watanabe to back up the conspirators' false alibis. Thereafter, he'd used Makela to bribe Na'auao and controlled Watanabe's career with bribes, plum jobs, and coercion.

Through the years, Gommes made a fortune through his dirty development deals. He'd bought the KonaWili development to extend his wealth. Whether he learned about the fumarole before the purchase, Koa didn't know, but before the development proceeded he'd ordered the fumarole filled in with rocks, then sold the parcel to the DOE, and finally arranged for Boyle to cover the volcanic vent in concrete, oblivious to the risks to children who would go to school there.

Over the years, Gommes must have sensed Witherspoon's bouts of conscience. From the search of Witherspoon's office, Koa guessed the architect had told Gommes he'd secreted a confession. Gommes must also have known of Boyle's depression. With wealth beyond measure, Gommes could easily have doled out forty thousand dollars in cash to Leffler. A master planner and enforcer like Gommes could have hired Leffler, buying himself an insurance policy long before *Pele* wrecked the KonaWili school. That could explain why Boyle had been killed so soon after the disaster.

It hung together like the flowers on a *lei*, pointing to Gommes as the man who'd paid Leffler to kill Boyle and Witherspoon. There was just one insurmountable problem. Leffler had tried to kill Gommes.

But if Gommes hadn't hired Leffler, that left only two contenders—Naʻauao and the governor. Koa supposed either of them could have tired of living under Gommes's thumb and turned on him. They had money, so forty thousand dollars would have been no impediment, but neither of them shared the history of violence Watanabe and Makela attributed to Gommes.

Koa wondered if he could get Leffler to talk. Maybe the man would trip up and drop a clue, shedding light on the mystery. He had the jailers bring Leffler up to one of the interview rooms, and asked Basa to join them. Basa had an uncanny ability to read people, and Koa needed every edge he could get with Leffler.

Before they began, Koa and Basa watched Leffler through the glass observation window for several minutes.

"That's one ugly scar," Basa said, studying Leffler's face.

"Yeah," Koa responded, "his service record says he got it in Afghanistan but not in the line of duty."

"Maybe when he raped one of the local women," Basa suggested.

"Maybe."

They entered the interrogation room together. Leffler, again chained to the table, glared at them with hostile eyes.

"You ready to tell us who hired you?" Koa asked.

"I ain't no snitch."

Koa pulled out a copy of the hit list taken from the safe in Leffler's girlfriend's apartment and laid it on the table. "Who gave you these names?"

Silence.

Koa slowly read the names: "Boyle, Witherspoon, Makela, Watanabe, and me."

Silence.

"And someone gave you another name—one that's not on the list—didn't they?"

More silence, but this time Leffler blinked twice in what Koa read to be confusion or surprise. He wasn't sure.

"Come on, Leffler, who told you to go after Gommes?"

There it was again, but this time Leffler's whole body seemed to tense. The man appeared surprised they knew of his attempted hit on Gommes.

"How'd you do it, Leffler? That's a nearly impossible shot. Downhill in a crosswind from 1200 yards."

Leffler's eyebrows narrowed, as though he were confused. Koa could almost see the wheels turning in Leffler's head as he tried to work out some puzzle.

Koa tried again. "What weapon did you use? The DesertTech SRS A-1 sniper rifle?"

Leffler opened his mouth to say something but then retreated into silence.

Koa tried several more times, but he'd hit a wall. Leffler wasn't going to talk.

On Koa's signal, the two police officers stepped outside. "Did you see his eyes when I asked him about Gommes?" Koa asked.

"Yeah," Basa responded. "The eyes, his facial muscles, and that ugly scar."

"He seemed surprised we knew about his attack on Gommes," Koa guessed.

"Maybe," Basa responded, "but I think there's more."

"Like what?"

"He kinda acted like the whole thing was news to him, especially when you started asking about the gun and the shot itself."

For a second Koa wondered if someone else had fired at Gommes, but then another thought struck him.

"Come on," he said to Basa and hurried toward the police evidence room, where they'd stored the evidence taken from Leffler's Mauna Kea cabin hideaway.

Koa knew a lot about guns. He'd qualified as an expert with a variety of weapons during his Special Forces days. He'd never been a sniper, but he knew how they operated. The scene at Gommes's place had puzzled Koa, and he'd wondered how Leffler had made the nearly impossible shot. The *pu'u* from which the shot had come stood at a considerably higher elevation than the house, so the shooter had been firing downhill. The bullet would nevertheless have followed a curved trajectory, requiring the shooter to point the rifle above his line of sight so that the bullet would fall in a long arc toward the target. At over 1000 yards, even with high-powered ammunition, the drop would be measured in feet, not inches, and even a small error in estimating the distance would produce a clean miss. Wind velocity and angle, humidity, temperature, as well as the characteristics of the ammo, would affect the trajectory. Getting everything perfect on the first shot without a range finder and wind measurement tools was nearly impossible. Expert snipers typically attempted such a shot only with match-grade or specially crafted ammunition and used tools like a Kestrel applied ballistic calibration system.

The Army had trained Leffler, putting him through various specialized training, including the tough Q course, but he'd been rejected for Special Forces and become a supply sergeant. Leffler's military service record showed no sniper training, and the rogue soldier had never served as a military sniper. While the search of Leffler's cabin hideout had turned up a DesertTech SRS A1 sniper rifle, the police had found no ballistic calibration system. True, Leffler could have performed basic ballistic calculations with a smartphone app, but range finder apps on smartphones without a laser attachment were close to worthless at long distances. And Leffler's smartphone wouldn't have given him the wind speed or direction.

Ammunition was another problem. If Leffler had fired from 1200 yards out, he must have been using .338 Lapua Magnum or .50 BMG cartridges. Those were big, heavy bullets and would have ripped a huge hole in a wooden target like the front door of Gommes's house. Yet, as Koa had seen in person and on the video from Basa's body cam, the actual hole in the door, while substantial, hadn't been made with heavy ammunition.

By the time Koa and Basa got to the police evidence room and retrieved the stuff taken from Leffler's cabin, Koa had convinced himself that Leffler had not shot at Gommes. They found the clincher in Leffler's stuff. When Koa examined the DesertTech SRS A1 rifle, the only sniper weapon Leffler had stolen, Koa realized it had never been fired. It still had the original manufacturer's grease in the barrel.

No one shot at Gommes from that *pu'u*. Koa suddenly realized *no one* at all shot at Gommes. The devious bastard staged the whole thing. He'd killed Dante, his own butcher's dog, to make the police think Leffler was after him. Yet, the truth was 180 degrees different—he'd hired Leffler. What a treacherous douchebag.

Koa wondered if he could get confirmation. An idea occurred to him, making him grin. Perhaps, he could be more cunning than Gommes. They left Leffler sitting in the police interrogation room for nearly two hours.

When they finally returned, Leffler appeared agitated. He jumped in his seat. "Jesus, man, I gotta take a piss," Leffler shouted.

"Tough shit, Leffler," Koa said. He sat casually, staring coldly at Leffler. He wanted the killer to be as uncomfortable and emotionally off-balance as possible. He sat still for nearly two minutes watching the man squirm. Judging from Leffler's reddening face, the man's blood pressure threatened to go through the roof. Finally, Koa spoke. "We've got you by the balls, Leffler." Koa let those words hang in the air for several seconds before he added, "Gommes ratted you out."

Leffler bolted up out of his chair, restrained only by the chain holding his cuffed hands to the iron ring in the center of the table. "That rotten son of a bitch," Leffler shouted. "I'll kill his double-crossing ass."

Koa grinned. He had his man. Gommes hired Leffler. No doubt about it.

CHAPTER FORTY-SEVEN

KOA AND ZEKE wracked their brains trying to figure out how to get the goods on MJK's killer. With no statute of limitations on murder, they could charge the person who choked MJK provided they had a witness or other evidence. Witherspoon's written confession wouldn't cut it—it wouldn't even be admissible in court absent his testimony.

The other men in the room that night, as well as Na'auao, could be charged as accessories to murder and conspiring to submit false reports to the police. Makela and Watanabe became accessories by lying to the police. The statute of limitations on those offenses precluded prosecution unless those crimes were part of a continuing conspiracy. They could prosecute those crimes only if Zeke could prove some act in furtherance of the crime—like a continuing cover-up or payoffs to avoid disclosure—within the past five years.

Beyond MJK's murder, there were the public corruption charges for those who facilitated the building of the KonaWili school and murder charges for the deaths of the students and teachers. There, too, Zeke needed proof. He couldn't rely solely on the testimony of Cheryl Makela and Tomi Watanabe. The murder of MJK and the subsequent cover-up had empowered Gommes to exert his will over the others, enmeshing them in the KonaWili conspiracy, but they needed evidence tying the crimes together.

Remembering the urgency in Sally Medea's voice when she offered her help to bring Witherspoon's killer to justice, Koa came up with the idea. He'd need her help for his plan to succeed, but he laid out his ideas for the prosecutor.

"Jesus, you have a Machiavellian mind," Zeke responded. "But it just might work." They batted the idea back and forth and refined the pieces until they had it right.

Zeke arranged an appointment to see Judge Hatachi, warning the judge they had a criminal matter of enormous sensitivity and would need a couple of hours of his time. The judge saw Koa and Zeke alone in his chambers. There, Koa laid out the history of the Kona-Wili school project, emphasizing Gommes, Makela, and Na'auao had all known about the fumarole.

Zeke then presented the results of their interview with Makela, revealing the long-standing conspiracy between her and Gommes to hide payments to Na'auao and Watanabe. Judge Hatachi, a seasoned jurist and keen observer of Hawai'i politics, had been around the islands his whole life. "You don't really believe those payments stopped with those two, do you?"

Although Zeke hid his feelings well, Koa saw the gleam in the prosecutor's eyes. "Well, Your Honor, the payments might have stopped with Na'auao. She's a real power in the state, but we already know that Watanabe transferred his interest to a trust that distributed the proceeds."

The judge nodded. "And they put those children in danger for money . . . for unrestrained greed?"

"That's undoubtedly part of it, Your Honor," Zeke responded, "but as Detective Kāne is about to explain, there's much more to this story."

Koa described how MJK had died, the police investigation, the false statements, and the conspiracy to cover up the murder. Then he laid Arthur Witherspoon's confession on the judge's desk. The judge read the document and sat silently contemplating Witherspoon's words for a long time. Finally, he said, "Tell me what you need." Zeke laid copies of the warrants needed for their eavesdropping operation on the judge's desk, and Judge Hatachi signed them.

In working out the details of their plan, Zeke bemoaned the fact that Witherspoon hadn't named the murderer. "This would be a whole lot easier if we knew who actually choked MJK."

Koa grinned. "Who's to say that Witherspoon didn't name names."

Zeke looked puzzled. "What do you mean?"

"We could rewrite the confession to put in the murderer's name. If we get it right, we'll get confirmation. And if we guess wrong, it'll smoke out the guilty man."

Zeke paused, then he, too, broke into a smile. "It's brilliant, Koa. Where do we stage this little party?"

"The East Hawai'i Cultural Center would be the perfect place."

Zeke laughed. "Arthur Witherspoon would love it."

They timed their operation to occur during the annual Merrie Monarch festival. The festival, held every year in Hilo, featured three days and nights when *hālau*, different teams of young men and women under the direction of *kumu hula* masters, competed for the top prizes in traditional and modern *hula* performances. *Hālau* came from all the islands and many other places. A *who's who* of Hawai'i society and government would attend.

Koa called Sally Medea. "You still want to help catch the man who ordered Arthur's murder?"

"Do I ever."

They met in Zeke's office to explain step-by-step what they proposed and what they needed her to do. Sally agreed without hesitation. They prepared scripts, and Sally rehearsed her lines until she had them down cold. Finally, Koa asked if she was aware of the risks of going through with the operation.

"I'm not just ready. I can't wait for revenge against the man who ordered Arthur's murder," Sally responded. "I want the bastard."

They set Sally up in an office with a telephone attached to a recording device. Both Koa and Zeke wore earphones so they could hear both ends of the conversations. Koa watched as she dialed. A servant answered the phone, and she asked for Gommes.

"What's this about?" the man asked politely.

"Tell him it's about Mary Jane Kinnon." That brought Gommes to the phone.

"Mr. Gommes," Sally began, "I was Arthur Witherspoon's personal assistant. I have the confession he wrote about the death of a coed at UH in 1975—"

"I don't know what you're talking about," came the interruption.

"Oh, you know exactly what you, Spooner, Boyle, and the man pretending to be Abercrombie did and how you covered it up."

There was a long pause before Gommes said, "I'm listening."

"We need to meet to talk about whether I give Arthur's confession to you or to the police."

"You want money?"

"We can talk about what I want when we meet. Tomorrow night at the East Hawai'i Cultural Center. Eight o'clock sharp, and don't be late. I'll be wearing a red jacket." She hung up.

Sally then made a similar call to Francine Na'auao, and then to the man Koa had identified as wearing the red wig—Governor Bobbie Māhoe.

Enlisting the aid of Cap Roberts, Koa and the tech services chief spent the day at the East Hawai'i Cultural Center. After they shooed the staff away and placed a CLOSED sign on the door, Koa looked around the current exhibition in the lower gallery. The photographs of Kīlauea's Halemaʻumaʻu crater glowing at night, coastal scenes with giant red steam clouds above lava pouring into the ocean, and pictures of rivers of molten rock setting fire to the forest and houses in Puna provided just the right apocalyptic tone for the evening's festivities. After all, they were, in Tony Pwalú words, talking about *Pele*'s revenge.

They hid pinhole cameras in the frames of the photographs, and microphones in the light fixtures. Koa then checked the monitors they'd set up in the projection booth in the theater on the second floor. The screens gave him a good view of the main room below.

Although confident in his plan, Koa worried about the possibility of violence. He and Zeke would hide in the projection booth for the night's festivities, but he placed Basa and three patrolmen behind locked doors just outside the main room, ready to respond to the first sign of violence. Koa also positioned an unmarked police van and a plain-wrapper police SUV in the parking area behind the historic building.

Concerned one of the invitees might try to scope out the place before entering, Koa positioned his troops by six o'clock. Basa and the patrolmen stood ready to spring out in the event of trouble. Koa stationed more cops in the windowless van parked outside. Koa and Zeke, behind locked doors in the projection booth at the back of the second-floor theater, watched the feeds from their cameras and listened to the hidden microphones.

Francine Naʻauao arrived first. She entered through the unlocked front door and peered around nervously. Governor Māhoe arrived second. Koa noted the surprise and alarm on his face when he saw Naʻauao. "Frannie, why are you here?"

"I got a call from some woman claiming Spooner left a confession. What about you?"

"Same thing. Did Spooner really write something?"

"I don't know, but the caller had Mary Jane's name."

"This can't be good."

Gommes arrived last. He looked around at the others. "You all get calls from some strange woman. Something about a confession?"

The others nodded affirmatively.

"Is she here?" Gommes asked.

"No one's here except the three of us."

"Has anyone checked upstairs?" Gommes asked.

The governor looked at Frannie before responding, "No."

"Everybody hold tight." Gommes headed for the stairs. Gommes made a circuit of the second floor, checking the locked doors before returning to the group. "We're alone. There's nobody upstairs."

"I don't like this," the governor said.

"Don't panic," Gommes responded. "I don't know what this bitch wants, probably money. Just let me handle it."

"Like you've handled everything for the last forty years?" Frannie asked.

"I kept your ass out of trouble, haven't I?" Gommes responded.

Koa pumped a fist into the air. Zeke grinned and made the okay gesture with his thumb and forefinger. They had all three of the surviving witnesses to Mary Jane's murder in the same room. Now they just needed to see if Sally Medea could extract a confession.

Showtime. The room below went silent as the microphones picked up the sound of the back door opening. The cameras showed a poised and confident Sally Medea, dressed in a red jacket over a white blouse and black slacks, enter and face her three protagonists. "Good evening. My name is Sally Medea. I was in love with Arthur Witherspoon, and he loved me. You all knew him as Spooner."

"What's this all about, Miss . . . Miss Medea?" Gommes sought to assert control.

Not at all intimidated, Sally responded, "It's about the crime the three of you committed forty years ago—the murder of Mary Jane Kinnon."

"That's bullshit," Gommes shouted.

"Let's hear her out," the governor responded.

All three of them looked to Sally, who withdrew a piece of paper from her pocket, unfolded it, and began reading: *"May the Lord forgive me for I have sinned."*

"Oh, my God." Na'auao's hand flew to her mouth.

Sally ignored the interruption and continued reading: *"It has haunted me all my life . . . what we did that night . . . the six of us.*

"I was high. We all were. The girls were naked, swapping partners, competing for the best climax, each goading the other on. Mary Jane was so beautiful, so sexy, so wild."

Sally paused for effect. Koa had rewritten Arthur Witherspoon's confession, and she started to read the first altered paragraph: *"Howard Gommes was on top of her, fucking her, choking her, she was gasping, begging for it, playing a deadly game . . ."* Again, Sally paused.

Gommes broke the silence. "That rotten son of a bitch. I should have known he'd squirreled away something like this. Fuckin' Spooner always was the weak link."

Koa watched their faces. Na'auao, pale as an albatross, stared wide-eyed. The governor bore a grim look. Gommes radiated anger.

Sally continued reading Koa's insert: *"Gommes killed her, he choked the life out of Mary Jane—"*

"That's a goddamned lie. Bobbie choked her. He killed her!" Gommes screamed.

"Shut up, you fool," Governor Bobbie Māhoe ordered.

Undeterred, Sally kept reading: *"We should have gone to the police, but we didn't. Howard fixed the whole thing, the fake suicide, the lies, the false witnesses. He got Frannie to lie. He paid Babylips and that little Japanese bartender to say we were at the KitKat. I should never have gone along. The worst mistake of my life. I was scared. We all were.*

"Howard screamed at us. He wouldn't let some slut ruin his life. He had money and knew how to fix it, how to set up the alibi, how to get to the coroner, how to make everyone believe Mary Jane committed suicide. Poor Mary Jane. I didn't believe it would work, but it did."

Koa stared at Gommes's image on the monitor as Sally recited Arthur's indictment of the developer. He had a hard, determined look. Koa could almost see his mind hunting for a way out of the disaster unfolding before his eyes.

Sally continued, once again, adding Koa's words to Arthur's confession: *"We became his puppets, richly rewarded pawns in dirty deals, locked into a lifelong trap. We did his bidding at KonaWili. He used Makela and money from the change order to bribe me, Boyle, and the governor—"*

"Jesus, you told Spooner about the bribes?" Francine Na'auao pointed accusingly at Gommes.

"Don't be stupid. Why do you think Spooner and Boyle went along in covering up the vent?" Gommes snapped.

Koa and Zeke high-fived each other. They had their confessions. Bobbie Māhoe had killed Mary Jane, and Gommes had bribed Witherspoon, Boyle, and the governor, to build KonaWili atop the fumarole. They had enough, but Koa knew that Sally was going for more. She wanted each of them in a noose, like they'd put on MJK.

Still, Sally continued to read: *"Those poor children, dead because we built a school on top of a volcanic vent, covering it with concrete—"*

"Give me that!" Gommes demanded.

Sally let the paper fall from her hand to the floor. "Take it. It's a copy. The original will go to the police unless I stop it."

"How much do you want?" Gommes demanded.

Sally calmly flipped the question back. "How much do you think it's worth?"

"A million dollars," Gommes responded.

"And the others? What are they offering?" Sally asked.

Na'auao and Māhoe looked at each other, trying to decide what to do. Then the governor turned on Gommes. "This is your fault. You said you had taken care of both Boyle and Witherspoon and destroyed anything tying us to that night in Mary Jane's room. You fucked up, Gommes. You pay the bill."

"That won't cut it," Sally said softly. "Either everybody pays up or you all go to jail."

Koa marveled at her poise. He couldn't imagine how she could play this high-stakes poker with such skill and determination. But then Sally had a powerful personal motive.

"Alright . . . alright," Māhoe gave in, "a half million."

Sally nodded. "Frannie?"

"Half a million."

Zeke gave Koa the high sign. They had a lock on Mary Jane's murderer, the killings of Boyle and Witherspoon, the bribery of state officials, and murder of the children at KonaWili. And there'd be no statute of limitation issue. Mary Jane Kinnon's death connected everything and the participants were still offering huge sums of money to cover up their crimes. Now all the cops had to do was go downstairs and make the arrests.

CHAPTER FORTY-EIGHT

SALLY MEDEA'S SCREAM screeched through the speakers. On the monitor, Koa saw Gommes take Sally in a headlock putting a 9 mm Beretta to her ear. "Listen, bitch," he said, "you tell us where the original is or you die right now."

"Code red. Code red," Koa gave the emergency signal. "Gommes has a gun to Sally's head."

Basa from the east side and two patrolmen from the west emerged from opposite doors and trained their guns on Gommes. "Police. Drop your weapon," Basa shouted.

"One step forward and the bitch dies," Gommes shouted back.

"It's over, Gommes," Koa said calmly using the building's public address system. "We have it all on tape, the murders, the bribes, and KonaWili."

Unruffled, Gommes scanned the room. "I'm not going down."

"There's nowhere to go, Gommes."

"My plane's at the airport, fueled, and ready to go far beyond your reach."

Bobbie Māhoe stepped toward Gommes. "I'm going with you."

"Fuck you," Gommes snarled. "I've been carrying your sorry ass for forty years." Still holding the Beretta to Sally's head, he released her neck to reach for his cell. He had the number preprogrammed and spoke sharply into the phone. "Ten minutes. End of the runway ready to go."

"You bastard!" Māhoe screamed and lunged for Gommes.

Dropping his phone and grabbing Sally's arm, Gommes brought the gun around and pumped two slugs into the governor, dropping him to the floor. Naʻauao screamed and ran to the governor's side. "Bastard!" she wailed.

Koa had underestimated Gommes. The man was an animal, and Koa had no way to take him down in such confined space without risking Sally's life. Speaking quietly into his headset for Basa to hear, he said, "Don't try anything. We won't risk harm to Sally."

Gommes had double-crossed all his co-conspirators and planned an escape leaving them behind. And, Koa thought, it might even work. With his own private jet, he could make it to South America, refuel, and disappear to any number of countries lacking extradition treaties with the U.S.

Koa tried to picture Gommes's next moves—forcing Sally out the front door into a car, racing across town, crashing a barrier into the airport, driving to the end of the runway, mounting the stairs to his private jet, and disappearing.

He turned to Zeke. "Take charge here. Delay them as long as possible. And call the airport. Have them block the runway." Then Koa stepped to the window, slid it up, and climbed onto the fire escape. At the bottom of the ladder, he grabbed two patrolmen—Kealoha and Horita—from the unmarked van. Together, they ran for the unmarked SUV. Moments later, they were speeding toward the airport, trying to stay one step ahead of Gommes.

When Koa reached the airport, Gommes's plane sat on the taxiway just off the end of the active runway, its engines running. The onboard stairs extended to the ground awaiting Gommes's arrival. Koa scanned the runway but saw no emergency vehicles in position to stop an aircraft from taking off. For some reason, Zeke's efforts to get the runway blocked had failed, and Koa wondered if Gommes had an accomplice in the airport administration. If so, his plan wasn't going to work.

Koa flashed his badge at the gate and sped toward Gommes's plane, approaching from its rear, where the pilot couldn't see the car. Stopping a dozen feet behind the aircraft, he and Kealoha jumped out and took off running under the jet headed for the stairs. Officer Horita backed the car away before turning and retreating out of sight. Koa and Kealoha scrambled up, boarding the aircraft. Inside, the cockpit door stood open, and the two officers had their weapons pointed at the pilot and copilot before they could react. Koa closed the cockpit door. Kealoha guarded the pilots while Koa watched through the cockpit peephole.

Less than five minutes later, Gommes's Mercedes raced to a stop at the foot of the airstairs. Gommes got out and directed Sally up the steps at gunpoint. Through the peephole, Koa saw them enter. Gommes pushed Sally into one of the seats before moving to retract the stairs and close the cabin door. Pressing a button on a communications panel, he ordered the pilot to "get us the hell out of here." He then took the seat across the aisle from Sally. Koa had hoped Gommes would put his Beretta away, but instead, he left it nestled in his lap. The plane began to taxi. Unbeknownst to Gommes, Kealoha directed the pilot to taxi toward the terminal and not toward the runway.

Gommes grinned. "Home free."

At that moment, Koa stepped through the cockpit door, his Glock aimed at Gommes's chest. "You're under arrest for the murders of Boyle, Witherspoon, and Governor Māhoe."

Shock registered across Gommes's face, but not for long. "Put the gun down, Detective. I'll make you a rich man."

Unmoved, Koa held the gun on Gommes. "Raise your hands, Gommes."

"Ten million. You can retire."

Gommes's hands remained in his lap, close to his Beretta. Koa guessed Gommes would try to fight his way out. So be it. Koa would shoot him the moment his fingers touched the gun.

"Why, Gommes? Why build the school on top of the fumarole? Why endanger schoolkids?" Koa asked, his Glock still leveled at the developer.

"Had to plug the fuckin' vent," Gommes answered. "It kept those Paradise assholes from developing the property, and I wasn't gonna let it ruin one sweet project. Covering the vent needed a big structure, and a school fit the bill. That's why I sited the school over the vent. Besides, that way, I got the DOE to pay for covering the fumarole. Saved me a few million bucks. Never thought the fuckin' thing would actually erupt."

Gommes's hand inched toward his gun. "Don't do it, Gommes," Koa said, his voice hard as steel.

Gommes pulled his hand away from the Beretta, and Koa thought he might have a chance to take him alive. Without warning, Gommes let out a shrill whistle. Just as the sound reached Koa's ears, he caught sight of a giant black blur racing up the aisle toward him. Virgil, Gommes's remaining Rottweiler, launched into the air. The dog's bright yellow eyes, open mouth, and razor-sharp teeth hurtled toward Koa. In that instant, Gommes dropped out of sight.

Koa fired twice in rapid succession at the airborne dog and dove for cover on the opposite side of the plane, but he wasn't fast enough. Virgil's teeth caught his shoulder, ripping through his shirt and tearing into his flesh. The impact spun him backward, knocking the Glock from his hand. His head slammed into something hard. His vision blurred.

Half-dazed, Koa heard Gommes coming in for the kill following the Rottweiler's attack. Koa searched frantically for his gun, but it wasn't within reach. Looking up, he saw Gommes standing over him . . . then the business end of Gommes's Beretta. Gommes had a triumphant expression on his face.

"You killed my goddamn dog, you son of a bitch, and now it's your turn."

Koa thought of his brother. He'd rescued Ikaika from prison and given him a new lease on life, but now they would never be together again. He tried to think of something to deter Gommes, but he could formulate no words.

The sounds of the gunshots—one, two, three—amplified in the confined space of the aircraft blasted Koa's ears, but the terrible pain he expected never came. Instead, confusion clouded Gommes's face. His grip loosened, and the Beretta hit the floor. Moments later, Gommes crumpled and fell backward.

Koa used a seat to pull himself up off the floor. Sally stood in the aisle with a small automatic in her outstretched hand. "I've been waiting a long time to kill that bastard."

Locking eyes with the woman who'd executed Gommes and saved his life, Koa said, "Arthur would be proud."

EPILOGUE

THEY WAITED AT Hilo airport while the jet from Honolulu taxied to the gate. Koa and Nālani, Māpuana and Alana. Even Koa's middle brother, Mauloa, came. A spirit of excitement electrified the air like Koa had rarely ever felt. Ikaika was coming home a free man.

It seemed to take forever for the attendants to get the jet bridge in place and for the passengers to exit the plane. Māpuana, as nervous and as excited as a young girl on her wedding day, waited for her youngest son. Finally, Ikaika emerged from the jetway into the terminal. Bandages covered his head, and he looked tired, but he wore a childish grin. He embraced Māpuana, shook hands with brother Mauloa, and even bestowed a kiss on Nālani's cheek.

Then he turned to Koa, grabbing him in a big bear hug. "*Mahalo*, big brother. You know when you told me about your crazy-ass plan back in the hospital, I figured you were smoking dope, but you pulled it off. I should've known you would come through for me." His words brought tears to Koa's eyes.

The following day, Koa took his youngest brother to lunch at the Hilo Burger Joint. Robyn served them double orders of burgers, fries, and shakes, which Ikaika devoured like a starving man. Afterward, they walked beneath the banyan trees through Liliʻuokalani

Gardens. "You know," Ikaika began, "I can never repay you for the money and time you've wasted on me over the years."

"You're alive and free . . . and Māmā's happier than she's been in a decade . . . that's all I need, little brother." Koa paused. "But you need a job and a place to live."

"Who's going to give an ex-con like me a job?"

Koa put his hand on his brother's shoulder and stared hard until Ikaika met his gaze. "That's your old way of thinking. *Mai noʻonoʻo pēlā.* Leave it behind. In the past, you were sick. Today you're healthy and you've got to act like it."

"So, what do I do?" Ikaika asked.

"My fisherman buddy, Hook Hao, is willing to rehire you as a deckhand, and you can live on his boat."

"Really?"

Koa saw a spark of hope in Ikaika's eyes. "Really. And the folks up at Hale ʻŌhiʻa, near Volcano, are looking for a gardener. It's a start."

"*ʻAe.* It's a good start," Ikaika responded.

When they parted, Ikaika stood a bit taller with his shoulders squared.

*   *   *

A week later the whole family gathered again, this time in Koa's Volcano cottage around a flat-screen television. Walker McKenzie introduced the evening's "From All Angles" segment: "Tonight we're going to bring you the life story of a most remarkable police detective, a story culminating with the inside scoop on an extraordinary forty-year-old murder—a crime ultimately responsible for the deaths of fourteen grade-school children and four teachers in the infamous KonaWili school disaster."

Koa and Ikaika had given Walker McKenzie the whole story from beginning to end, and McKenzie had turned it into a blockbuster. Koa Kāne was about to become a police legend in his own time. He wasn't sure how he felt about that, but he and Ikaika had paid their debt to Walker McKenzie.

After the news cycle ran its course, and the press moved on to the next story, Koa returned to the tiny cemetery behind the little white church on the hill in Hāwī. He stood over Hazzard's grave paying his respects to the man he'd killed. He would never escape the guilt he felt for what he had done, but in the tangled world of human behavior, his guilt had once again driven him to find justice, not just for the *keiki* and *kumu* at KonaWili, but for his brother, mother, family, and *kūpuna,* his ancestors.

AUTHOR'S NOTE

There is no KonaWili school on Hualālai Mountain. There was no eruption of a volcanic vent under an elementary school, and thus no children died in such an eruption. The disaster portrayed in this book is a product of the author's imagination.

Of course, that is not to say that it couldn't happen. Although Hualālai Mountain has not erupted in 200 years, it remains a serious threat, and its geological history is accurately portrayed in this book. The USGS says Hualālai is "a potentially dangerous volcano that is likely to erupt again." Other volcanologists are convinced it will again erupt and, because of its location perched above Kailua-Kona, such an eruption could cause significant loss of life and serious damage.

It may seem strange that anyone would build a home or a school or a fire station within the danger zone surrounding Hualālai, but just as the Japanese built the Fukushima-Daiichi nuclear plant in a known tsunami zone, and Italians have built whole towns on the slopes of Mount Vesuvius, so too have Hawaiians built the coastal city of Kailua-Kona in the shadow of an active volcano.

And they seem mostly oblivious to the risk. Surveys in 2003 concluded that only a minority of those living in Kailua-Kona believe that Hualālai might erupt again, and only about one-third realized that lava from Hualālai might reach their seashore in three hours' time. Strangely, this despite the fact that residents and tourists fly in and out of town from an airport built on the last major lava flow from Hualālai. This seemingly odd characteristic of human behavior sparked my interest in fashioning a novel highlighting people's peculiar perception of the risks associated with the likely repetition of catastrophic historical events.

I have also been fascinated by the long-term effects of secret criminal behavior on the human mind. Koa Kāne, my protagonist, represents one end of the spectrum—a man driven to make recompense for his unintended, but reckless, killing of another human being. Having devoted his life to finding justice for murder victims, he visits the gravesite of his own victim after every major case.

Other characters you meet in this book represent other points on this behavioral spectrum. There are characters who drown their criminal memories in psychotropic medications. Personalities who go to great lengths to excise years'-long experiences from their resumes, while others seem inured to their crimes, all too willing to continue to profit from them. Finally, there are people who would use their common criminal history to control others. And fear of exposure grips them all. This mix of characters tainted by human warts and their reactions in the highly stressful aftermath of a natural, but human-enhanced, disaster makes for a fascinating crucible in which to explore these Big Island players.

I hope you enjoy reading *Fire and Vengeance* as much as I enjoyed writing it.